—— Praise for ——

Yet, Here We Are

"Moving nimbly across the middle decades of the twentieth century, from the bustling nightclubs of Chicago to the fledgling co-ops of Minneapolis, this absorbing and keenly observed novel is part romance, part mystery, and part social commentary. With tenderness and eloquence, Massman explores how the secrets we keep—from our communities, from our families, and from ourselves—shape us forever. The wisdom these characters accrue will stay with you long after the last page is turned."

—**Kaethe Schwehn**, author of *The Rending and the Nest*

"Poignant, engaging, and often humorous, *Yet, Here We Are* immediately pulls in readers with its lyrical prose, surprising twists, and vividly drawn characters who slip into your heart. Massman has penned a truly compelling story of love, betrayal, and irrepressible hope. A deeply evocative novel that stays with you long after turning the final page."

—**Pamela Hamilton**, author of the award-winning novel *Lady Be Good*

"Massman's *Yet, Here We Are* weaves a gorgeous, heart-wrenching, and very real tale of love and resilience in a fascinating historical time. The engaging plot peels back the layers of a complex woman and her family as they engage in a fight that will change the course of history. *Yet, Here We Are* is a thought-evoking, compelling, and memorable read."

—**Dianne C. Braley**, author of *The Silence in the Sound*, winner of the 2022 The New York Big Book Award

"Massman creates an interwoven narrative exploring one young woman's artistic and cultural awakening in the late 1940s and her daughters' subsequent ecological awakening in the 1970s. The strong female characters in Massman's debut novel are richly developed, and the storyline is well-rooted in our current era's environmental angst. *Yet, Here We Are* would make wonderful grist for any book club discussion."

—**Glenn R. Miller**, author of *Doorman Wanted*

"In *Yet, Here We Are*, Massman captures the yearning for love and liberation among two generations of rural women thrown by chance into urban landscapes, offering both breathless freedom and unsettling chaos. Amid the lost innocence sparked by personal and political upheaval, Massman delivers an inspiring message of courage, perseverance, and hope."

—**Craig Cox**, author of *Storefront Revolution: Food Co-ops and the Counterculture*

"This vivid and moving depiction of a mother and her two daughters explores their personal and cultural histories in the heartland of the Midwest. Overlapping narratives braid two timelines—post–WWII and post–Vietnam War—to tell the stories of three women. Elizabeth, Louise, and Sage are linked not only by blood but by their own distinct needs for authenticity and for life-affirming and creative responses to the times in which they find themselves. Taken as a whole, this strong debut novel is a rallying cry to embrace each moment, to participate in community life without surrendering what makes us open-hearted individuals."

—**Leslie Schultz**, author of *Still Life with Poppies: Elegies*

"Massman has crafted an immersive novel that transports readers through time and space into realistically portrayed historical lives. With lush prose, Massman paints vivid portraits of each character and draws readers deeper into their hopes, dreams, and struggles. Overall, *Yet, Here We Are* is a compelling tale of love, loss, resilience, and the enduring search for meaning that fans of literary drama are sure to enjoy."

—**Micheal R. Vukelic**, International Speaker, Success Coach, and CEO, Outrageous Success LLC

"An honest story about the joys and sorrows of a woman's life and the hopes and dreams of her and her daughters. *Yet, Here We Are* is a beautifully moving dance between eras, an echo of life in the mid-seventies and the post-war years that rings true to the times."

—**Soren Petrek**, author of the Madeleine Toche historical fiction series

Readers' Favorite **5 Star Review Recipient**

Yet, Here We Are

by Brenda K. Massman

© Copyright 2024 Brenda K. Massman

ISBN 979-8-88824-301-5

All rights reserved. No part of this publication may be reproduced, stored in a retrieval system, or transmitted in any form or by any means—electronic, mechanical, photocopy, recording, or any other—except for brief quotations in printed reviews, without the prior written permission of the author.

This is a work of fiction. All the characters in this book are fictitious, and any resemblance to actual persons, living or dead, is purely coincidental. The names, incidents, dialogue, and opinions expressed are products of the author's imagination and are not to be construed as real.

Published by

3705 Shore Drive
Virginia Beach, VA 23455
800-435-4811
www.koehlerbooks.com

Yet, Here We Are

Brenda K. Massman

VIRGINIA BEACH
CAPE CHARLES

This book is dedicated to my husband and children.
Thank you, always, for your encouragement and for your love.

Prologue
— October 1948 —

How far removed I am. Elizabeth sat straight-backed upon the wooden stool, hands folded protectively over her newly purchased clutch, eyes casting curious, apprehensive glances across the smoky dimness of her surroundings. After months of dreaming, months of longing anticipation, she had arrived here in Chicago, not a single person known to her. Bewilderingly, lavishly alone.

She raised her hand briefly, unusually eager for a drink, the essentiality of it extending solely from the novelty of her situation. But the barkeeps were oblivious to her gesture as they moved swiftly, adeptly, pouring crystal clear and amber-hued liquor from bottles that lined a wall of mirrors like soldiers ready for duty. The clinking of a cube, a splash of whiskey, a nimble stir. A wave of naivety passed through Elizabeth.

Turning her attention instead to the opposite end of the elongated room, she noticed a quartet assembling upon the stage, its instruments testing the air in preparation for performance. In the center stood a woman wearing a neatly fitted dress of shimmering fire, her back to the audience as she addressed the men who would accompany her. Captivated, Elizabeth watched the knowing fingers of the bassist pluck at taut strings, glistening beads of sweat peppering his broad forehead, dark as morning coffee, closed eyes shuttering away any thought but that of his music. The longing of the sax and the tranquil pulse of drums keeping pace in keen harmony as the band moved fluidly from warm-up to performance.

A powerful alto emanated from the singer as she slowly turned to face the audience, demanding those in conversation to pause, to peer over their shoulders for a glance at this presence who serenaded the patrons of the Blue Window from the depths of her soul. One couple stood, slowly engaging in dance beside a table laden with empty snifters, with highballs holding a finger's width of bourbon yet to be quaffed. Nearby, a woman with a high gloss of blond hair reached languorously toward the man beside her, trailing a smooth, knowing finger across his shoulders. *Yes, tonight.* Songs of love, songs of desperate hope saturated the air with intrinsic comfort. The result was dazzling, if not surreal: easy romance melded with a hint of precarious danger, each individually distinctive yet somehow remarkably dependent on the other.

Elizabeth worked her way through the crowd closer to the stage and settled at a small table, well enough secluded next to a sturdy wall of red brick. In front of her, a handsome man wearing pressed black pants and a white collared shirt joined a small gathering. She watched as he placed his suit jacket over the back of a chair, his eyes meeting hers for a wink longer than a passing glance.

And in that singular moment, in an enchanting basement lounge in the city of Chicago where she found herself breathing in the music like the necessity of oxygen, a flicker of love no larger than a mote of dust landed on Elizabeth's heart. Gracefully, without suspicion. It was a spark that would set into action a most unthinkable direction in her life. One of extravagant joys and one of abysmal sorrows.

An experience she would never wish to exchange.

Chapter 1

—— Elizabeth, October 1948 ——

When the day of my departure arrived, Sage was nearly six years old, Louise just three, and the birth and death of my son ten months past. I ascended the wooden box steps that led into the cavernous passenger car of the Midwest Arrow, which would soon escort me away from the bucolic existence I'd always known. With haste, the steward pointed me in the direction of coach seat D14, and I walked as quickly as my new dress shoes allowed before dropping gracelessly into the stiff seat.

Through the small window beside me, I peered out at the gathering of folks staying behind. An elderly man with thick-framed glasses stood alone, his hand slowly lifting toward the train, and nearby a woman, perhaps a few years younger than I, blew a kiss into the air as the toddler in her arms writhed for its freedom. My own small family formed the rest of the paltry crowd: Will holding Louise aloft, her face turned toward the sky where she was no doubt watching a flock of geese glide overhead, his own lackluster eyes loosely committed to the engine car up ahead. The touch of my daughter's desperate hugs and kisses still lingered, her good nature having quickly morphed into short-lived confusion as the reality of my leaving came to fruition.

It was Sage who looked pointedly at the train, at the very window behind which I had settled myself, though my eldest child couldn't possibly have known that I would be in that particular spot. I waved upon the smudged glass of the window, adding my mark to those of the travelers who'd preceded me. Sage mirrored the wave with her own little hand, and I was sure I saw a smile come across her face.

As I looked at them, a poignant ache nipped at my heels. It would be the first time that I had been apart from my children for more than a day, the first night since my wedding that I would not lie in bed beside my husband. Will did not—perhaps could not—understand my need to go away, though only for a short while, yet I understood his hesitancy. Things had changed between us; I had changed. But I had prepared myself for this moment, for anticipated pangs of melancholy during these next three weeks, packing them away in a separate, invisible piece of luggage that I would try not to open too often yet would keep nearby for when needed.

The train set into motion with a begrudging jerk. I was off. After a year of hopeful expectation, in half a day's time I would be transported from the banks of the Mississippi River across the state of Wisconsin, landing in Chicago by nightfall. The slow movement of the gulping engine gradually picked up speed and smoothed its rhythm, the noise settling monotonously into the background. In front of me, the seatback blocked any forward view, and from above the diamond-shaped lights lining the wooden walls and ceilings flickered uncertainly. I turned back toward the window. It didn't take long for the landscape to change from buildings and billboards to open country with generous foliage painted in comforting russets and lively apricots, with glimmers of ruby like pockets of hope—a brief respite from the otherwise endless expanse of summer green, of winter white.

After a while, I turned away, the silhouette of the landscape quickly fading from sight in the dim light of the car. I realized that I still held my ticket, the date prominently stamped at the top: October 4, 1948—ten months to the day since Frankie was born, a day that remains etched upon my spirit.

The morning had begun with a fluttering of pure, splendid snow as I walked with unwarranted trust over the virgin ice of the creek bed. The isolating crunch of each step broke the stillness of the early winter air, competing only with the occasional trill of a bird or crystal-like tinkling of snow meeting the surface upon which it fell. Layers of white blanketing the ice of the shallow creek bed formed a labyrinth of sorts around mounds of stones, like dogs curled in sleep, which I navigated with quick guesses to avoid the surprise of a soft spot.

It was nearly half a mile, perhaps farther, that I had laid tracks before stopping to rest on the trunk of a fallen tree. There, as I sat in the stillness of the wooded creek, I considered the dream from which I'd awakened that morning, one in which a young boy stood before me, his nascent brown locks having grown in fine waves that parenthesized tender hazel eyes. "Be happy, Mommy," he had said, the only words he spoke.

I considered what may have been behind the seemingly simple message. Were they words of caution? If I couldn't be strong enough to summon joy, would the pain bear down on him? How could I, a pregnant woman, be mired in despair during this exceptional time in which strength was so necessary? My previous pregnancies had held no fear, no sadness. They were simply the gift of being a woman.

Sage had been born at home, a surprising first birth. Labor had begun midmorning, shortly after I'd finished a cup of black coffee and a warm roll slathered with freshly churned butter. There had been no introduction to labor other than a restless night of sleep, but a sudden, rapid seizing of my abdomen followed by the breaking of my water sac was a less-than-subtle hint that this child would soon be born.

Will had been at the kitchen table with me and immediately ushered my petite, albeit very pregnant self to the bedroom. He rang Dr. Grimmsrud, who had suggested that my husband take me to the hospital. But I wouldn't leave—couldn't leave—for the rapidity of the contractions.

Dr. Grimmsrud had agreed to come out to the farm after seeing his morning patients, letting Will know that it would be several hours of labor, as it was with first births. Two hours later, the doctor had not yet arrived. In his stead, Dorothea, from the farm just past the east bend in the road, managed the birth with Will as her assistant, my husband a calming sedative to my outbursts of agony.

Sage arrived quickly, went to the breast quickly, and has been quick of mind ever since.

"Sage? What is in such a name?" Our few relatives were astounded that the baby girl—our firstborn—was not given a Christian name, a family name. Louise, perhaps, after my own mother, or Emma after my grandmother, God rest their souls. "What kind of name is a spice, dear?" they asked. "Where is the honor in such a name?"

"She's not named after a spice," I calmly replied, without remarking that sage is an herb. "Sage means wisdom. Look at her eyes. There is wisdom in them."

"The only thing different about her eyes is that they are not blue like most babies."

Will wasn't terribly enthusiastic about Sage's name, either, though his disapproval was surmounted by my insistence. I was her mother; I knew this child, and I knew she was Sage.

The dubious welcome that Sage received eventually turned away from the oddity of her name and toward the joy of a new child in the Ley family. Our second daughter was born three years later on the fourteenth of August at Winneshiek County Memorial Hospital.

"This is the day we have been waiting for since Pearl Harbor. This is the day when Fascism finally dies, as we always knew it would." The sound of President Truman's voice lacing through radio speakers sparked immense celebrations throughout America as I cried out in laborious joy, my uterus wrenching in pain over one of the most powerful contractions yet. From outside the door of my hospital room, Will whooped, jumping into the air, thankful for God's victorious right hand. The world was celebrating with kisses and confetti; in my mind, at least a small part of the celebration was for our perfectly healthy, perfectly named daughter, Louise.

My pregnancy with Frankie had felt discernibly different from the previous two. Although the experience had been physically similar, a chasm of bleakness had settled in my heart, crowding out the unrecoverable joy of parenting two astonishingly developing children. Tucking my daughters into bed after telling a bedtime story, strolling through the woods during cool summer evenings—none of the usual ways of inveigling happiness back into my spirit had been effective. I couldn't seem to find the enthusiasm needed to change anything. Or even try, really.

Returning my thoughts to the present, I stood from my spot on the fallen tree and turned back toward home, unwilling to continue considering the previous night's dream any further. I navigated the frozen water with extra care, clutching tightly onto immature tree trunks as I pulled myself up and out of the creek bed once I neared home.

Will and the girls were at the pond where Will had just drilled a hole in the ice with his new auger so that he could teach the girls how to ice fish. I hung my coat on the hook by the door and set my hat and gloves on the register to dry, then went into the bedroom where I wedged myself under the blankets of the freshly made bed to catch a quick nap. But no sooner had I closed my eyes than I felt the first stab of unreasonable pain stretch across my abdomen.

I stiffened, unsure of what was happening—several weeks of pregnancy still remained before my child was due to be born. My abdominal muscles remained taut as if to prepare for the waves of pain that were about to wash over me like the methodical flow of a tide. A lapse of time passed in which I felt as if I had been strapped to the mattress, and then from the kitchen door I heard Will's voice.

"You caught three, Louise! Three fish!"

"Yeah," said Louise. I could almost hear the smile in her voice. "Fwee for Mummy."

"And Sage, your mother will be so proud of the big bluegill you reeled in!" I envisioned Sage carrying the small milk bucket half-filled with water that sloshed over the edges, giving the fish a bumpy ride as she focused intently on getting them home.

"Set down the bucket and I'll go find her. Stay quiet now."

"Shhh," Louise said.

I heard the hinges of the door and the *thwup* of Will's work boots being pulled off, followed by giggles from the girls as he tiptoed through the kitchen and toward our bedroom. But when my husband opened the bedroom door, his stealthy footsteps came to an abrupt halt, his eyes widening at the sight before him.

"Betty!" he called out in hushed astonishment.

I looked toward him just as another crushing pain seared through my abdomen. Blood had now soaked the bed with the stain of despair, encircling the greater part of my pale, tense body, the metallic pungency of it rippling throughout the air of the small bedroom.

"Betty, what's happening? Is it the baby, Betty?"

But at that moment the cramp, immense in its grip, welled up even stronger. Like the snapping of a rubber band, my legs jerked involuntarily toward my abdomen causing my back to arch like a tautly strung bow. Though my eyes were forced closed, my mouth opened as if great, vocal waves of anguish were about to discharge. Yet, silence ensued, the pain too powerful to allow the relief of a wail. Will reached for me, cradling his hands behind my head, his forehead touching mine until the pain passed moments later.

"Betty, honey. The baby. Did you call Dr. Grimmsrud? Does anyone know what is happening?" he asked in a whisper.

I slowly moved my head to the side and back again.

"Betty, listen to me," he said, moving his broad hands to either side of my face as he looked down at me. "I'm going to call the doctor. I'll be right back."

I blinked and Will rushed from the bedroom, having forgotten about Louise and Sage waiting to debut their fish. I could hear his voice speaking with an urgency that the operator had likely not heard in some time as he commanded her to get Dr. Grimmsrud on the line immediately.

"Dr. Grimmsrud, Will Ley here. Listen, Betty needs you right away. There's blood all over. I'm pretty sure it's the baby coming too early. It doesn't look good, Doc. Betty doesn't look good."

By the time Dr. Grimmsrud had arrived fifteen minutes later, hours seemed to have passed in a confluence of fear and agony. I remained mute, my gaze focused on Will's, who insisted he be in the room with me.

"I'm here, honey. We're going to move through this together. Breathe, now. Just breathe."

Frankie lived for four minutes. Not yet six months in utero, my boy was unprepared to enter the world. During the span of his short life, I held him without pause, refusing to let go after Dr. Grimmsrud handed him over to my yearning arms. His eyes never opened; his skin was transparently thin over his delicate body. His heart, at first beating rapidly with life—in fear or effort, we would never know—far too quickly slowed its pace. As I held my son, I was sure that my own heartbeat was rhythmic with his. Sure that mine, too, was ebbing its pace and ready to cease in one last, tragic beat.

It wasn't until the final, quiet tick ceased that a swell of grief erupted from me. Grief for my son. Grief for myself, for our family. A numbness of physical sensation commingling with the blistering pain of loss spread swiftly throughout my body. He was gone. My boy, he was no longer.

I told the others to leave, had insisted on being left alone with his still body, the only opportunity there would ever be to hold him, to feel his flesh, his essence. Will nodded at Dr. Grimmsrud and the two walked out of the bedroom, closing the door quietly behind.

The air was once again flush with stillness, with searing noiselessness. I closed my eyes and heard the sound of my own breath. Felt the air move freely into my lungs, out of my lungs. Felt my heart knock at my chest and my abdomen rebel with indiscreet interrogation, wallowing in the punishing pain. I should've listened more closely when he had warned me of the shortcomings of the future, for surely it was little Frankie in my dream. "Be happy, Mommy." I should have realized, should have done something, should have changed somehow, right then and there.

When I opened my eyes, I could look only at my son, lying statically in my arms. I drew my knees toward my chest, deliberately this time, and adjusted his body so that he lay close to me upon my inclined thighs. With a feathery touch, I traced over his delicate eyelids, continuing the movement over the curve of his dainty ears, passing downward over his cheeks, his chin. After long, indulgent moments, I cupped the back of his silken head in both of my hands and leaned toward him. I kissed his forehead gently and whispered a mother's goodbye, knowing that his evanescent soul was leaving me, gliding along an unreachable path that, in that moment, I longed to follow.

Three days later, we buried our son. The organ remained silent, as did the few folks who had scattered throughout the pews of St. Benedict's Catholic Church. When the Mass ended, I walked unceremoniously down the aisle beside Will, who carried Louise. Sage walked in pace between us, and at the opening of the doors, we turned in the direction of the nearby graveyard where we laid to rest our only son.

Upon arriving back home, I prepared plates filled with the food offerings we had been given by neighbors and friends—green bean casserole, pickled beets, chicken and dumplings—then retired to my bedroom. I closed the door, turned the lock, and opened the window a few inches despite the December air. Facing the rectangular mirror that alighted upon my grandmother's vanity, I removed the dark blue suit I had been wearing, along with the white slip and drab undergarments beneath. And there I stood, naked in front of myself, gazing at the reflection of my body.

My rounded breasts were full, aching with the remains of superfluous milk. My uterus had only just begun to contract during the past few days, and extra weight remained settled like a protective sheath over my abdomen. Turning my backside toward the mirror,

I twisted my neck to allow a long glance at the side of me to which I rarely gave notice. A small bruise darkened my shoulder; I did not remember the occurrence. My waistline was thickened to the point of nonexistence and my buttocks slightly sagged, though I could still detect youth within the sculpture.

In the distance I heard the din of a car motoring down the road from the east, a milk cow lowing for her calf—each seemingly a peal of consequence. My emotions bounced like a neglected ball searching for a place to settle, a place beyond where it had already been.

Facing front once again, I drew my hands delicately upward from my hips, pausing to caress the thickened skin of my abdomen before shifting toward my breasts. A reactive wince breathed forth as my fingers touched hardened nipples, knowing that they would never feed the hungry mouth of my baby boy. As if of their own will, my hands continued to roam upward over my slim neck and into my hair that, during this last pregnancy, had darkened a shade or two from its golden-brown color. A reflection, I thought. Lifting the thick waves, I turned to the side and pursed my lips, still colored with lipstick, and felt an unwarranted swell of desire. It wasn't Will that I was imagining. It wasn't any man, or anyone at all. The desire was simply there, without reason.

A frail breeze wafted in through the window, brushing the cold air against my exposed skin. Embracing the chill, I remained in place, wondering where life would go from here. For there was now something more that I needed. I had married a man who was faithful. He was good to me, successful in his farming career. I had a comfortable home, endless outdoor space, and kindly enough folks surrounding me. I had given birth three times with no desire to foray into the experience again. And I was rife with a daunting cheerlessness that had only compounded over the past three days.

The breeze elevated momentarily, brushing a few loose strands of hair along my shoulders. I ran my tongue along my lips, ignoring the bitterness of lipstick, and turned to face my other side, holding hostage no single thought. Simply being, listening.

It was then that something elusive began calling to me, a dreamlike voice that I couldn't identify yet understood that it would somehow heal me—from Frankie's death and from the vacuum into which I was being drawn. I released my hair and squared myself to the mirror.

A brief interlude; a different life.

I listened.

Chicago.

An explanation didn't follow, but the idea swooped in powerfully and uninhibited. Far different from the imaginative daydreams I'd had as a teenager of a trip to the city of Minneapolis, Chicago was an inexplicable demand. But by whom? I had the girls, Will, the farm . . . I couldn't just leave.

Maybe you could.

I just lost a child. I am in mourning.

This is different because today you are different. Your life is now different. Which is why you must go.

No. I must be wise.

Be wise. Go. Live.

How could doing so possibly be for the better?

Living is always for the better. Go.

But . . .

Go. To Chicago.

Chapter 2
—— April 1975 ——

Louise had just ripped the binding string from the sack of hulled barley and began pouring the brittle grains into the bulk bin when a raised voice brought her to a pause. In the two years she'd been volunteering at the food co-op, Louise couldn't recall having ever heard a voice elevated—both a blessing and a curse in her opinion.

"You'll have to check elsewhere." Mark's voice held a note of restraint, which is exactly why Louise knew this was more than a question from a neighborhood shopper as to why no sugar was to be found in the store. She set down the bag, the weight causing a spill of grains across the ninety-year-old fir floor that by all appearances hadn't had a facelift since its inception. Louise slipped off her wooden-soled clogs and knelt, feeling the tickle of barley slip into the flare of her bell-bottom jeans.

"You know why you don't have a can of kidney beans? You know why?" The anger in the stranger's voice distilled the air with silence.

Louise, sweeping the barley with her hands into a scoopable pile, paused again. *This is getting interesting.*

"Well, sir, I have a feeling you're going to tell me why I don't have a can of kidney beans, whether or not I want to hear it," Mark replied in his serene, mellifluous voice. Louise could envision his calm countenance: Steve McQueen eyes, the expressionless set of his mouth, hands stashed in the front pocket of his tunic.

The anonymous speaker was quick to respond, as if a long-awaited stage debut had finally come to fruition. "You don't have a *can* of fuckin' kidney beans because you're a fuckin' *elitist*, you good-for-shit *hippie*."

Louise could hear the jingle from the strap of bells on the door, a terrified shopper getting the hell out, no doubt.

"Hmm," replied Mark. "You see, I thought I didn't have a can of kidney beans to offer you because we have a *philosophy* about selling only *pure* foods. But thanks for correcting me; I'll immediately change our bylaws to include 'don't sell *cans* of kidney beans because we're *elitist*.'"

Mark turned toward the scant aisles of food wares, calling out for Sherrie and Louise to grab the fictional co-op bible and immediately ink in the newly revised bylaws.

"Absolutely, right on it," Sherrie said, her voice laced with ennui.

"I'll rustle up a quill and bottle of ink." Louise giggled, playing along from her place in the back corner of the room, while still wondering over the oddity of the verbal assault. She'd heard that some of the guys from the Cooperative Organization had made a bit of noise over the past month, but today was the first time she was privy to an actual performance. Personally, she didn't understand why it was so important for the Cooperative Organization, or CO as they were known, to join all the food co-ops in the Twin Cities under one roof, so to speak. Living Waters had been running just fine without them, and Louise was glad that Mark was standing his ground. She was also happy as hell she'd picked up this shift from Peck to witness the amusement.

"You all think this is funny shit, but you don't know. You just *don't know*." The obtrusive stranger left on that note, slamming the door in a reverberating exclamation point.

"And . . . let the good times roll," said Mark.

Louise hopped to her feet, leaving the last few grains on the floor, and made her way toward the front of the store. Mark stood up from the wooden stool next to the cash register and walked nonchalantly toward the door, watching the irate intruder return to his mud-colored Pinto and peel away.

"You know, they're probably not going to stop making these friendly visits," said Sherrie, approaching the front counter. "Maybe we oughta let the cops know, just to give them a head's up. Maybe they'll patrol the area a little more often."

"Right, because they'll surely prioritize a kidney bean argument," Louise responded with a wink. "If anything, they'll stop in out of curiosity and leave all the more disappointed once they realize there are no doughnuts for sale."

Mark chuckled, and Sherrie turned aside to wipe a sticky ring of honey from a shelf. Despite the growing number of visits from CO, Mark didn't seem particularly alarmed. But then again, a tornado could touch down across the street and he would probably stand by the window and watch with his familiar slow nod and half smile.

"You know, I heard that Real Food Co-op joined the enemy," said Mark. "I'm surprised. Jake doesn't seem the type to cave. Man, wonder what was in it for him."

Word around town was that ever since the CO formed, their worker bees had been buzzing around to various co-ops trying to sway them toward centralizing with the idea of uniting the working class against capitalists, of making food cheaper—even if not pure—to bring in more shoppers. But Mark wasn't having it. The reason he'd opened Living Waters Co-op was because of the food—wholesome, locally raised food available to everyone.

Having turned the cardboard sign from *Open* to *Shut*, Mark made his way back to the front counter and lit up an ever-present joint. He pulled in the smoke, his eyes squinting in thought, then handed it off to Louise.

"Wonder what's in it for anyone, really," Louise said, feeling the smoke dance in her lungs, a familiar loosening. She tossed her head back in exhalation, her short blond locks brushing the top of the oversized wool sweater that hung on her slim frame like cloying drapery. Passing the joint back to Mark, she leaned her head onto his shoulder.

"Have you ever asked?" called out Sherrie, now at the back of the small store where she'd moved on to scrubbing the door of the small refrigerator. Without Sherrie, Living Waters would rarely experience the touch of a damp cloth.

"Asked what?" replied Louise.

"Asked what's in it for us if we sell the fuckin' kidney beans."

"Oh yeah, they let us know at their last visit," Mark called back. "'A system of democracy that excludes no one, a store for all the people.' As it is now, we're exclusive—haven't you heard? We're like a yacht club, catering to the elite."

Louise laughed at the analogy, imagining Thurston Howell stopping by for a bag of organic lentils and a bundle of red chard to cook up for supper with Lovey. Maybe even add a touch of fresh, pungent goat milk brought in by the Sandersons that afternoon.

"What's all the laughing about?" called out Randy with a wide smile as he walked through the doorway and toward Louise. He reached out with one arm and pulled her into his broad-shouldered body, simultaneously reaching his other hand for the joint.

"We're exclusive," Sherrie said, walking up to the front of the small store to join the others. "We'll have to see your invitation before entering next time."

Randy, though smiling at the unknown joke, nonetheless looked at Louise for an explanation. Louise immediately knew that he was questioning whether this was another racist remark despite the fact that it came from Sherrie. It was hard enough for him to get around town, even law school campus at times, without having racist bullshit thrown in his face.

"No worries," said Mark before Louise could answer. "The only black we won't allow in here is the bean type that comes in a can. The CO paid another visit."

"Ah, Weezy told me that rats have been stirring in the streets. Who this time?"

"An unknown. Likely some new bloke trying to prove his mettle," replied Mark.

"More noise?"

"Yeah, I guess."

Mark turned to the register and removed the few bills it held, though not enough to warrant counting. He placed the money into a leather zip bag that he kept under the counter, securing the flimsy lock with a key that hung like an ancestral locket around his neck. The spare was held by a magnet behind the calendar in the office on the off chance that Mark wasn't around at opening or closing time.

"Time to go, man. Maybe I'll call a meeting one of these days and get the collective thought on what, if anything, we oughta do," said Mark. "Just . . . let me be the one to tell Peck."

"No problem there," replied Louise.

She and Randy each took a final drag of the stunted joint before stepping out into the late spring day to walk the few blocks to their home.

"Airspeed," Jim instructed rather than inquired.

"One hundred five knots," said Sage.

"Altitude?"

"Thirty-five hundred."

"Make a thirty-degree turn to the right."

"Check."

The numbers displayed on the various gauges and instruments of the plane were a breeze for Sage, the calculations second nature, even though she'd been taking ground lessons for just three weeks, air for two. It was the breadth of the land far below that tempted her into distraction. Patterns created by man and nature displaying geometrical grids of black dirt fields sidled up to shades of emerging spring green and amoeba-shaped bodies of water. Miniature vehicles on outlying roads moved forward like dedicated ants, leaving curious clouds in their wake. Yes, here is where Sage felt on the top of the world, a relieving contrast to the complacency of her everyday life. Here in the Cessna 172, life as she knew it became a hazy memory.

"Ms. Ley, check your altitude," Jim commanded in a rugged voice that bordered on anger. Sage had no doubt he was wondering why she wasn't at home with a husband and a couple of kids. "Blasted youth these days," she could almost hear him thinking.

Even though she wasn't married, at least she wasn't running around the city on a quest for "peace and love." No disrespect to her sister, but it just wasn't her thing. Not that she ever thought her thing would be hovering above the earth in an engine with wings. Even that came as a surprise to Sage, and it absolutely bewildered Louise and Mother. She was Sage, after all: the cautious one, the wise, level-headed daughter. The one who preferred orderly knowns to unreasonable unknowns. She was the research librarian who craved knowledge as if it were a parching thirst that could never be fully quenched.

"All right. Let's take 'er down," Jim directed, his voice softening a smidge.

Sage sighed and glanced downward again for a parting impression of today's outing, then adjusted the rudder with growing certainty.

Minutes later, having once again returned to solid earth—to standard, ordinary life— Sage scooped a handful of water from the sink of the modest airport bathroom and splashed it onto her face. The whoop of icy water distracted her from the adrenaline of flight before she made the twenty-five-minute drive to her home, the upper floor of a two-story Foursquare on St. Clair Avenue, where she quickly realized that she had exhausted herself enough during the day to consider an early bedtime.

The waning sun momentarily shone through the clouds, jetting a ray of light into the high pocket window of her bedroom. Sage sat before the dressing mirror running the prickly bristles of a hairbrush through her long, tangle-free chestnut hair, an exact match to her eyes. She silently reviewed the day's lesson—crosswind navigation—that, though she'd understood the concept during the classroom lesson, had been entirely different in practicum. Feeling the downward pull of the plane as she manipulated the rudder to press against it ignited her adrenaline, to be sure. Yet sluicing through the air, no matter what the situation, somehow managed to release the perpetual wheel-spinning of her mind, erasing the murmur of anxious energy that insisted every corner of her life be properly tucked into place. It was as if the distance from the earth allowed her an empathetic distancing from the disquieting reality of her life. From the moment she had first felt the rumble of the engine under her seat and saw the earth drop from beneath her, Sage knew without a doubt that flight was her ally.

Chapter 3
— Elizabeth, October 1948 —

"May I assume you had family see you off?"

The voice, rich and silken like freshly skimmed cream, came from the woman across the aisle from me, also seated alone. She wore a cocoa-brown tweed traveling suit with an ivory-colored blouse that reflected her blond locks and light complexion. Surprising red earrings dangled from her lobes, mirroring her lipstick and fingernails. Though I'd seen women in magazines with colored nails, I'd never had a close-up look, and I found myself responding to them rather than her.

"I did. My daughters are five and three," I said, forcing myself to look back up at her.

"What adorable ages," she replied, overlooking my awkwardness.

"Yes. Sage—she's my oldest—is really something. She is so sweet and so smart at the same time. And Louise, she's probably still staring after the geese in the sky, always interested in what's outside."

I averted my eyes to my lap for a moment, realizing I had begun to blather. But the woman's smile and raised eyebrows encouraged me to continue.

"Will you be away from them for long?"

"Three weeks."

Regret pricked at my chest; I'd never been away from them for more than a day. I asked whether she, too, had children. Though if she did, I was sure they would have been much older than my girls. She appeared to be in her forties.

"No." She continued smiling, though her eyes, I noticed, lost a degree of light. "I do have a dog, however, that is very childlike at times."

I laughed and glanced down again before replying. "We have two dogs, though they're not in our house. They're hunting dogs."

"Oh, what is it they hunt?"

"Pheasants, ducks, raccoons. We sell the hides of the coons. I think they're made into coats and hats and the like, though I've never really cared to ask for details."

I could hardly bear to look at the hides stacked in the corner of the basement, let alone discuss their ultimate use.

"I've seen ladies with such collars on their coats. Men as well," replied the woman.

I shuddered at the thought of those hides touching any part of my body.

"That must be it then. Maybe they were wearing an authentic Will Ley coon."

She laughed. "And probably paid a right eye to get it."

I laughed, too, and felt myself relax. I'd never been in conversation with a woman of such class.

"Your husband is a hunter then?" she continued.

"He's a farmer, but he hunts during the hunting seasons. In the seven years we've been married, he's always given us a fresh wild turkey for Thanksgiving."

"Ah, the best."

"I do always look forward to it. Are you married, too?"

She paused for a beat before replying with a simple "Yes."

I nodded, unsure of whether I'd touched on a topic she would rather not discuss.

"I'm Betty," I said. Then, "Elizabeth Ley."

"Helena Graham. Lovely to meet you, Elizabeth."

"You too. You know, I hadn't even thought about what the train ride might be like when I imagined my trip to Chicago. I guess I just couldn't get the possibilities of the city out of my mind."

"Chicago will do that to a person."

A steward, dressed in black pants and a jacket with a starched white shirt, stopped in the aisle just short of us. "Lunch will be served in ten minutes. The dining car is three back. Can we expect you to join us?" he asked, looking first at Helena, then at me.

Helena nodded, I said yes, and the steward moved on before I could ask about the menu. I had no idea what to expect during any part of this adventure.

"Have you been to Chicago often?" I asked, resuming our conversation.

"Yes. It's a fairly easy trip. A woman needs to remove herself from the everyday now again, doesn't she?"

"That's exactly what's been on my mind! Though I don't know if Will believes in that idea as much as I do."

"Is this your first time away?"

"Yes. It shows?"

"No. But I can imagine your husband might have been quite surprised at the idea of your leaving. Unsure why it was necessary, perhaps?"

"Will is very . . . stable. In all ways, but especially in not wanting to upset the flow of things. He doesn't see why I can't just go on a long walk and refresh myself or kneel in prayer and ask God for help."

I surprised myself by revealing this much and hoped she wasn't taken aback by my confession.

"I'm sorry. He's a really good man. I didn't mean to make him sound bad."

"Oh, I can hardly believe you'd be married to a curmudgeon. And, I do understand your plight."

Her empathy instantly buoyed me. There was no one, no other

woman with whom I could discuss the reason for my need to experience something beyond the everyday. It was the loss of Frankie, yes, but it was so much more than that. It was a need to discover who I was—as a woman, as a wife. It was a rescue tube that landed before me as I flailed in deep waters, searching for land. I wondered whether Helena ever felt the uncertainties that I had about marriage, about love. Can a man who is so good still be the wrong man? The idea had begun to drip into my thoughts in recent months. It was an unsettling thought, and certainly not a logical one, yet it continued to rally against me.

Helena and I dined together at a Formica table rimmed in ripple-edged stainless steel, similar to my table at home, though much smaller in size. Each table, I noticed, was bolted to the floor, as were the wooden benches with their high backs closing off the space between diners. Complimentary gin or vodka with tonic water was offered, which we declined, followed by slices of bread and butter. By the aroma in the air, I surmised that chicken might be served soon after.

"Can I ask where you live, Helena, or what your husband does for a living?"

"Of course. I live in St. Paul, on Summit Avenue. Are you familiar with St. Paul?"

"No. I've only ever been to Minnesota a few times to places just over the border from where I live outside of Decorah. In Iowa."

"Well, I would encourage you to visit, should the opportunity arise. St. Paul is a worthy city. Many changes have occurred since the war's end. The arts scene is blossoming, more parks are being developed. People seem to care about the place in which they live more so than in years past. It really is becoming quite lovely."

"Is it anything like Chicago?"

Helena slowly tore off a corner of bread. "Only in that it is a city, though of course St. Paul and Minneapolis together are much smaller. But Chicago just . . . has its own life, its own personality, I guess one would say. It undoubtedly leaves an impression on those who visit."

As I ate from the plate of food set before me—a slightly dry chicken breast with gravy and baked butternut squash with onions—I imagined the grand city Helena continued to describe: the bustle of cars and people, the sharp incline of modern buildings leaping toward the sky, lights that never entirely dimmed, the tarry smell of the wooden pier. It was simply a Midwestern city, yet it was also a foreign world, so far beyond the borders of my bucolic life. Exhilaration coursed through me at the realization that I would soon be there; my much-anticipated trip was no longer in the future.

After our meal, Helena and I returned to our seats where she retrieved a book from her bag—*Middlemarch*—and I a magazine. Reading proved to be a challenge to my equilibrium, and after a short while I set aside the magazine and once again closed my eyes.

I awoke as the steward was announcing the Midwest Arrow's impending arrival at Union Station. Through the window, distant lights were becoming more prevalent. We were almost there. I had almost arrived.

Soon enough, the train slowed its pace and came to a crawl. I pulled my fleece cloche over my head, though the weather was far too mild for it, and gathered my nearby belongings. The steward worked his way one last time toward our seats, indicating with an upturn of his hand that we were to exit. Upon disembarking, a second steward near the door handed me a picture postcard advertising the Midwest Arrow. I tucked it into my purse and reached for the handrail as I stepped into the evening air of Chicago.

Before I had a chance to look around, Helena wrapped her gloved hand around my elbow and led me through the station. Around us, people swarmed. The din of voices, the clicking of shoes on the marble floor, and the sounding of a train whistle consumed the air, reverberating off the walls like a dissonant symphony. Travelers walked in every direction through the grand open space, mostly men with small black bags in hand and some women, a few with children. Everyone seemed to wear a different expression, everyone en route to their own important lives.

We exited on the opposite side of the station into the electric evening air, where the action was no slower. Cars with headlights and taxi cabs topped with simple roof signs carried people away in a grand, confusing rush. Helena raised her arm and approached a taxicab without hesitation.

"The Dominican," she directed, as the driver placed my baggage into the rear of the car.

I turned to her, feeling at a loss for words. "Helena, I can't tell you how happy I am to have met you."

"Likewise, dear Elizabeth. May your stay be all that you wish for—and beyond."

I was unsure whether to shake her hand or pull her into a hug until she made the decision for me. And as we embraced, I dearly hoped that fate would allow us to cross each other's paths again.

The driver pulled the taxicab into an opening of burgeoning cars, all of which seemed to be driven with haste. An unexpected ticking emanated from a meter at the front of the car, and the driver spoke as if by phone into a handheld device, indicating our destination.

During the twenty-minute ride to the hotel, I looked out at the blur of sights passing by. Dissipating were any lingering concerns over leaving home, the city an invisible eraser, replaced by a hint of joy to which I'd become unaccustomed. By the time we arrived at the Dominican, the scenery made me feel as if I'd been transported to the other side of the world.

Will had insisted I stay in one of the nicer hotels, for he'd assumed my safety would be better guaranteed in such a place, and I was certainly glad he had. Never had I seen a building made entirely of marble as was the Dominican Hotel: enormous white slabs stretching five stories upward like a palace inserted into a city block. Entering the foyer was like walking into the center of a marvelous fountain with marble here, too, cascading from the ceiling downward and across the expanse of the pristine floor. Drapery saturated in lush layers of violet-colored velvet dramatized windows that reached higher than my humble house, and I had to restrain myself from rushing over to sweep my hand across the Victorian-era furniture finished in various shades of crimson- and plum-colored fabrics. Instead, I stood in place, surely gawking.

Reminding myself to relax my shoulders, I finally stepped forward and followed the porter, who had begun carrying my luggage toward the front desk. I'd made more than one stop at the local library in preparation for this trip, and during the short snippets of time I'd had while the girls preoccupied themselves with picture books in the children's section, I read what I could find in the newspapers about happenings in the great city—fashions, theater reviews, advertisements of restaurants. I pored over Emily Post's advice on etiquette, surprised to learn that tips were expected for many in service—waiters, concierges, porters—and that conversation with service staff was to be initiated by me if it went beyond the initial inquiry of help.

After checking in, the porter guided me up the iron-barred lift and down a wide carpeted hall to my room near the east end of the fourth floor. He pushed open the door and stepped aside to await my entrance, then followed me in and deposited my luggage on the metal stand. I placed a dime in his gloved hand, and he backed out, softly closing the door behind him.

Like an ebullient child, I swung around to examine the room that I would call home for the next twenty-one days. A rug the color of tender lettuce shoots spread across the floor and floor-to-ceiling curtains matching the rose-blossom bedspread welcomed me. Next to the bed stood a night table fashioned of dark walnut, and an elegantly carved bureau had been placed along a short wall beside the doorway to the bathroom. Two wing-backed chairs encased a small table in front of the single window. The furniture, the artwork, the vase of mums atop the bureau—every detail appeared to have been designed with thoughtful attention.

I made my way into the private bath that was largely consumed by a white clawfoot bathtub with a thick, rose-colored towel draped over its edge and was tempted to run the tap immediately. But, not yet seven o'clock in the evening, there was no trace of exhaustion within me.

Perusing the hotel services guide, I spotted a list of nearby establishments, intrigued by the name of one a mere block away: The Blue Window, boasting "performances by some of Chicago's finest jazz and blues artists." Without hesitation, I opened my suitcase and pulled out my clothes, hanging them in the closet, and set aside a pale-blue double-cotton dress with just enough of a V-neck to subtly expose my still-tanned neck and chest. I layered on a brown cardigan and was about to complete my outfit with the locket necklace that Will had given me for our fifth wedding anniversary but couldn't find it in my handbag. I must have left it behind, I realized, and instead wrapped a short scarf around my neck before fishing out my lipstick and painting my lips cherry red. With naive eagerness in my step, I left my room and walked out into the streets of Chicago.

Chapter 4
—— April 1975 ——

*I*t was a day of new snow, and a smattering of desperate leaves clung to the aged oaks, their darkened branches a silhouette of geometric lines against the late-season white sky. The trees formed a makeshift border around a graveyard toward which Daddy, Mother, Louise, and Sage walked. Young Sage could smell the rich bouquet of Mother's jasmine perfume wafting from her left and the certain grip of Daddy's hand on her right. "Careful," Daddy cautioned, pointing downward, averting her attention from the sight of an eagle soaring overhead. Implanted in the ground before her, Sage saw a miniature cross, its emerald-green paint weather-worn, revealing patches of exposed wood the color of angry clouds. A cross not marking any obvious gravesite. When she looked up again at Daddy, she saw that a teardrop had fallen from his eye.

With startling awareness, Sage heard Louise's voice from the passenger seat, chattering on about the new waitress at the café in which she worked. She felt the insistent cold of the driver's seat seep through her new denim jeans and into the back of her thighs and saw the car key in her hand hovering before the ignition. She blinked, feeling the drip of what must have been a snowflake languorously carving a path down her right cheek, and brushed at it as her thoughts drifted back into awareness.

"Sis, what's up?" Louise asked.

Sage didn't respond. *What in the world just happened*, she wondered, the sudden scene before her having come out of nowhere. Surely there was an explanation, a reason for this anomaly. The sugary Orange Crush she'd had for lunch, maybe, or a flashback from a dream last night. Perhaps it was as simple as her mind wandering. Something organic. Something reasonable.

"And why are you crying? The new girl isn't *that* bad."

Sage glanced at Louise, her brows furrowed, then looked in the rearview mirror. Indeed, a single teardrop was tracing its way down her cheek from the outer edge of her right eye. She leaned forward to get a good look at the sky, and though it would no doubt begin snowing within the half hour, not a single flake was yet falling.

Impossible! she thought, drawing in an audible breath. It couldn't be a tear. Sage did not cry, and she certainly didn't cry for no reason at all, like closing out an afternoon of shopping and lunch with her sister. Sure, it would be entirely logical if this had happened to Louise, but for Sage to have a preternatural experience was, well, incomprehensible at the very least.

Realizing that her sister would not simply dismiss any further oddities from her, Sage inserted the key and turned the ignition. She slid the temperature lever to red, flipped the fan on high, and began backing out of their parking spot as quickly, yet safely, as possible. She could feel Louise's eyes boring into her as she moved the column shifter from reverse to drive and maneuvered her car toward the street entrance in the direction of Louise's place. Clicking on the radio, Sage was pleased to hear Captain and Tennille's latest hit and began to sing along, a distraction from what would no doubt soon turn into a deluge of questioning from her sister.

Bono strolled languidly into the room, his shaggy golden-haired head lowered and pendulum-like tail keeping time with the Sunbeam clock that hung above the couch.

"You ready for a walk, old boy?"

Bono stopped and looked up. Though his hearing had begun diminishing, "walk" was one word he was still able to decipher, and he turned and led the way down the stairs and toward the front door with a slow, arthritic gait. Sage loathed to see Bono's decline. She'd only had the Labrador retriever mix for four years after adopting him from a couple that had given birth to a beautiful, bouncing, dander-allergic baby boy. At that time, Bono was already nine years old, and she'd made the stroll through the neighborhood with him faithfully every day since. Today, however, she needed the outing more than Bono did, needed to unpack what had occurred as she and Louise had left the mall.

Sage tied the laces of her new white sneakers and grabbed the leash from the pegged coat hanger. Just as she opened the door, the phone rang. She paused, Bono giving a gentle tug in his motion forward. Whoever it was could call back later.

"I think Sage is fucked up."

"Louise, you know I don't like it when you use that language," Elizabeth said as she shook a blend of flour and baking soda from the sifter into the bowl of gooey chocolate.

"Okay . . . Sage was acting like she was stoned the other day," Louise said, grabbing a can of Tab from the refrigerator.

"Louise . . ."

"I'm just using an analogy I'm familiar with."

"Louise! How about you just tell me what's on your mind."

"That's what I'm trying to do," said Louise, rolling her eyes as she hopped her backside up onto the counter and opened the can with a *phoosh*. "We went to the mall yesterday and when we were about to drive back home I was talking about . . . I don't know, something . . . and Sage didn't even start the car right away, although it was really cold.

She just sat there and got really quiet. So I looked at her and she was just staring straight ahead like she was confused or scared or something. And then she just started the car and drove away, hardly talking on the way home. She was weirdly distant."

"Distant in what way?" Elizabeth had stopped stirring the batter, her eternally slim figure draped in a faded green apron adorned with miniature flowers of white and blue that had once been her mother's.

"Just a weird sort of quiet. Like she was suddenly in a different groove."

"Did you ask her about it?"

"Yeah, but she just shook off the question and turned on the radio."

"Then I'm sure everything is fine."

"But there was a second there when I looked over at her right before we left, and a teardrop rolled down from her eye. as if spontaneous crying was perfectly normal for her!"

"Was she crying, or was it just a teardrop?"

"Just one. But a teardrop—for no reason! Eventually she tried to convince me it was a snowflake."

Elizabeth turned back to the bowl, remaining silent as she dropped in walnuts and gave it another stir. "Then it was likely nothing of concern. Sage is a grown woman. If she wanted to talk about something, I'm sure she'd have let you know what was on her mind."

"But, it was just so . . . heavy!"

Elizabeth scraped the brownie batter into the well-worn metal pan and slid it into the preheated oven.

"Louise, I don't know what's on Sage's mind, though I must assume she wasn't terribly bothered by it. Maybe she just needed to work through something."

"But she's always told us everything!"

"Louise, you have a penchant for magnifying certain things that aren't always worthy of doing so." She began wiping down the glossy wooden countertop. "And that's perfectly okay, but it's also important not to assume that everyone else's unusual actions require analysis. Do you understand what I mean?" she asked, her voice gentle.

Sometimes Louise felt as if she were still a five-year-old around her mother. And her sister, for that matter. "So, you think it's me? You know, the Universe . . ."

"The Universe places into our minds what is meant to be said. Is that how it goes?" Elizabeth smiled, her eyebrows raised teasingly.

Sarcasm—nice, thought Louise and rolled her eyes again. "Can we get back to Sage here?" she asked, leaning back on her hands." What do we do about her?"

"Well, she hasn't talked to either of us about it, so I suggest we leave it at that. Like I said, if something is bothering her, she'll let us know if and when she is ready."

So, that's the bit of wisdom I get from Mother this morning, Louise thought. *What a downer. I could've stayed in the sack with Randy for all the good this did.*

Louise hopped down from the countertop and finished off the Tab, tossed the can into the trash, and walked toward the front door, peering into the sewing room where she caught sight of her mother's latest quilt. She stepped in to take a closer look. On the table lay a broad swath of black wool that had been built up with layers of scrap fabric and novelties of various sorts. Dozens of meandering lines of thread covered the surface with rounded shapes that otherwise softened the rigidity of it. In some ways, her mother's quilts were not unlike her own esoteric murals. She knew her own reason for using themed abstraction—her paintings were often ignited by dreams—but she couldn't decipher the meaning behind her mother's work or from where the inspiration came. It was always only the method and materials that were discussed, never the gist.

"What's the story on your latest quilt?" Louise called out.

Her fingers traced the faux pearls on one end and noticed on the other end a red satiny ribbon looped again and again into the shape of a rose, a small rod of iron—perhaps a tip of a garden post at one point—acting as the stem. The femininely curved lines of the ribbon spoke of womanhood, Louise understood, but what of the fishing hook next to it, she wondered, and the decidedly sharp lines of the scraps?

"The theme is still in the making," called out Elizabeth. "Do you like the background?"

"I'm diggin' it. It really got my attention. Why so much color this time?"

"I think winter this year wore me down. I started it last month when it seemed the leaden sky wouldn't leave."

"And . . . you're planning a fishing trip this summer?"

Louise leaned out of the doorway to smirk at her mother, knowing she would never consider going out onto open waters. Mother wouldn't even acknowledge the idea of a cruise aboard a luxury ship for fear of needing constant sedation, let alone a fishing boat bringing her within reach of the horrifyingly calm waters beneath her. Louise thought it strange, but she supposed everybody has their aversions.

Chapter 5

— Elizabeth, October 1948 —

A hesitating glow of streetlights chartered the course toward my destination, the Dominican moving into the distance. It occurred to me what an extraordinary leap this walk was from the inky jaunt I'd taken to the chicken coop early this morning. Here, a blush of lights hinted at dazzling displays in storefront windows: antiques from distant Europe and women's wool dresses with coordinating gloves and broad-brimmed hats. *Free fitting! On sale! New shipments in!* Words beckoning to passersby, goods that I would never have laid eyes on in the select few stores that lined Decorah's main street.

It wasn't until I happened to glance up and notice a dingy wooden sign hung above a nondescript door that I realized I had arrived. Painted in ironic red lettering were the words, *The Blue Window Entrance*, with a small window near the top of the elongated door that was far too high to peer through. Two women who looked to be about my age exited, entwining their arms at the elbow while the *clickety-clack* of their heels carried them in the opposite direction from which I'd come.

I grabbed ahold of the handle before the heavy door closed and skirted into a corridor barely wider than the narrow entryway. There, lackluster lights hinted at faded business names that had once been advertised on the brick walls of what may have been an alleyway: *Schelling Clothiers, Liberty Bank*. I walked several paces before an opening to the descending stairwell appeared and worked my way down numerous steps before they took a sharp left and immediately revealed a door the color of a late summer's midday sky. On it was painted *The Blue Window. Please Open. Please Shut.*

From behind me, a man's sudden burst of laughter gave me a start, and the provocative voice of a woman trickled down after it. I quickly pushed my way into the dim light of a sepia-tinted room, where my eyes once again were forced to adjust. Inside, electric lamps cast a tenuous glow through thick, milk-glass shades, and a haze of beigy-blue hovered like an early autumn fog, permeating the room with the sweat of cigars and elegantly long cigarettes. Tables crowded with self-engaged patrons claimed the space within, with men dressed in dark clothes and women even darker, the only obvious sign of color the ubiquitous red lips of the women. I regretted not opting for my navy skirt and sweater instead of the powder-blue dress I was in.

Undeterred, I worked my way to the bar counter, where I assumed I was to place a drink order. I settled onto a stool, but after brief observation determined that waiters would also provide this service at a table. Though few were empty, I found a small one situated against a wall midway between the stage and the door and keyed in on the conversation of those beside me.

"Fred! Where the hell have you been? My Sophie's been climbing all over me to find your whereabouts!" The burly man who had spoken appeared alarmingly large next to the small, stocky woman at his side.

"Ah, Sophie. You're too good to me," the other man responded with a smile that grew wider by the second. "You're the only woman I know who actually looks forward to seeing me." His manner was one of jovial camaraderie.

The gentleman named Fred was shaking the hand of another who appeared to be Sophie's husband, then turned aside. "Stephen, good to see you again, old chap," he said, switching to a British accent as he jutted his hand toward this man too. "Herb. Neil." He leaned in toward the last two that stood among the small group.

Intrigued, I continued to listen in and steal quick glances at the growing assemblage of smartly dressed men and women as I studied the drink menu. It seemed that Stephen, the tallest of the group, dominated Fred's attention, as well as mine. I was enraptured by his refined accent, indicating a home across the ocean, and noticed that he wore three rings on his right hand, which hung by his side nearest me. On his other side stood a woman in a neatly fitted dress that flared at the waist, reaching just past her knees. Ruth, she was called. Her arm had been linked through Stephen's until it seemed that she could no longer keep herself from touching the garrulous man, too, and at a most suave point during the conversation, stepped between the two and gave each a peck on the cheek, as if she had suddenly transformed from a sophisticated woman to a giddy teenager. Her relocation blocked my view of the others at their table almost entirely but also gave me an opportunity to ogle a bit longer, unnoticed, at the trio directly before me.

"What would you like from the bar, madam?"

When I realized it was me to whom the waiter was speaking, I immediately ordered a glass of beer, the first item listed on the menu. "Oh, and a glass of water, if you don't mind. Please, sir."

Please, sir? Had I just set a glowing beacon atop my head?

To my chagrin, I noticed the man named Stephen glance back at me and nod briefly before resuming his conversation with the others. I felt a rush of heat in my face and turned my focus instead on the musicians who were about to begin the next set, their assemblage eliciting a subdued din. The beer and water arrived promptly as the lead singer—a Black woman whom I guessed to be in her midthirties—belted out the first notes of an unfamiliar song. I was immediately mesmerized.

How unlike the music that emitted from the speaker of the Admiral that sat upon the bookshelf in our living room, its static tampering with the art of fine musicians. Instead, buttery chords emanated from her, gliding the scale from hauntingly tender to thick and boastful. I did not—could not—turn away.

At the closing of the first song, the woman immediately turned to signal to the musicians behind her, then quickly scanned the audience as the swishing of a drum set the beat for the next song. Her gaze landed upon mine as she began to sing again.

"Excuse me, madam." I heard the voice before seeing its source. "May my old chum here borrow this chair from your table, or are you expecting others to join you?"

The man with the British accent stood before me, his hands resting atop the chair by my side. I noticed that the nearby group had found a second table to accompany the growing number of people within their cluster.

"No. I mean, yes. Go right ahead. I am by myself tonight."

The smoke from his cigarette drifted directly toward me, forcing an unwelcome cough, the result sounding more like a hiccup, which I felt was about to begin as well.

"Well then, might you consider joining us?" he asked, overlooking my embarrassment. "We could quite easily make room."

I looked more closely at him and noticed a spark of green in his otherwise mink-colored eyes. From my vantage point he appeared even taller than I had first thought, though whether because of my seated position or his engaging British accent, I couldn't determine just then.

"Oh, no. That's just fine, really. Please take the chair. I'm just fine right here, watching the band and listening to the music. But thank you for the very nice offer."

Again, he lowered his head in a single nod.

"If you change your mind, we'd be delighted to accommodate you."

With a quick smile, he turned back to his group, holding the wooden chair in one large hand and reaching out to cup the elbow of a passing waiter with the other, promptly placing an order. "Thank you, sir," he added before sitting down once again.

It wasn't until the musicians finished their set, the absence of their soulful sound leaving a poignant lack in its wake, that I broke away from the spell I had been under and settled into a heightened awareness of my surroundings. There I was, in a cavernous pub in the city of Chicago. Beer, with its bitter aftertaste on my inexperienced palette, had eased my tangled mind into a loose knot. A handsome Englishman, who had a short time ago offered me a chair at his table, now sat across from me, the petite woman with whom he had arrived having taken leave with the man to whom she had earlier sidled up. The realization of my current situation was suddenly disquieting, and I was decidedly aware that I wanted to leave, to take the easy walk back to the Dominican where I could lie in the comfortable bed awaiting me.

"Stephen, I must leave," I announced. "Thanks for your kindness and for talking to me, but it's time for me to go."

"Oh, must you? I was about to order a proper nightcap." He appeared genuinely disconcerted by my attempt at dismissing myself.

"It's just that it's been a long day, and I think it best to go back to my room and dream about my sweet little daughters."

"Oh yes, family. My dear wife left with Mr. Chase to meet with his brothers at Rudolph's on Hastings downstreet. You see, we've just returned to the city after some time away, and she can hardly wait to 'ditch' her husband, as they say, in lieu of friends. Fancy that!" He paused, forcing a wan smile. "I'm quite surprised they didn't choose Giarro's. It is a lovely little spot that stays open until the wee hours for us merry folk. Might I be able to interest you in a meal before you rush off?"

Food. How tempting the thought of it was after what had been a relatively long hiatus from the meal I'd eaten on the train.

"I think I need sleep more than food. I should go. Thank you though."

As I pushed my chair back, another man—a fraction of a man, really—whom I had noticed circling the room throughout the evening, swung a chair up to our table and straddled it in one fell swoop.

"Well, well, it's not time to leave already, is it?" He glanced at me with daring eyes, then quickly turned toward Stephen who had begun, with intentional alacrity it seemed, to raise himself to a standing position.

"Betty, this is Neil. Neil, Betty," he said, turning his head toward each of us in introduction. "Neil, I see you intend to close the club tonight. We, however, were just about to leave."

"First your wife, now you. What sort of return party is that?" The contrast between Neil's deep voice and his small stature caused me to stare at him a blink longer than was appropriate.

"I can't speak for Ruth, but as for this chap, it's all about hunger. Please excuse us, Neil. I'm sure I will see you in good time."

Stephen stepped behind me, holding the back of my chair as I pushed myself up, and together we made our way toward the exit.

"That was a sudden departure," I commented once out of earshot. "Is that man a threat?"

"Ha ha! Neil? Ha! No. He is harmless as a ladybug."

"He gave me a look that made me feel . . . uncomfortable."

Stephen's eyebrows raised momentarily. "I assure you, strip away his uncouth glances and lift the pitch of his voice, and you'll find him as friendly a fellow as there is." He placed his hand on the small of my back, ushering me through the doorway. "Now Giarro, he is a man to watch out for. And by that, I mean the food he prepares will forever remain in the palate of your memory."

I could feel my hunger take the lead.

"Pasta primavera, sizzling with sweet handmade sausage imported from Naples. Rosa sauce so rich with heavy cream and perfection of spice that you simply cannot stop until the last noodle has been savored." He kissed the tips of his fingers and thumb. "The most heavenly taste you will ever experience."

Never had I heard such an exotic description of food, and I began to count the number of hours it had been since I had eaten the overcooked chicken and lukewarm squash. Certainly, a friendly meal could do no harm.

"I'll go, but just for a quick supper," I quickly decided.

We had begun to climb the steps when I heard a greeting from behind.

"Hello, my name is Wini."

I paused and casually turned toward the voice, assuming that the introduction was directed toward Stephen. To my surprise, there stood the vocalist, smiling at me, her hand outstretched in my direction. Having never been so near a woman of color, I was taken aback by the magnitude of her close-up beauty, of the midnight black hair pulled tightly back to reveal a heart-shaped face and skin as smooth as cocoa milk. Deep-set dark eyes were accentuated by the longest lashes I'd ever seen.

"I'm Betty," I said, reaching for her hand. "Your performance was really nice. I mean, it was beautiful. I've never heard a voice like yours before," I managed to eke out.

"Oh, thank you. The good Lord put it there, and Mama made certain I would never let it waste away. Is this your first time here, if you don't mind my asking? I sing here often and can't say that I've seen you before." Her speaking voice had a soothing quality to it, a slow drawl reflecting that of her music.

"I've never been here before tonight. I'm not from here, just on a vacation," I said and noticed a look of concern on Stephen's face.

"Well, I'll be here again next Saturday night," Wini continued. "Every Saturday for the month. Are you planning to return?"

"I don't know just yet, but I will surely try to," I replied, not having thought about what I would be doing on any given day, let alone a week from now. Yet, I wanted to return. The opportunity to hear her sing again was suddenly as important to me as the vacation itself.

"I look forward to seeing you if you do."

"Yes, well, the lady and I must leave now," Stephen interrupted, a trace of indignation in his voice. "Betty, shall we?"

He held his elbow askance, onto which I placed my hand ever so lightly. I flashed a quick, uncertain smile at Wini, nodding briefly as Stephen and I finally made our way back out into the streets of Chicago, turning in the opposite direction of the Dominican.

Chapter 6
— April 1975 —

Though the Minnesota Historical Society was Sage's workplace, Louise was no stranger there. It was late on a Friday afternoon when she hoisted open the heavy, wood-framed glass door and entered, pausing in the lobby to toss her sunglasses into the knit bag draped over her shoulder. After her eyes adjusted to the incandescent light, Louise wound her way up the wide granite steps to the third floor, where she found her sister exactly where she'd expected: at her desk, bent over a mammoth-sized book of bound newspapers. Louise approached with stealth and tossed a copy of *Sensationally Alive* upon the orderly desktop, causing Sage to bolt upright.

"Louise! Why did you do that?" Sage scolded in a hushed voice.

Louise winked and sat on the edge of the desk, ignoring the question. "First, tell me what *you* did last night," she said in a whisper, leaning in. "Then I'll tell you what *I* did."

"Um," Sage replied, wearing a sarcastically foolish look, "Let's see. First, I walked Bono. It must've been for at least a half hour. Crazy, huh?"

Louise rolled her eyes. She never could understand her sister's need to live such a staid life, as if repetition and sameness were royal orders imposed upon her by an imaginative queen.

"Then I made supper and cleaned up the kitchen immediately after. It was spotless! And then . . . hold tight . . . I got stoned."

Louise's eyebrows shot up, as did her voice. "You did?"

"Shh," Sage scolded. "I sure did." She leaned in conspiratorially toward her sister, whispering, "All of it except the part about getting stoned." Sage winked and sat back in her chair.

"Damn you!" whispered Louise, her slight fist thumping the magazine, causing Johnson, from his desk next to the corner window, to finally look up. A fleeting glimpse at Louise and he turned back, unamused, to his occupations.

Sage noticed that the couple gracing the cover of *Sensationally Alive* had just pushed off into the Boundary Waters, ready to take on the northern river in their sturdy canoe. Each wore a backpack that was nearly as big as the young woman who had a head of remarkably iron-flat hair. Flat, that is, until Louise's fist put a delicate wrinkle in it.

"You know, sis, I can dig that you're not into smoking weed, but you really ought to go out with me some night. Downtown. Have some drinks."

"Okay."

This time it was Louise who bore a sarcastic look. "Fool me twice, shame on me."

"No, really. Let's go have drinks. It's not like I don't touch the stuff. There's just never much occasion for me to do so."

"Far out."

The Depth on Fifth and Sherman was decided upon, and Louise immediately hopped up and headed back toward the steps, seemingly too astonished by the acceptance of her sister's invitation to reveal what she had done last night. But no doubt, Sage would be given the details later.

As Sage swiveled the wooden chair back toward her desk, her elbow brushed against the magazine, causing it to slip to the floor where it landed open to an article entitled "Earth's Influenza" with the subcaption "Earth Day: a cause for celebration or apology?" Earth Day . . . there was a ring of familiarity to it, though Sage couldn't recall why. A news article from a few years ago?

She wondered if this was the article her sister wanted her to read, the reason for her visit, and smiled to herself at the thought of Louise's short attention span—like a butterfly always flitting from one thing to the next. Sage picked up the magazine and set it aside, unwilling to be distracted from research. Her investigation into the historical shipwrecks of the Great Lakes was nearly complete, and she would deposit her summary, neatly outlined, onto Ned's desk where he could "take it to the next level." She wondered whether he would make additional edits this time or simply add his byline once again.

The Depth wreaked of days-old booze outmuscled only by cigarette smoke thicker than the dank air of the space that entertained a concoction of college students, droves of dancing couples, and a few obligatory drunks who could be anywhere between age fifty and seventy; it was difficult to tell by their rough, sallow faces.

By the time she'd finished her second drink, Sage was discoing with a guy named Marco. Or maybe Mikhael. After the third, Louise finally revealed what she had done last night: slashed her bra with a machete at the latest equality rally downtown, still refusing to sport one now. Sage, or rather the vodka, exclaimed over the chutzpah of her sister as if she were the most audacious woman that had ever walked the streets of Minneapolis.

"Believe in a cause," Louise said, "and you'll do whatever it takes to do what it takes."

The two sisters toasted the impromptu adage then broke into a fit of laughter over the ridiculousness of it. Louise followed up the toast with a gulp of her Jack and Coke before plunking the glass down with a thud, having suddenly recollected a tucked-away thought. She turned toward Sage, a Holmes-like gleam in her eye. "Where the hell did you go the other day?" she demanded.

"What? What're you talking about?"

"When we were driving home from the mall on Tuesday. You were checked out, totally gone. Where were you?" Louise leaned in, now inches from Sage. "And did that have anything to do with you agreeing so quickly to a night of drinking with good ole Lou? Fess up, sis. It's girls' night out."

"No," Sage answered coyly after a beat. "I just wanted to do something different."

She took another sip of the vodka tonic in her hand and looked toward the dance floor, her shoulders wagging awkwardly to the beat.

"Are you going to tell me what was up with you, or do I have to wrestle it out of you?" replied Louise. "I'll tickle you right here and now if you don't tell me. You know I will! Admit it, you were completely freaked out over something."

"I wasn't freaked out, Louise. I just had a funny little . . . dream."

Someone dropped a bowl of popcorn on their table, and Sage gave herself time by stuffing her mouth full. Cheeks bulging, she raised her eyebrows and shoulders as if to say she was incapable of speech.

Louise's already narrowed eyes formed into even smaller slits.

"Fine," said Sage, realizing it was probably a good idea to let someone know what had happened, just in case it was some sort of medical condition—or, god forbid, a brain tumor. "It was no biggie. It was just this dream, like a daydream, I guess. We were young, and our family was walking along in a graveyard, and it started snowing."

"And . . ."

"And that's all she wrote."

Louise's eyes slowly widened in pace with her grin. "You had a vision!"

"Well yeah, I guess you would call it that."

"A psychic vision!"

Again, Sage looked toward the dance floor and pushed aside her empty glass. "I'd hardly call it that. It's not like there was any foretelling of the future."

"A vision doesn't have to be of the future, sis. Just so you know."

Sage grimaced.

"What else happened?"

"Nothing, really."

"Which means something else happened. Tell."

"Well," Sage sighed in concession, knowing from years of experience as Louise's sister that nothing would slip past her. "When the 'vision' left, I felt a teardrop falling down my cheek."

"You told me it was snow!"

"Well, it maybe could've been! I don't know for sure."

"Yes, you do. It wasn't snow—it wasn't even snowing! It was a tear that appeared out of nowhere, and you don't know why the hell it was there."

"Gee, thanks for clearing that up for me. Now I don't have to wonder about it anymore."

"Could you feel the snow in the vision?" Louise continued, ignoring the sarcasm.

"No, not really. Whatever it was ended with a snowflake falling onto Daddy's right eye, and when it was over, it felt like a snowflake had fallen on my right eye. Or eyelashes. It was just kind of weird, you know, and I was just a little freaked out for a while after that."

"Freaked out how?" Louise urged. Sage purposefully tossed another handful of popcorn into her mouth and chewed slowly, but her sister remained oddly patient.

"It surprised me, I guess," Sage admitted. "Not a lot of surprises happen in my life."

"No kidding," said Louise.

"It just got me thinking about stuff, and I lost track of . . . oh, I don't know . . . myself, I guess. I needed some time to get it out of my mind." Sage realized that she hadn't spoken with her mother in a couple of days. "Is Mother worried that I haven't called?"

"You know Mrs. Ley. She's cool as a fucking cucumber. One of these days we'll get her feathers ruffled over something. But don't change the subject. I want details."

Sage conceded and gave up every particular she could muster—which were very few considering the brevity of the occurrence—none of which satiated Louise's curiosity. Instead, Louise was convinced the two needed to visit the psychic on Hennepin Avenue.

"Madam Soleil is outta this world. She can help you find the right path, you know? Awaken you, as Siddhartha would've said. Why the vision? Where is it leading you?"

"I told you, Louise, I'm not going to a psychic, and Siddhartha can go teach a rock. I've let it go, okay? Just sit on it. Don't get yourself all worked up over this just when I've been able to set it aside."

"Sit on it?" A peal of laughter erupted from Louise. "Nifty try, but it's not working for you, sis."

Sage, too, rippled with laughter, realizing how ridiculous she must've sounded. She wondered what Daddy would have thought of Louise today: her eccentric ideas and unhinged lifestyle. Maybe he would've expected it; she'd always had a brightly colored thread running through the fabric of her makeup.

"Hey, Lou," she said, knuckling a tear of laughter from the corner of her eye. "Who would Daddy choose to be? You know, if there was an afterlife and in it you really did get to choose?" She paused for a moment. "Someone heroic. An astronaut?"

"Nah," replied Louise, immediately taking up the question as if one she was commonly asked. "He would've been a big oak at the top of a rolling hill, a protective shelter for wild animals," Louise paused in consideration. "Or is that enough? I don't think that's enough."

"An angel, guarding a fragile old woman through her days of living alone after her husband dies. She lives in the country and her children are far away in New York, inattentive and uncaring. The jerks," Sage countered.

"No, no. You can't choose to be an angel."

"Why?"

"Damn, sis, it just doesn't work that way." Louise rolled her eyes dramatically as if Sage should know "the rules of the afterlife" by now.

"Okay, fine. Daddy was protective. Remember when he showed us how to use the rope swing in the barn for the first time? He wanted us to be bold, swing far and wide, but didn't want us to crush our bones doing it. A few days before, he'd piled all that loose hay right in the middle of the loft and told us it was because it was easier to feed the cows that way. I remember how Mother had smiled and turned away when he said that. I didn't realize till much later that he'd had to haul all that hay over to the hatch fork-by-fork to drop it down below and from there do the same thing to spread it to the cattle. Bales would've been so much easier."

She noticed how intently Louise listened, absorbing memories of their father like rain on parched soil.

"Remember how you went first with a running leap to the rope?" Sage continued. "I swear you swung right over to the other side, practically out the window. Then on my turn, I freaked out immediately and let go, landing smack in the haystack. He knew."

For a moment, both were silent, Louise looking into her glass, stirring the ice in a centrifugal motion. Out on the dance floor, a lanky woman wrapped her arms around her much shorter dance partner as they swayed to their own rhythm. Nearby, three guys laughed so heartily that one fell from the booth onto the disgustingly filthy floor.

"An eagle," Louise said. "That's what Daddy would be."

Sage thought about this, about the way an eagle soared overhead in her vision, certain and graceful. "An eagle," she agreed.

That was the last vivid conversation of the night before Sage was back at home, too wired to sleep and too tipsy to care. *Matty? Mack? Mercury? What was that guy's name?* The question of whom she had danced with continued to nag at her as she turned on the burner underneath the tea kettle and pulled Louise's magazine from her bag, opening it to the piece on Earth Day.

> Open your eyes, you, the ignorant, abusive travelers of life! Look outside the opaque cocoon you've so carelessly woven and you'll find the earth crying out for help! Help in overcoming a debilitating influenza, a pandemic that humanity alone has sown by stampede into its land and its waters.
>
> As you are reading this article, a mere three years have gone by since our planet Earth was honored with a day in her memory, but nearly two caustic decades of her poisoning by us have passed discernibly unnoticed.

Intrigued, Sage poured steaming water into the swirl of gray and blue clay that made up the ceramic mug Louise had given her as a birthday gift last year, splashing only a few drops onto the counter, which she wiped up at once. She went into the living room and sat on the couch, one leg folded underneath the other.

So many questions came to mind. What exactly is this "debilitating influenza" the writer—a one Peck Wells—is referring to? Where, specifically, are the signs of this disablement? Could this issue really be as pressing as he makes it sound when not even the *Twin Cities Times* has reported on it? What credentials, if any, does he have, or is he just another revolutionary looking for a cause to clutch to? Likely the latter, Sage thought as she flipped to the masthead to see who Peck Wells was. "Publisher, Editor, and Senior Writer. Well, there you have it, a do-it-yourselfer."

Even so, she turned back to the column and picked up where Mr. Wells had just given credit to Rachel Carson and quoted from her book *Silent Spring*.

> "These sprays, dusts and aerosols are now applied almost universally to farms, gardens, forests and homes—nonselective chemicals that have the power to kill every insect, the 'good' and the 'bad,' to still the song of birds and the leaping of fish in the streams, to coat the leaves with a deadly film, and to linger on in soil—all this though the intended target may be only a few weeds. Can such a barrage of poisons coat the surface of the earth without making it unfit for all life? They should not be called 'insecticides,' but 'biocides.'"

"Hmph, that's a pretty potent accusation from Ms. Carson that he's quoting."

Bono moved in his sleep, pushing against Sage's leg. She set down the mug and continued reading, finding herself surprisingly disappointed when she reached the end. She added the magazine to the small stack placed neatly on the coffee table and, now sufficiently tired, called it a night.

Chapter 7

—— Elizabeth, October 1948 ——

Like the Blue Window, Giarro's, too, hosted a thick assemblage of patrons, though the aroma that permeated the air was in delightful contrast. As Stephen and I stood near the entrance waiting for the return of the host, I looked in awe at the busyness of the place during this late hour. A waiter crossed in front of us, his hands and arms laden with white bowls piled high with pasta in unfamiliar shapes and coated with sauces colored both red and white. I could feel my salivary glands unfold in anticipation, my stomach now begging for food.

"I can see you are already enjoying my secret hideaway?" Stephen asked, noticing my gaze follow the plates. "I'll familiarize you as we wait," he continued. "There is a quaint, yet frantic, kitchen beyond the door to the back," he said, leaning toward me, then gestured at a different, two-way door. "A second seating area is just through that opening, and two private rooms lay beyond."

I glanced at the rooms he indicated, wondering if all were as busy as the one in which we stood. The host quickly approached, already gesticulating with an energy far more zealous than Stephen's earlier animated description of the food.

"Mr. Stephen, Miss, come-a my way. We have a taay-ble just-a for you, signore, signora. You will like-a the nice special tonight. Primo! I will tell-a you as we walk. Very busy."

The young man hurried us over to a corner table as he spoke rapidly, as much with his hands and arms as he did with his voice, using words for food that I'd never heard. "Mama has made-a meatballs today of-a veal sausage and-a mushrooms and just the right touch of-a fennel." He pinched together his fingers and quickly fanned them out as if he had composed the description into music. "But I give away no secrets! Tonight you have-a penne and-a roasted garlic vinaigrette smothering on-a your pears. Now, we serve-a you Chianti that come-a from the homeland."

He turned to the table beside us and asked the man sitting at it if he would move ahead in his chair so that I could squeeze into the space left between it and the table. Just as quickly he raised his arm and with a fillip of his fingers summoned the attention of a nearly identical-looking waiter. It seemed that we had an urgent need for wine after all.

"The tiramisu you will-a find room for at the end, and-a you will-a leave happy as a possibility!"

We settled into our chairs, and wine glasses were plunked onto the table in front of us, our supper having been decided for us. Conversations echoed around the room, with the occasional calling out from a waiter to the kitchen rising above the din.

"My, this sure is a hectic place," I observed.

"Yes, it is rather lively."

"The food looks really good. I don't think my husband would have much of a taste for Italian cooking. What a treat for me to be here."

"Well then, I am extraordinarily happy to have introduced you to Giarro's. But now, you must further introduce yourself to me. Tell me about your life in Iowa. I haven't yet made it there in my travels."

As I took the time to really notice this man with whom I sat, with whom I was about to share a meal, I saw that his eyes were kind, his expression one of interest. A loaf of warm bread was set on our table, and I was glad that I had ignored my earlier concern over coming here.

"Well, let's see. I have a husband and two children—girls," I said as I picked up a slice of the bread, noticing there was no butter dish on the table, only a bottle of greenish-colored oil. "Sage is the oldest; she's five. Then there is Louise May, who is just three. We live on a farm near Decorah, which I suppose is very pretty with trees all around and big hills, but sometimes that's just difficult to see, you know? When you've always lived in the country, it isn't as easy to appreciate it."

Did I just say that? I thought, feeling a rise of heat. *Why would this man even care whether I could see beauty anywhere, let alone on an Iowa farm?*

Stephen, even though he bore what I interpreted as a quizzical look, seemed intent in his listening. I realized how nice it was to spend time with a stranger, to have another person to talk to, as I had with Helena on the train. So far during this trip, it was proving to be quite easy to get to know people, even though that had not been my intention nor my expectation.

"A farm is a lot of work that just never seems to end," I decidedly continued. "The girls aren't old enough to help with the crops and animals yet, so we have a hired man, but I still have to help out too. And that is along with watching over the kids and keeping up the house and the garden. I guess they're things I'm used to doing, but more and more I realize that I'll be doing them forever. Anyway, I guess everything really wore on me to the point where I felt like I just had to get away. My husband, Will, said to me one day, 'Just go. If you feel that you absolutely must, just leave for a while. Go to whatever city you think you need to go to.' He didn't mean this in a bad way, as if he never wants me to come back. He just finally realized how important it is that I have a change."

I paused, peering out at the lit-up street beyond, embarrassed by my divulgence. "I'm sorry," I said. "I'm sure you didn't ask me about my life to hear about my troubles."

But when I looked up again, I saw that his expression held a degree of empathy.

"Certainly do not apologize! I am intrigued." He leaned forward and placed his elbow on the table, his hand supporting his chin—a pose that I wouldn't have imagined such a refined Englishman to settle into.

"If you don't mind my asking, what are you searching for in the city?"

I could feel my shoulders release ever so slightly as I considered how to put my longings into words. Stephen had poured a spill of the green oil onto his plate and was dipping his bread into it. I followed his lead. The bread was oddly chewy, unlike the fluffy loaves I churned out weekly.

"When I was young, I always savored any magazine that I could get my hands on. If it was *Good Housekeeping*, I ignored every page that had to do with a house and stared endlessly at the women in the advertisements, how they were dressed, how they were posed. The rare times I got ahold of a magazine like V*ogue*, I spent hours wondering what the lives of these people were like. *Life* carried my imagination to places like California and New York and even London. When a new issue of *Life* appeared on the coffee table, I would spend days living in a bubble of anticipation for what my future might hold."

I could feel the glow of remembrance as if I were back at Grandmother's house, lying on the divan after supper, imagining the boundlessness of my future.

"It was the same with movies. When I saw a flick starring Myrna Loy or Ginger Rogers, I became them in my mind, even changing the way I spoke and walked—at least as much as a girl could. I filled myself up with those images, looking toward the day when I could finally leave Grandmother's farm and become a woman of the world. But in St. Timothy, people just don't—"

"Ah! Penne and-a meatballs, just-a for you!"

I was startled by the waiter's sudden reappearance. In a grand reception of food delivery, he placed bowls of steaming food before us and artfully spooned onto each a heap of finely shredded cheese, which I later learned was called asiago.

"This will bring-a you much pleasure!" he exclaimed. "I fill-a your wine, signora. Drink-a your wine with-a your pasta, and the taste," he made another kissing gesture with his fingers, "you will-a treasure like-a your grandmother's ring. Buon appetito!"

"Grazie," called Stephen after him as the man rushed back to the kitchen. I looked at him with curiosity, then at my ring.

"From the look on your face, I shall assume that it is indeed your grandmother's ring?" Stephen asked with an amused smile.

"Why, yes. It is."

"No need for concern. Anthony works during the day as an antiques appraiser. He knows his periods."

I laughed, relieved that I wasn't dealing with a gypsy, and inhaled the scented steam of the food that sat before me, using as much grace as I could muster in taking a first hungry bite.

"Please, continue your story, Betty. Betty, is that short for Elizabeth?" Stephen asked.

"Yes, Elizabeth is my given name, but I've been Betty forever," I said, dabbing the corner of my mouth with my napkin.

"Elizabeth has such a fine ring to it, does it not? I see you more as an Elizabeth than a Betty. Do you mind if I call you Elizabeth?"

"Of course not; please do. It'd be a welcomed change."

This request, though small, felt like an acknowledgment of who I was at my core. Betty had always felt so ordinary, but it was the name I'd been called since childhood. Elizabeth, however, could be any woman she wanted to be. Elizabeth is who I would be here in Chicago, I decided. A gentle smile crossed my face.

"As I was saying, people in St. Timothy just don't pack their bags and move to New York—unless they've joined the military. They stay near their families, get married, and carry on with tradition. So that's what I did: I quit school after the tenth grade to help Grandmother Josie on her farm. I still dreamed, though. That, I never stopped." I paused to take a sip of wine and found that the dry, fruity taste of it was an extraordinary complement to the meal, just as the waiter had implied.

"You did not complete your education?" Stephen asked.

I shook my head, having just taken another forkful of food, and continued after a moment. "In St. Timothy it's not too unusual for people to quit school early. Boys will help on the farm or girls will work for mothers with young babies. Things like that. You don't always need to finish school to find work. But I guess for me I just didn't like school; it felt like a distraction for some reason. And, I had grown up with my Grandmother Josie—my parents died when I was very young—so quitting school didn't seem like a sacrifice, especially with her arthritis as bad as it was."

I looked at him to evaluate his interest, which appeared to remain steadfast.

"But I've always spent a lot of time in local libraries. It's not that I wasn't interested in learning; I was just more interested in some topics than others. In fact, I had made up some of my own clothes designs back then and sold a few things that I'd sewn to the ladies around town. I saved some money and thought I would try to sell them in a city one day too. But then I met Will, and I guess we . . . Well, anyway, I became a little more realistic and down to earth after that. I married him and we moved to our own farm. And truthfully, I lost interest in designing clothes. I still sew dresses for my daughters, but that's not the same."

Stephen continued to watch me as he sipped his wine. "May I ask if you have been finding what you were searching for here in Chicago?"

I thought about this for a moment, even though my immediate feeling told me that yes, I was already beginning to.

"I can hardly believe I left Iowa just this morning! I feel somehow at home here with all these nice people like you and Helena—I met her on the train—showing me the ropes and making me feel comfortable. Will was so fearful that something bad would happen to me here. To him, the city is a place of wild times and constant crime. I see the city as a stage made for entertainment."

It was unusual for me to talk at length like this, especially about myself, but Stephen was an objective listener, interested in the directions my life had taken and the decisions I'd made along the way. Sure, Will listened on those occasions during which I'd opened up about my feelings, but he never asked questions, didn't understand why I couldn't appreciate my life for what it was. And while my neighbor Dorothea was probably the closest thing I had to a friend, she would tell me to leave my burdens at the feet of Jesus, who would provide me with all the answers I needed. Stephen, however, who had appeared so formal upon our meeting, seemed to have morphed into an amiable comrade with an authentic interest in my life. Between the delicious food and surprisingly comfortable companionship, the outing certainly felt fortuitous.

"Now it's your turn. Tell me about yourself," I said, adding a few brief shakes of salt to the last of my supper.

"Ah, but I was so enjoying your story." He pushed away his bowl and sat back in his chair, twirling the stem of his wine glass as he observed the movement of the wine. "In fairness of exchange, I will share with you a tale or two of my own. But the hour is quite late, and I'm sure you are eager to turn in. Could I interest you in joining me at the lake tomorrow, where I could regale you with the stories of my banal life?" He smiled. "I have a sailboat that I could give you a tour of. Or we could simply sit in the nearby park."

"But don't you have plans with your wife and friends? You did just get back to town," I reminded him.

"There is a fashion show tomorrow that my wife is attending with her friends and would not miss for the world. I have been left to wander the streets by my lonely self," he replied with a mock look of sadness.

"No plans with your other friends? Neil seemed very eager to spend time with you."

"Nothing set in stone. Our gatherings are typically quite casual, 'spur of the moment' as they say here in the States."

"Okay, well, I guess I don't have anything planned either, if you're sure your wife won't mind."

He confirmed with a nod and a noticeable smile.

"Then let's do it. Let's take a nice walk in the park. Maybe you could point out some of the highlights of this city, give me some suggestions for what I should do?"

"Indeed, that sounds lovely. I think you'll find that our lives do mirror one another's to a degree."

Though I could not begin to imagine what those similarities might be, I felt the zing of anticipation and already looked forward to the new day.

Chapter 8
— June 1975 —

The back porch with its aromatic cedar siding became for Elizabeth a substitute for the outdoors on days like this. A southern front carried in dutiful moisture, the pitter-patter of rain displacing the trill of warblers and wrens. She had been completing the final detail on a quilt, using delicate threads removed from the veil of her mourning hat worn during Frankie's funeral to stitch six black stars above an equal number of wells constructed of tin: one for each month of pregnancy. She finished the final star before removing herself to a small desk situated in the corner of the living room, knowing that she must not put off updating her business ledger any longer. The amount of money people were willing to pay for her unique art—especially considering the abstract nature of it—was still a surprise.

She had just opened the ledger when there came a knock at the door. Elizabeth couldn't imagine who would be calling on her at midday but was happy to have a distraction from the task at hand. Money management was something Will had handled, and his meticulous ways lent, in part, to the success he'd had as a farmer. For her, it was a chore of necessity.

She pulled open the door, the pace of her heart quickly elevating in recognition of the man before her. His hair was now streaked with silver, and wrinkles of time spread outward from the corners of his eyes, but the black suit and shoes could have easily crossed the gap from when she last saw him twenty-some years before. Chicago. Age had insisted upon certain alterations of his look, but he was otherwise unyieldingly the same. A sudden feeling of nausea clutched at Elizabeth's stomach, her mind aswirl as she fought to regain her composure.

"Neil?" she said in an exhale.

"Yes. You remembered."

His voice was the same as she recalled from their brief encounters back then, a deep tumble of words that sent a shudder coursing through her.

"What are you doing here? How did you find me?" Elizabeth scanned the driveway, the car. *Could it be possible?*

"I am alone, Elizabeth. Or do you prefer Betty once again?"

She pulled her inquisitive gaze back, eye level with this man whom she never imagined she'd see again—and certainly never desired to.

"I am in the area on business," he said through the straight, unmoving smile pasted upon his lips. "I saw an exhibit of yours. In Chicago. There was something about one of the quilts that stopped me. It seemed . . . well . . . familiar."

Her mind raced to think of which one it could be, which of them were even in the exhibit, but it was lost to her as if a temporary memory block had barricaded any sense of reality.

"It had a purple sweater with pearl-colored buttons on the neckline. Right in the middle of it. The only time I'd ever seen a woman wear a sweater like that was that day on the boat. Stephen's boat."

Stephen. He spoke his name as familiarly as if the two had dined together just last week.

"Come in."

Elizabeth opened the door fully and worked her way unsteadily down the two steps that led into the sunken living room, where she sat in the nearest chair. That day, within the cabin of the *Winsome Lady*, was crystal clear in her mind, as was every moment with Stephen. It was the day they had been caught off guard by Neil's sudden presence. And now, here was this same man with his shadowy appearance walking into her home. She recalled the unsettling feeling that arose when she had met him, first at the Blue Window and later on the boat, as if he were a tomcat slinking toward the barn, scratching at the night for prey.

"It seems I've given you quite a shake-up," he said, closing the front door. He removed his black fedora and raincoat and hung them on the coat rack, then looked over the space, expressionless, before asking whether he could join her in the living room.

"Of course. My apologies. I must admit seeing you at my door took me off guard." Elizabeth stood somewhat shakily. "Can I offer you a glass of water? Coffee?"

"No, thank you. I won't keep you long."

She made her way to the open kitchen and filled a tall glass with tap water for herself, carrying it with both hands back into the living room, where she placed it on the end table next to where she sat.

"Your home is . . . refreshing," Neil said, his unreadable look remaining in place as he leaned back into the chair nearest the door. Again, he scanned the room, its sparsely decorated white walls trimmed in wide planks of pine that matched the wood floors. A newly purchased sofa of woven sea-green fibers sat next to an armchair, its needlework pattern worn from decades of use. An oversized Pollock imitation consumed the space of the wall behind her desk.

Elizabeth waited to respond, not wanting to engage in small talk but only to know the reason for his visit. But after a few moments of hovering silence, she acquiesced.

"Do you often drop out of the sky?"

Neil turned back toward her.

"No. No, I don't. But in this situation, I thought it might be necessary." He continued, straight-faced. "There are things, Elizabeth, that should be discussed."

He stood and pulled what appeared to be paper of some sort from his shirt pocket and carried it over to where she sat. Elizabeth bristled, thankful that she was sitting as he handed her a stiff white envelope that gave no clue as to its contents. She held it taut for a moment before noticing that the tips of her thumbs had paled. She looked back at Neil, who had returned to his chair, and lifted the unsealed flap, revealing a second envelope tucked inside. Across the middle, in familiar, elegant script, was written *Mrs. Elizabeth Ley*. Her hand involuntarily went to her lips, a brief sense of lightheadedness returning.

"Stephen," she muttered, surprised at hearing her own voice speak his name.

"Sorry to have caused you upset." Neil paused. "I should have . . . It wasn't the best way to give this to you."

More than twenty-six years of time had passed, and while memories of Stephen would always be a part of her life, like a scar, they'd faded with time. Ephemeral memories. Yet, now in her hands she held something concrete, something that by all appearances had come from Stephen. Something that he had touched, had written, had been a piece of him.

"Read it when the time is right."

Though Elizabeth heard the words spoken, her senses darted from corner to corner, desperately in search of reason. For what the contents of this token from the past would reveal. For why this man was sitting here in her living room.

"While it is true that I am here on business, the main purpose of my visit is to have conversations that are overdue," he continued. "Your story hasn't come to an end. You must trust me on this. You know little of me, Elizabeth, but I ask for your trust. For Stephen."

His dark eyes seemed to have softened, but what did she know of his eyes? Of his purpose, his chicanery? Elizabeth looked again at her name written on the envelope.

"Stephen's handwriting."

"It is."

"Where did you find this? Did he give it to you?"

"There is much to be told."

"Do you know where he is?" Her hands shook visibly now, her

voice tinged with a note of desperation.

"There's not a simple answer to that."

"What do you mean? Is it yes, or is it no?"

The shrill ring of the telephone cut through the air, causing Elizabeth to startle for the second time within minutes. She stood, her heart now racing. Neil made his way toward the door.

"As I said, there is not a simple answer. I will leave you now but will be calling on you again."

The door closed with a silent click as the phone rang out its final call. Elizabeth pressed the letter onto the end table and took a step back as if the paper were Stephen's own flesh materialized before her, Neil a figment of her imagination.

She looked again at the handwriting on the envelope, recalling a moment at the corner deli when Stephen had pulled a fountain pen from his jacket pocket, its gold trim catching the light, and wrote on the bottom of the menu: *Stephen Covington, Hotel Bellwether*, along with the hotel phone number. She'd smiled at him and reached her hand out for the pen that he'd returned to his pocket. He retrieved it and slid it across the table to her. *Elizabeth Ley, the Dominican Hotel.*

She had pushed the menu back toward him and noticed the contours of his face soften as much as his smile widened. It was the only time she'd witnessed his handwriting, outside of the poem, but she had never forgotten its schooled script. It was a part of him, as much as the shape of his hands or the sound of his voice was a part of him.

Mrs. Elizabeth Ley.

It had taken several years to let go of him, but her path had once again become a straight one, corners with their sharp, distressing angles unwelcomed. And now, suddenly, a new corner appeared, one around which she had no idea how to navigate.

Elizabeth turned away from where the envelope lay and quickly made her way to the bedroom, where she flung open the closet door. Kneeling, she inched forward, setting aside the few pairs of winter shoes in the back corner of the small space, along with the rug underneath them, before unhinging the small door on the floor. She reached inside and felt for the hatbox, which she grasped with both hands and removed gingerly, as if it would crumble should she do so with haste.

Elizabeth reversed her crawl and, once out of the closet, leaned back against the door, the box still in place between her hands. She needed to compare, to find proof that could validate or invalidate the authenticity of Neil's delivery. Had it truly been composed by Stephen? Or was it a trick of Neil's, a relative stranger who had made a sudden, mystifying reappearance in her life?

She got up and hurried back into the living area with the hatbox, where she extracted the envelope that Stephen had given to her at the Dominican, placing it beside the one she'd received today. She inspected the penmanship of both, considering the loop of the *l* and the slender bulge of the *b*, the ratio of letter height—anything that would prove the inauthenticity of it. But indeed, the handwriting was the same.

Twenty-six years. Every one of them spent in a state of speculation.

Had he survived? Had he returned to England? Or did he choose Chicago?

Had he survived? Had he searched for her? Had he remarried? Did he think about her?

Had he survived?

Perhaps within this newly acquired envelope was a note that had been written back then, during those weeks in October 1948 when they spent most every day in each other's company. But maybe he had written it much later. Even last week.

Elizabeth knew she must put her thoughts in order, be prepared for whatever its contents would reveal. But not now. Right now, she didn't have the wherewithal to learn the fate of Stephen, if that was indeed what she was to learn. No, not now.

She picked up both envelopes and carried them with fastidious haste back into her bedroom, where she placed them on the bureau and left the room, closing the door to form a temporary barrier.

"Close the door."

Sage had just returned from lunch when Bernie called her into his office. She did so and lowered herself onto the stiff edge of the nearest chair as she considered the possibilities of this unexpected request. Historically, her supervisor had treated her decently, but she'd overheard his temper flare occasionally during meetings with a select few of her coworkers.

"Sage, how are ya?" Bernie asked from his position near the window, transforming his face into an obligatory smile.

"I'm fine. Thank you."

Stifling air consumed the small space, taking an additional toll on her Babe deodorant.

"Good." He paused, continuing to grin, and she noticed how the bags under his eyes spilled over the tops of his cheeks when he smiled. Caught between his two front teeth was a yellow-gold morsel, from a peanut no doubt—he ate them like candy—and Sage briefly considered ways to discreetly drop a box of toothpicks onto his desk. She wished he would shut down that smile.

"Look. Here's the thing," he finally said, the pull of gravity returning the loose skin of his face to its natural state. "Peterson is taking off for a couple of months. Going off to god-awful China, of all places, to adopt a baby with the missus. We've gotta fill his space, and there's only so many extra hands in this place. So, I'm thinking I want you to help with that."

Bernie placed his hands into his trouser pockets and walked over to his desk as he continued talking. "He was supposed to get a jump start on gathering up some vittles on the history of food cooperatives—co-ops—in the state. They just started up in the past couple of years or so, really, but seem to be spreading god-awful quick, and we wanna stay on top of it. I know you're working on the shipwreck background for Freeman, but I wanna get right on top of this one. What do you think, you in?"

"Of course I'm in," Sage replied matter-of-factly. How she'd longed for the day when she would have her own assignment. "I'm one hundred percent in."

Bernie turned back toward her and finally sat down in his chair.

"Here's the thing, Ley. When I say we don't have enough hands around here, I mean you'd have to take this one on your own. Background, research, writing, editing. The whole kit and caboodle."

The oddity of the expression occurred to Sage, how *caboodle* hadn't even been a word until someone decided that it sounded more poetic when combined with *kit* than plain old *boodle*. How all words, really, were fabricated at some point in time.

"I think I could manage both the kit and the caboodle just fine."

Bernie emitted a brief chortle. He was a tall man—perhaps too tall for the short, unsteady chairback that creaked as he leaned into it—yet his amiable nature was surprisingly reserved when it came to laughter, much more serious than jovial. Stress was surely the reason, thought Sage.

"I knew I could count on you, sweetheart. I got word this morning that there's growing tension between a couple of the food co-ops around town. Might be nothing much there, but the media will probably be checking it out at some point, seeing what kind of trouble the hippies are stirring up now. We'll likely be getting some calls for background info."

He smiled, and Sage once again had to force herself to avert her gaze from the stuck morsel. "I know of one co-op. Do you have a list I can reference?"

"Yeah. There's a guy named Mark at Living Waters over by Augsburg. Nice enough guy, it seems. He's one of the originals of the god-awful co-op scene and knows what all's out there. I can't say for sure if he'll cough up any info on the group they're in shenanigans with right now, but he might. Like I said, nice enough guy."

"Living Waters, that's the one I'm familiar with. My sister volunteers there."

"Huh, you don't say. I wouldn't have taken you to be the co-op type."

"Well, no. I've never been there, but Louise and I aren't exactly twins when it comes to our interests."

Bernie closed his eyes and gave them a hard rub. His hair was evolving weekly, dropping from his head at an uncanny rate as if preemptively fleeing from its predetermined demise. "All I've heard is they're putting up their dukes over white bread. Sounds god-awful petty to me but seems it's turning more serious. Political stuff. It's always political, isn't it?"

"Yes, I guess in the end it is. I'll get started on this today."

"Great. Thanks for kicking in, Ms. Ley."

Sage returned to her desk, thankful that the air conditioner perched in the window had been dusted off and set on high. She cleared the stacks of newspaper and began a rough outline of questions she wanted to find answers to, then deposited the notebook into her bag and took the steps down to the back door.

Outside, the heat was amplified in the sweaty stillness of the air, her polyester pants entrapping it against her skin. She was glad that she'd worn strapped sandals today rather than the usual loafers. But the heat didn't hinder the elation she felt over her new assignment, and Sage found herself singing along to "The Night the Lights Went Out in Georgia" as she drove toward the St. Paul Public Library. She'd only had time enough to listen to one more song on the radio before arriving.

The street in front of the marble behemoth was nearly empty during the midafternoon hour, and Sage pulled up alongside the curb. As she hustled up the steps leading to the entrance, she could smell grease fumes from the vent of a nearby restaurant which, as if by reflex, made her crave French fries. A handsome man with dark hair buzzed nearly to his scalp hurried out the library door as she was about to enter. He paused and held open the door. *How chivalrous*, Sage mused.

Inside, a tingle of anticipation coursed through her as she retrieved the spiral-bound notebook and pencil from her bag, having found an open table situated in a quiet corner. It was time to dig. She was about to begin ghost hunting, the anticipation of discovering something elusive, something previously unknown to her on the horizon.

Sage headed toward the nearby magazine section, where rows of periodicals lined several wall shelves, but she stopped to peruse a few that had been left on a table. She opened the cover of *Today's Farmer* and saw a two-page Rid-Away layout consuming the prime advertising space and wondered whether this was what the author of the Earth Day column was referring to when he had quoted, "Without chemicals, life itself would be impossible," before ripping apart the theory. She flipped to the next page and perused the table of contents.

"New Corn Hybrid Promises Highest Yields Ever"

"A Closer Look: Pork Production on an Industrial Level"

"An Interview with Three Generations of Iowa Farmers Moving up the Ladder"

Curious, Sage carried the magazine to a corner table, along with a couple of others that might provide insight into how modern food is produced. Technological advances were making headlines more and more, and she had a feeling the movement was in direct opposition to what food co-ops were preaching.

"Excuse me," spoke an unfamiliar voice at her side soon after she sat.

Sage looked over in dismay at the unexpected presence. She didn't like disruptions—thus the library, thus the corner. It seemed like an obvious statement. Before her stood the man who had held open the door. His face still claimed the hurried look it had a few minutes ago, and his eyes burned with intensity.

"I was just wondering if you might've seen someone riding a red bike as you pulled up?"

He stepped an inch closer, and it took Sage a second to realize what he was asking.

"Um, maybe. What did the person look like?"

"I don't know. I leaned my bike up against the shrubs just outside the door, and now it's missing. I think someone stole it. Did you see anyone?"

"Um, let's see. I . . . I don't think so. I was kind of preoccupied with my own thoughts, so I wasn't really paying attention."

He continued staring as if the answer wasn't good enough.

"You say it was red?" Sage continued.

"Yeah. Like a dodgeball, kind of dark red."

"You know, I don't think I did."

"Are you sure? Because I was only in here for about ten minutes, so there wasn't much time for someone to get away with it."

"Yeah, I'm sure. I had just pulled up and was singing along to the radio—"

"What were you singing?" he asked.

"Um, first it was 'The Night the Lights Went Out in Georgia.'"

"Was it on the radio, or were you playing the eight-track?"

"On the radio."

"Have you ever seen Vicki Lawrence in concert?"

"No." She looked askance to see if anyone was nearby witnessing this bizarre conversation. "You?"

"Yeah. Outside at a summer fest last year."

"Was she good in concert?"

"Not bad. The best part was that it was raining like a bat outta hell, even hailing, and the whole crowd just stood there singing along like nothing was going on. Then she took a break and some girls started mud wrestling, and a bunch of guys got into it, too, and soon half the people there were rolling around in the mud. It was awesome."

Sage couldn't imagine mud wrestling at a concert, but the conversation proved to be entertaining.

"Do you go to many concerts?" she asked.

"No, only been to a couple."

He slid out the chair across the table and sat, dropping his backpack on the floor beside him.

"Oh. What do you spend your time on here?"

"Kicking industrial ass," he replied.

"Hmm. Just how do you go about that?"

"Through exposition. I read the gloating reviews of achievement in the latest periodicals and then write my own version of what they *forgot* to mention—the leftovers. The pollutants, the poisoned watersheds, the garbage left behind. You know, stuff nobody wants to think about."

His fervent tone sounded newly familiar. Sage cocked her head and asked, "Did you, by chance, write an article last spring for *Sensationally Alive*? On Earth Day?"

"Yes!" He leaned in toward Sage as if he were about to propose a conspiracy of sorts, and she quickly became aware of just how handsome this man before her was. Not just nice looking, but there was depth to his looks. His short hair revealed a smooth forehead and square jawline that came off as both masculine and compassionate, and bronzed skin accentuated enchanting sea-green eyes that were nothing if not impassioned.

"I'm Peck Wells." He thrust his hand toward Sage.

"Sage Ley."

"You read it? Don't take this the wrong way, but you don't look like the type to subscribe to *Sensationally Alive*."

Suddenly aware of her prim polyester outfit, Sage realized for more than one reason that she was not "the type."

"Yes, I read it, and no, I don't subscribe. My sister left it on my desk at work."

"What are you doing with the notebook? Are you a writer too?"

This man, he's like a pinball machine, thought Sage. "Sort of. I mean, I'm researching an assignment," she answered, feeling her cheeks flush as if she'd been caught in a flat-out lie.

"What?"

"What did I say, or what am I working on?"

"Both."

"What about your bike?"

"Shit." He paused then quickly decided. "It's gone. I'll deal with it later."

The interrogation having been set in motion, Sage spoke tentatively about her background at the historical society and the newfound assignment she'd been granted. The revelation sparked a discussion that would last for the next hour, meandering from food co-ops to farming and back again. More than once they were hushed, as Peck riled himself over the disdain he held for the chemical-intensive farming methods that had become so prevalent. It was clear to Sage that Peck was authentic, true to his personal and hugely broad cause of saving the earth. His exclamatory style was keenly different from her own objective, informative style, but she found it easy to get caught up in the fireworks.

"Hey, do you have some free time?" Peck asked. "I want to bring you somewhere to meet a friend."

"Yeah, I guess I don't have any plans. The day's nearly over anyway."

"Great. Mind if you drive?"

Chapter 9

—— Elizabeth, October 1948 ——

An inimitable hue of blue saturated the sky during the midmorning hour, the air already comfortable enough to shed my sweater and soak in the diminishing warmth of autumn. I'd pulled back my freshly washed hair with combs, and my face welcomed the fresh, tranquil sunlight as I turned onto St. Francis Avenue toward Lakeshore Park. As I walked, it occurred to me that, from the moment I'd stepped down from the Midwest Arrow with Helena by my side, this particular place in which I had landed was just where I was supposed to be during any given day, at any given time. As if a player on my team, the pleasant weather punctuated my certainty.

I stepped up my pace and took notice of my surroundings. Few people were on the sidewalks, and those who were seemed to be in a hurry, with the exception of one elderly man who sat upon a wooden bench near the park, Whitman in hand and golden retriever at his side. The lack of a crowd was understandable: it was Sunday, a family day. The thought of my own children without me by their side at church, five hours away by train and another one-and-a-half by automobile, made me long for the touch of their warm little hands, their exuberant embraces. I became uncertain whether this impending outing was a wise decision after all. Maybe it was the wine or the divine food that had swayed my decision the night before, or perhaps the release I'd felt in conversation with Stephen that made the idea of spending the day with him seem harmless enough. I had also been remarkably comfortable around him and had the sense that he was a true gentleman. Of course, I understood that propriety called for his wife to be present, too, but his reassurances that she would welcome the idea of him busying himself with his own interests felt genuine. And, this was Chicago; things were different here.

But now here I was, ambivalent and apprehensive, a married woman meeting a relative stranger—a man—in a city far away from home.

"Elizabeth, dear! Hello!" Stephen called out from a short distance away, walking briskly in my direction. "Oh dear, you look perplexed," he continued as he stopped before me, his smile replaced with a look of concern.

"No. I was just thinking of my children, so far away on a Sunday." I looked down. "I'm sorry. That wasn't a very nice hello, was it?"

"Well, if it is any consolation to you, Elizabeth, I did not see my wife this morning either. She is sleeping it away with a terrible headache before dashing off for a day of frolicking with the ladies, in the name of fashion. I'm afraid she was a bit too zealous in her festive endeavors last night. Though it is no surprise, I suppose," he said, peering out over my shoulder toward the lake. "I do believe she was deposited home by Mr. Chase around five o'clock in the morning."

Five o'clock! I thought. *Unimaginable!*

"I don't suppose hearing that helps you feel the least bit better about missing your children. However, perhaps it might lighten your spirits knowing that you now have a mission. A discarded old gentleman requires your entertainment, keeping both of our lonely selves happy."

It saddened me to hear him hint at a broken relationship, yet I was surprised to feel a surreptitious wave of warmth coil through me before slithering off with the breeze that moved in off the water.

"So, which one of these boats belongs to an 'old' gentleman like you?" I asked, looking toward the pier. Surely, he couldn't have been more than thirty-eight years old, forty tops.

"Ah, yes. We elderly fellows tend towards a finely crafted vessel such as the one settled there," he said, pointing to the nearest one on the second dock. "Would you like to take a closer look?"

"Yes, I sure would! But is it okay if we have something to eat first? I guess I wasn't all that hungry when I left this morning, but suddenly I'm starved. I think I saw a sandwich shop just over there on that street."

"Certainly. They serve a terribly delicious chocolate milkshake. I am never one to forgo an American milkshake."

As we began making our way toward the restaurant, I again exclaimed over the savory food we'd eaten at Giarro's, still relishing the recollection of the new flavors on my amateur palate. Stephen spoke of the many artists of cuisine that toiled in the great restaurant kitchens of Chicago, an unrelated set of flavors to the blandness of London eating establishments, he explained, where seasonings seemed more of a concept than a reality.

"Might you be interested in tasting the finest Greek food you've ever tried, say tomorrow evening?" Stephen asked as we passed through the park.

"The finest? Like the finest Italian food?" I laughed. "Do remember, I live on a dairy farm where we eat meat and potatoes almost every day. I've never even tried Greek food, let alone had the opportunity to compare Greek food."

Stephen held open the door to Martha's Diner, our laughter trailing in behind us. The understated interior of the small restaurant smacked of familiarity and comfort. The daisy-print wallpaper and chalkboard menu could have been any one of the three sandwich shops in Decorah. The tangy smell of barbecued beef sandwiches enveloped us as we walked past a glass-fronted pie safe with seven varieties of pie encased within before sliding into a booth near the window.

After ordering a meatloaf sandwich with potato salad and apple pie à la mode for myself and Stephen a chocolate milkshake, bowl of chicken noodle soup and, at my urging, macaroni salad with pickles on the side, we resumed our conversation as if we were friends of old recently reunited. And as we did so, it occurred to me how odd it was that two people so disparate in lifestyle had been chanced together at adjacent tables in a hidden lounge of an enormous city. How unlikely that those two people shared a great deal of commonality, as I was beginning to understand. And how fascinating that, though both married, within a short period of time each found more delight in conversing with each other than with their very own spouses. Dangerously fascinating.

I'd never been on a boat—any boat of any type—but as a young woman I'd fallen for the posed images in magazines in which models expressed their good fortune of sailing along the shore, smiles wide and carefree hair tousled by the wind. Their lives, I had been certain, were perfect, as unflawed as their white linen suits and flowing summer dresses. And now, I of all people, was about to step onto the deck of a vessel docked upon the shores of Lake Michigan.

Stephen offered me his hand, which I held tightly as I straddled the short distance from the dock over the low railing to the wooden deck. Just before me stood the captain's wheel, two small benches, and what looked like a miniature house rising from the middle. Surprisingly tall poles held layers of fabric, presumably the sails. I was curious about it all and didn't hesitate to ask many questions, which Stephen patiently and happily answered.

"What's in there?" I asked, pointing to the miniature house.

"That is what's called the cabin. The living quarters, as it is." Stephen smiled at my enthusiasm. "What do you say we tour in reverse, starting with the cabin then make our way back up here to the deck?"

"Lead the way, Captain."

He opened the hatch, and I climbed down the short ladder, holding tightly onto the wooden sides. He followed behind me.

"Do excuse the dust. I confess," he said, "it has not been in use for some weeks now."

"Oh, that's okay. There's not too much to see. I mean, there's just not much room, so it's easy to see everything quickly." I felt my naivety usher forth in the form of a blush. "But I like it all just fine. It's very nice in here."

I turned hastily toward the nearest space, eager to remove the focus from my awkwardness. "I'm sorry. Please do give me a tour. Is this the parlor we are in?"

Stephen chuckled softly as he tutored me on the correct terminology. "We are now in what is called the salon. And yes, it is a parlor of sorts, though diminished in size, as you can see. The galley is the kitchen just beside us, and the head, or loo—the bathroom as you know it—is through the small door beside you."

The tour was illustrated by an occasional head nod or hand gesture, both of us having remained standing in the same spot.

"Through the aft door is the sleeping area known as the v-berth," Stephen continued. "And on the starboard side near the front of the boat," he motioned to the right, "is another bunk. The engine is below the floor and the cockpit and deck are above the ceiling. And there you have it. That concludes the grand tour!" He chuckled at the brevity of it. "Feel free to roam the castle."

Several more questions poured forth, and after a while we worked our way back up on deck. What exactly does "v-berth" mean? Where is the anchor? How and when does the sail go up? How does steering work with a sail?

My questions didn't go unheard. Stephen introduced me to further vernacular unique to the world of sailing—mainsail, headsail, clew, huff, leech—all of which I found intensely interesting, even the minutiae. As I took it all in, I secretly hoped that I'd have a chance to go on a sail. But if not, even if this was where it was to end, it was an experience that I never, after having married, imagined that I would have. It was as if I had just awakened from a long, restless sleep and was taking in that first delicious stretch.

Sailboat terminology was only the beginning of an unexpected education. Over the course of the next several days in Chicago, Stephen acted as my guide as we toured the city obsessively, our friendship growing stronger with each day. We ate not only Greek food but French and Chinese dishes, too, along with steak and Guinness pie—a staple in England, he explained. We rode an elevator to the top of a new skyscraper and saw men hovering on beams as they built another next door. We rode the El to the Chicago Museum of Art, where I was taught how to differentiate between a Monet and a Manet; where I learned terms like *chiaroscuro*, *deconstruction*, *pointillism*; and where I nodded in puzzlement as I considered the concept of pieces in which figures were blatantly distorted. As I stood in silence before one work in particular—a colorful painting by the artist Jackson Pollock—it was impossible not to reflect on the argument I'd had with Will the evening before I departed for my trip. One that, though on the surface was about art, clearly emphasized our differences.

"This is maddening!" I'd called out, admittedly with more annoyance than was necessary as I rattled the pages of our hometown newspaper.

"And what is it that is bothering you now, honey?" Will had asked, his inquiry laced with an obvious tinge of exasperation.

"Listen to this: 'Home Happenings: Mrs. Robert Swenson (Eloise Swenson) and her two children, Roberta and James, left Sunday to spend the week at the home of her parents, Mr. and Mrs. H.R. Grimes, at their estate nestled upon a Lake Harriett cove in Minneapolis.' Honestly, who cares? Why are we paying money to read this nonsense? And this: 'Mr. and Mrs. Bob Galloway spent the weekend as guests of Mr. and Mrs. Herbert Hewitt in Des Moines. Mrs. Elliot Severson, recently widowed, opened her home to her brother-in-law, Gilbert, and his new wife, Ann, for a weekend visit.' Why does the newspaper print this stuff? Is there anyone out there who betters their life by knowing Bob and Joan went to Des Moines? Really!"

"Can't argue that," Will said. "Same goes with this new artist, Jackson Pollock. Seems he drips paint onto canvas and now is rolling in dough. 'Is he the greatest living painter in the United States?' Ha!"

He set aside the latest issue of *Life* magazine, and my eye caught the image of the cover: a mother gleefully raising her infant son into the air. I quickly turned away.

"Everyone has their authentic interests, Will. If putting on a suit each day, or a pair of overalls for that matter, isn't his thing, maybe getting people to see life in a different way through art is."

"Is that first-hand experience?"

I looked at my husband, a man fashioned with patience, and realized how his calm demeanor had been replaced by morsels of frustration these past weeks. But pity was not my priority on this night. I had been too mired in my own troublesome blend of irrational blues and eager anticipation over my upcoming trip to Chicago to act on anything but my own self-interest.

"Even though I'm not an artist, I happen to appreciate how art impacts our world. And, if canning tomatoes and washing clothes doesn't complete my life, so be it. It's okay to have other interests. Everyone does."

"Yeah, art. You picked a high-quality one. Very important in bettering one's life."

"And what do you call that image of *The Lord's Supper* on our wall? You seem to be fine with keeping it displayed as the first thing seen when walking into the house."

"*That* is of God. *That* is a reminder of what He sacrificed for us. How can you compare a sacred image like that to a bunch of paint splatters, Betty?"

"It's not a comparison of the two—of one being better or more important than the other. It's the fact that they're both important. To you, being reminded of the sacrifices of Jesus is close to your heart. Another man might need to release his anger, his stress, by feeling understood through splattering paint onto a canvas, as you put it."

I stood, the chair cushion suddenly feeling like a rigid board, and folded the newspaper I'd been reading in a haphazard way, tossing it back onto the lamp table between us.

Will gave me a sidelong glance. "Yeah."

The usual brightness in his blue eyes had faded during recent months, weariness an unsolicited replacement. A surge of guilt rushed through me, and I made a mental note to add my failure as a wife to my list of transgressions. Yet even that wasn't enough to overpower the headstrong stance that had meddled with my mood.

"Look at what Louise does when coloring with her crayons," I said, standing before him with my arms folded tightly in front of me. "Last week she was so excited over drawing a carrot because it is her favorite food, and the other day I found her trying to draw a fish. She told me it was the fish that died outside the bucket. She looked so sad, Will, and she hugged me so hard and told me she wanted the fish back."

I paused, unwilling to become choked up over the memories of that day, the day Will and the girls had come home after fishing. The day he had found me in the bedroom, straining against the pain of giving birth.

"Have you ever noticed that when Louise feels strongly about something, she draws it? It's how she expresses herself. It's her way of figuring out her own life. I'd call that important."

"She'll grow out of it. She's three."

"I hope she never grows out of it!"

I could feel the froth of exasperation growing. How could he dismiss art as if it were a thistle among flower beds, a weed in his precious fields?

"I wish you could enter my mind, my life, for just one day," I said, shifting my line of vision outside the living room window to the fields beyond.

"I'd get lost!" he responded with a laugh, a feeble attempt to recover the more amicable tone of previous conversations we'd engaged in that evening. "Give me a compass and atlas, and I'd still need a flare gun."

I felt the sting of tears, tears that so often hovered on the brim of my eyelids, guardians refusing their escape. "There's something inside me, Will. It's hard to explain. It's as if I'm being lured upstream to spawn, an instinctual need. I didn't create it. It's just there. Maybe it's always been there."

"But you have kids who need you to be here for them. They can see it, Betty. They can see that you've stepped into a mud puddle and ain't bothering to get out of it."

I spun away from him and went into the kitchen. The yeasty aroma emanating from the loaves of bread in the oven had begun to waft into the living room, a sign that they were nearly done baking. Though it was well into the evening, I still wanted to add the lace onto the new Sunday dress I'd sewn for Sage, the finishing touch, before I left in the morning.

"Not everyone finds fulfillment in farming or farm life, Will. I'm different. I'm sorry," I called out from the kitchen. "Or maybe I'm not. I just am who I am. And being surrounded by women and newspapers that thrive on gossip is just dreadful. I want to look at art, up close, every detail of every brush stroke—or splatter. I want to discover for myself what it means."

I peered into the oven, noticed the honeyed color of the bread, and remembered how little I'd eaten for supper.

"I've always had visions of life being more than . . . I don't know, just more . . . grand."

I closed the oven door with a heavy hand and glanced into the living room as I set the bread on the table to cool. Will was facing the window. I knew I had crossed a line, but this time the needle of guilt with which I poked myself was duller than those more sharpened instruments of the past. I was tired. I was excited. I was about to pirouette for the first time, I was sure, but the strength needed to stand on my toes had felt more challenging on this night than the others leading up to this trip that I had so anticipated.

"Well then, I'm sure you'll find a whole lot of grand in Chicago. Aren't you lucky."

Will pushed himself up from the wingback chair, snuffed out his Lucky Strike, and clicked off *The Abbott and Costello Radio Show* that had been playing in the background. The only remaining sound was the commentary echo of his footsteps as he walked toward the bedroom.

That night, for the first time since we'd been married, we did not say "good night" to each other, did not caress each other's feet underneath the white cotton sheet. And we certainly did not make love.

And now here I was in Chicago, exploring everything that held my interest with a man who cared about it as intensely as I did.

A full week had passed in a whirl, the momentum of experiences forming a strong bond of friendship between Stephen and me. I had been too absorbed in the newness of it all to consider the occasional slip in Stephen's demeanor. Though usually jolly and present, there were times when he became quiet, when I would catch him gazing off into the distance or looking at me with questioning eyes. And so I was taken aback when, as we stood at a street corner waiting for a taxicab to carry us to the baseball district—a look at Wrigley Field was a necessity, he insisted, and I quickly agreed, wanting to describe it to Will upon my return—he surprised me with an announcement.

"Ruth has filed for a divorce," he said without segue. "She has departed for New York with the man of her interest, stating that she is 'no longer willing to maintain a marriage for purposes of putting up a facade.'" He delivered the news while hailing an approaching taxicab. "And a crumbling one at that. She has a better life to live, and with a better man, she informed me."

The taxicab pulled next to the curb and Stephen opened the door for me, directed the driver, then quieted, as if worn out from the sudden admission.

"We don't have to go to the stadium," I said, looking forward, unsure how to appropriately handle this news.

He turned toward me, nonplussed. "Whyever would we not go?"

"Do you want to go somewhere else? Talk about the situation with Ruth?" I asked, looking back at him.

"No, dear Elizabeth. I want to view one of the finest baseball stadiums in the country, with you on my arm. My time with you has been, and continues to be, thoroughly enjoyable. I want nothing more than to be right here with you."

Once again, I felt a glow of heat. I had made assumptions that their marriage wasn't perfect—whose is, really?—but we had talked so little about his personal life that it caught me off guard. And it made me feel vulnerable. I was now in the company of a man who was no longer wrapped in the safety net of marriage. A single man, for all intents and purposes.

As the car surged forth into traffic, the sticky hands of guilt from which I had thus far managed to disentangle myself wrapped their fingers around me. I didn't want this declaration to upend the time that I was earnestly enjoying in the company of Stephen. I knew such a thought was selfish, yet it was there, and I wondered whether he, too, felt the same.

My feelings toward Will hadn't changed; he was a good man, and I understood that I was lucky compared to some other women. But the uncertainty of how we could move forward with vast differences in our ideals had only been emphasized during my time in the city. My husband was a dear, kind friend, but he was not my love. It was a truth that grew more evident with each day that passed. Chicago was a place in which he would never belong and one in which I longed to remain.

Chapter 10

— June 1975 —

Living Waters had been a distant thought in Sage's mind until today. Even though she knew Louise spent a lot of time there, she'd never stepped foot inside the place. But today she'd been twice reintroduced to it by both Bernie and Peck.

Peck directed her to park across the street from an aged Craftsman-style house with faded wood trim exposed by layers of weather-peeled paint. They crossed the street and the grassy front yard in need of a mow toward a set of steps that led to the door of a four-season porch. Sage noticed the sign above.

LIVING WATERS
FOOD CO-OP
EST. 1973

Near the foot of the steps sat a woman, her eyes closed as she swayed to the tune of the flute she was playing.

"Hey, Mary," Peck said as they passed by, though she was oblivious to the greeting, and he and Sage continued up the steps and onto the porch that was filled with shelves of seedlings, flowers, and plants of several varieties.

Once inside, Peck was greeted with a smothering hug by the cashier, a woman named Sherrie, whose shiny black locks sprung in tight curls at all angles. He asked over Mark's whereabouts, to which Sherrie responded by pointing her thumb over her shoulder, indicating the back of the store.

Sage took in the setting as they walked. Overall, there really wasn't much to the place, at least not compared to Novotny's Supermarket down the street from her duplex or the SuperValu on Selby Avenue. The produce section here consisted of a decent supply of greens, bundles of fresh herbs, and a few other vegetables—some unfamiliar—along with a small pile of rhubarb and gobs of strawberries. The heads of iceberg lettuce were like softballs compared to the volleyball-sized ones at the SuperValu. Peck paused to grab a small handful of string beans and handed a couple to Sage.

"Um, I'll pass."

To her left were large round cardboard bins with *whole wheat*, *kamut*, and *spelt* written in magic marker across the lids. Sage wondered over their uses. Bread? Cake? Her own preference was the soft doughiness of the loaves from the Wonder Bread store, also a convenient few blocks from her home.

Next to the bulk bins was a shelf lined with jars of nuts and seeds and another above it displaying a selection of handmade soaps and candles that she recognized as the beeswax type Louise made. Last was a refrigerator, with a handwritten sign taped to it that listed the contents within: *farm-fresh eggs, bottled milk, goat and dairy cheeses.*

The air held the earthy scent of food blended with the rudimentary odor of humanity, but it also carried an almost palpable buzz. A small cadre of neighbors and students from the nearby campus had gathered to shop, many of whom Peck introduced "Louise's sister" to. Sage wondered if the co-op was for them, like for her sister, a step toward seeking control of what had perhaps become uncontrollable: their revolution.

At last, she and Peck reached the back room.

"Hey, Sage. Nice to meet you, man." Mark's voice was like molasses, his easygoing mannerisms a sharp contrast to Peck's. Tall and long-haired with round wire glasses, he was, Sage thought, just the kind of man she expected to find working at a food cooperative.

Mark was the glue of the store, she learned, the one who kept the books, kept the schedule, and as of late, kept the peace. She couldn't imagine how Mark managed all he did, considering the sloth-like pace with which he spoke and moved.

"Guess who's planning to pay a friendly visit?" he asked Peck, his lips forming a smile that conveyed a confusing mix of pleasure and angst.

"No shit," replied Peck, the lack of words between the two confounding Sage.

"Yep. Seems the bean fiasco a couple of months ago was their introductory warning, a step up from petty annoyance. Word's out that they're prepared to try to close down shop if we can't come to terms with the community guidelines."

"There's no way the CO can do that," Peck replied, his posture stiffening. "We can run our store any damn way we please. There's no way those assholes can squash us!"

"Whoa, take it easy, man. No one's squashing anyone." Mark set his hand on Peck's shoulder. "We'll get it worked out."

From across the store, someone called out Mark's name.

"Listen, I gotta go, man, but come hang out more often," he said to Sage, then turned and walked back into the store.

Sage could see the tension in the muscles of Peck's face and arms. He guided her through the back door to a small cement parking lot, where grass had forced itself through myriad cracks in the cement and a few hungry crows dined without pause on an indiscernible food morsel as if they, too, were a part of the sustainable living design.

Once outside, Peck stopped. He looked down, settling his hands upon his waist. "Shit. What an idiot."

Sage's eyebrows furrowed. "Everything okay?" she asked, hearing a hotrod rev up on the street out front.

"Yeah." He let out a short chuckle and looked up at her. "I was gonna walk you to your car and then maybe ask if I could see you again sometime. You know, like on a date."

"Oh," Sage wasn't sure what to say, not knowing whether it was an offer or whether he'd considered a date then quickly recoiled from the idea. The prolonged silence carried the weight of chagrin, causing Sage to feel around for a diversion of topic.

"Do you think Mark will have time to talk with me yet today, or is there someone else I should talk to? I mean, my assignment isn't due for a while, but I guess if I could get a jump start on it since I'm here, that would be fine too."

"Mark's the man, but we'd better try another time. It's pretty busy this afternoon." Sage noted that he used the word *we*. "Anyway, I'm an idiot because, well . . . we didn't park back here."

Peck smiled sheepishly, and Sage, realizing that she hadn't considered where they'd parked either, let out a burst of laughter.

"Perfectly okay," she reassured him. "Well, I should go. I'm sure Bono—my dog—is tearing up my place by now." As if Bono would have the gall, let alone the energy to do so.

"That's a great name."

"Thanks. Did you see Sonny and Cher in concert too?"

"Not yet," he said and smiled at her.

Another moment of awkward silence ensued before Sage once again led the conversation. "Well, it was great to meet you. I'll stop by here again soon to talk to Mark. Maybe I'll catch up with you then. Can you get a ride?"

"Don't need one. I live there." Peck pointed back at the co-op, at the upper floor. A set of semidecrepit wooden steps along the side led to the second story, where a white door held a dried-out wreath. "Let me walk you to where your car is actually parked."

Together they circled back toward the front of the house.

"Listen, you wanna grab some grub this weekend?" he asked.

Sage felt her breath catch.

"Before you answer, I should probably tell you that I'm a vegetarian."

"Thanks, but I'm pretty sure that won't hold me back from saying yes. Unless you're planning to ask me to cook the meal."

"Not this time. Nothing El Triunfo can't do for us. Seven, Saturday?"

"Sure." She paused and wrote down her address and phone number, tearing off the corner of the page and handing it over as if she'd been doing this for years. In reality, she'd had but a handful of dates, each of them about as satisfying as eating a bowl of flour.

Louise lounged in the small square of grass on the streetside of the Power Station Café, her shift having ended, before stepping into the Corne next door where she could be out of the sun. Originally the Corner Bar, years of a missing "r" necessarily renamed the rundown establishment the "Corn-ey."

"Hey, handsome, what's happening?" She wrapped her arms around Randy's broad upper back.

He turned and placed his own arms around her waist. "Shit, what time is it?" Randy himself rarely drank, but the late-afternoon clientele was entertaining enough.

"It's nearly four-fifteen. I thought you'd forgotten me," she said, her lips turning downward in a fake pout.

"Darlin', I'd never forget you." He pulled her toward him, his eyes glowing despite their deep chocolatey color. "Just sidetracked is all. Don was telling me a little more about the CO happenings around town. Steward and East End have been getting the stink eye too."

Randy turned back to Don. "Wish I was set up at a law firm already."

"They've just been chewing on a bone," Don said. "Looking for the marrow, their next piece of meat. But they won't find it at Living Waters. They've got a good thing going over there," he said, looking at Louise. "You know that better than anyone."

"Damn straight," Louise said. The thought of anyone threatening the store that was like her baby, having helped give birth to it by way of joining on as one of the first volunteers, was unacceptable to say the least.

"Thanks, man." Randy stood, patting Don's shoulder. "I'll fill you in on the way, butterfly."

As they walked toward home, the potency of the midafternoon heat had begun to ease noticeably. Randy's tall afro leaned comically to the side in the occasional gust of wind as they sauntered through Minneapolis's West Bank, its curbs dotted with cigarette butts and an occasional scattering of Pepsi cans and flattened McDonald's bags. A fair share of the houses, most of them built closely to one another, were in various states of disrepair, but the Augsburg College campus gave respite to the claustrophobic feel of the neighborhood, with its open grounds and manicured campus.

Randy had been updating Louise on Don's co-op news when a sudden succession of rubber tires coming to a hard brake disrupted their conversation. They stopped and looked at each other, realization setting in as to where the sound of car doors being slammed was coming from.

Randy grabbed Louise's hand and together they ran ahead, turning into the alley and entering the co-op through the back door, where they were met by an older couple scurrying out. Louise saw Mark near the front of the store and let out a sigh of relief. If anyone could handle this, he could. But before she had a chance to finish her thought, a man with a shock of red hair strode through the front doorway, a small gang of cohorts enshrining him.

"Mark," he called out more loudly than necessary. "It's time we get this straightened out."

Mark took a step forward, holding an overflowing box of spinach in his arms. "Dude, as far as we're concerned, Living Waters doesn't have anything to straighten out. We're set, man. We're fine with the way things are."

"Well, you see, you're not. We're all in this together. No one works outside of the CO." Now the red-haired man stepped in closer. "Your elitist practices forget the most important people—the working class—and you gotta get your shit together."

"Jerry, we've been through this, and our views haven't changed. What you're claiming is a nonexistent agenda that you need to let go of. We're here for everyone, man, and our customers support us."

Mark walked past him toward the small produce section and began pulling the bundles of spinach from the box, placing them at the end of the counter.

"How's that, by forcing them to work at your store?" Jerry's voice elevated as he moved further into the aisle. "It's a business, man. You have to run it like one, and the CO is here to see that you do. That we all do."

"Jerry, like I said, we're good."

"Well, we don't happen to think you're good. In fact," he said, glaring up at Mark, "you *will* stick with the guidelines. You *will* work with us, or you won't operate at all."

"Are you threatening me?" Mark turned toward him with uncharacteristic swiftness, his body looming over Jerry's by a six-inch advantage.

Louise could smell the adrenaline in the air. She squeezed Randy's hand with her own sweaty fingers and felt the rapid beat of his pulse.

Jerry took another step forward, closing the space between the two. The only sound was the *shush* of shoes shuffling against wood as the small horde of men waited for action. "You can think of it in any way you want to, but we're not backing down."

"Dude, it's not about control. It's about food—pure food—and it's about the earth. It's how we began and how we intend to stay, man. The people who work here, who shop here, they're cool with the way things are."

"Yeah, we're just fine," came a woman's voice from beside Louise: Hilma. "You can push your agenda elsewhere, but we, the people who shop at Living Waters, have no problem with the place. We very much like it, in fact."

"So you're okay with social elitism, with turning a palm to the working class?"

"Do I look like an elitist to you?" Hilma asked, her stained cutoff denim shorts cinched onto her aging body by suspenders, a faded blouse underneath.

"An argument could be made if I were to venture in that direction."

"I am here to tell you, not only am I *not* elitist, but I am a neighbor and a supporter and a customer at this store, and I would have it no other way. You and your cronies can put yourselves back into your tough little cars and drive on off to wherever you came from. We're not buying what you're selling."

A ripple of murmurs arose from those standing behind Jerry, but a raise of his hand shut them down. "Miss, I'll respect you because you are a supporter of the cooperative movement, but I realize that you likely don't know what's going on behind the scenes. This establishment, you see, is forcing volunteerism—an illegal action for any business. And trust me here: with the prices that are charged, the working class is gonna be pushed right out of here before you can say Living Waters is coming down. So, we're gonna leave here now and let you think about that for a while. But rest assured, we'll be back."

"You want working class, son?" she retorted. "You found her. Right here, filling her basket with goods from Living Waters."

Jerry ignored the comment. "There's an element of community that co-op supporters understand, and together we'll move forward. Those who choose not to," he looked at Mark, "will soon find themselves singled out not only by the CO but by the people." He turned toward the front door and redirected a final order to his group. "The righteous always win!"

At that, he left, followed by the others who had opened a path for him like the parting of the Red Sea. Mark ambled over to the door and silently watched them speed off, leaving a cloud of smoke and a can of Blatz in their wake. He picked up the box of spinach and resumed stocking.

Chapter 11

—— Elizabeth, October 1948 ——

It was, perhaps, inevitable that a swell of attraction would inveigle its way into our iridescent hearts. The sun will follow the moon across the sky, and the heart will slow its beat at night, predefined rhythms of nature disregarding man's desire for control.

It was a Tuesday afternoon, and Stephen and I had planned to meet once again at the pier where the *Winsome Lady* was docked, now ten days after my introduction to her. The early afternoon sprinkling of rain had subsided, and a temperate breeze was pushing the remaining clouds east as I walked toward the marina, having come from the library where I'd just finished reading *Jane Eyre*.

Upon my arrival, Stephen invited me below deck. I stood near a high, narrow window that provided enough light to peruse the titles of a modest collection of books that occupied a small shelf above a maritime chart. He approached and reached over my shoulder to point out a volume of French poetry, his chest momentarily brushing against my back. It was a mere hum of a touch, though a disorienting one that sent a current of energy coursing through me. I briefly reeled, reaching toward the shelf to steady myself, but the small space of the salon left no room for the electricity to dissipate. In a faltering voice, I quickly excused myself to the head.

"Yes, of course," Stephen replied in a near whisper.

I hastily stepped away, his eyes pulling after me, and stood hesitantly in the doorway before closing the door between us.

The spark of energy, the rush of feelings—surely my own development—crowded against me in the cramped space, encouraging my imagination to flourish. I peered into the silver-speckled mirror above the sink, its round shape like a halo surrounding my flummoxed reflection, and forced myself to breathe in deeply despite the musty air. I grabbed ahold of the finger upon which my wedding ring had remained in place since the day I married Will, the diamond biting into my palm, and continued to inhale strength, exhale the red of desire. But my silent self-commands were proving ineffective against a truth that frayed at the edges of my resolve, against the fusion of color that enlivened my world when with Stephen.

Time seemed to still as I unfolded my thoughts, but I couldn't stay there, couldn't remain hidden away. After a quick moment I straightened myself and slid the wooden door back into its nook, then reentered the salon.

"Elizabeth," Stephen said, standing promptly.

I lowered my gaze to the floor beneath us that shone with luster.

"Elizabeth, may I say something to you?"

I nodded, unable to meet his eyes just yet. "Yes, but I must leave very soon."

"Elizabeth, I feel quite flustered about speaking my thoughts, and certainly they are inappropriate. Yet, I have this distressing feeling that if I do not utter them quite quickly, I shall never again have the opportunity to do so." His words tumbled forth with haste.

"No." I stopped him. "I don't want to be rude, but if what you're about to say has anything to do with me"—I shook my head and whispered—"please don't."

"Just look at me for a moment. I beg of you." He took not a step toward me but away, and I remained silent. I could hear the audible click of a swallow.

"There is a feeling I have for you, Elizabeth, that I have never experienced—not even for my wife. And it has happened so immediately, so powerfully, that I cannot simply will it to pass." He paused. "I married Ruth because it was convenient. Because I was supposed to. I loved her well enough, but had we not married I would have been equally as satisfied remaining friends with her. 'Pals' as you say in America. But one marries when in that circumstance, especially at the age I then was, thirty-five.

"We've not been faithful, Ruth and I . . . to one another." Stephen laughed, a short, pathetic sound that held no joy. "I must be mad for telling you this, and perhaps you have already scurried back up the companionway, but I will nonetheless blather on." He stepped in yet closer to the shelf of books, a place that had seemed innocent enough just minutes before. "This is new for me, this feeling I am having for you. Elizabeth, I cannot help but wonder . . . to believe . . . that what I am feeling may be the embryo of *true* love."

A thunderous silence ensued, my ability to breathe having fled at hearing his words. All at once, I wanted to dance in delight, shirk away in fear, roll back time, and run forward into the future with him. It wasn't just me who felt a growing passion, but this man—this wondrous man before me—shared those same affections.

A displaced wind gusted directly against the boat, rocking it gently yet nonetheless upsetting my already questionable balance. I reached for the table and sat down hard on the bench beside it. Stephen now turned toward me, and I looked at him, waiting, though I wasn't sure for what.

Just as he had done with Ruth, I, too, in my flawed humanity, had put on blinders and jumped into the depths with Will, unaware that the water would later be drained, the wellspring left dry. Now, as I prodded my way around this new experience, I realized that those blinders were removable. And in the revealing light, the world around me had become new.

I understood, too, that if I were to move forward with Stephen, this change would not easily be understood by others, if at all. That the world is stubborn in accepting love's dissipation, reserving cheers for those whose marriage succeeds for a lifetime, jeers for those whose don't. A world that believes what God has brought together, no man shall tear apart. One that says you must make a marriage work yet doesn't reveal how to summon back love when it has absconded into unreachable corners. Nor do they suggest that it is important. What matters, it says, is that you've committed and must continue to trek forward. Yet, isn't letting go when there is an honest recognition of love's absence the fairer thing to do?

In those brief moments of silence, my thoughts vacillated between conviction and confusion, the only certainty my daughters. Despite what I wanted, they came first.

"My life is different from yours, Stephen," I began, breaking the quiet. "I have children. They don't disappear when I go away. They are very real."

"I do understand."

I hesitated momentarily but knew I had to continue, to be as honest with him as he was with me. "Yet I, too, admit that I have feelings toward you. I feel something that . . . that is miles from anything I've ever felt before."

His eyes brightened.

"When I was younger, before I got married, I dreamed of how I wanted things to be, as I told you about that first night at Giarro's. I dreamed of ideals that a girl in my situation had no right to dream about, of a world beyond the tiny piece of it I knew. And of a partner who I could experience the world with.

"I set those dreams aside when I said my vows. I mean, I changed it, because it was a dream. It wasn't real. That's how it was where I grew up and how it still is. You work hard. You get dirty and wear yourself out before the day ends. You do it beside your family and your neighbors. And you don't consider what might have been because dreams outside of those in your sleep aren't necessary. They aren't what *is*."

I looked for his reaction and saw that the intensity in his look remained.

"Yet, even though I set aside my dreams, I never could fully cut ties with them. And now here I am, Stephen, suddenly *in* my dream. I can touch it now; it's right here. You're right here. But," I shook my head slowly. "I'm afraid it may be too late to be a part of it."

Stephen stepped toward me, his head nearly skimming the surface of the low ceiling, and took my hands into his, kneeling before me. "Elizabeth, I cannot think that we were brought together and both of us so properly swept up by these feelings we clearly share, only to believe that words we had earlier spoken out of duty to another must stand in our way." His voice raised not in pitch but in intensity, and a frown was now etched onto his face. "I cannot believe that!"

He reached up to grasp my arms, his touch gentle yet robust, the electricity of it once again pulsating throughout my body. I yearned to be closer to him, to unzip the outer shell of his being and step inside, to become as much a part of him as he himself was. My attempt at conviction of right and wrong was waning briskly.

Stephen stood, raising me with him. My foot moved forward, as if by its own will, bringing our bodies together. I slid my arms around his lean frame and touched my cheek to his chest. I felt his fingers rest softly under my chin as he lifted my face toward his. Our lips met, and all thought blurred into the ether.

The kiss was but a gauzy effort to convey our rising emotions. It wasn't about an insatiable desire to lie together but was one soul speaking to another in a language that is soulful, universal. For so long, I'd been living in a merciless drought, the once verdant leaves of my garden wilted, seeds lying dormant when I should have been witnessing the blossoming of flowers. Now, a youthful tulip began to lift its head from the dark soil below, still folded at a graceless angle, particles of dirt scattered upon it. A bud, fresh and new with the promise of exceptional beauty.

"Stephen," a deep male voice called out from the deck above, drawing us hastily out of the spell that had been cast upon us. "I've come with a nice surprise."

We pulled apart, the metronome of our private world silenced.

A man wearing a pair of black, patent-leather shoes was working his way down the ladder-like steps into the cabin. My hand sprang to my lips, where I brushed at whatever lipstick may have remained.

"I thought I'd see if I could catch . . ." he began, stalling as he turned around and took notice of me. His eyebrows shot up, and a look of familiarity crossed his face as he churned out a greeting and dipped into an old-fashioned bow at the waist.

I'd expected a man of generous size to appear, as the deep and rather boisterous voice had implied. Instead, before us stood one of about my height, dressed entirely in black from the fedora upon his black hair to his black pants and shoes. Even his crisply ironed shirt was dark as midnight.

I immediately recognized him from the Blue Window as the man whose offer for revelry Stephen had declined when we were preparing to leave for Giarro's. It was obvious by the sight of the two bottles of liquor in hand—one scotch and one gin—that he was ready to re-up his previous offer.

"Elizabeth, this is Neil," said Stephen politely, casting a quick glance his way.

"Yes," I replied. "Hello." I was still dazed from the moment we'd just experienced and couldn't think of a single pleasant comment. After all, there didn't appear to be much pleasantness about him.

"Well, well, well," Neil replied. He didn't hesitate to freely roam his gaze from my face to my feet and slowly back up again. "Elizabeth . . . yes. I believe we've met before, Betty. Now Stephen, why didn't I know about this? Come to think of it, you've been awfully evasive since that night at the Blue Window. And you, sweetheart, must be the reason why."

"Neil, that is no way to greet a lady. At what time this morning did you begin nipping at the bottle?"

A brief roar of laughter burst forth in reply as he plunked his waif-like body onto the bench. There was a nick in his self-assuredness that underlay his confident appearance, as if he were a child playing grown-up.

"I suppose it was early, but it is . . . What day is it again? It is Wednesday after all, the hump day of the week."

"Aren't you to be working today?"

"No, sir. I took the day off to have a few drinks with my pal Stephen. Now, tell me about the young lady and why the two of you are hiding on this boat like a couple of stowaways." His mouth turned up in a half smile as he uncorked the gin.

It would be untruthful to say I was altogether disappointed that Neil had appeared out of nowhere, as it offered me the opportunity to excuse myself, to give myself time to think. I bid a hasty goodbye and climbed the ladder, Stephen following closely behind. Above deck he implored me to stay, but the need to clear my mind was the more insistent, the call of the city holding its hand.

The sun warmed my shoulders as I walked on solid ground, the sound of my thick heels transitioning from wood to cement, the surrounding trees of the park enfolding me into the comfort of their home. Despite my certitude over what had transpired moments ago, I knew that I had woven myself into a web, and as pleasant as the silk threads felt next to my skin, they were also entrapping.

Will, my innocent husband, who only wanted me to love him as generously as he loved me and to give to me what most any other woman back home would have gladly taken: a gentle, secure, hard-working man. Why could I not accept his love? Why could it not secure its hold on me, a woman who was raised to expect nothing other than this? Will possessed no selfishness, only solidity.

Stephen was the living representation of my longings: sophisticated, worldly, and also entirely kind and generous. He was a man toward whom my heart lunged, who had resuscitated my spirit. Why had

Stephen and I chanced together when neither of us were looking?

An outburst of activity from a busy few squirrels averted my thoughts, and I sat on a nearby bench watching them encircle the ample trunk of the maple tree in a game of subterfuge.

My thoughts turned to Sage and Louise. How did they fit into these two very distinct lives? A father on the one hand, the only man they'd ever known to be paternal toward them. A man who loved them exceptionally—and they him. And on the other hand, Stephen, a man unknown to their world who quite possibly had not even the slightest interest in my offspring. And what type of friends did he keep? Was I feeling affection for someone of whom I had no real knowledge? Who, perhaps, was an entirely different person than I was supposing him to be? Surely not. Surely, these many days we'd spent together had revealed his true character.

I stood up and began to pace, the squirrels a streak of gray as they raced away in alarm. My gaze shifted toward the towering buildings of the city skyline. *I could leave right now*, I thought. Cut the ties to Chicago with a single snip of the shears and return to the life that was expected of me. Yet the thought of it—the thought of leaving Stephen—felt like a punch.

And what if I had, in that moment, declared emancipation from my dreams, left the city and returned home? What if I had?

Chapter 12
— June 1975 —

As Sage walked from the carriage-house-turned-garage to the front door of her home, she noticed that the color of the sky had turned from silver to gray, pregnant clouds drooping with the weight of water. The leaves of the ash tree in the front yard revealed their lighter underbellies that fluttered in the increasing wind. She opened the door, and an anxious Bono rushed outside as fast as his stiffened body would allow. Sage watched him from the front stoop. Across the street stood a house that looked as if it had been dipped in mustard, from which Mr. Young stepped out and circled his finger in the air, a signal to his teenage son to wrap up the mowing. With a leggy gait, the boy pushed the mower into their garage, appearing oblivious to the thunder and lightning in the near distance that had begun an ostentatious display.

"Bono, come!"

The dog walked over to where Sage now stood holding the door open and, within moments of reentering the house, angry rain began to pelt the rolled glass windows. As she walked into the small kitchen, the ringing of the phone added another layer of noise, though she wasn't about to answer it in this electrifying weather. Then, as if on command, the lights powered off with the last ring.

"Not again," she muttered in frustration.

Sage opened the refrigerator and quickly removed a jar of mayonnaise, not knowing how long the power would be out. A spoonful added to a can of tuna and a generous sprinkle of salt and pepper would make do for a tuna sandwich supper.

Giving in to the notion that her relaxing evening would be taking place in the relative dark, Sage set her plate on the coffee table and lit two half-melted candles. She plunked herself down onto the worn leather sofa and spread out her legs and arms like a starfish, the touch of skin-on-skin unbearable in the stifling second-floor heat. Bono jumped up beside her.

"Hey, sweet boy." Despite the heat, Sage couldn't help but place her clammy hand on his soft coat. She took a bite of her sandwich and closed her eyes while chewing, recalling the activities of the day: the research assignment, the introduction to Peck, the happenings at the co-op. It was all so unexpected yet not unwelcome. Maybe surprises are fortuitous at times, she considered, her thoughts lingering on the handsome face of this man who had appeared out of nowhere.

Then, all of a sudden, she was back in the graveyard.

In the middle of a cemetery, young Sage walked with Mother and Daddy on either side, Louise holding Mother's other hand. In her peripheral vision, she saw a gravestone, while ahead lay an open field, newly planted, the dirt blackened by the moisture of rain. The organic smell of it wafted toward her, and she looked down at Daddy's hand, marked with patterns of sun-deepened freckles. Sage gripped it tightly, absorbing its warmth. She turned toward his face and saw tears just beginning to roll down his cheeks but was confused: Daddy was never one to cry.

Sage shot up and looked around. Bono was still there beside her, his eyes locked onto her sandwich. Lightning continued to flash, and rain still fell. The kitchen light flickered on momentarily, then remained off for what would be the rest of the evening.

The air felt thicker now, challenging the stability of Sage's breath as she gained a growing realization that she lacked control over these unwanted clips of a different life. But control was what slowed discomforting thoughts from racing through the passageways of her mind. Control is what kept her life in check. It was why she'd registered for flight lessons: to understand that she *is* in control. And now this—whatever this was—had begun to usurp it.

She hadn't fallen asleep—of that Sage was certain. Maybe she was developing a brain tumor. But surely there'd be more symptoms than a couple of offhand visions. Had she read anything unusual? *The Odessa File* was on her coffee table; that could bring graveyards to anyone's mind.

Still, it felt like a crime to be so authentically there with Daddy, even if just for a few seconds, when all these years she'd had only distant memories to rely on, memories that could not harness him in. Now, within these unlikely visions, she could fully sense him, even though that was, of course, impossible.

The phone rang once again. This time, she went into the kitchen and answered it, the brunt of the storm having passed.

"Hello?"

"Hey. Peck here."

She drew in a sharp, muted breath, a tingle of anxious excitement reaching all the way down to her fingertips. "Hi. How are you?"

"Good. That was a hell of a storm, wasn't it?"

"Yeah. Did your lights go out too?"

"As always. Hey, I found my bike."

"Wonderful. Where was it?"

"Strangely enough, at the library, but ditched in the back. Some kids must've taken it for a joyride."

Peck spoke at a slower pace than he had earlier that day at the library, but his words still held a certain sense of urgency. Sage imagined him in his apartment above the co-op drinking coffee, eating supper, watching the news, jotting in a notebook, and talking on the phone all at once.

"It turns out that Jerry, the asshole with the red hair, came back to Living Waters later, his buddies holding his hand. Fluffed some more feathers is all."

Sage and Peck talked briefly about what had occurred and how the CO was throwing its weight around the cities in its quest to take control of all the food co-ops. Sage took notes, getting more background information from Peck to help her have a better understanding of just what the conflict was about.

Living Waters, like some of the other co-ops in town, was designed to revolutionize the food industry away from mass-produced food tainted by chemicals and additives. The Cooperative Organization, which had already taken over several of the start-up co-ops, ran by a set of strict bylaws that not only allowed the sale of foods that are far from healthy—like sugar—but also required member stores to purchase their goods from the CO Warehouse.

"And where do you get your products from?"

"Locals. Farmers, mostly. And craftspeople and gardeners, foragers and bakers. We pick up the bulk items like flour and grains from the People's Warehouse that sources everything locally too."

"So, you're about local and organic, and the CO leans more toward supermarket style. I don't get why both can't just do their own thing."

"Exactly. We don't care how they run their business, but we do care about ours. We can't quite figure out why it's so necessary for them to have us all under their thumb. Other than the simple fact of control." Peck paused for a beat. "Hey, I want you to meet up again with Mark. I think you'll want to hear about where he's been. I mean, not places, but stuff in his life, his work with co-ops. Pretty cool guy. If those assholes at the CO would leave him alone, he might get somewhere with his cause."

"Yeah, I'd really like to talk to him."

"Oh shit." A few muffled sounds and a loud crash came from the background. Sage could hear him talk to her from a distance, but she had no idea what he was saying.

"You there?" he asked, now back.

"Yes."

"My supper tipped on my lap. Black beans. Hot."

Sage laughed. "Are you drinking coffee and writing, too, by chance?"

"No, lemonade. Why?"

"Forget it." She laughed again, this time to herself.

"Hey, what would you say to pulling some strings for us, for Living Waters?"

"Why, because as a female research assistant at the historical society I wield unlimited power?"

Peck ignored the comment. "You know some of the writers from the *Times*, right? Work with them once in a while?"

"Sure, now and again. I help them with some backup info for their stories. And usually bring them cups of coffee to boot, lucky me."

"What I'm thinking is that the *Times* is a major area newspaper. A lot of folks still think that food co-ops are hippie hangouts and too 'out there' to bother with. The CO assholes causing trouble isn't helping any."

"You say assholes a lot."

"Yeah, I know," Peck replied without losing a beat. "So, what Mark and I have done is to set up Living Waters on a different level."

"You and Mark own the place together?"

"Well, not exactly own, but run, yeah. He's the head honcho and I'm sort of the sidekick. Now quit interrupting me, young lady."

Sage laughed and remained dutifully silent as Peck continued.

"We set up Living Waters so that anyone can go there without feeling like they're shopping at just another supermarket. They learn that we support our farmers. They're taught why that's important. And we talk *a lot* about the importance of eating whole foods. We're thinking that maybe one day more people will buy shares, and we'd use the funding to grow. Don't want to keep the business running out of a house forever."

"And if this was explained in a newspaper story, you might bring in more members."

"Yeah. You gotta remember, we're in our infant stages. All of us in the food co-op business are still trying to figure out how to make this work for the long run. And those from the CO, before they resort to bullying, present what sounds like a logical, cooperative option."

"Because of the lower prices?"

"Yeah, mainly that. They say it'll help us grow."

"Does the CO also buy from local farmers?" Sage felt like she was beginning to get a better grasp on what was happening.

"Sort of. Communes out in the country and a couple of other forward-thinking farmers around the Upper Midwest. But again, only if the farmers are willing to take part in their little buying club, selling at discounts—but in this case, deep discounts. They're reminded that they're part of a cause and have a promise of more money in their pockets once a certain level of profit is met."

"So, with time comes more money, but they have to discount now in order to get a foot in the door."

"You got it. And, they have more relaxed standards for how it's grown."

"So, like you said, the standard for Living Waters is local, as well as additive- and chemical-free."

"Yep. It's all from Minnesota, so long as it is an upright farm."

"How do you know they're upright?"

"Because we know the farmers. Most of us at Living Waters have been to or helped out at the farms in one way or another. We call them organic farms—that's the chemical-free part."

Sage recalled Randy having mentioned picking up produce from area farms. Surely Louise had been with him on more than one occasion.

"Those who run the CO are upset over the fact that we won't sell shit, like canned and processed foods. They claim that we're catering to the middle class, making it unaffordable to the masses. It's all bullshit. We're paying fair prices for the food and selling for only enough profit to keep things up and running and to pay Mark and a couple of others a fair wage. Farmers need to make money, too, without sacrificing their own standards." The tempo of Peck's voice had begun to pick up.

"For over two years, this has been Mark's baby. His way of saying we don't have to live by anyone else's rules, for the good of the people. But when the CO came along, they wouldn't listen to his ideas, even though Mark had opened the same kind of store with a hell of a lot of success in San Francisco a few years ago. Instead, they're using the same scare tactics on him that scared the shit out of most of the competition."

"Would they make that much money off Living Waters if you buy your goods from them?"

"Sure as hell wouldn't. That's the part we haven't yet figured out: why has their need for control become so out of control?"

"So, you think if I can convince a reporter to publish an article in the *Twin Cities Times*, some folks might be more open to what you're trying to do?" Sage asked.

"Exactly. We're not in this for the money, though a higher profit margin would help us grow and therefore educate more people. But it could really give us a boost toward getting more shoppers pure food at reasonable prices that also allow a reasonable profit for the farmers. A boost toward changing the way people think about how they eat and what they're doing to the land, and not just relying on what the government tells us to think. It shouldn't have to be such a fight for people to have this essential freedom, but it is."

More and more, Sage's understanding of the situation was settling in. She realized, too, that Peck's passion for this topic wasn't because of a certain doggedness in his psychological makeup or even a desire to make a small business achieve reasonable success, but it was to keep consumers educated and power in check. Yet, there was still so much for her to learn.

The ringing of the phone once again broke the silence during the early hours of an otherwise calm morning. *What's with all the phone calls*, Sage thought as she scrambled out of bed and ran into the kitchen. On the other end of the line was a man with a strong German accent who asked if she was the Decorah gal, Sage Ley. Sage was befuddled; she'd forgotten that she could be considered a resident of Decorah. Living there had been so far in the past.

But once she acknowledged her identity, the man, whose name was Hans, released a torrent of unsolicited information for the next ten minutes. A neighbor had given him their names, it seems, and Hans was now living on the farm that had once again changed hands.

"I have something of yours that you might vant," he said.

"Really." Sage's mind raced for ideas of what it could possibly be. A box of buried doll clothes that she swore she'd never give up? The trim of the laundry room door that they'd used to measure how much they'd grown each year? It certainly couldn't have been anything of value. They had moved away from the farm more than twenty years ago and would've missed it by now.

"It's the cross, from the field. It came up vhen I ran over it vith the plow and threw the gears out. A piece like this—I knew it must be special. It looked like it'd been through a thousand years of time vhen it came up. But Siri, she cleaned it up and it's been sleeping in our basement."

What the heck is he talking about, Sage wondered, *or am I still half asleep?* She continued to search through her memory bank but was only able to think of the twig crosses that she and Louise had made for the cats that had died over the years. She glanced out the window just to be sure a freak snowfall hadn't occurred out of the blue. And then she pinched herself—she was definitely awake.

"Well, um, what's it look like?" she asked.

"You don't remember? I didn't think a person vould forget a cross like this. Maybe your mother remembers?"

"I don't know, maybe. Could you describe it to me?"

"Vell, okay," he said with an air of frustration, as if he were talking to an idiot. "It's about two feet long and made of thick iron. Still a little rusty, but Siri, she got some of that off. She's a good cleaner, Siri is. Let's see . . . very heavy, lots of carving in it. The name *Ley* right there on the front of it."

"What? Did you say *Ley*?"

"Vell, yah. That's your name. You know the cross now?"

Try as she might, Sage couldn't recollect an old iron cross, had not even an inkling of it. Daddy and Mother bought the farm from the Ford family who'd owned it for decades before them.

"Was there anything else along with this cross?"

"No. Just the cross." In fact, he was starting to sound a bit cross himself. "Vell, at least I don't think so. I vas pretty blazing mad that it had ruined my plow and didn't exactly think of looking for nothing else."

"And the name *Ley*, L-E-Y, was inscribed on it?"

"Yah. You don't know it? Maybe it belongs to somevone else."

"Oh, no, I'm sure it's ours. I was just a young girl when we moved, you see."

"Yah, that's vhat I thought."

"If you could send it to me, COD of course, I really would appreciate it." Sage gave him the details of her address, hung up, and wondered what was happening to the quiet, static life that she'd so recently had.

Far too awake to fall asleep again, she turned on the TV and started the percolator before completing her Saturday chores, after which she showered and changed into jeans and a button-up blouse. Today was another flight lesson, and she always wore one of two nondescript white blouses in hopes of appearing as serious as she felt about the lessons.

Leaving Bono with a kiss on the nose, Sage made the twenty-minute drive to the Lakeville Airport, situated in a rural area south of the Twin Cities. She had been surprised at how natural flying had felt within a short period of time, controlling the stick and rudder second nature, soaring amid the plumes of cumulus clouds that curled in the air around her a remarkably peaceful experience.

Today's lesson was a review of landings, the first one routine. Sage set the flaps at forty degrees, and the plane began its descent. Despite her natural ability to handle the craft, she was still unable to overcome the feeling that the runway rose up to greet her a bit too eagerly. Yet, she executed another smooth landing. A small victory, for the day's lesson in emergency landing had not yet begun.

Back on the ground, Sage removed her sunglasses as a cloud passed overhead, dimming the morning light, and felt a shower of adrenaline course through her. Next to her, Jim seemed particularly eager to move on to landing number two.

"Review the procedures, Ms. Ley," said Jim, looking down at his lesson plan as he spoke.

"Stabilize and plan. Attempt an engine restart. Execute the best landing possible."

It was another fifteen minutes of running through procedures before Sage propelled the Cessna 152 upward, leaving behind the perfectly straight line of the airstrip. After reaching an altitude of one thousand feet, she banked the plane to the left, circling back to the west.

"Ready, Ms. Ley?"

She gave the affirmative. Jim reached over and cut the engine, the silence a red alert. She was on.

Airspeed at ninety-five knots, Sage pulled the stick toward her, knowing she would lose speed but gain valuable altitude. Below, roadways and fields became potential landing sites, should the lesson ever ring true, but for today the airfield appeared in the distance and she aimed toward it, the craft quietly obeying. Sage checked the fuel tanks, calling the levels into her headset while ensuring the primer was locked and the mixture set to full rich.

"Open carburetor heat, change magnetos," she recited.

"The prop has stopped spinning, Ms. Ley. Try starting the engine."

"The engine will not start, Mr. Frank. Prepare for an emergency landing. Mayday, Mayday, Mayday. Cessna 152 over east Lakeville. Engine failure, coming in for emergency landing."

Sage set the transponder to squawk code 7700 and focused on her target ahead. With the Mayday call made and the air traffic controller aware of the trial run, the plane glided toward the runway.

"Aim for the thousand-footers, Ms. Ley."

"Sighted and approaching." Sage kept her focus on the white markers ahead and began the descent.

"You're looking a little high. Not too fast or you'll float down the runway."

"Making a single spiral to lose elevation."

"Good."

Sage circled left and aimed again for the airstrip.

"Full flaps," said Jim.

Sage pressed the flap lever down, causing the nose to pitch forward while maintaining the airspeed, now at fifty-five knots.

"Ready?"

"I've got this," Sage replied.

She pressed the right rudder, maneuvering the plane into a sideslip. She could feel the drag of the position but was losing altitude much faster than she'd expected. Sweat sprang from her armpits as the reality of the situation took hold. Undeterred, she held the angled position and kept the thousand-footers in sight. Getting too close to the ground in this configuration would result in a very undesirable situation, yet at the same time she had to continue downward to a certain point.

"Okay, pull her back. Here we go," Jim instructed.

Sage took a deep breath and pulled back gently on the yoke as she smoothed out the plane.

"Good. Steady. Keep her steady."

After what felt like an endless amount of time, the tires gently kissed the pavement, the muscles of Sage's body releasing like the unclenching of a fist as she brought the plane to a halt. The final lesson was complete.

I did it. I did it! She looked over at Jim with a wide grin on her face, then surprised him by pulling him into a hug.

Chapter 13

—— Elizabeth, October 1948 ——

I pulled out a steely gray skirt and rose-colored blouse from the small closet and reached down for the oxford lace-ups that would be comfortable enough in which to spend plenty of time on foot. It wasn't my nature to surprise someone, but the city had bequeathed me with a sense of boldness that reminded me of my younger days. It was due time I took up the invitation from Wini, the vocalist I'd met briefly at the Blue Window, who'd asked me to return.

An apple sufficed for breakfast as I left the hotel and retraced my steps to the Blue Window, hoping that either Wini would be there practicing or I could learn where she might be found at this time of the day. To my surprise, the owner of the establishment was there reviewing his books, and at my request, he pulled up her address card and jotted down the information.

"The neighborhood in those parts ain't like the neighborhood in these parts," he said, looking not at me but back at the ledger before him, and continued tracing his pencil down a column of numbers. He didn't elaborate, so I thanked him and made my way back up the steps and down the long, dim passageway, exiting the door and heading south.

Though Wini's address was a mere eight blocks from my lodgings, it wasn't long before the neighborhood took a surprising turn. Gone were the lovely storefronts and beckoning restaurants, replaced with brick apartment buildings and dingy dime stores. The air felt heavier somehow, oppressive, and I pulled my handbag in closer, increasing my stride as much as was reasonable without appearing to be in a purposeful rush.

As I neared the apartment building that matched Wini's address, I came upon three girls with the darkest skin I'd ever seen, perhaps eleven or twelve years old, singing a tune about flying rocks while jumping rope. The rope came to a halt, and the girls silently watched me as I passed by. Nearby, a handful of boys were hitting an empty food can with a stick up and down the street. I was, no doubt, broadly noticed by them, too, but unlike the girls, none of them looked me in the eye. I couldn't help but wonder if these children had ever witnessed the vast openness of the country, inhaled the sweet scent of a freshly cut field of alfalfa, or wandered through thick woods with birds flitting from tree to tree. I realized, too, how relatively little I knew about the world at large, having been confined to my microscopic corner of it all these years.

I slowed my pace and began to look in earnest for number 1212, having easily found it, the number etched into a cement panel near the door. Upon entering, I was met by the smell of what I assumed was food cooking—an unfamiliar pungency of spices combined with onions, perhaps—and worked my way upward through the chilly stairwell, feeling thankful that there was some amount of daylight streaming in through windows that were in need of a good cleaning. Once I'd arrived on the third floor, I walked down the hall by the insufficient light of a single bulb that dangled from the ceiling, black wires exposed, squinting to decipher the numbers on the doors until I came to the one I sought. I gave a soft knock on the marred wooden door. It was opened quickly, and an unfamiliar woman stood before me. Yet, she knew me.

"Miss Betty, what a surprise!"

Her smile was wide and her invitation to enter was welcoming. Had it not been for the voice, I would not have known her to be Wini. In performance her hair was rolled and coiffed and shone heavily with pomade, but now ringlets of black strands sprang freely outward. A lack of stage makeup further disguised the person I was expecting to see, though there was still an evident beauty about her.

"You look like you just saw a yellow-eyed creature from the deep dark sea!" She laughed, not at me but at herself. "It really is me, Wini, who I'm guessing you came to see. Come on in, Miss Betty."

I blushed as I stepped through the doorway and immediately announced my lunch invitation.

"Of course! I can't believe you came all the way over here to see me!" She then apologized that her room was not spic-and-span. "Cuz truly, it's never spic-and-span," she said with a laugh and asked me to nonetheless make myself at home.

"I would have rang you, but I was given only an address," I explained apologetically.

"The day I own a phone will be the day a man flies to the moon," she exclaimed, followed by another chuckle. "I'll keep myself to myself, thank you, and don't need nobody to hear my business."

"Oh," I stammered. "I didn't mean to assume . . ."

"No, no. No apologies needed. Just because that's the way the world spins don't necessarily mean Wini's gonna hop on for the ride. That's the number one thing to know about Wini."

She winked at me then, and I couldn't help but think of Will, of what he might say if he witnessed a Black woman winking at me. Or what Stephen would say, for that matter.

"I got my own directions to follow. And right now, they're telling me to go that-a-way and get myself looking presentable for an outing with Miss Betty!"

As she walked into the one other room in the small apartment, I smiled, truly intrigued. There was nothing bashful about Wini, as I might have surmised from the power in her voice when on stage. Yet, she also had the rare ability to laugh at life with the carefree spirit of a child.

The apartment was, if nothing, a bold representation of contrast—certainly not what I would have expected when walking through the building. Black-and-white photographs of Ella Fitzgerald, Nat King Cole, and Bessie Smith, to name a few, were hung upon walls painted in bright orange and red. A small rug with circular markings in deep shades of gold hung on the wall above the worn sofa alongside another in a zig-zagged pattern. Four wooden masks, surely from another continent, lined the adjacent wall that opened to a kitchenette with a counter not nearly long enough to turn out bread dough. I didn't have enough time to even begin to comprehend a unifying theme before Wini returned, now with a searing yellow scarf hiding her great mass of hair beneath. I could only think, this is a woman who is *alive*—and not afraid to show it. Wini was just what I needed on this day.

We left her apartment and sauntered along the city blocks, our conversation birthing a friendship as we sought out a place to lunch together. The combination of my ignorance and Wini's confidence mistakenly allowed us to believe we'd be able to eat together publicly. Wini accepted each of the abrupt turndowns with grace in the face of humility. Though I knew of the disparity between Whites and Blacks in our society, until now I hadn't had a close-up view of the indignity that went along with it.

We finally settled on hotdogs from a late-season vendor and were immediately met by a group of hungry seagulls tentatively hopping toward the park bench upon which we sat. Wini showed me how harmless they were, and soon I was tossing bits of bun into the air, laughing as the birds leaped with wing-assisted strides to gain a prized morsel slathered in ketchup, mustard, and relish.

"You know, Miss Betty. I didn't think you'd take my invitation to visit seriously, let alone track me down." She shook her head slowly as if in amazement, then looked at me. "But I appreciate that you did. I appreciate it a whole lot."

I raised my eyebrows in surprise. From my perspective, Wini was a stage star. Though her name may not have been Billie or Ella, her voice certainly rivaled theirs. I was a mere fan, just as astonished that she wished to spend time with me.

"That man you were with when we met—he didn't look too kindly on my invitation."

"Stephen?" I paused, surprised to realize that this was the first time I'd thought about him since entering Wini's apartment. "I guess he really wasn't very friendly toward you. I'm sorry about that, but he's an awfully nice man when you get to know him. He's from England, you know."

Wini nodded thoughtfully, taking another bite from her hotdog.

"Please, tell me. What is it about Stephen that bothers you?"

I had taken a leap here, unsure whether she was bothered by him or simply stating an observation. But my question sparked something in her, a thought that she was eager to share with me.

"Those men—Mr. Stephen and his group—they're at the Blue Window quite a bit. I been singing there for over a year, so I seen all kinds of people sit at those tables, drinking all kinds of booze, making all kinds of conversation. And I can tell you, their talk's not always clean talk, if you know what I mean. Mr. Stephen's group stood out to me, mostly because of one man. He'd been in a few times with some other fellows before I'd ever seen Mr. Stephen join them, and he just gave me the heebie-jeebies. It was the way he looked—and spoke. Made me feel unsettled."

I turned on the bench to fully face her.

"The first time Mr. Stephen came in with his wife—I believe her name is Miss Ruth," she continued. Again, I blushed, and she respectfully turned back toward the open park. "That first time there was quite a celebration going on. We'd just taken our last break of the night, and I sat down with a glass of water at a table near the stage. Their table wasn't too far from where I was, and their voices carried real easy.

"Miss Ruth wasn't feeling well by this time, she'd told him, and this other man, the loud one whose name I can't seem to remember, offered to give her a ride home. I don't know why Mr. Stephen wasn't the one to bring her home, but it all seemed to be neatly arranged. I clearly remember the way this man spoke her name. 'Ruth!' his voice boomed, stretching her name into bumps. It was obvious he'd had several drinks by this time."

"Wini," I stopped her. "Was the man you refer to dark-haired, maybe sort of outspoken?"

"Yes ma'am. Like I said, he's an odd little fellow who's at the Blue Window most every Saturday night. As if his small size and big voice weren't enough to remember him by, he always wears dark clothes. Like he got the devil in him. You remember him from the night you were there?"

"Yes, I do. And I met him face-to-face, when I was with Stephen," I admitted. But I quickly realized I'd said too much. There was no need to let Wini know that I'd become smitten with this man of whom she seemingly didn't approve. I didn't want to divulge my feelings toward him, but I did want to learn what more Wini had to say about Stephen—because she knew him in a different way than I did—so I remained quiet even as her eyes lingered on mine for an extra beat.

A sudden refulgent ray of sun broke through the passing sheet of gray and shone directly upon us, giving hope that the damp chill in the air might pass.

"'Stephen,' Miss Ruth said to him. 'Neil'—that's his name, I remember now—'Neil is going to race me home so that I can lie down. My head... you understand, I'm sure.' Mr. Stephen gave a quick nod, then turned away from them and lit a smoke. Miss Ruth got up from her chair real quick, and she and the other man immediately set off. For some reason, Mr. Stephen happened to look right at me while he was working on lighting his smoke. Chance, I'm sure, but I was trying to be discreet about listening in, and he caught me red-handed. I looked away and waved to an invisible person on the other side of the room. I could feel him continue to watch me for a short while before he called over the waiter for another round of drinks. I got myself up then and went back to the stage. That was my first encounter with Mr. Stephen, my introduction to him, I guess you'd say."

"And the look he gave you made you feel uncomfortable?" I was unclear where she was going with this.

"Let's just say that a Negro woman knows when she's being looked at by a man because he's hot for her, and she knows when she's having darts thrown at her because she's a different color. Mind you, I didn't feel threatened," Wini said, turning from a head shake to a nod. "But darts were flying."

"I'm sorry, Wini. That must've been difficult."

"It was what it was. Nothing I can do but wring it right out of me when I sing the blues."

Again, I was astounded by where our society had landed. A woman with the most magnificent talent, a stranger who exuded kindness, could never be "good enough" in the eyes of the world in which she lived simply because of the pigmentation of her skin.

I stood and walked a few steps away in thought. "And you saw him often after this first encounter?"

"I certainly did. Every couple of weeks for the next few months. Why anyone would want to spend winter here in Chicago and not England, I'll never know." She loosened her wrap. "Anyway, I been born to bear this kind of treatment, and I don't know why I remember this one encounter so clearly. But it does stand out."

I waited for her to continue.

"I have to be honest with you, Miss Betty."

"Please," I interrupted, "just Betty."

She smiled warmly. "All right then, Betty. To be honest, I'd love more than anything for you to be at the upcoming performance, sitting at the table right next to the stage. But no one looks too highly upon a White woman and a Negro woman befriending each other. You saw what happened as we were looking for a place to eat. As much as I disagree with the way folks look at my kind like we're below the lowest class, I fear for you. A woman all alone in a big city, spending time with the likes of me—you don't want the wrong person witnessing that."

"Wini, I was at the Blue Window the other night, and I sat and watched you and felt completely at ease."

"But we never met before then. Now people will know we're acquainted."

"You mean Stephen."

"I mean Mr. Stephen. And his friends."

"Do you really think he would care about my being at the Blue Window to see you?" I was beginning to feel as if a seam were coming apart, a slow tear in what had felt like a perfectly stitched piece.

"It's not just that." Wini's forehead morphed into a frown. "I got no right to direct any person's actions. Well, except those hooligans that cover my front steps like they a bunch of ants." She laughed, relieving some of the tension that had been building, but the equanimity in her voice immediately returned. "I would be concerned that if you went to the Blue Window when Mr. Stephen was there, you'd get lost in that group of people. And I just think you're too beautiful a soul to have that happen to you."

I was honored by her praise though felt unworthy of it. And as much as I wanted to gain a full understanding of her insights, I was also afraid of hearing something that couldn't be revoked. But in the end, I was compelled to continue.

"Exactly what is it about them—him—that you don't like, Wini? Stephen gave you a look, but he didn't say anything to you, right?"

Two lanky young men walked past us taunting Wini with casual name-calling, just loud enough to be heard. Though her face stayed calm, her dark eyes grew discernibly wider, momentarily flashing with anger.

"I don't know how much experience you have with Negros, Miss Betty—Betty—but as you can see, most Whites don't got any great love for us. As much as I know in my heart that's not right, it's the way it is," she said. "But it won't be that way forever, I can tell you that much."

"I'm sure sorry you have to go through this."

"Don't be sorry. It's my plight, the plight of my people. There was a time in most every culture when some group cast disgrace on a portion of its people. This is just that time for the American Negro. But this, too, shall pass. Lord, yes, it shall pass."

I thought about this. Would it pass? Surely it must. Surely our country couldn't go on laced in disapprobation forever. What would it look like on the other side? My musings were brief; I wanted to finish the conversation we'd begun.

"Would it be okay with you if we continued walking?" I asked.

"I'm a fool for a long walk."

The sidewalk that led away from the park entered a neighborhood of small square houses neatly arranged in rows, all of them new, with a handful of empty lots yet to be built upon. I wondered whether they were a part of the post-war housing efforts I'd read about.

"Stephen gave you a look that made you feel uncomfortable," I reiterated, picking up from where we'd left off. "And he has friends that seem . . . well . . . not like us. But I have to ask, has he ever done or said anything directly to you? Don't get me wrong, I'm not challenging you, but I have come to know him somewhat, and he doesn't seem to be a man of hatred."

Wini nodded her scarved head. "That's a good question, Betty. To be honest, no. He's never hurt me directly. But I can feel it in my bones that, if I were wrongly challenged, he would *not* come to my rescue. More likely, my prosecution."

A wave of anxiety passed through me as I listened to her words. How could this man be the same one I had come to know? Stephen would do anything for me; I was sure of that. Yes, he'd been curt with Wini at the Blue Window that first night I'd met him, but still, he was a good man. This dynamic was so new to me.

"What about the others in his group? Do you get that same feeling?" I asked.

"Mr. Neil I wouldn't trust with a rubber sword. And another man, Mr. Walter and his wife Miss Rebecca—well, let me just say that they seem like powerful people. Most don't pay me any attention, which I prefer."

"So, if you consider the whole group, where does Stephen fall in the line-up of evildoers?" My expression, I'm sure, was one of consternation, my questioning like a detective hot on the trail of his suspect.

Wini looked at me and quieted for a second, then let loose a generous whoop, throwing back her head and raising her hands. "Hallelujah!" she exclaimed.

A seagull flew off at the unexpected disturbance, and I smiled, confused, until her laughter eased.

"Oh Betty, you are the color yellow in the arch of a rainbow. You're a warm and reasonable soul, you are," she said, still grinning widely. "And you're right. I have no proof that Mr. Stephen is an evil man, and it just might be that I've come to see the smallest spark as a wildfire. I see him as being of his group, and the group is not of me. And I now admit—and admissions don't come easy for Wini—that maybe I've been too harsh. Maybe I have. And if so, I give you credit for opening my tainted eyes."

Her smile dropped then, disappearing as swiftly as it had arrived.

"But maybe I haven't labeled him harshly. Just in case, you be careful. Don't go getting yourself tangled in their web. Life is too short to be spent finding your way out of sticky webs, if you don't mind my saying so."

I nodded. I understood webs more than she realized.

Chapter 14
—— July 1975 ——

Mark's honeyed voice, waltzing alongside the strumming of his guitar, quieted the conversations of the small group that had collected in a circle on the front lawn of Living Waters, their hands now woven together as they sang along to the music. Louise couldn't help but smile as she looked around. There was Peck, his uncertain singing voice belying a confident demeanor. Larry, in his ever-present round-rimmed sunglasses and leather headband, which by now was surely a biological attachment. Sherrie, singing clearly as she looked toward the sky. Hilda from next door, Living Waters' first and most frequent customer, humming along. Paul, sweet and quiet, ever ready to please. Mark, their guiding light. And Randy, her lover, her best friend, her future. All of them, an extension of family.

Louise closed her eyes and swayed to the melody, sensing her energy open wide and a surge of love beginning to course through her like a dazzling light glowing from within. But a single word brought the moment to a halt.

"Shit."

Louise opened her eyes and noticed everyone looking up the street, where a crew of men approached—eight, ten perhaps—aiming toward their target: Living Waters. She immediately recognized Jerry from his previous soap-box moment. She couldn't believe this was happening again.

Mark stood, waving a hand behind him to indicate that everyone else was to remain seated on the grass.

"It's unanimous," said Jerry as they entered the yard. "Everyone—all of us at the CO—have decided. You agree here and now to conform to the CO guidelines or you close your doors. If you follow the rules, we walk away. If you don't . . ." He took one step closer to Mark, a sarcastic smile punctuating the slimy threat. "Well, let's just say you've been given your final warning."

"C'mon, man. You're gonna use force on us to get your way? Like war? Like 'Nam? You can't be real. Let's talk this out."

"Talk? You wanna talk?" Jerry shook his head and shot Mark a look of incredulity. "We've tried talking, man, and it just doesn't seem to be working in that polluted mind of yours. This isn't about you. This is about *everyone*. This is about a *serious revolution*."

A grumble of approval came from a few of those standing behind Jerry. Larry shot up; Paul and Sherrie followed. Louise hoisted herself up, the serenity she'd felt just moments ago shattered by a bolt of human lightning. Together, they formed a line on either side of Mark, linking arms in camaraderie.

"Good one," said Mark. "I still haven't heard any valid reason why you can't just let us be, man. Leave us to our own little corner of the world. If we succeed, we succeed. If we fail, then you can laugh at us all day long. Let's put this behind us, man."

A handful of people began murmuring at once, and Peck, who'd miraculously remained quietly sitting until now, jumped up in response, elevating his voice above the others.

"You still think threatening us is gonna get the results you want? Think again," he said, shoving his finger against Jerry's chest. "This group's not going anywhere, and hell if we're gonna change our ways."

A man in a red T-shirt stepped toward Peck, his short sleeves like a rubber band over his inflated pecs, a lead pipe in his hand. "Maybe this'll make you change your mind?" he asked, tapping the pipe on his palm with a steady beat.

"Just because you're the bigger crowd and brought along big bad toys doesn't mean you'll get your way," Peck retorted, his body like a lion ready to pounce.

"You obviously want to mobilize the co-op scene, but why, really?" said Mark, taking back the conversation. "You have a direction with your stores, and I embolden you to follow it, man. Sell your goods to whoever you want. Buy from your exclusive warehouse sources. But don't try to break down what other devoted people are doing to bring their own brand of change to the community, man. When we opened the first co-ops, they were for a cause, they were something new. And that's exactly what we're continuing to do here. Don't discourage the people who are trying to walk in stride *beside* you and your efforts. And c'mon, man, how often does violence really ever win over peace?"

Another rumble of voices resounded, from one side accord, the other defiance.

"You know, Mark, I'm tired of your sink-me-to-the-bottom-of-the-fuckin'-ocean voice trying to tell us that this is all about peace and we need to be the ones to give up. If you really want the peace you talk about, *you* give it up. We're not budging. So it's gonna be up to you. We're just here to keep the co-op scene cohesive."

"Don't you think you've scared away enough people from your stores with your ideals of cohesiveness?" Mark asked.

"Doesn't say much for your values," Peck added.

"I'll show you my fucking values." The man in the red T-shirt lurched toward Peck who, too curled for the cause to consider consequences, mirrored his charge. Just as quickly, a variety of weapons were displayed: wooden bats and lead pipes, a thick metal chain. Randy grabbed the hands of Louise and Sherrie, forcing them away from the scene. Louise pulled Hilda along with them as they made the short dash to the edge of the yard.

"You stay out of this, all of you," Randy directed them. He turned away and began to sprint back toward the group of men where a shoving match had begun in earnest.

"Randy, no!" Louise retorted, equally as commanding, knowing the consequences for him could be dire. No law firm would hire a Black man with a record. And no cop would let a Black man off the hook.

He stopped.

"No," she repeated, her forehead furrowed, her eyes now begging.

Randy's fists clenched as he stared at the men in the yard. This fight could not be his, and Louise was sure Randy understood that too. There'd been too many battles he'd already incurred to get to this point in his life, and as passionate as he felt for the cause, it wasn't worth the ruination of his future legal career. He looked back momentarily at Louise, his wide nostrils flaring, then again at his friends. Louise held her breath, exhaling only when she saw him retreat and walk backward toward her. She reached for his hand, grabbing it firmly.

"Go. Please," said Louise. "I mean it."

Randy let go of her hand and broke into a jog toward the alley. She knew the angst that leaving would cause him, knew that this was one of the toughest decisions he'd made in a long time. Louise watched him run, momentarily disappearing behind Hilda's house, then reappear, his stride now full speed in the direction of their home. Hilda, too, was trotting toward her house with haste.

"Stop! Calm down!" Louise's attention snapped back to the situation at hand, Mark's voice now having taken on the tone of a plea. His hands were flailing to no effect as the tangle of men displayed their brawn. Neighbors had begun to step out of their homes and into their yards.

All at once, the cool evening air leaned torrid as the first fist landed with a blunt thud on human flesh. Two men plunged to the ground, their bodies locked in a grapple of power, the others caught up in a mass of bodies that had begun drifting toward the store.

Louise couldn't think of what to do other than to remove her macramé belt, a desperate tool with which to defend herself. Sherrie stood beside her, fiercely evaluating the situation.

The sound of shattering glass stung Louise. It seemed that the weapons wielded by Jerry's group were intended for something other than bodies, and she watched with alarm as bats were thrust with abandon upon her second home, methodically destroying each window of the porch. Tall shelves within toppled, shelves that had been built from the wood of an uprooted tree in the yard that displayed flowers grown by dedicated farmers. A rainbow of color tumbled downward as the men moved farther inside.

Blaring sirens pierced the air from the south, and Louise noticed a Corvette from down the block pull away from the curb, its driver concealed by the closing of the tinted window as it sped away.

"Cops!" an unfamiliar voice shouted, an echoing warning.

One by one, men burst through the doorway and ran for the hopeful escape of their cars. A trickle of dark red blood marred one man's face. Another was being shepherded as he hobbled away, leaving Louise to feel a dagger of deservedness for both. Within moments, their cars were racing away from Living Waters as the sound of sirens intensified.

Louise and Sherrie made a dash for the door but were forced to slow their steps and pick their way across shards of broken glass and upended pots. Inside, clouds of flour dust hovered in the air. Popcorn seeds and lentils lay spread across the floor, and shelves that had displayed a colorful array of vegetables just minutes before were now toppled or destroyed, having given way under the pressure of madness.

"Oh god," Louise muttered into the silence.

Paul sat on the floor next to a broken slab of slate: *Granola, 40 cents/lb.; Wild Rice, 35 cents/lb.; Dried Cranberries, 30 cents/lb.* His head was leaning against one of the few remaining intact shelves, blood trailing from his nose. On the other side of the room, Larry was on his knees, listlessly picking up bunches of radishes. Mark stood near the back, panning the chaos of the store.

It was Peck who kicked a loaf of bread, sending it skittering across the floor, and slammed his fists against the checkout counter, breaking the eerie quiet.

Louise reached over to flip on a light switch just as two policemen walked through the doorway, their hands clutching their respective clubs that dangled menacingly at their sides. The two looked from one side of the room to the other.

"Doesn't look like you won. Where's the rest of 'em?" one of them asked.

"The assholes ran off like the little fuckin' chipmunks they are," Peck said.

The officer turned toward Peck and looked at him a hint longer than necessary as he smacked his chewing gum.

"So, uh, who's responsible for the new arrangement?" the other, taller officer asked.

"Just someone hoping to stir up trouble," Mark responded. "But it's over. We'll take care of things."

"The other team? The Warehouse group?" the first one asked, a smirk forming on his lips.

This time it was Mark who fixed his look on the officer, and Louise wondered for a moment if he was going to punch the guy. It was common knowledge that the cops wanted every one of the hippies to pound the hell out of each other and beat it out of town. The law could then go on living in their idealistic world of writing out parking tickets and hauling home teenagers who managed to escape their white picket fences after the ten o'clock curfew. Instead, Mark responded with a simple "No."

The officers looked around one last time and decided there might be more pressing crimes to attend to, though perhaps not nearly so amusing.

"Anything you want to tell us about this?"

"No," Mark again responded.

The officer paused again. Louise could feel her chest tighten.

"Looks like you got yourself in one hell of a pickle. You get this cleaned up before anyone else comes through this door."

And with that bit of sage advice, they turned to leave. The quieter of the two placed a card on the front counter and gave Mark a brief nod before they picked their way out through the rubble.

This time it was Mark who kicked at a kohlrabi before he squatted down, his hands locked behind his head as he took deep breaths.

"Fuck!" yelled Peck. "Just fuck! Leave our store fucking alone!"

Everyone else remained quiet. A small watermelon fell to the floor with a *thunk*, punctuating the stillness.

"Okay," Mark said as he stretched back to his full length, brushing aside a brick of goat-milk soap, its edges crumbling. "A little worse for the wear, but not taken down."

"Yeah, we're not, but everything else around us is for damn sure taken down," said Paul, his nose now stuffed with the corner of a handkerchief, making him sound as if he'd suddenly caught a bad cold.

"We can't let that include our spirit, man. There's always going to be challenges to be met in life." Mark said. "The bat's either gonna knock you down or knock the ball out of the ballpark."

Larry looked up at Mark. "The sun doesn't rise for another nine hours. Wanna get started on the clean-up?"

Mark smiled down at him. "No, man. We'll leave it. Let's hold off. Let's all go home and get some rest. It's been a hell of a day."

As the others worked their way up off the floor, Louise moved toward Mark. "I'm sure Randy will gladly help sort out anything he can on the legal side." She paused. "You know, he wanted to be here . . ."

"I know, Lou," said Mark, nodding his head. "We all know. And if he would've been here, I'd be one angry jackass right now."

Louise nodded. "Thanks, Mark."

The crunch of footsteps making their way toward the front door resounded. Louise hooked her arm through Mark's as they turned in the opposite direction and left through the back door and toward her home.

———◇———

"Elizabeth, have you taken a row in that charming little canoe that sits near your gazebo?" asked Neil, standing by the windows in the porch, where the most prominent view of the lake was had.

"What was that? I couldn't hear you over the dishwasher. It's quite a handy appliance, but I'm finding that it sure does make a fuss." She glanced over at the sink to ensure the hose of the new appliance was attached snugly to the kitchen faucet before adding a cup of sugar and a pouch of Kool-Aid to the pitcher of water. The powder drifted upward, tickling her nose like a cherry-scented feather.

"The canoe. Do you use it?"

Elizabeth glanced over at him. He was dressed in surprising blue jeans and a short-sleeved tan-colored shirt today that made him look out of character, too cheery for his somber personality. She looked out the window, where a peek of red metal gleamed from behind the gazebo, a birthday gift from her daughters some years ago. "No."

"Is that mildew I see?" Neil was now leaning closer to the glass of the French door, as if shortening the distance by a few extra inches could help discern whether it was indeed mildew that had formed.

"Yes, likely."

"Only water from the air touches it then?"

"Yes, only water from the air. I choose not to use it. Or to venture out onto the lake."

"Yet you've chosen to live on a lake."

"Indeed, I have," she replied, giving the drink a final stir. "I choose to have a view of water rather than the view into a neighbor's house. And life."

"Hmm." He continued to look outward. "Stephen will . . . would've been impressed."

Elizabeth's eyes flickered toward him. Neil had shown up with a bottle of red wine bearing an Italian label with which she wasn't familiar. This second appearance was not unexpected, nor was it welcomed. Yet since this surprise guest first showed up two weeks ago, her mind had been teeming with questions, with recollections of

Stephen and renewed wondering over his fate, still unknown to her after all this time. She couldn't allow herself to turn away the possibility of answers—of closure. But she also hadn't been able to bring herself to open the envelope that Neil had given her on his first visit. It couldn't end this way, with Neil the bearer of the news—if that is what the envelope's contents were to reveal.

But Elizabeth had also considered the opposite, that this could be a new beginning. If so, what would that mean to her, in her current life? She had no husband—there was never another man after Stephen, after Will. Though she had inched her way toward closure, there were, she reminded herself sadly, remaining inches ahead of her. A person could push away the past for only so long before one's muscles ached from the effort of it. Whether or not the contents held any answers, she had no idea. But Neil likely did. Was this a game for him, Elizabeth wondered, one that she was unversed in how to play? She and her opponent circling around the question of Stephen, taking turns rolling the dice. She obediently following his lead.

"How long are you in the area, Neil?" *How long must I endure this game?*

"It seems it may be a bit longer than expected. Did I mention to you my business venture?"

"No, you didn't."

Elizabeth set down a tray of iced red beverages on the coffee table and sat. Neil took up his glass and remained standing above her, his steady gaze locked onto hers in such a way that made her want to turn away, to step outside for a breath of fresh air.

"I've begun to dabble in the wine distribution business. Mostly, I'll be bringing in wines from the French and Italian countryside to those parts of our country that are just beginning to develop their palette. I'm also working with a few forward-looking landowners in your area who are starting their own quaint little vineyards."

She'd heard of one family who lived just outside of Northfield that had begun to clear the trees from a hillside with such intentions.

"But of course it will take years, decades perhaps, to perfect their own blancs and ports," he said, holding up the glass of Kool-Aid toward the light of the window. "Meanwhile, wines from the finest wine-growing regions in the world are being made more readily available, in part thanks to my endeavors."

He took a drink, then held the glass away with an outstretched arm and observed it. "This is certainly a sweet yet oddly refreshing beverage."

"Your venture will have you in the Twin Cities for another week then?"

"It's unknown just yet. It really depends on my main reason for being here." He looked over at Elizabeth.

"And what is that?" she asked, hoping her voice didn't belie her hesitancy.

"My main purpose for being here is for an architectural project I'm assisting with."

"Those are two very different interests."

"They are. I would call it a transition. Maybe not too dissimilar from yours? Farm wife to artist?"

Elizabeth was unsure whether his directive had a hidden meaning or was simply meaningless conversation, but the thought was replaced by what this indefinite period of stay could mean for her. Was it his intention to draw out this game? Would she find it within herself to use a trump card?

She leaned back and crossed her legs, returning her glass to the tray. "Neil, what does this mean to you?"

"My visit to your pretty home, I presume you mean," he said without missing a beat. He reached forward and replaced his near-empty glass next to hers. "How about we venture outside to talk. The breeze has made for a nice afternoon."

"Sure."

Elizabeth rose immediately, leading the way out to the wooden deck, down the steps, and toward the patio. She noticed that Neil had walked straight ahead rather than follow her. He stopped in front of the canoe, where he bent down and rubbed away a small patch of mildew.

"Mind if I turn her over, take a look?" he called back.

She nodded and made her way over to the side of the gazebo, watching Neil hoist the canoe up and over, its interior catching the sun, sending off a flash of blinding light before it settled into place. His hands roamed the aluminum body, pausing at the bolts that held it together, then moved to the bow and sighted the line.

"She looks sturdy. A fine piece of work."

Elizabeth was surprised at his estimation, for she had always assumed this was an inexpensive canoe, considering the fact that Sage was just out of college when her daughters had bought it for her, Louise working her first restaurant job. She did not comment but instead surveyed the lake. Its glassy surface looked inviting, but she moved no nearer to the shore.

"Have you ever been in a canoe, Neil?"

"Me? No. Well, not since I was young. I'm more of a skiff man."

"How about Stephen, would he have enjoyed a canoe?"

It was out. She'd broached the topic that Neil had so cleverly avoided.

"Canoe, skiff, sloop, ocean liner—a man of all watercraft. Learned to use them all while growing up on the coast in the family home."

"The family home in England?"

"None other than Brighton."

Elizabeth eyed him cautiously. "Does he still sail, after the accident?"

Neil's hand brushed along the outer side before he finally stood, sliding his hands into his pockets. "I don't know."

"You don't know if he sails, or you don't know if he goes out on the water?"

"I don't know."

"Because you don't see him?"

"That is correct."

She considered this but didn't—couldn't—further inquire. Tiny daggers had begun to stab at her lungs, her mind unable to think clearly.

"Excuse me." She made her way back to the house, silently willing this man to have the decency to take leave of her place—her home, her safety net.

To her surprise, within moments Neil was at the door, this time the front door. With his hand on the doorknob and one foot over the threshold, he leaned in and surrendered his visit.

"Before I go . . ." He paused. "You haven't mentioned the letter I brought to you. May I ask whether you've read it?"

Elizabeth was surprised that it had taken him this long to inquire, causing her to further wonder why he was there, what his motive was. She went to her desk and opened the middle drawer from which she pulled the envelope and walked to where he stood.

His eyebrows raised in expectation, but Elizabeth remained quiet.

"I know that Stephen holds a special place in your heart," he said. "He does in mine too. A dear friend."

"Then perhaps he has told his dear friend about the contents of the letter," Elizabeth challenged him.

"When it comes to matters of the heart, he has never been revelatory."

"So it follows that I ought not to reveal the contents."

"This is different."

"Oh? Why?" she asked, cocking her head to the side.

Neil studied her for a moment. "Because Stephen cannot be reached. And I, too, am concerned about him."

"If he can't be reached, how is it that you came to deliver an envelope from him?"

"It was sent to my address, with no return address."

"And from where was the postmark? Surely, you looked at that."

"Of course I did. It was postmarked from England. However, there was no note inside for me, only this envelope. It was long ago that this came to me."

"I see. And you were never inclined to open it?"

"No. It wasn't mine to open. But it also wasn't mine to throw away."

Plausible, thought Elizabeth, yet something about his response didn't feel right. Rehearsed, maybe. Why would he not have opened it all these years? Could he really be that honest? That loyal?

"I see." She walked back to the desk. "To be honest, I have not yet opened it," she said, tucking the envelope back into the drawer. "Surely you understand if I would rather not talk about it right now. And I don't want to keep you from your commitments."

"Of course." Neil smiled tersely and nodded. The door clicked shut behind him.

Elizabeth realized then that she had no idea how to reach him. Not yet knowing what may or may not be revealed in the letter, she couldn't afford to lose his acquaintance. Not now. Not after all this time. She rushed toward the door.

"Neil!" she called, catching his attention just as he was about to close the door to his car. "My daughters will be here for dinner on Sunday." She blurted out the first thing that came to mind. Would you join us?"

He accepted her invitation, then started the car and drove down the lane, a rise of gravel dust disappearing into the hedges.

Chapter 15

—— Elizabeth, October 1948 ——

As I returned to the Dominican, my spirit was simultaneously refreshed and dismayed. Companionship with another woman! Will and I gathered with the neighbors for card games, occasional suppers, or winter sledding, but there was not a woman with whom I could communicate deeply, with candor. From my perspective, my female acquaintances were living their lives as expected, relishing in the fullness of their families, their farms, church socials, and the busyness of their lives—with a healthy dose of gossip on the side. Unlike me, they didn't appear to be daydreamers, wondering what else was out there or, more poignantly, noticing what was missing.

In contrast, Wini and I talked not about warding off garden pests with a border of marigolds or how to work an oil stain out of a pair of jeans; instead, we compared our lives growing up—me in St. Timothy and her Charleston. She described her musical training from an early age and the way the ocean carried folks from different walks of life across the world to South Carolina or washed them away in a riptide of grief. How a hurricane had them on their knees, praying for safety, and how houses had not only been built upward, but spread wide to accompany large families and their "help" that had been brought in so many years ago. I sat wide-eyed while listening to her chronicle the highlights of her former lives in the cities of New Orleans, San

Francisco, and New York, and felt gratitude that she had landed in Chicago, at the Blue Window, directly in front of my eyes and ears. With Wini, there was no feigning interest in uninteresting topics and no tedious small talk simply for the sake of avoiding silence. She was a force of life, effervescing in a world that worked so hard to contain her.

Yet once in my room, as I dropped onto the bed, the day's delights began to mirror the waning light outside my window. Wini was clearly a woman of certain wisdom, which was precisely why I couldn't mindlessly wave away her cautions about Stephen. At the same time I reminded myself that her initial perception of him had been garnered over a few inches of time in his presence, taken from observation, not communication. And, she did look more favorably on him as the discussion moved forward. So what was the flutter of uncertainty that I felt? Was it a reaction to the indecorous position in which I had placed myself? Or was it a cautionary warning? And why, despite her concerns, did my yearning for him continue to surge like a swollen river soon to spill over its banks?

That evening, there came a knock at my door just as I had finished bathing and dressing for supper. Upon opening the door a crack, I saw Stephen standing there, a bright smile on his face.

"Stephen! What a surprise!"

"Hopefully a nice one?" he asked, his eyebrows raised into arches.

The weight of consideration that I'd been carrying with me since the moment Neil appeared on the boat scattered away as if a balloon had been pricked. I was also relieved that Stephen had not been deterred by my abrupt and rather rude departure from the boat.

I opened the door for him and noticed that he held a rectangular package the size of a shoe box, crimson in color and wrapped in ribbon dyed in an even deeper shade of red, the length of it spilling over again and again into a luxurious bow.

Having seen me glance at it, Stephen held out the package. "For you," he offered, then pulled it back. "But not to be opened just yet."

I couldn't help but feel amused, unused to gifts received outside of notable dates on the calendar. I invited him in, and he set the box upon the bureau, its reflection in the attached mirror doubling my curiosity.

"I came to you, Elizabeth, to apologize for what happened the other day. And in desperate hope of finding you here." He took my hands in his. "I was terribly afraid that you might have absconded all the way back to Iowa."

I bowed my head, wanting to find the right words in response. I should be the one apologizing; I was the one who had left.

"My apology is for the appearance of Neil. But that is the only thing for which I feel regret." Stephen slowly raised my chin, a similar action to the last time I'd seen him, to the moment we were about to kiss. "The words I spoke, the kiss we shared—those I cherish, Elizabeth."

Stephen paused, then leaned in hesitatingly as he looked deeply into my eyes. I closed my eyes and offered my lips to his.

When we finally pulled apart, a smile immediately set in, one that felt as if it would remain in place forever, as long as I was with this wondrous man.

He excused himself and went to the door, where he retrieved a bottle of wine and one of scotch that he had left just outside in the hallway. "I didn't want to appear presumptuous," he said, "but I guess I've now exposed myself."

I gathered two wine glasses that had gone unused these past several days and carried them to the small table situated by the window. Stephen took up the corkscrew and opened the bottle with a practiced air, then poured two generous servings.

"For the lady." He handed me a glass.

The wine emitted an aroma of yeasty fruit, and he instructed me to press my nose into the glass and inhale deeply.

"What? Put my nose right into it?"

"Indeed, darling. To get a true sense of the bouquet, it is necessary."

I did as I was told, despite feeling foolish, and inhaled a tart, earthy scent redolent of blackberries.

"Ah, you are a natural."

"And cherry, I think." I was surprised at just how aromatic the wine was.

"Excellent!"

I took a small sip, seeking out specific fruits and spices as Stephen made suggestions. Pear? No. Cinnamon? Perhaps.

"This is an exceptional bottle, produced in France before the war."

"Oh?"

"I'm afraid the French vineyards didn't fare well during the war. In fact, they were quite hard hit, many of the grape crops devastated. Relatively few bottles remain."

I gripped the stem of my glass a bit tighter. "How did you find it?"

"This bottle, my dear, is compliments of Neil."

My jaw tensed at hearing his name spoken again, but I drew in another sip and allowed myself to relax into the warmth of the evening.

"He may not have brilliant timing, but he certainly has a knack for fetching a fine bottle."

As if on cue, a light rap at the door sounded, reigniting my discomfort.

"Relax, darling," he said, setting down his glass and placing a hand on my leg. "Room service."

"Didn't want to be presumptuous, you say?" I said teasingly.

He grinned and went to the door as I sank back into the chair.

"Yes, there on the table," he indicated to the maître de and passed him a coin.

Stephen picked up my glass and poured another inch of wine before lifting the lid of the silver tray. Inside was a row of sliced sausages and a trio of cheeses: a familiar-looking one in a deep hue of golden yellow, another marbled with purple strands, and a third rounded in shape and enveloped in a rind. A slender loaf of uncut bread and a bowl filled with a spread that reminded me of buttermilk frosting, though flecked with black specks, were also neatly arranged on the tray, sprigs of parsley placed artfully in between.

One at a time, Stephen introduced me to the varieties, educating me on how the Bordeaux we were drinking heightened the individual nuttiness or earthy undertones of the various cheeses. Until now, I had never considered that eating bread and cheese could be such a palatable experience.

"Tell me, Elizabeth. Have you ever seen a sunset that popped a flash of green at the very moment the horizon swallowed it up?" he asked as we continued to sip and nibble.

I wondered from where this thought had come. "What do you mean, the sun turns green? I think I would have remembered that."

"In a sense, yes."

"No, I can't say that I've even heard of such a thing." I visualized the pumpkin-orange glow over the west bean field but couldn't realistically imagine a green sun. The thought of it rather chilled me as I recalled the sickly shade of green that colored the sky before the tornado of 1942. "A big pop or a little one? What shade of green?"

"Oh, very small. A flash that is not even a second of time. And a brilliant green, my dear."

"Stephen, does the sun really flash green?" I knew by now that he had a rather quirky sense of humor, but I wasn't quite sure if this conversation fell into that spectrum.

"It does, but just the very tip, or maybe above the tip. Or perhaps the sky above the sun. One really cannot say with certainty, as it is quite quick."

"But why? A rainbow-like effect?"

"An atmospheric effect, one would suppose."

We were quiet for a moment, respectively considering this unusual phenomenon, before Stephen spoke again.

"When I am sailing, whether along the shores of Lake Michigan or circling the isles of the Channel back home, I always watch for the pop of green. It is said to be a harbinger of great fortune."

"And . . . are you here to herald the coming of riches, Mr. Covington?" As I looked at him, I noticed how his dark blond hair had dulled near his temples, setting off his magnificent brown eyes even more so—eyes that explored my face, my hair, my own eyes.

"Riches have already been found."

"Yes," I agreed. "They have."

Stephen pushed himself up to an abrupt stand. "But, my darling, I cannot simply 'spill the beans' and reveal the many secrets of a green sunset. That would belie the laws of mystery," he said, pouring the last of the wine into my glass and decanting the bottle of scotch for himself.

Our conversation continued along unmapped terrain, twisting along curvy roads and settling, at times, into coves overlooking broad valleys. He talked about his favorite parts of England, and I told him stories about Louise and Sage. I found that sharing snapshots of my children's lives and seeing his interest in learning about them was immensely satisfying.

"I now have a distinct image in my mind of your two treasures," he said after a while. "Perhaps I will have the chance to meet them one day and see if those images are befitting."

I was bewildered into brief silence. Sage and Louise were my life, but my other life, one that belonged to Will. Stephen was like a foreign object in that scene, a giraffe in the Alaskan mountains.

"Elizabeth, I know your time here is not indefinite. At some point, I would like to discuss what might become of us. For why were we brought together so certainly, so extraordinarily? Surely it is not only to depart from one another in just seven short days and go on with our lives as if we had never met?" He took my hands into his. "You are lodged in my heart, dear Elizabeth."

This time it was I who stood, stepping toward the bureau where the box remained unopened. One of the ribbons had a slight tear at the edge, a flaw I hadn't noticed earlier.

"No, I don't want to walk away. You are important to me—very important. I know that . . ." I hesitated. "Well, I don't know anything, really, about what to do once this trip ends." Straightening my shoulders, I turned back toward him. "Honestly, Stephen, here in Chicago I've been living a different life. I have a life back in Iowa, but you are my life here."

We, both of us, absorbed the impact of my words. For me it was a simple, startling truth. For Stephen, I believe, it was an affirmation of us. I felt as if I were about to either combust into a cloud of confetti for having found this perfect man who was right here before me—or sink into a pit of quicksand at the thought of leaving him. What had we done? How could this possibly end well?

"Stephen, I haven't thought about what life will be like seven days from now, when I'm not here. I'm sorry, but I've just been . . . I don't know what else to say other than . . . living."

"Do you deserve, Elizabeth, to live beyond a week from now?"

"Of course, yes. But . . ."

"We both deserve to live, and happily so."

"But what will we do, Stephen? Really, I'm sorry I haven't put a great amount of thought into it. My life has been so full here, and I've been determined to take in each day so completely that I haven't allowed myself to think too much about the future. Have you?"

His chest expanded, and he closed his eyes as he exhaled. "Darling, during my moments away from you I have thought of almost nothing else."

Stephen set down his glass and stood, drawing me toward him. Our bodies connected with magnetic force, the light from the overhead chandelier casting a glow over the nearby bed. Muffled voices from beyond the door and the screech of the El coming to a raggedy halt a short distance away echoed around us. He slid his hands up my arms and along my back, pausing at my waist. He looked at me with fervor such as I had not yet seen in him. "I love you, Elizabeth. With my whole self, I love you."

The ambient sounds vanished, leaving behind just us—Stephen and me. Nothing but us.

As I took in his words, a luxurious flame ignited inside me, burning away bewilderment and doubt. His sentiment reverberated throughout my body, down to my very cells, and a whisper of promise pressed at me from inside, eager for liberation. His lips brushed against my cheek, my neck, my lips, compelling my own to open and reciprocate his passion. He slid his hands underneath my sweater, and I felt every racing beat of my heart as we slowly, yet greedily, removed each other's clothes, scattering them unabashedly upon the rug until we were skin-to-skin, succumbing to a level of passion that I hadn't known existed. All I could think was, this is how desire is meant to feel, how love is meant to feel. *This.*

Chapter 16

— July 1975 —

The first thing Louise noticed as she approached Living Waters was cardboard in lieu of glass in the front windows, causing indignation to restart its engine. Though shards remained embedded in the yew shrubs and the dirt below them, she didn't have to pick her way through the porch like she had last night. Inside, a few of the shelves had been propped up alongside the front counter, and a handful of salvaged vegetables were packed snuggly into woven baskets. Someone had been at it early. Louise wondered if anyone had been able to get a decent night's sleep.

Peck came around the corner with a broom in hand, his headband already dampened with sweat. They exchanged glances, and Louise was about to ask if he'd done all this alone when Mark followed, juggling several cardboard boxes in his arms.

"Hey Lou, give me a hand?" Mark called out.

"Yeah, of course." She grabbed the top two.

"There's tea in the back."

"I'm good. What should I do with these?"

"It all goes. Separate the food from the debris."

Louise saw a handful of beets lying in a basket. Nearly everything that was ready to be sold yesterday was now food waste.

"Oh, and watch for glass and nails."

Louise pulled on a pair of gloves and got to work. Larry arrived, and soon after Sherrie stopped in with bagels and juice before starting her day shift at the University of Minnesota Hospital, where she interned. No doubt any others who were able to help would show up shortly.

By midafternoon, the inside of Living Waters had begun to take on a less dire look. Everything broken had been cleared out, leaving a refrigerator and the original long counters lining the walls. Peck and Paul were in the yard reconfiguring two sets of freestanding shelves into one, the grating of the hand saw gnawing at Louise's nerves. Mark had spent a good part of the day measuring and talking on the phone. He was now sitting on the stool at the front counter, where he had scratched out a map of the room, trying out various configurations for a new layout using tiny strips of cardboard.

"How about an H on its side?" Louise asked.

"Not a good use of space."

"An X?" she suggested, with a teasing jab.

"Ha ha."

"We could form an L-W for Living Waters!"

"Funny girl today, Lou." Mark continued adjusting the cardboard as he sized up the room. "I think the existing counters are hindering the space. Maybe we pull those out and start fresh."

"Everyone loves a fresh start, even counters."

"That just might be the thing. C'mon." He got up. "Let's take a break outside. Larry, grab the tea!"

Louise heard Larry's "Yup" from the back room, and she and Mark went outside together to where Peck and Paul were working.

Mark looked at their project and nodded. "I like it, man. Great height too. Those the braces you're using?" He pointed at a small pile of L-shaped metal pieces that looked to Louise as if even trampling elephants couldn't bend them.

"They could even double as crowbars," Peck said, eyeing Paul, who shook his head and laughed a short, nasally sound, his swollen nose and black-and-blue eye a reminder of what the backswing of a crowbar can do to a face. "Ooph," he groaned at the ironic pain of laughter.

Larry came out with a board holding sun tea and paper cups, his skinny arms buried by the mass of it. Peck guzzled his and laid back, pulling off his headband and closing his eyes against the sun. Mark thanked everyone for committing and talked briefly about his ideas for the inside as well as what all needed to get done before Living Waters could reopen for business.

"Let's all try to keep our thoughts solid, man. Don't trip over what happened. If we focus on warring with the CO, then it's a war we will get. If we focus on peace, peace will come our way. But it has to be done together—no one steps away from the circle."

More than one person looked at Peck.

"With all due respect, Mark, 'peace not war' hasn't gotten us too far, in case you haven't noticed," Peck replied. "If these assholes wanted Living Waters to break, then Living Waters needs to return breaks both bigger and deeper."

"Yeah, man. We gotta do something that'll send a clear message that we won't stand for this," said Larry. "What's it gonna say to them if we just clean up the mess and ignore them? 'Come and get more, we've got lots of brooms?'"

"And what about safety?" Paul asked. "Louise and Sherrie could be working here alone when they come back. Or what if it was just me, for god's sake? I've got the body of a waif and the wits of a fairy. Who's to say how far they'll go next time?"

"Or the rest of us, for that matter. I've got a little kid at home who I need to feed. I'm not gonna work too well if my arms are ripped off," said Tim, sitting away from the group on the front stoop.

Until now, Louise hadn't thought about it in that way. Still working on quelling her anger over the multiple gashes the CO had inflicted upon Living Waters, she considered this idea and realized that the guys were right. There was no denying that Living Waters had quickly become a dangerous place to work. She and Sherrie were probably most at risk. And definitely Paul. On top of that, they had no idea just yet how their community of patrons would react once a match struck fire on the tinder of talk.

Louise jumped up, her petite frame a short reach above the sitting bodies of the guys. "Hey! I think I've got it!" She stepped back to get everyone in sight. "The CO isn't out to hurt us. They just want to hurt our *business*."

"Is that why my nose is continuing to swell?" Paul asked, briefly removing the ice cube he had pressed against it.

"Here's what I'm thinking. The Warehouse group showed up pretty damn tough-looking with their bats and pipes, as we all saw, and came on to us hell's bells. Yet no one here was hit with a weapon, right? Except for you, Paul. But like you said, you happened to be behind the guy when he swung."

"Right."

"There were a couple of fist fights, but hey—you're dudes, and dudes do that. The weapons, however, were only used for the store, and when that started happening, everything became really loud. When you guys were inside, just before the cops came, some of the neighbors started coming out of their houses." Louise looked each of them in the eye in turn as she spoke. "To see what the racket was about. Imagine what they saw!" She threw her arms up in the air at the declaration. "They saw an enormous group fight and heard glass breaking, along with a good amount of swearing. Combine that with Living Waters being a 'radical' grocery in a quiet neighborhood run by a bunch of groovy hippies, and what you get is an 'I'm staying the hell away from there' attitude. Do you see it?"

Peck opened his eyes and looked her way, using his hand as a sun shield.

"So maybe they aren't jerks enough to have hurt us as badly as they could have, but they're out to ruin our reputation so that we hang it up," Tim suggested.

"I gotta admit, it makes sense," said Peck.

"Wait a minute—aside from Paul, *did* anyone get hit with a

weapon?" Mark asked. No one acknowledged that they did. "You know, it did seem like it could've been a lot worse. There were what, ten or so of them and about six of us? Them with weapons, us without?"

"And maybe they're responsible for the police call too," said Paul. "Sure, it could've been a neighbor, but the cops came quickly, you know? Maybe they had someone stay back to make the call at the right time. Like Louise said, people didn't start sniffing around until just before the cops got here."

"You might be onto something," Mark said. "They would've known we wouldn't narc on our own kind. But they could use subterfuge and do so themselves."

"Assholes," Peck said.

"We don't know with certainty if ruin by reputation was their intention, but it has potential." Mark looked toward the sky, a telltale sign that he was considering things from multiple angles. "If so," he continued calmly, "here's where the idea of peace can play an even more dominant role."

Peck rolled his eyes.

"Our focus needs to be on peace, but peace with the neighborhood. Now more than ever, we need to show them that we are trustworthy and that our goal here is of pure, wholesome intention." He paused and took a long drink of tea. "I think the first step we need to take is to trust ourselves and each other *and* trust that the Warehouse group will bring no more physical harm our way. We need to establish that in our minds and in our hearts."

"And our bruises," Paul added.

"Paul, I want you to consider taking a few days off, to heal. I know you're capable of working with your booboos," said Mark, the others laughing in response, "but we don't need our customers to see them. We need them to see quality food.

"Which brings me to my second point. I need anyone with a vehicle to join me in making food runs over the next few days. Peck, can you and Paul finish the shelves by tomorrow? I think I have a good plan for a new midsection layout that'll work better, and we'll only need one solid rack of shelves. I'll make some calls, and you can meet me here at nine o'clock. Will that work for everyone?"

Louise was the first to raise her hand in agreement. "Randy and I will be here," she said, followed by Paul and Larry's assent. "Aye," said Tim. Peck was a given.

A noticeable shift in energy had transpired as ideas continued to come forth, and a solid plan began to form. In the end, it was decided that there was soon to be a newly designed store, complete with a "Thank-God-We're-Living" Waters Day that would follow, putting a humorous twist on the situation. A revitalized business was about to emerge from the sea of broken glass.

Louise sat next to Randy in the Chevy pickup, its tailgate wired shut and wheel wells rusting at an ever-increasing rate. They bumped along the short gravel road that led to Elizabeth's home before Randy turned into the curved driveway where surrounding hardwoods were lush with emerald-colored leaves that veritably dripped oxygen into the air. As they wound their way toward the house, Louise noticed that Lake Bells was soothingly calm, the reflection of the clouds unmarred on the amoeba-shaped body of water that loosely resembled two handbells connected at the handles. She was glad to be here today, far away from the city.

Randy parked next to the mosaic path that led from the front walk down a slope to the garden beds behind the house, where a weathered bistro table and chairs were artfully situated within a fragrant flowerbed. It was there that Louise often found her mother planting, weeding, or pruning beds of tulips, peonies, roses, or asters—depending on the season.

"I see Mama Betty's been at work," said Randy.

"As usual, the flower beds are flawless," replied Louise.

The house, too, mimicked the tranquility of the setting, with its shingle siding the color of a gentle afternoon rain and abundant French-paned windows that invited daylight to glaze over the quaint spaces within.

"Hello!" Louise called out as they entered, setting down her bag and slipping off her thong sandals.

"Oh," Randy murmured.

Louise looked up and caught her breath. A man was standing next to Mother. Right there in the kitchen . . . a man! He was clearly overdressed for the occasion, wearing gray pin-striped trousers, a dark gray shirt, and a black vest. *Is that a tie?*

"Louise, this is Neil. Neil, my youngest and her boyfriend, Randy," said Elizabeth.

"Nice to meet you, Louise, Randy," the man said, greeting them with a bow of his head.

"Hi?" Louise glanced over Neil's shoulder at Sage who stood in the kitchen behind him. Sage quickly shook her head and shrugged while struggling to remove a corkscrew from a bottle of wine. Louise slid her hands into the back pockets of her jeans, feeling the rough knots of thread from the recent flower embroidery experiment she'd performed on the pockets.

"Your timing is punctual, as usual. We were just about to serve," Elizabeth called over her shoulder as she pulled a bowl from the upper cabinet. "Wash your hands and bring the salad to the table, would you?"

Louise and Randy walked into the bathroom, where they whispered their astonishment while washing up. A *pop* resounded, and they returned to the dining room, where Sage was dividing the wine into five equal servings.

"Would this chair from the corner here do for an extra seat?" Neil asked. "By the looks of this fine dinner, I may need more elbow room."

"Yes, that one is good," replied Elizabeth.

Neil moved it to the side of the table for four that held five place settings and pulled out a chair for Elizabeth, though not her usual place at the head of the table, which he instead occupied. Randy mimicked the chivalrous gesture with a smirk, to which Louise rolled her eyes.

"So, let's get right down to business," Elizabeth said, holding up her wine glass. "Randy, we couldn't be prouder of you. The challenges you've hurdled throughout law school, and now having passed the bar exam—you are an inspiration to us all." She smiled proudly at him. "To Randy."

"To Randy!" Louise reached over and pecked him on the cheek.

"To Randy," Sage joined in the toast.

Neil nodded and brought his glass to his lips.

"Thank you, Mama Betty, everyone. If it wasn't for my butterfly and her sweet family, I don't think I'd have made it. You all don't realize what you mean to me." He raised his glass again. "To family."

"To family!"

Randy had been a part of the family for more than two years now, he and Louise having met when he made his first delivery to Living Waters from the Smith farm. It was a brief visit that ended in a date; three weeks later, they signed a lease on an apartment. At the time, Randy had just finished his first year of law school.

Sage asked Randy for details about his exam as Elizabeth passed the plate of sliced meatloaf to Neil. Louise gathered up the bowl of potato salad from the opposite end of the table and served Randy a heaping spoonful. After the bustle of food service had passed, Elizabeth took advantage of the pause.

"My dear family is, no doubt, wondering over the guest in our presence," she said, adding a slice of bread to her plate. "Neil has come in from Chicago. He is in the cities on business and stopped in for a surprise visit." A polite, though curt, smile crossed over her face as she spoke.

"And I suspect that the foremost question on your mind is, how did I come to know Neil?" she continued as she scooped a pat of butter from the butter dish and began slathering it onto the homemade bread with quick swipes. "To tell you the truth," she continued, "I've known

Neil for many years now. Nearly twenty-seven." She glanced at Sage.

"That's a long time. Where'd you meet?" asked Randy.

"Chicago," chimed in Neil. "In fact, Chicago is the only place we've ever met before a few days ago, when I arrived here in Minnesota."

"Chicago?" Louise asked in disbelief, setting her fork down with a clang. "When were you in Chicago, Mother? I know you exhibited at a gallery there, but you refused to go. I never did get that."

Elizabeth again looked at Sage, who appeared to be searching through her steel-trap memory bank. "As I said, it was twenty-six years ago, this past October. I traveled there by train and stayed for three weeks."

"Right on, Mama Betty. You—" began Randy.

"Forgive me if I'm the only one who thinks this is a little odd," interrupted Louise. "But you took off for Chicago for three weeks and never told us about it? And now, all these years later, you're introducing us to a man you met there? Neil? What is this all about?"

Randy set his fork down.

"I can understand your surprise, Louise. Never thought old Mother had any curiosities in her life, right?" Elizabeth said, setting her fork down too. "It was a complicated time in my life, and I needed a getaway. Your father was a very successful farmer, especially after the war ended, and the timing was right. It wasn't unheard of, Louise. People did travel back then."

"Yeah, but to a great-aunt's house in Cedar Rapids maybe. You just took off, alone, to a major city—you, who had never been outside of your little spot on the earth? And you never told us?"

"Yes, me—a woman with needs to fulfill and a desire for a vacation. The living was different back then, but people were still human. We had the same basic needs then as we do today." Elizabeth's voice remained calm, but a rise of tension had begun to niggle its way in. "And, you did know about it at the time, of course, though you were quite young. I've just chosen not to speak about it since."

Neil sat back in his chair.

"I met several people while there. Neil, Helena, Wini . . . Stephen."

Louise narrowed her eyes, suspicious of the pause in the list of names, but her interest in the man in their presence overcame it.

"Is Helena your wife?" Sage asked.

"I've never heard of her," said Neil.

"How about Wini?"

"No. She is not my wife," he responded brusquely, with a fastidious glance in Randy's direction as he straightened his tie.

"Is she a Black lady?" Randy's mouth pulled back into a smile. "She's Black like me, isn't she?" He tossed his head back and laughed.

"Randy, knock it off," said Louise. "Why do you even think that?"

"I can read looks. Black people have a second language. Not one of us can't read a look of disgrace on a White man's face. That's okay, dude. I'm cool with it. I'm cool in my own skin." Randy laughed again, shaking his head. "So where does this Wini lady live, Mama Betty?"

"Forget Wini! Wini comes later!" Louise threw Randy a sharp look, and he picked up his fork once again and dove into the roasted green beans.

"Louise, take it down a notch. Let Mother tell her story," said Sage.

"Well, it seems I've been revealed," Elizabeth continued. "This Midwestern lady has indeed had diversified friends."

Again, Louise rolled her eyes.

"But stories are for another time. Today I would like all of us to get to know Neil. He is my guest, as it seems you have forgotten, Louise," Elizabeth said, then turned toward Neil. "Neil is on the architectural team that designed a new building near downtown. Very modern apartments, right Neil?"

"Yes, the Riverside Plaza."

"I've heard of that building. We have a file begun at the historical society where I work," said Sage.

"You're a historian, then?" asked Neil.

"Well, sort of. I'm a research librarian at the Minnesota Historical Society. We're in close touch with city councils, community development groups, news organizations . . . that sort of thing. We have a pretty good idea of what's new, if it has history-making potential."

"I have no doubt this building will make history. It is the latest in modernity; there's nothing else like it in the state," replied Neil, raising his chin to a lofty angle. "I began in the business just as the war was starting—the Second World War, not Vietnam. It was a slow beginning, but as soon as it was over there was an explosion of construction in cities across the country. People wanted to get back to a sense of normalcy."

"Sounds like you've had a long career," Louise observed.

"I've had some interesting opportunities in the business. Lately though, I've been dipping my toes into a new venture," he continued. "I've taken part ownership in a small chain of stores. Stores that sell wines from around the world."

"If this is the wine you're selling, I'm buying." Randy lifted his glass in the air, a solitary toast.

"It is indeed. A Rhone direct from France. The other is a red Bordeaux."

"And you're opening one of these stores in the Cities?" Sage asked.

"If my search for a proper location results in success, yes."

"How'd you find Mother's address? Or have you two been in touch all these years?" Louise asked, setting the conversation back on track.

Neil had just taken a bite of meatloaf and was nodding while chewing as if to rush along his task of pummeling the food to a digestible state. The clock on the wall behind him ticked just a notch too loudly as everyone waited for his response to what Louise had considered the most important question posed thus far.

"Excellent question," he replied, then paused to swallow a second time. "I saw an advertisement for a quilt show in one of Chicago's downtown galleries some time back. I had no idea that a quilt could be considered art, and I was curious. I went to the gallery with an old friend and was wandering the exhibit rooms."

An old friend, Elizabeth noted.

"I caught sight of one particular work that seemed like a bright star in comparison to the others. It was reminiscent of an abstract painting but made of cloth. As I considered it, I began to make out a person—a man, specifically—standing off-center with a field of corn behind him that blended into a lake. As I studied it more closely, there were real kernels of corn used to create the effect of lightning. I was mesmerized! I then saw the artist's credit and accompanying photo, and I was certain that she was the same Elizabeth I had met long ago. Elizabeth, from a farm in Iowa."

Sage noticed the flash in her mother's eyes.

"And when business brought you to this area, you easily found her in the phone book?" Louise continued.

"Yes." Neil smiled, exposing teeth in the early stages of aged yellowing. He turned to Elizabeth. "And now here we are, having a meal together. I don't believe we'd ever had a chance to dine together those twenty-six years ago. I think this deserves a toast."

A stiff smile appeared on Elizabeth's face. "Of course."

"A toast: to reunions, introductions, and unexpected happenings," said Neil, raising his glass.

Elizabeth raised her glass and immediately turned the focus back to Randy, asking whether he'd had any leads on law firms that may be hiring, thereby ending any further conversation about Chicago.

The meal moved forth and was followed by the clearing of dishes. Neil insisted on helping with the clean-up, so Sage took advantage of the opportunity for which she'd been waiting.

"Lou, Randy, help me retrieve something from my car, would you?"

"Well, well, well. If it isn't the woman of mystery," said Louise. "What's up, sis? Got yourself a secret admirer hiding in the trunk?"

"Cute, but no admiration is coming from this surprise. I can tell you that."

Sage inserted a key into the latch and turned it until a *pop* sounded, releasing a wave of heat from the trunk. Inside sat a nondescript cardboard box that had been taped shut and subsequently sliced open. Louise reached for a flap, but Sage immediately swished her hand away.

"Patience!"

"Here, let me get that," said Randy, hoisting the box up and out. "Shit, you dig up some gold for yourself?"

"Yep, you guessed it, Randy. Nugget after nugget, buried in my yard."

Sage led them around the side of the house and toward the picnic table out back where Randy set the box down. There, she made the two of them wait until Elizabeth and Neil arrived before giving out any clue as to what was inside.

"This must be the mysterious package you hinted at. It looks quite heavy," observed Elizabeth, leaning in to look at the return address. "Is this from the farm, Sage?" A look of bewilderment crossed over her face.

"It is."

Elizabeth returned upright, her confusion remaining evident.

Sage began the tale of how the box came to sit upon her mother's table, recalling the bizarre phone conversation with Hans and repeating his story of how the object inside had damaged his plow upon its discovery.

"I bet that didn't go over well," said Louise. "Now c'mon. What is it?"

Sage pulled back the cardboard flaps and lifted the iron cross from its newspaper swaddling.

"Whoo-ee! That gives me the heebie-jeebies," said Randy, stepping back with his index fingers crossed.

"Randy, you can't ward off a cross with a cross," said Sage. "Besides, it's not alive. It's a chunk of metal."

"You calling that a plain old chunk of metal after telling us where it came from?"

"It came from a field."

"Our name!" exclaimed Louise, pointing at the *LEY* emerging from the rusted iron.

"Yeah, pretty funky to see, isn't it? And notice the hash marks."

Sage pointed to the lower section where four marks had been etched in. Unlike the cross itself, these were irregular in size and spacing, like a drawing of grass made by a young child.

Elizabeth remained quiet as she watched her daughters take in this anomaly.

"Maybe the marks are from the plow," said Louise.

"They seem too irregular for that. And too aged, for that matter. Here, let's turn it over." Sage lifted the top of the cross, Louise the bottom, and pushed aside the box before setting it back onto the table. The reverse side revealed nothing out of the ordinary, only a slight flaw in the ironwork.

"Must've made one hell of a sound when Farmer Hans's plow scratched it up," said Randy.

Lacking interest, Neil drifted toward the gazebo. Soon after Elizabeth, too, turned quietly from the table and stepped away.

"Cripes, she's gone from being a nervous Nelly to acting like she'll lose her dinner if she sees this thing for another second," Louise said in a hushed tone.

"That's a bit of an exaggeration, Lou," said Sage.

"What, you didn't notice that she was bugged out?"

"Want me to take out Neil? I got karate skills," Randy whispered, forming an X with his forearms.

"Dream on." Louise elbowed him, and he tickled her back in revenge.

"Okay, focus you guys, would you?"

"Yes, Ms. Sage."

"Sorry, ma'am," added Louise.

"Cut it out. Now back to the cross—"

"Wait, she's coming back," said Louise.

"Mother, do you know anything about this?" Sage asked, once her mother returned.

Elizabeth closed her eyes and inhaled slowly. "I do," she replied, exhaling in a sigh before reopening them. "But it's not likely what you want to know."

"We want to know anything. It's just so mysterious," replied Sage.

"Yes, it certainly is," agreed Elizabeth. She sat down hard with an uncharacteristic dearth of grace. "What I know is that it was buried in the northeast field. But I only know that it was there because I tripped over it. It was the day your father's accident occurred." She looked at Louise. "It was the day you brought home a sack of skunks. Do you remember?"

"Of course. They were super cute."

Elizabeth shook her head. "I had just set out to carry the babies back to the woods when I heard him shout out. That was not like your father. I'd never before heard him in pain, and it scared me tremendously."

Elizabeth stood, crossing her arms, and looked out at the lake. "I ran toward the field, scared of what I would find. But before I had even arrived, the shouts had stopped, and I could only think that he was gone. That I couldn't handle another loss." Her voice caught, and she took another deep breath before continuing.

"I saw the tractor in the near distance and ran in its direction. The ground was soft, and my legs carried me over it with as much speed as they could muster. I was almost there when I tripped and fell. When I heaved myself back up, I noticed a piece of iron extruding from the soil. And I began to run again."

Elizabeth paused, the memory bringing weight to the fresh summer air.

"I'm sorry, girls, if this is too much."

"No, keep going. Tell us," said Sage, touching her mother's arm. "It's okay."

She nodded. "I ran the last few steps before I reached your father. He was lying on his back. Alive, of course, but in tremendous pain. The pesticide from the sprayer was burning his skin, searing him right before my eyes. I could feel my panic rising and ran back to the house to call the doctor, begging Will, begging God, 'Please don't die. Please don't die.'"

"Oh, Mother." Sage moved her arm across Elizabeth's shoulders.

"I remember that day. God, it's been years since I've thought about it. Louise and I were outside, and we heard Daddy call out too. We didn't know what was happening, but we knew it wasn't good."

"I remember too," said Louise. She thought back to how her mother returned for a pitcher of water, still rushed and scared-looking, and ran off again. She'd started crying but stopped when Sage told her that Daddy must have been thirsty. She'd believed her sister, a hopeful truth.

"It was the first year that your father had used the new pesticide, recommended by neighbors, guaranteed by the salesman. I knew instinctively that it wasn't a good idea—it just didn't feel right. Will promised that if the spray didn't increase our yield that year, he would never use it again." Her hand brushed across her forehead. "But that wasn't the day I'd discovered that what I had tripped over was a cross. That came later.

"Your father was in bad shape. I remember Dr. Grimmsrud arriving, and I remember the neighbor, Bob, stopping his truck at the edge of the field and running toward us. I heard the wail of a siren, and the next thing I knew, Will was inside an ambulance being rushed off to the hospital."

Elizabeth's shoulders rounded as she folded further back into the memory. "His burns were terribly severe, but that was curable. It was the residual effects that changed him." Again, she shook her head as if still in disbelief all these years later. "The burns scarred, but other things cropped up too. Headaches became frequent. And he just . . . he just wasn't himself."

Sage and Louise knew the story of Daddy, but the specifics had rarely been talked about and certainly not thought about in years. They knew that his ill health had been a grim time in their lives, largely because of the continued casseroles dropped off by neighbors and parishioners from St. Benedict's, but their mother had talked so little of it in the years since.

"I remember that, after he returned from the hospital," said Sage.

"I kept thinking he'd gone from being a hare to a turtle. And that the turtle kept pulling his head in, hiding. I'd assumed he was still in pain."

"When did you go back into the field?" Louise asked, memories of Daddy more distant than those of her sister and eager to get back to the mystery of the cross.

"It was while your father was in the hospital, a week or so after the accident, that I went back. I traced my footsteps to where they'd crossed over the dirt. The object—I didn't know what it was just yet—was still protruding from the ground, though I could only see one arm. I tugged at it, curious about its unusual shape, but it wouldn't budge. So I went back to the shed, got a spade, and carried it with me back into the field." Her hands clenched as if holding onto the handle. "I dug it up and saw that it was a cross. A familiar one." She looked in turn at both Sage and Louise. Louise leaned in. "It was your father's, passed down as a family heirloom of sorts years ago."

Randy let out a low whistle.

"I didn't know how it ended up in the field. When we'd moved there, Will mentioned storing it away in the shed, and I hadn't given it a second thought since."

"It is an unusual shape. Do you know anything about that?" Sage asked. "Or the hash marks etched in?"

"I don't know if there's significance to the shape, just that it was an heirloom. As you know, your father lost his parents early in life. He didn't talk about them or the cross very often. Almost never, really."

"Did you ever ask Uncle Roy?"

"I called him once, but he didn't know much about it other than that it existed and was given to the eldest: your father. Though he did recall that there were two hash marks on it, marks that Will had etched in to commemorate their parents."

"Two? But there are four," said Louise, looking again to reassure herself that she had indeed seen more than two.

Sage also moved in to inspect the cross more closely and confirmed that there were four marks. "Do you think Daddy might've marked

Frankie's death?" she asked.

Elizabeth nodded thoughtfully. "He never mentioned it to me, but yes, now that you suggest it, I am certain he would have done that."

"So that leaves one mystery mark," said Louise.

"Mother?" Sage asked.

Elizabeth shook her head. "No, I don't know. Roy is alive, still in California. I can't think of anyone else who it could represent."

"What did you do with the cross after you dug it up?" asked Sage. "Hans said he found it in the field. He reminded me more than once that it wrecked his plow."

Elizabeth tucked her hair behind her ear in an effort to keep her hands occupied, looking out at the lake once again. So much of the past had been flung back at her in recent days.

"I . . . I buried it again—immediately. Once I saw what it was, I couldn't . . . well, I never wanted to see it again, with your father's accident so fresh and so many unknowns at the time." She looked at Louise then Sage, whose gaze she held. "I dug deeper into the earth and covered it entirely, hoping never to see it again."

Chapter 17

— Elizabeth, October 1948 —

I awoke the next morning in my hotel bed, Stephen lying at my side with his eyes still closed, the golden glow of the brass bed rails like a promise of good fortune.

Though dawn was just breaking, I began to think about the many activities I wanted to fit in before my time in this transformational city would come to an end. There was shopping to do, another visit to the Blue Window to see Wini, and—most compelling—time with Stephen. Any second of time that I could squeeze in to be with him.

Beside me, Stephen rustled in slow wakefulness, his knee brushing up against my thigh. I turned onto my side to face him, to see what he looked like when first greeting the day, but his look was expressionless in the subtle light. My pulse quickened. What did this mean? Was it a look of satisfaction? Uncertainty? Regret?

"Are you frightened of me, darling? Is it my bed hair?" he asked.

"No." I giggled with relief. "Just trying to read your expression. Are you okay?"

"Of course I'm okay, love. I'm literally the finest I've ever been."

"Oh," I said, further relieved. "All right then." I looked at him intently. "Do you always awaken this way, with no expression?"

"Well, I suppose I do. Don't we all? Am I to open my eyes and shout out peals of laughter? Ha! Ha ha!" He tossed his hands in the air and began to writhe playfully, like a child being tickled.

"Oh, you!" I reached down and kissed him before he could close his mouth, feeling the vibration of his throaty laughter as our lips met, my tongue finding its own pleasure as he had taught me last night. He pulled me closer and began stroking my body exactly where I yearned for his touch, his own body responding in sync until, feeling emboldened, I positioned myself on top of him.

The layers of my cocoon of melancholy had been pierced, and I had emerged, dazzled by this new life into which I had entered, by the dramatic shift that had taken place. No longer was I Betty Ley, listlessly tagging along with life. I had *become* Elizabeth, the woman I'd imagined myself to be, living the life to which I'd long been drawn. And this man with whom I had spent the night was the man I loved.

The complexities of our situation had not changed, but an invisible wand had wondrously erased any trace of doubt from my mind. Stephen was who I wanted to lie next to in my bed, whose expression upon first awakening I wanted to see, whose laughter I wanted to fold into, and whose body I wanted to make love to on a Wednesday morning, on any morning. Stephen was the man I loved. I loved him with demanding certainty.

In time, we roused ourselves out of bed and readied for breakfast. Together we walked hand-in-hand in the direction of the hotel dining room, where crisp white linens covered round tables and the smell of bacon caused me to salivate with hunger.

I had crossed an irreversible line and, euphoric as I was, I knew that impending conversations were necessary—starting with a conversation about Ruth. We had to delve under the surface to offer each other full exposure of our triumphs and our failures.

"Stephen, I'm sorry if bringing up this topic is uncomfortable for you. But Ruth . . . Are you sure there isn't anything you want to tell me about your marriage? It just seems that maybe you'd want someone to talk to about it. I'm comfortable with listening."

Stephen looked aside, letting out a paltry "ha" of indifference, and tightened his grip on my hands. I remained quiet. After a beat he shook his head. "There is little I wish to say on this topic, darling."

It was, perhaps, no coincidence that our table held in its vase a late-blooming black-eyed Susan—the flower of encouragement—and so I tried again. "There is a saying my grandmother had that I suppose applies to all sorts of things in life. She would say, 'Just because you don't acknowledge it, doesn't mean it's not there.' I know that your divorce just came up recently, Stephen. It's okay for you to feel whatever it is you feel. You don't have to shut it out."

He released his hold on my hands and leaned back into his chair, searching his thoughts. "Very well then, darling," he began after a moment. "With utmost honesty, I feel relieved. I've battled with love for Ruth for quite some time, and I don't believe in love and war together in one sentence. Those words are of two distinct and opposite meanings and are simply not meant to be housed together. Love is beauty. Love is the grandest of emotions."

He looked tenderly at me, and I folded my hands together on the table and leaned in, eager for him to continue.

"Do you know, I've told her that I loved her but twice in all this time? Yes, two times.

"The first was the moment of our engagement. It was late in the morning, and a great fog had surrounded the villa in which we had unwittingly found ourselves during a weekend drive. The fog created a marvelous sense of security, a closeness that prompted me to feel as if I would be unable to live a reasonable life without her in it. I told her that I loved her, and I asked for her hand in marriage. She accepted the proposal but did not reciprocate the acknowledgment of love. I had assumed this was her way, that she did not use the word with ease. Frankly, it didn't even seem like a necessity at that moment."

Our beverages were delivered, and he poured the hot tea into his cup. I sipped my coffee and listened to the continuation of his story.

"The second time was our wedding day." He added a splash of milk to his tea and gave it a single stir. "Though she spoke the word in our vows, when I expressed my love to her that night, she responded with an endearing smile but again did not return the sentiment."

He set down the spoon and folded his hands underneath his chin. "I recently came to learn, however, that she does indeed utter the sacred words. They appeared to flow with ease the night of our return to the States, while at the Blue Window when she and Walter sidled off to a wall near the back, not realizing that I was passing by."

Love, how it flows with stealth, I thought. Swirling in circles around one, whisking past another with inscrutable dismissal.

"Why do you think she married you?" I asked, though I might have guessed the answer.

He removed his pipe from his side pocket and filled it half full of tobacco, which he tamped down and lit with practiced efficiency. A sweet, earthy ribbon of smoke drifted toward me, and I hoped that it would infuse my blouse so that I could sense his presence for hours to come.

"Why did she marry me? Status, perhaps. Comfort. Security. With me she did not lack for any measure of material goods or for the luxury of travel. And why did I marry her, you may wonder?" He looked at me with a pipe smile, the left side of his mouth a comma. "I believe that I understood, but did not acknowledge, her lack of love for me. She was—is—an intriguing woman, and I was a single man properly racing toward middle adulthood in a fashion that did not please me: alone."

"If only you'd had Grandmother's wisdom sooner. Guess you should've been seeking out an Iowa farm girl all along." I reached out for his hand.

"Yes, yes. They surely are of innocent ilk, are they not?" He shot me a teasing smile and once again took up my hands in a marvelous grasp.

"Grandmother also said, 'Just because you think something doesn't mean it's true.' Ruth could very well have loved you, Stephen. Or still love you for that matter. But maybe she loves Walter more. Maybe she loves you both in different ways."

"Such precarious words you speak!" he exclaimed with intentional drama. "You might well be sent directly to the convent if anyone other than me heard you utter such audacious thoughts!"

I grinned at his silliness.

"Ruth has now hired an attorney," he continued after a moment, the tone of the announcement more like a notice being read from the *Chicago Tribune* than a life-altering disclosure. "The paperwork will be sent here to the States and should arrive within two weeks."

"Oh, my."

"But a very good 'oh, my.' I am ready to release what should never have been captured to begin with." He took another sip of his tea and sat back into his chair, as did I.

"Thank you for opening up, Stephen," I offered to him. "I'm sorry that I don't really know what to say." Knowing he would soon be an unmarried man was a step forward on the complicated path toward our future together. Perhaps the easiest step.

"There is no need for you to say anything; however, I do appreciate your having asked. It does provide a sense of relief to have talked about this."

"That makes me happy to hear."

"How about I show my appreciation by way of an outing on the *Winsome Lady*?" Stephen asked in a sudden turn of conversation. "What does my dear little winsome lady say to that?"

"Yes! Yes, I would like that very much!" I immediately reined in my excitement, wanting to ensure I was respectful of the conversation we were having. "Stephen, would you like to talk further about this? About the divorce? About Ruth?"

"Why, I do not believe I would, thank you. It is a thing that must be, and one that is desired by both of us. A formality I fully expect to move along swiftly."

I momentarily wondered what Will's reaction would be if I, like Ruth, declared our marriage in ruins, told him that a different life was awaiting me far away, across the ocean even. But I crumpled the paper-thin thought into a ball before it seeped in further. I would not go there just yet. I would be right here, right now, and nowhere else.

The waiter returned to refill my coffee, apologizing for the delay in our breakfast.

"Perfectly acceptable," replied Stephen and nodded at him. "Darling! Your gift still awaits its unveiling."

The waiter immediately returned with the red box, which he set on the table before me.

"You sneaky man," I said to Stephen, astonished that he had set up this ruse while I was readying myself for breakfast.

He watched as I pulled delicately at the long ribbons, unraveling them fully before I lifted the lid. Inside was an envelope with my name penned across it. I glanced up at him before opening it, and he nodded in encouragement.

Inside was a single sheet of rich linen paper, the color of a white rose, with his name and address embossed at the top: *Stephen L. Covington, Brighton, England.* The space below was filled with his handwriting, script that rippled with elegance. Again, I looked at him before reading the words.

"For you, darling."

I held the paper gently in both hands and silently read.

Just as snow falls from the heavens,
whispering wings of angels curling soft flurries into singular patterns,
their destiny given from above, yet dedicated to the earth,
laying claim to every barren inch below;
just as this do I love you,
with lavish artistry,
with elusive mystery,
with infinite abundance.

———◇———

Before I had even opened the door to the Blue Window, I could hear Wini's voice on the other side, its perfect pitch echoing across the empty room during a midweek rehearsal. I closed the door quietly behind me and stood nearby to watch.

Though her eyes were closed, I could sense the music coursing through her body, her hand conducting an invisible force as she sang the lyrics to a song that was rife with longing. Had she ever been in love, I wondered? Had she ever experienced that wondrous freefall into an abyss of pleasure when with another?

I listened briefly, not wanting to interrupt, and left as surreptitiously as I had entered. My questions went unanswered, but I was to see her again on the penultimate night of my stay, when I would attend another full performance. I scampered up the steep wooden steps and back into the zealous daylight. There were but a handful of quickly passing days before me to check off my list of reasons for coming to this magnificent city, distractions aside.

I recalled a children's shop two blocks north and set out in that direction. The girls would delight in a gift, perhaps easing the discomfort of having missed me these past several days. I considered a new wooden puzzle for Sage and maybe a sock monkey for Louise, smiling as I imagined the delight of my little ones.

"Elizabeth! Is it you?"

I turned in the direction of the voice that held a familiar ring and discovered my companion from the train, her hand waving as she hurried gracefully toward me.

"Helena! I can't believe it's you!" I said as she neared, the astonishment of her appearance causing baffling tears to prick at my eyes.

"Nor can I! Oh, give me a hug, darling!" Helena wrapped her arms around me then applied a kiss to each cheek, careful not to mar them with the fuchsia-colored lipstick she wore.

"Tell me—oh, I can see it in your glow. Your trip has exceeded your expectations. Am I right?"

I felt a teasing blush warm my face as if Stephen were standing beside me, our hands clasped in exposed lovers' egotism.

"You were certainly right about the city having a lot to offer. I've experienced so much," I exclaimed, my hands spreading outward in illustration. "But I'm disappointed that I have to leave in less than a week."

"Then you must return. On the Midwest Arrow, of course!"

I nodded as my thoughts briefly flitted back to the memory of our introduction.

"Oh, dear! I just remembered . . . I have something for you."

As Helena rummaged through her fur-encased purse, I wondered what she could possibly have for me, for surely neither of us had expected to run into one another. She began pulling out a long silver chain that soon resulted in a necklace punctuated with a locket. It was the locket that Will had given me for our anniversary, inside a photo of him that I had proudly shown to Helena while on the train. The locket that I had not given thought to since my first night in Chicago when I was unable to find it in my purse. I blinked rapidly, attempting to stave off tears.

"My dear. I am so very sorry . . . I found it on the sidewalk next to the taxi after you left. I should have returned it to you at the Dominican much, much sooner."

I held tightly onto it and wrung my way through a few words of gratitude. "No, please don't worry about that," I managed. "It's just that . . . well, this is such a surprise. Seeing you is so wonderful."

She rested her hand on my elbow. "As it is you, Elizabeth. I hope the necklace brings you much joy."

I smiled politely, wiping away the few tears that had escaped. What Helena didn't realize was that my tears weren't for the loss of an object.

"I would love to hear all about every minute of your time here, but regretfully I have a meeting I must attend and am running slightly behind."

"Oh, of course. I do want you to know how happy I am to have run into you. And, thank you for returning the necklace. That means a lot to me."

"A brief, though fortuitous reunion! You are most welcome." Again, Helena air-kissed both my cheeks and walked off with another wave of her hand toward the life that awaited her.

The sterling silver of the locket was still polished to a shine. I did not bother to open it, but instead deposited it into a hidden pocket of my purse. I snapped the clasp closed and resumed walking in the direction of the children's shop.

The sounds of construction became more pronounced as I neared the shopping area, the latest high-rise building the city to new heights. I arrived at Stanhopes and stepped into a world emblazoned with color. As I closed the door behind me, the noise of construction disappeared as quickly as my wandering thoughts. I had landed in a world of whimsy, where trains chugged along on tracks that encircled the room and porcelain dolls were dressed in capes and stoles created from top-notch fabrics. The discordant sound of the plucking of a keyboard extended from the back of the store, and I considered whether Louise might prefer a musical instrument over a sock monkey.

I wandered around considering the many options, when my attention was captured by a young boy, perhaps age five or six, standing before an easel. A barn in traditional red had been painted directly in the middle of the paper, a ball of yellow sun above. He was now working on a tree, painted in bright green with splotches of purple.

"That's a nice tree. What kind is it?" I asked.

He kept up with his task, remaining silent. His cheeks were the color of tulips that stood out stunningly against white skin.

"Is it a crabapple tree?"

His head moved slowly from side to side.

"Hmm. Is it a plum tree?"

No.

"Am I getting warm?"

His lips formed a shy smile, and he began working on a stream across the bottom of the scene.

"Can I eat the purple off the tree?"

This time his head moved up and down quickly before he paused and frowned.

"This is my son, Eddie."

I turned toward the voice of the proprietor and introduced myself, commenting on his son's artistic abilities while noticing that the red hair of the boy was not due to the genes of his father.

"He likes to paint the scenes that he saw last spring when we drove into the countryside. Lived in the city all his life with everything he could need around him, but a trip to the countryside—he hasn't let go of it."

"The country has an appeal," I turned back to Eddie. "I live on a farm."

He looked up at me, bright with hope as if I were going to sweep him away into this magical land that he was creating.

"And my farm looks very much like your painting, Eddie. The barn and the stream both. But I don't have any mysterious trees with questionable fruit growing from their branches."

Eddie smiled and finally revealed his secret. It was a cherry tree in blossom, the idea taken from a book on George Washington, his father explained, and one he thought looked just right on his colorful farm.

"It sure does look just right! I wish I had thought of that for my farm."

"Time to clean up, Eddie. Your mother will be stopping in for you very soon. Thank the nice lady for her kind words."

Again, the boy smiled at me, his shining eyes more than enough thanks before he dashed off through a doorway leading into the back of the store. For Louise I bought a paint set, undeterred by the number on the price tag.

Chapter 18

— July 1975 —

Sage was relieved when she received a call inviting her to supper at Rosario's. She hadn't heard from Mother since dinner with that Neil guy, during which time her sly glances toward Sage hadn't gone unnoticed. Sage had sensed that something was off, but Sunday dinner hadn't been the time to inquire. And, if there was one thing Sage knew about her mother, it was that if she were going to divulge information—which had always been a baffling rarity—it would be in her own good time.

When she arrived, ten minutes early, Elizabeth was waiting with a half-empty margarita before her. Sage greeted her with a questioning look.

"Everything's fine," Elizabeth said as she stood to air kiss her daughter—a mannerism that Sage had known no one other than her mother to display.

She complimented her mother's new hairstyle—the feathered look was flattering—and noticed that the pink cotton dress she wore, a leftover from the late fifties, was still fashionably fitting.

"Dos margaritas! On ice for señora," the waiter declared with an exuberant smile as he handed Elizabeth a glass filled to the brim with golden liquid. "And for señorita, margarita blended." He stepped back, smiling at the drinks as if admiring either his ability to have carried them without spilling a drop or perhaps yearning for a draw himself.

"Gracias," the two said in unison, and he stepped away, carrying the tray under his arm.

"All right, down to business. What's going on, Mother? And don't say, 'Everything's lovely,' because I know you better than that. You're about to begin your second margarita for goodness sakes, and I just got here!"

"That's quite a greeting. I didn't realize I was giving off such worrisome vibes."

"And I can't say that I've ever heard you use the word *vibes* before."

"Well, it seems I'm now a hip woman."

Sage looked at her solemnly, and Elizabeth's smile quickly faded as she shored up her posture, a sure sign that the conversation was about to take a serious tone.

"I'm sorry if I worried you by not calling sooner. But I'm glad you're here."

"Happy to be. So, what's going on? You seem a little . . . unlike yourself."

Elizabeth shuffled her silverware, neatly aligning the knife, fork, and spoon upon her napkin before her words began to spill across the table. "There are some things I want to share with you, Sage. About my past. Things that resurfaced as the result of a visitor I've recently had."

"Neil?"

Elizabeth slid the fresh margarita closer and traced the straw through the liquid, the ice swirling precipitously close to the top of the rim. From a table somewhere in the back of the restaurant, shouts of "Feliz cumpleaños!" were heard, while a toddler called out for his own reasons from another table.

"Sage, tell me what it was like for you growing up. What was your perception of our family—before your father passed away?"

"Well," she said, her eyebrows raising in surprise over the question. "I guess it seemed pretty normal. I mean, Daddy was outside a lot in the fields and in the barn and wherever, and I know that you took care of Louise and me. Took care of the house. I guess that was just normal stuff."

"Yes. But how did it all feel to you? I realize you were still quite young when your father died, not yet eleven, but what did life *feel* like for you, before and after?"

"Wow, Mother. There were so many differences." Sage wasn't sure what she was getting at but was willing to follow her lead on what had, until very recently, been somewhat of an obscure topic of conversation.

"Before Daddy died, life was different. I mean, we lived on the farm and were surrounded by a small but certain group of people, if you know what I mean. I had no expectations, so it all seemed normal. When we moved to the city there was a new group of people in our lives, so the mood changed because of that, and because of his death, of course. I'd say the two can't really be compared."

"Yes . . . I suppose."

"But if I were to try to describe that mood, those feelings?" Sage continued, seeing that there was more her mother wanted from her. "It's weird, but I'd have to say life after Daddy— though of course sad—had in some ways become more satisfying. Don't get me wrong—" She glanced alarmingly at her mother. "It wasn't because Daddy was gone. I still miss him."

Reassured by Elizabeth's gentle touch, Sage finished her thought. "But there seemed to be a lightness, a loss of a foreboding . . . I don't know how to describe it. Maybe *foreboding* is the wrong word, but I remember that the years after he died were when I began to feel like the world opened up somehow. Maybe that just goes along with becoming a teenager. Maybe that had nothing to do with the changes that were happening in our lives."

"There is maturity, yes," Elizabeth replied, again with hesitation.

Sage took a long draw of her margarita. *God it's a strong one. Perfect.*

"I don't know how to pinpoint the mood, but—and I really do think this is outside of the maturity aspect—it was . . ." She paused. "Fresh. Yes, that's how I would describe the difference between the two times. It felt fresher." She noticed the waiter heading their way with a tray of food. "Wow, I never realized that until now."

He arrived, lowered the tray from overhead, and set a steaming beef burrito with rice and beans before Sage and a colorful plate of chicken and black bean enchiladas sprinkled with tomatoes in front of Elizabeth.

"Could you bring two more margaritas, please? In about ten minutes?"

"Make that just one," said Sage, in further disbelief that she was witnessing her mother imbibing.

"Sí!"

"I don't know what's gotten into you," said Sage after the waiter left their table, "but I think you'd better make this the last one."

Elizabeth agreed, even though the buzz she had begun to feel was a welcome relief to the disquiet of recent days. "So, what do you think may have caused that freshness of mood, as you described it?" she asked, furthering the conversation.

"Well, I suppose it was in part due to being in a new place. And—again, please don't take this the wrong way—but I think that you really changed after we left. At first you were withdrawn, not so much when it came to Louise and me, but toward others. At least that's what it had seemed like. I'm sure it was hard on you—losing your husband, having to make a living for us three—but after a while, you became more of who you are now, more comfortable in your skin, I would say."

Elizabeth took a bite of her food.

Sage wasn't certain where this conversation was going, but now she, too, considered it a necessary one.

"I was very saddened by your father's death, Sage," Elizabeth said after a moment. "That is true. But more so, it was guilt that I felt."

"Why would you feel guilty? You were a great wife."

Elizabeth set down her knife and fork, again lining them up, this time on her plate.

"I felt guilty because I wasn't always the wife your father deserved to have. He was a most loving and giving husband, and to be honest, I didn't reciprocate as I should have. Because I couldn't."

"Why? Or why not? I mean, you loved him, right?" Thoughts of her mother and Neil came to mind. *Oh, god.*

"Yes, of course I did. I loved him and appreciated him. But . . . this isn't easy to admit. Sage," she said, lifting her chin a notch.

Sage braced herself. *How could she? How could her own mother fall for a fool like Neil?*

"I was never passionate about my relationship with your father. There are some people in this world for whom appreciation and respect are enough, and there are others who require a deeper connection. No matter what I had tried, I couldn't seem to summon that deeper vein of love for your father. Passionate love, like he deserved."

A loud peal of laughter from the booth behind Sage felt like an insult to their conversation. She wished that she had ordered a second margarita after all and considered summoning the waiter, who was never too far away.

Elizabeth, seemingly oblivious to the ambient noise, continued. "When I was young, I had a lot of dreams for my future, ideas of who I wanted to be and how I wanted to live. I thought I'd live in the city, find a job in a creative field. But these dreams weren't realistic, considering where I was raised. And then, a few years after my marriage to your father, I found myself walled in by a state of unbreakable sadness. I realized that I would never live that kind of life. What I wanted, and what your father and I lived, were two very different scenarios. When I married him I just always assumed we would grow old together, and that would be that, satisfied or not."

"Have you ever talked to anyone about this?"

"A doctor? Oh, no! I can hardly believe I am telling you these things now."

"So, you feel guilty because you married a man who wasn't your Romeo? I hate to say it, Mother, because this man happened to be my father, but I don't think you're alone in the world."

Elizabeth cocked her head to the side. "You mean you're not angry with me?"

"Angry? How could I be? You're human."

A frown formed on Elizabeth's face, her eyes narrowing as if trying to peer point-blank into her daughter's thoughts. "I have to say, I am surprised. And . . . very relieved. But I want you to know that I would have stayed with your father, had he survived."

"So again," Sage shook her head, "why the guilt?" She had a feeling that the lid had only begun to be twisted off this jar of secrets.

Elizabeth brushed a stray hair behind her ear. "Sage, do you recall my mention of a trip to Chicago during dinner on Sunday?"

"Well, yeah! You never go anywhere. It was definitely a surprise. Though I do have the slightest recollection of your having been away for a while when I was young."

"The thing is, I went to Chicago to refresh myself." Elizabeth spoke cautiously. "I couldn't shake the feeling that something was missing, that this wasn't how I was meant to live. That I had landed in someone else's shoes. Parts of my life I wanted to hold tightly onto and never let go—you and Louise, of course—yet I felt a calling to set out on a treasure hunt for my own spirit. In part to release Frankie, if that was even possible."

Elizabeth's eyes dampened. Sage had no idea that after all these years, the memory of Frankie would still carry such emotional weight.

"Even before his birth, I'd been out of sorts for several months. And then, on the day of his funeral, I had a moment . . . There was an experience." She pushed away her plate and took a sip of her margarita. "What I mean to say is, I knew . . . I knew with certainty that I had to explore life in a different way. How did I know that I wasn't really living a different life elsewhere?"

"Mother—"

"I know," Elizabeth interrupted. "It sounds ridiculous, but life growing up in St. Timothy—it was so different from what you experienced. There weren't the choices back then that you have now."

"Mother, you have a stream of liquid dripping down the front of your dress." Sage handed over her napkin. "Here, dip and dab."

Elizabeth looked down in surprise and made a feeble attempt at removing the stain.

"There probably weren't as many options back then, but you're starting to sound like Louise. Living a different life elsewhere?"

Elizabeth made one last attempt at removing the stain, then set down the napkin in resignation.

"What would you do if your life had turned out differently, Sage? What if, instead of working in research, you were pumping gas at the Corner Mart because you didn't have the opportunity to go to college? Would you hold the handle of the gas pump, letting flies buzz around you day after day? Or, would you take off the blue overalls and walk down the street to find something different?"

"If you put it that way, sure I'd move on, I guess. I mean, I know what you're getting at. It just sounded weird how you put it. But go on." Sage had the urge to retrieve a notebook and pen from her purse and record the coming conversation for later review.

"At first, your father was against my going. He could see that there was something wrong and, having always been the more practical one, suggested I talk with Dr. Grimmsrud. But a doctor couldn't prescribe how to fill the void within me, and he knew it. So after a while, he agreed to let me go away for a few weeks."

The waiter stopped by their table, offering a dessert of churritos or fried ice cream. Sage and Elizabeth declined, and he gathered their plates onto a single arm and returned to the kitchen.

"The first few days of my stay, I fell in love with Chicago. Oh, Sage, there were women dressed in the latest cuts, with hats of the most fantastic designs. There were buildings—businesses, hotels, theaters—that I could never have imagined. Lights and bustle were everywhere. I littered the bureau in my hotel room with napkins and paper covered in notes, which I clearly instructed the maid to leave because I wanted to remember all of it."

"Do you still have them? I'd love to see."

"No, they didn't make it home with me."

"That's too bad. What else did you do, other than gawk at other women and bricks?" Sage asked with a teasing smile.

"I probably was gawking! I was awkward at that time. Big dreams, no experience. But to answer your question, yes, I 'gawked,' though at a lot more than clothes and brick. There were museums, Sage, with works of some of the world's greatest artists: Van Gogh, Matisse, and emerging artists like Motherwell. Works of art that back then I had never imagined I would see in person—right there before me. There were fancy foods I'd never even heard of and certainly had never tasted. Live theater. Taxi cabs. Businessmen rushing about the city. Musicians. So much sophistication. It was like nothing I'd ever seen and everything I wanted to be a part of.

"And there was the water . . . Seeing Lake Michigan was a dream come true for me. You may not believe this, but ever since I can recall, I've been drawn toward the idea of large bodies of water—lakes, oceans, seas. This was my first experience with one, and almost a day did not pass without my taking in the lakeshore."

"Wait, did you just say you are drawn to water? You, who refuse to climb into a canoe?"

"Well, I didn't say I'm drawn to being *in* the water."

"Hmph, now that is an astonishing revelation!"

As she watched her mother describe the city, Sage noticed how her forehead softened, how her eyes opened wider. "What did you do at the lake?" she asked. "It was too cold to wade in, right?"

"Oh yes, far too cold in October, though mostly the weather was lovely during my stay. Anyway, it wasn't an area in which one would wade. But there was a pier, where rows of sailboats were docked."

The waiter set down the check, crowded hash marks alongside the word *margarita*. Unhesitating in her story, Elizabeth opened the clasp of her purse and pulled forth bills from her wallet while he stood nearby, his smile unrelenting. The expansive dining area, Sage noticed, was now nearly empty.

"I was rolling along on the wheels of glee in the city," Elizabeth continued. "I even went to a lounge alone at night to listen to music. Can you believe that? Back then I wasn't apprehensive about doing so. Now, I wouldn't dream of doing such a thing."

"I assume you met people there? There was Neil, of course," Sage said, leaving an opening in hopes that her mother would take the bait.

"Yes, there was him. Though he was a sidebar, if you will. I never spent any time with him while in Chicago. In fact, we'd spoken no more than a handful of words to each other during my time there."

Thank god, was Sage's first thought. Then, *how odd*. She'd assumed that her mother and Neil had forged some manner of friendship, considering his recent visits.

The bell on the restaurant door rang yet again as the last of the remaining patrons exited.

"I think we'd better leave, Mother."

Elizabeth looked around the restaurant, noticing the dearth of patrons. "Oh, but . . . Well, I suppose I can't exactly drive myself home, can I?"

"No," Sage said, shaking her head. "You, Mother, will stay at my place tonight. We'll stay up until all hours of the night if we must!"

"Like a slumber party with my daughter."

"Like a slumber party. C'mon. Let's go."

The two walked arm-in-arm outside and into the parking lot, stopping first at Elizabeth's Falcon to lock the doors, then crossing back toward Sage's lonely sedan under the lamp post. The cool air was refreshing, and Elizabeth was glad there were no more margaritas to order. The intoxicating effect had felt good for a while, but she could foretell the appearance of a headache in the not-so-distant future.

It was a short drive to Sage's apartment, where Elizabeth took in the surroundings of the place while Sage brought Bono outside. It had been quite some time since she'd last been here. There was a lingering smell of morning sausage combined with vanilla-scented candles, and the place was unsurprisingly tidy. She moved into the kitchen and turned on the tap, filling a glass half full.

Moments later, Bono clickety-clacked his way back through the doorway and bounded arthritically toward Elizabeth with an excitement that belied his age. Bono, whom Sage had rescued from the side of the road just four years earlier, had since been the most loyal of dogs. The missing patches of golden fur and ribs that had been hungrily exposed against his matted coat were now replaced with healthy fullness.

Sage and Elizabeth plunked down onto the sofa, Bono jumping up to nestle between the two.

"Stephen and I met at the Blue Window," Elizabeth began once they'd settled in.

"Stephen? Who's Stephen? Do you mean Neil?" Sage asked, assuming the slip was an effect of the margaritas.

"No, I mean Stephen." There it was, the eggshell cracked open, its amorphous contents ready to be released.

Elizabeth spent the next hour walking Sage through the distant story, from the moment in which she'd felt the first whisper of attraction and subsequent surprise of love, to the yearning to be with this man she'd known for but a glimmer of time. Despite the many questions that arose, Sage listened intently as the pent-up fountain of memories was released, imagining the unfamiliar characters act out a surrealistic tale. And in the end, when her mother's confession came to a close, there was just one question that Sage was compelled to ask. One that she felt she somehow deserved an answer to.

"Was he more than Daddy?"

Elizabeth returned Sage's steady gaze and took her daughter's hands into her own. "Different from Daddy. I'm being completely open and honest, sweetie. Different, for there isn't a comparison. Your father fulfilled the part of me that needed to be a mother. Stephen made my heart dance in a way that I'd never before experienced, that I didn't realize was possible."

Sage got up and walked to the window, looking out into the dark of the night, absorbing this new information. Bono sighed a stuttering exhalation, unaware that she had left his side, and the wall clock across the room struck twelve. A new day had arrived, and Elizabeth's secret now demanded to be relabeled.

"I invited Neil to dinner so that you could give me your evaluation of him."

Sage turned back toward her mother, conflicting emotions playing tug-o-war in the aftermath. "I don't understand."

"Your opinion of him as a person. Does he seem untrustworthy or honest?"

"Untrustworthy or honest?"

"Yes."

"Mother, you just told me you were in love with another man named Stephen, and now you want me to tell you what I think of his friend Neil?"

"I understand how strange this must sound." All at once she stood, somewhat off balance, and covered her face with her hand. "It must sound mad. But I'm not asking for your opinion because I have romantic feelings toward Neil. That would never happen. It's just that . . ." She dropped her hand and turned away for a moment, composing herself. "There was an accident. The last time I was with Stephen, there was an accident," she said with resignation. "And I want your opinion of Neil because he is the only person that may be able to tell me whether Stephen survived."

Chapter 19

—— Elizabeth 1948 ——

I let down my hair, its loose waves laced with auburn streaks, lightened by the long months of sunshine, and stepped gingerly into the satin dress. It was the color of midnight, with a length of fabric that nearly kissed the floor and a butterfly-cut neckline that dipped daringly low. A generous bow at the waistline emphasized my curves while detracting from maternal flaws, and matching gloves covered my hands and forearms to a point just over my still-roughened elbows.

Stephen was the one who had first spotted it while shopping together two days prior, insisting that it had been designed with me in mind. His eyes lit up when I walked out of the fitting area, his look reassuring me that the search was over. He was right. Now, as I looked at my reflection in the mirror, I felt as if I could hold hands with Aphrodite.

A taxicab met us at the Dominican just as a light rain began to fall. I had come to wonder if the city was somehow immune to water loosening from the clouds, for the weather had been nearly foolproof to this point, but clouds had moved in surreptitiously during the afternoon, gathering untimely.

When we arrived at our destination, the driver came to a stop and waited in line at the entrance, as did several other taxicabs, Packards, and even a Cadillac limousine. Once we had neared, Stephen, with one hand holding an umbrella and the other upon the small of my back, ushered me from the car into the Civic Opera House, where *Otello* was about to perform.

Inside, Roman columns stretched lavishly from the marble floor to the steeply arched ceiling, one that was smothered in gold gilt and held an array of oversized chandeliers that floated daringly above us. Elegantly dressed women and men milled about, some in conversation, others being entertained by a small grouping of musicians playing their string instruments, their music hovering in the air like a serene fog. The walls surrounding us matched the color of the wine that flowed freely about the glamorous room. Stephen garnered two glasses from a white-jacketed waiter as he guided me toward his friends with whom we would be sitting.

"Elizabeth," he said, pausing once we'd reached familiar faces. "I would like to introduce you to Julian and Dora, long-standing friends."

Julian bowed briefly in a friendly hello, and Dora gathered my hands warmly into hers.

"It is so very lovely to meet you, Elizabeth. And I must say," she paused, admiring my gown, "you must share with me where you found this treasure."

"I see another check to write in my future," said Julian, winking at Stephen. The two chuckled.

"Maxwell, meet Elizabeth," Stephen said, nodding toward another man who had neared our little group. Maxwell reached out to grasp my hand from underneath and pulled it toward his lips. I wasn't sure how to react and so smiled and remained quiet. He inquired to Stephen whether he'd been out for a sail in the warm weather.

"Elizabeth and I will be giving the mighty lake waters a run tomorrow. I have no doubt her introduction will be a fortuitous one." He moved me yet closer to his side.

Neil soon approached us, rounding out our oddly numbered group. "Betty," he greeted me with a nod.

"Hello, Neil. How are you?"

He smirked and not without obvious intention remarked, "Very well, overall. Though a little unsettled from a meatloaf sandwich I indulged in today at a corner café. If you've never had one, you should give it a try."

Once again, I responded with silence.

"Henry, Marie," said Stephen with a nod. "I hope you are well. May I introduce you to Elizabeth."

"Hello," replied Henry, though Marie raised her eyebrows and without a word turned toward Neil, who was lighting a cigar.

I didn't expect to be received open-armed by anyone, but Neil's snub and Marie's look of disdain nonetheless jolted me. I could feel my shoulders begin to droop and my smile turn wooden. *What am I doing here?* Dress shopping with Stephen, the hours of afternoon preparation, the refinement of the opera house—it was all a fairy tale. It wasn't my life; none of this was my life. An owl was descending swiftly upon me, its talons ready to burst the thin, glittering bubble that I'd been floating in, leaving behind a sticky residue on my satin dress. I was all of a sudden back at home, scrubbing stains from Will's work shirts and bumping my way out to the fields in the tractor with a lunch basket. That was my *actual* life, the one where opera was a foreign word, where clothes were worn for function, not display.

"By the way," Stephen leaned in and whispered in my ear. "Marie is a bloody nutter. A real-life Bertha Rochester." He winked, and I covered my mouth to stifle a laugh, setting aside the undue fret.

The fluctuating emotions of the previous evening had been washed away by the rain and the sun that once again brightened the corners of the city. I walked toward my destination, pausing to peer through the windows of shops displaying colorful spines of books and fashionable shoes polished to a brilliant gleam, even hardware with gadgets and tools I'd never seen. Stopping by the deli, by now a familiar eating spot, I ordered two ham sandwiches with a side of macaroni salad and a lemon bar. The bell on the door reverberated as I exited and turned toward the marina.

Several boats floated stolidly in their designated slips as if awaiting their captains to bring them to life on what surely had to be one of the last of the lovely autumn days. I saw Stephen through the shadow of a maple tree, bereft of its autumn coat, where he sat upon the faded wooden seat of a bench, the sun shining on his heart side. Our eyes met in greeting, the catch of a flame burning away the single thread that distanced us until his arms were once again around me, the world around us flickering into an exquisite moment of nonexistence as we kissed.

"Hello, my beautiful Elizabeth."

"Hello," I greeted with further kisses. "And hello . . . And hello."

As we approached the *Winsome Lady*, I felt like a young girl about to experience her first pony ride. I could hardly wait to feel the glide of the boat through the calm water on this, my maiden voyage.

Together we untied the moorings, freeing her from the slip. Stephen then took his place at the captain's wheel, I standing behind him, and slowly motored the boat toward the open water, carving a path through the labyrinth of docks where I had a close-up view of several other craft, some smaller and others significantly grander. The noise and vibration of the motor surprised me, and I hoped that it didn't have to be running the entire time we were on the water.

Once we had cleared the harbor, Stephen opened a bench from which he pulled a handful of asters that were no doubt very recently in habitat at the nearby park. I broke off the length of one stem, allowing just enough of it to remain so that I could tuck it above my ear. He pressed my head against him and inhaled the balsam-like scent of the flower, and a rush of desire passed through me. But the day was all the way ahead of us.

With the compass set due north and the water a mesmerizing blanket of deeply colored teal, we headed toward the vastness of the lake. The breeze of movement carried with it hopeful anticipation for nothing other than the joy of living. Seagulls circled in curious loops of hungry hope before moving on, the last sign of life that we were to see for the remainder of the day.

My thoughts returned to the previous night at the opera, to Neil, who more than once had left me wondering what beneficial qualities Stephen saw in him, outside of his architectural expertise.

"Tell me, Stephen," I began. "Neil—have you known him for a long time?"

"Neil, you say. Well now, let me consider this for a moment." He paused to recollect time. "Was it in May or June those many years ago that I came to know the old chap? It was at a garden banquet, I can tell you that. Ruth insisted we attend during our first trip to Chicago, despite not knowing a soul there. Nor were we formally invited. If you knew the dauntless woman, you would understand immediately that such a triviality would not hold her back from getting what she wants. So that was the venue, the year 1938. It was the year oil was discovered in Saudi Arabia, though how the two events connect in my mind, I cannot say."

He reached for his cocktail.

"Neil." He released a quick, kindly laugh. "Neil introduced himself by handing my wife a glass of champagne, which immediately garnered her attention and created for him a cozy little spot in her good graces. Ruth thanked him brilliantly, immediately entwining her arm with his and steering him toward a group of unsuspecting attendants who were enjoying conversation near a trellis of climbing yellow roses. I remember the color, for it seemed the entire day was yellow with the promise of warmth and joviality."

"And what did you do while they kept company with each other?"

"Well, I'd like to say I found delight in those in attendance, having the time of my life, as you Americans are wont to say. But it was gazing upon the crowd from a surreptitious location near the garden gate that gave me satisfaction. I watched women gush over flowerbeds that matched the color of their pretty dresses. I watched a man with a wooden toothpick hanging from his lips overtake the conversation at any opportunity. I began a game with myself, studying others to determine whether the day would hold any surprises.

"Excuse me, darling," Stephen said as he stepped away from the wheel. He cut the engine, and I watched as he cranked a small wheel to unfurl the jib, setting it in place, then did the same to the mainsail. Though the breeze had picked up somewhat, I was still bewildered by the amount of air that filled the capacious fabric. He then moved back to the captain's wheel and maneuvered the sloop forward, the invisible power of the air propelling us toward the future of our day.

My palms broke into a sweat at the sudden speed with which we were moving. I stepped up behind him and placed my hands softly on his shoulders, kneading his muscles with intentional tenderness to take the focus off my own anxiety. He leaned back, his head nesting into my breasts, which immediately created a new energy within my body. I had nearly forgotten the question I had asked about Neil but was reminded by the flower that had untucked itself and fallen to the deck.

"And were there? Surprises?"

"Not one. Our debut event had been eventless."

I was let down, as I had thought that some revelatory information about Neil would be told. "So you were at a garden party. And Neil and Ruth became friends. And with you also?"

"Yes." Stephen lit his pipe, hunching forward to shelter a match, and the wide-open space quickly consumed the smoke. "Yes, we then became fast friends. He was different from the other men I'd met. There was something of an appeal to him, as if he were toting around a bag of curiosities.

"Soon enough, we began meeting with a crowd of merrymakers who frequented the lounges of Michigan Avenue with religious regularity. In Ruth's eyes, Neil became a source of great enjoyment, for he knew those to know, those for whom entertainment was of the utmost importance. She became the malt to his vinegar, stealing away with him and the bunch at any opportunity. And within a short time, whether I was with her did not matter so much as her being with them. The crowd."

There was no disappointment in his voice, simply a factual account.

"The old chap grew on me as well. Later that month he gave me a tour of the architectural highlights of the city, and I became enthralled with the art of it, with his art. And I found that he entertains with the wittiest comments when relaying the inside gossip."

"Really? Neil is witty?"

"Ha ha! Seems a bit of an oxymoron considering his look, doesn't it? But he is witty, yes."

I thought about this for a moment, as difficult as it was to imagine, then continued my questioning. "And since then, the three of you have spent a lot of time together?"

"Oh, absolutely. Whenever we are here in Chicago, he is an accoutrement."

"I have to say, he gave me goosebumps when I met him."

"Ha! Yes, he has a way of doing that. And do you know, darling, that after all this time I still cannot determine with certainty whether that self-display is a part of his 'witty' character, or timidity. I don't know if he intends to induce discomfort or if he is apprehensive. Indeed, he is a bit of an enigma."

It wasn't the first time that I found it difficult to keep up with Stephen's rich vocabulary, his fence-straddling ambiguity. "So, you think of him as a *very* good friend then?"

"A *very* good friend? Do I have those, I wonder? Or do I simply have friends without labels? Hmm," he said, laying his finger on his chin as if in deep thought.

I pulled my hands from his shoulders and whispered in his ear. "You would not call me a very good friend?"

He pulled me onto his lap, the scent of tobacco surrounding us like a shroud as he brought his lips to mine and pressed fully, enduringly.

Now out in the open waters, Stephen, eyeing the sun and the instruments, got up to adjust the sails in order to set us adrift. As I watched him, I realized how swiftly my time in Chicago was nearing an end. My longing for this man had grown by the minute, and I could no longer postpone a conversation about our future, as I had so hastily done the other day when he had broached the topic. But that delay had been a necessity; now the halcyon setting refrained from pulling me—us—in any one direction.

He finished his task and momentarily dipped into the cabin before sitting on the bench across from me. He had retrieved a bottle of champagne and uncorked it with a twist, pouring half a tumbler for each of us. I could have counted on one hand the number of times I had drank alcohol during the daytime—an occasional beer following a hot afternoon of baling hay—but certainly never champagne.

"Stephen, I'm sorry it's taken me so long to talk about this, but we do need to address things. What will become of us." I paused. "The train takes me back home in three days."

"That we do, darling." He waited for me to continue.

"I want to be with you, Stephen. I don't think that I can *not* be with you."

Speaking the words aloud made my heart quicken. I was stepping over a line from the hallucinatory life we'd been living to wide-awake reality. I had been so determined to be in the moment that I'd ignored the niggling question my mind had asked of me in recent days: the question of what would become of us. But we were now at a crossroads, the choosing of our direction a necessity.

"And I have made my desire clear. My intention is to be with you." Stephen took my hands into his, his knees bumping up against mine. "I also understand that your situation is far different from mine." He kissed my hands once, gently, and looked into my eyes. "Live with me, Elizabeth. Bring your children. Move here to Chicago, and I will relocate here permanently."

I looked toward the direction of my home that was so, so far away. "It's not that easy."

"I'm not saying that it is, darling, but it is unavoidable. We cannot live an ocean apart."

I knew in my heart that if it were just me, I would have said yes without delay. As painful as it would be to hurt Will, we would both survive and carry forth. But how could he and I, two parents, raise children with that kind of distance between us? Stephen moving to Iowa was, of course, absurdly out of the question.

"I can afford to have you usher them back and forth to spend time with their father whenever you see fit. Elizabeth, we will buy you train tickets at your whim. We will buy you a car. We will make it as comfortable for your daughters as can be."

With this suggestion came a flutter of possibility. Without the factor of affordability, and without the constancy that being a farm wife entails, it just might be possible to keep their father in their life, despite the distance. The girls were young enough to take on a new lifestyle without too much disruption. Here would be a new beginning for us, a life with Stephen. And here would also be Wini, a built-in friend.

"That would make it more doable," I said, but the hesitation in my words was obvious. I squeezed his hands. "I don't want to spend a minute without you, Stephen, but I'm sure we both realize that if we do this, it will take some time to settle. I don't know how long."

"If we hire Ruth's attorney, it could be mere hours!" he winked, resetting the mood. "I respect your desire to put things in order within that beautiful mind of yours, darling, but may I request that we reserve this conversation for later? I don't want us to lose the precious moments of this stunning day."

He was right, of course. This was not the time for a conversation that could just as easily take place in the dark of night. Already I felt lighter, possibility having woven itself into the splendid day.

"Cheers to us," I said, pulling my hand from his and raising my glass of champagne.

"À ta santé," he replied, lifting his to meet mine.

As I took my first sip, a stray gust of wind brushed my hair across my eyes, momentarily shielding my sight.

Chapter 20
— July 1975 —

There came a gentle knock at Sage's bedroom door followed by a head peering from behind. Sage pulled her eyes open—seven-thirty—and remembered that Mother had slept on the sofa, which was probably why Bono wasn't at her side expecting his morning rubdown.

"Hey, Mother. Sleep well?"

"Well enough, I suppose. Considering," replied Elizabeth with a wan smile.

Sage recalled the confession that had occurred last night—Chicago, Stephen—but it now felt distant, as if she and Mother had been characters in a movie playing out someone else's life.

"How are you feeling?"

"Similar to how I look, I imagine," said Elizabeth. "Sweetie, would it trouble you to give me a ride back to Rosario's for my car? I should get back home."

"Sure thing."

Sage roused herself out of bed and dressed and was soon backing out of the driveway. Fog had settled in overnight, giving the passing newspaper boy the appearance of an apparition.

"Please don't let my story bother you," said Elizabeth as soon as they began to move slowly down the street. "It's a story of my life, my mistakes—if that is how it's viewed. While the affair did, of course, alter the rest of my life, I consider my life to be a good one. But it changes nothing for you and for Louise because it is *my* story." She turned toward Sage. "Do you understand what I'm trying to say?"

"I understand. I do," Sage replied. "It's possible that it made your life—all our lives—better. It sounds weird to say that, but that's what I was thinking when I went to bed last night." She paused. "Sometimes things just work out in the long run."

Sage said no more, keeping her focus on the road ahead, relieved that the fog offered her an excuse to remain quiet, to process this new knowledge of her mother's history.

They soon arrived at Rosario's, and Sage remained in her car as she watched her mother exit the parking lot. She leaned into the steering wheel and exhaled a long breath. Underneath her calm guise, a sense of restlessness had begun on the drive over and was now jumping up and down for Sage's attention. But what good would it do to sit here, in an empty parking lot in the fog?

She sat up and grabbed the wheel. "Okay, oh wise one, move forward." But before she was able to pull the gearshift into drive, she had arrived again in the graveyard.

The thick, oppressive fog was palpable, spreading a layer of dampness across Sage's bare arms. There she stood in a field, Daddy in his denims and a white T-shirt beside her, a growing stain creeping along the front of his worn shirt. She felt his calloused hands holding hers as he crouched down to meet her at eye level. "Watch your step now. Don't trip. It'll be dark soon." His look was unwavering, his words not so much a warning as a directive. Sage noticed how his brows were furrowed, though whether in pain or concern she couldn't discern. A rivulet of tears streamed down his cheek, dropping off to the ground at the steep curve of his jaw.

Sage shook her head as she came back to the present. She was now certain that these visions—this being the third—were not a fluke. A tight clenching began in her stomach as she considered all that had transpired in recent days. A series of spontaneous daydreams appearing out of thin air would've been enough of a disruption to her steadfast life. Enough would've been the night she'd just spent with her mother, listening to her narrate her autobiography from long ago, her love affair. Enough would've been Louise's tale of the growing co-op brawl; she never did know how to step away from danger, and Sage worried for her safety. At this moment, it was all enough. No longer was Sage leading her life. Somehow, she had become a mere spectator in the peanut gallery. A puppet whose movements were not of her own will.

"Well," she said aloud. "Welcome, Surprising Secret Life. Please join my guests, Curious Hallucinations and Frightening Food Fights. Make yourself at home."

Desperate to get back to the comfort of her home, Sage angled the gear lever to *D* and exited the parking lot. But within a short minute came a resounding *hooooooonk!* She white-knuckled the steering wheel and pressed hard on the accelerator, squinting in anticipation of impact as her car blasted forward. But no crushing of metal resounded, and she tentatively widened her eyes, feeling her heart thud anxiously in her chest.

Despite the urge to stop the car right then, Sage willed herself to continue driving ahead until she could find a place to pull over. She passed by a small line of cars in the opposite direction that were waiting at the red light—the light she'd missed—drivers and passengers looking at her with curious judgment. A glance in the rearview mirror confirmed that the cross traffic was moving along once again.

Sage pulled into the nearest parking lot, far enough away from the store that the red Shopko sign was obscured by the fog, and shifted into park. A rise of tears gave way before she could even cut the engine.

"What am I supposed to do with all of this?" She slammed her fists against the hard steering wheel, welcoming the blunt pain—a manageable pain—and let the rising simmer of her thoughts boil over into tears.

She cried for Daddy, lost to her so long ago and now, once again, terribly missed. She cried for Mother and the deep losses that she had endured throughout her life. She cried for herself, for the unknown meaning of these disruptions in her life, and of where she was to turn. With the fog wrapped around her like the arms of a protective grandmother, she let the hot tears stream out of her.

At last, Sage shook the dust from her thoughts. She restarted the car and, with extra caution, drove out of the parking lot and back onto the street, this time in the direction of Louise's place.

Louise wasn't home when Sage arrived, nor was Randy. The door, however, was not surprisingly unlocked. Sage pushed it open, its aged hinges exhaling a drawn-out groan, and walked in.

As she looked about the room, she felt a surprising amount of admiration for the barrenness of the place, so different from that of her own rooms, where collections of objects lined the shelves. Here everything felt light, with no unnecessary burdens.

In the center of the room stood a couch with a one-legged ashtray next to it and a worn woolen rug in front. A small table and two chairs lined the opposite wall, with two plants cupped by green macramé hangers in front of the single window above.

Sage sat on the faded brocade couch, a well-used "new" piece since she'd last been over, and found her knees rising above her hips as she sank toward the floor. Lying down seemed the more comfortable option, so she propped a crocheted pillow behind her head and gave in to the sensation of her backside once again settling low.

Her thoughts turned to Louise, and Sage wondered over the uncanny calmness of her sister's life. Sure, Louise would be the first one to jump from her chair if a debatable topic was at hand, but at her core she was unshakable, remarkably at peace with daily life, with the little slice of the world she occupied.

Francis, the neighborhood cat, glided in through the open window and strutted toward Sage, leaping onto her stomach and touching his cool nose to hers. His long fur was as soft as the rabbits that Sage and Louise had pretended were their own children back when they lived on the farm. He purred loudly, dipping his head with the beginning of each slow stroke, arching his back as her hand moved downward.

The narrow trail of Sage's thoughts began to relax as Francis crawled onto her chest and curled himself into a comma, his purr a soothing vibration. She rested her gaze on the ceiling mural, Louise's ever-changing work of art that now had an eagle soaring in the middle. A bolt of black created the appearance of a crack in what could have been a sky made up of swirls of unrelated color—swirls that moved, impossibly, the more Sage stared at them.

After a few minutes, she lifted the slumbering cat and pushed herself up. She noticed the corner of *Sensationally Alive* emerging from underneath the couch. She picked it up, saw that it was the newest issue, and flipped through the first couple of pages in search of Peck's editorial, which she quickly found.

> **The Residual of War: Are Field Chemicals for Life?**
> By Peck Wells
>
> Thirty years ago, we knocked the shit out of malaria by dousing our mosquito-and-lice-infested soldiers with DDT: Dichlorodiphenyltricloroethane. As scientists and manufacturers do, they began to question what else this deadly combination of carbon, hydrogen, and chlorine could be used for, and eventually somebody's light bulb turned on (Paul Herman Muller's, to be exact) and he shouted, "Bingo! Field pests!" Not to mention blasting related pests out of gardens, animals, institutions, and even homes—a true wonder chemical. Bye-bye mosquitoes . . . and bees, and butterflies, and birds, and fish. What, they didn't think its detrimental effects would spread? Didn't

think word would spread?

But a few years ago, the Environmental Protection Agency said, "Wait a gol darn minute. This might not be so good for ya after all, dontcha know." So, we're no longer spraying it as liberally as an air freshener at the church chili supper, but we're now regulated to using, well, different versions of DDT. Herbicides like hexachlorocyclohexane and Rid-Away: same idea, different formula.

The thing is, the composition might be different, yet when will the next iteration of Rachel Carson come along and say, "Whoa . . ."? Yeah, yeah, I know—we've churned out a hell of a lot of crops because they weren't being chipped away at by natty pests. But is there really no other way to do so? No possible way to both feed our growing masses and protect the earth?

How long will Mother Nature allow us to recycle our mistakes? How long do we continue to bury our heads in the chemical-laced mud until we realize this isn't gonna cut it for long?

Forever isn't a real thing, folks.

Dang, thought Sage. *This guy's for real.*
She set the magazine on the couch and left the apartment.

———◇———

As Elizabeth rounded the curve of her driveway, she noticed first the car, then the man. Neil was waiting for her on the front stoop.

A pang of disappointment coursed through her—he was the last person she wanted to see this morning—but then she realized that his timing couldn't be better. She'd been playing the game of polite hostess, but Neil had not given her any real information—except a letter, if that's what the envelope contained. A letter that she could not open until she had told her story to her daughter. A letter that she would not open until after her unwanted guest left the city, left her part of the world.

Elizabeth wondered if he was waiting around for her to read it, but she couldn't discern whether it was to witness her reaction or in hopes that she would reveal its contents to him. Either way, she couldn't shake the feeling that there was an underlying fallacy about the letter, about Neil's being there. It was time to move past this prolonged visit. It was time to ask the question. Had Stephen survived?

Chapter 21
—— Elizabeth, October 1948 ——

Sailing amid aquatic splendor, the *Winsome Lady* carried us yet farther from land as she once again cut through the deep navy waters that broke into mellifluous shapes in our wake, shapes dappled by the blazing sun. Stephen stood certain at the captain's wheel as he skippered the vessel toward an indiscernible destination.

Though he had eased me into the experience of sailing, Stephen now toyed with me as he tacked starboard, the sail flapping noisily as it moved to the opposite side of the boat where it instantly reinflated. The sloop dipped wildly toward the water, and I clung to the railing, wide-eyed. But Stephen's laughter reassured me, and I laughed along with him, all fear having evacuated from my thoughts.

After a while, he made further adjustments to slow the boat, and once again we drifted quiescently. There, on our own little floating island, we sipped on champagne and shared a picnic of scones with jelly (his contribution) and sandwiches and salad from the cafe (mine). It felt as if we had been doing just this for years. Stephen had become my lover but also my closest friend. I could no longer imagine my life without him.

I moved toward the bow, my thoughts, my spirit both remarkably joyous, as if I'd been transported to a place of unparalleled freedom. I was in love—with Stephen, yes, but also with my life. It was a feeling that I hadn't experienced in years, if ever before.

"Oh Stephen, I never imagined, at least in my adult life, that such a dream could come true. This feeling of . . . oh, I just feel so alive, Stephen! Being right here," I said, opening my arms wide and turning a circle. "I can hardly believe I'm here, right now, with you."

"Yet, here we are," he said, his own look one of absolute contentment.

"Here we are," I repeated as I imprinted the entirety of the moment into my memory.

I walked back toward him and retrieved my glass, finishing off whatever remained of the champagne. My hair, which had been firmly set into place that morning with combs and several sprays of Breck, had nonetheless blown about relentlessly, and I now removed the feeble accessories one by one, fully releasing the remaining locks from their hold. I shook my head, liberating it to its wild, natural state, the lapping water like music encouraging me on.

Stephen reached for a handkerchief from the pocket of his knit vest and began to slowly undress my face, watching his own movements as he smoothed the soft cloth over my skin, erasing the powder, the red lipstick. I surrendered to his touch, closing my eyes as he brushed away the blue eyeshadow that I had applied with such care earlier in the day.

Greedy warmth began to spread throughout my body. I felt his lips on my chin, on my ear and my neck, and opened my eyes as he began to undo each individual button of my cardigan, his eager fingers striving to work slowly. With my sweater discarded, I took a step back and removed the thin shell from underneath, then reached behind to pull open the zipper of my skirt, letting it fall onto the sun-warmed boards before sliding my stockings down the length of my legs.

Stephen stepped forward and reached toward me, but I wouldn't let him touch me. Not yet. I wanted to complete that which he had begun, complete it for him.

I turned and moved my hips seductively from side to side as I lowered my panties, pushing them aside with my bare foot. I then undid my bra, holding it at arm's length before dropping it, too, onto the growing mound of clothes at my feet. With suggestive leisure, I turned toward Stephen, now fully exposed.

Stephen had already discarded his vest and underlying shirt, and now his gaze caressed the skin of my shoulders, the trace of my breasts, the gentle curve of my belly. I placed my hands on his chest and slid them down, rounding in toward the buttons of his pants that, once loosened, dropped easily to the deck. I removed his undershorts, his socks—my touch as soft as silk—and ran my hands along his legs, continuing upward until they once again rested on his chest.

He closed the space between us, the fullness of his lips urging my own open with ease. Tremors of desire coursed through me; I needed him desperately, in every way. Stephen lowered me to the deck, where our bodies came together. Within moments, a surge of wild abandon radiated throughout my body, the sky our only witness.

With a loud *schwupp*, the headsail reinflated to full height and thrust the boat forward. Though we'd redressed, I could still feel a savage nature continue to pulsate, accompanied by a growing sense of freedom that had unfurled deeply inside. Together, Stephen and I were the water through which we moved. We were the wind that fueled us. We were the sun whose warmth we absorbed.

Earlier, Stephen had produced a camera from below deck, and now I caught sight of him out of the corner of my eye, clicking the shutter release of the Kodak from a low angle, its bellows fully extended. He removed a sheet of film and stepped in for a closer angle, then another— he, too, wanting to preserve the moment in perpetuity. What I wouldn't give to have one of those photographs, to have been able to have seen whether they captured the sparks that were surely emanating from me.

The wind had begun to increase, and the surface of the water rippled more vigorously. Stephen began to prepare for our return to the city.

"It seems one can never have an entire day of perfection here on the regal lake," he noted as he hoisted the headsail too. "Last year Neil and I had a lovely outing, on a Wednesday in July, where we'd toasted the good fortune of the weather. By midafternoon, thunder had begun to roll in from the west, and we had to bugger back to shore. Then, wouldn't you know, the bloody storm ended upon our arrival at the pier."

"Midwest storms are nothing to fool around with. I would imagine especially here on the water."

"Indeed. It doesn't look to be terribly threatening today, however, wouldn't you say, darling?"

I looked at the thin white clouds that had begun to cast a veil over the warmth and light of the sun. "I can't imagine anything too bad happening in the middle of October. Now, if it was May . . ."

Stephen adjusted the wheel, and again I felt the power of the air as it caught the sails.

"I want to hear more pearls about this woman with whom I have fallen head over heels in love. Tell me something true about yourself, darling. I want to know anything and everything about you."

"Such as?" I asked, not having a clue where to begin.

"How about . . . What is your favorite blend of fabric?"

"What?" I laughed. "What an odd question!"

"Ha ha! Gotcha. All right then, how about your favorite color? Hollywood actress? Animal? Type of tree? Vegetable? Do you have an answer for any of those?"

"Okay, how about this? Pink, Vivien Leigh, cardinal, maple, and beet. Your turn."

"Hmph. You are certainly not in a garrulous mood at the moment, are you?"

"Just cutting to the chase."

"All right then. Have you different questions, or shall I answer my own?"

"Different," I said. "I want to know your favorite city, body of water, restaurant, store to shop at, and . . . sock color."

"Sock color! And you thought my questions were wonkery!"

We laughed at our private little game, and Stephen took a long draw from his scotch while organizing his answers.

"First, I do not understand how a beet can be a favorite vegetable of anyone."

I laughed again.

"Nonetheless, I will overlook the flaw." He paused a moment longer. "All right, I have my answers. Are you ready?"

"Ready and waiting."

"Venice, formerly the Mediterranean Sea but now Lake Michigan, Henry's on Rogue, and . . . what else?"

"Store and sock color."

"Ah, yes. David Halley's and navy."

"Just the answers I would've guessed," I joked.

"But of course. They were far too obvious."

I was amused by how our differences were vastly defined yet were also inconsequential. "My turn to answer."

"Well, well. My succinct little dear has suddenly found a desire to talk about herself! Very well then." Stephen thought up a new list of questions. "I want to know your favorite flower, time of the day, flavor of cake, and . . . are you ready for this?"—I nodded eagerly—"place upon your body on which you want to be kissed."

Had Will ever asked me such a thing—not that he would have—I certainly would have blushed wildly. But here, today, with Stephen, I whooped in laughter.

"My answers are lilac, five-thirty in the morning during the summer, angel food. And . . ." I stood and stepped in close to him, "mid-lower back, very low, in the curve. Would you like me to show you just where?" I whispered into his ear.

"By all means. I want to be sure to have the exact spot seared into my memory."

I lifted my sweater and pulled the hem of my skirt down a few inches.

"There?" he asked, my breath catching at the electric charge his touch sparked. "Ah, I see," he said. "Consider it never to be forgotten."

I turned back toward him. "My turn to ask again. I'm going to steal your question."

"My answer is milk chocolate."

"No," I giggled. "Where do you most want my lips to be on your body?"

"Any place you like, I like, my dear."

"Oh?" I took his face in my hands and kissed him fully, fervently, both of us immediately aroused. But a low rumbling of thunder to the west returned us to the moment and Stephen to focusing on our destination.

"I suppose we ought to be more earnest about moving our way ashore," he said, scanning the water for distant land. His grip on the wheel, I noticed, had tightened. "How about you gather up the life vests. You'll find them there," he pointed at one of the benches. "I'm afraid this new design on the weather may be here to stay."

Though I knew he was right, I couldn't help but feel disappointment, wanting this enchanting day to never end.

"One more kiss, here in the middle of nowhere?" I asked.

Stephen didn't hesitate. I thought I detected a hint of sadness in his eyes, but it was quickly forgotten as our kiss coursed through me, seeking out a secret space in which it could live, from where it could later be recalled. This kiss—it was my blue diamond.

—— July 1975 ——

Louise sat cross-legged on the long countertop at the back of the store, the palm of her hand cupping her chin as she searched for a dark gray cutout with an orange tip that began the fox, the irony of piecing together the *Carnivorous Animals of North America* jigsaw puzzle at the more-or-less meat-free co-op having not escaped her.

"What do foxes eat, anyway?" she asked Mark, who stood on the other end of the counter looking for the puzzle piece that would complete the back of a skunk.

"Little critters. Moles and mice."

"Hmm. I always thought they'd lean more toward a meat-free diet. More of a gatherer than a hunter."

Mark nodded. "Um hmm. What about the skunk? Gotta say, I didn't know he'd be a hunter."

"Weird."

They continued their search.

"Black and white," said Mark after a minute. "Seems like it ought to be a hell of a lot easier to find a black-and-white piece. But then again, when is anything really black and white?"

"Whoa. Deep, man." Louise winked at him.

"You know, that makes me think of—"

"The CO," Louise finished.

"Yeah. What if it isn't just black and white, in the metaphorical sense? What if it's not just about confining the co-ops to the Warehouse?" Mark looked up for a moment.

"As in?"

"As in, what if there's a lot more gray area between the storefronts and the supply store?"

"Found it!" Louise pressed the cardboard shape into place and gave it a light tap with her fist.

"Or what if it's all gray," Mark continued. "You dig me?"

"Not whatsoever. Boil it down, dude."

Mark began to pace. "What if they don't give a rat's ass about the co-ops at all? What if it's some other ruse, and this is the cover story?"

"C'mon! This piece has to fit!" Louise looked up. "I'm listening. Really!"

"I don't know, man. I keep getting a feeling that this whole ordeal is off somehow. That there's a leader who has his followers doing his bidding."

"Or her."

"Or her bidding. What if it really *is* some sort of malevolent group? What if the other co-ops have succumbed to scum?"

"You mean like a co-op cult? Gotta say, you're stretching taffy there."

Mark stopped pacing. "Yeah, you're probably right. I don't know how a co-op would fit into the script. Something just keeps nagging at me, though." He looked down at the jigsaw puzzle again. "How about you, Lou . . . Have you felt anything?

"Other than the shredding of my nerves when I can't find the right piece?"

"Puzzling, huh?"

"Very funny." Louise reached over and slapped his butt. "But yeah, the whole CO thing is sort of a puzzle too. I'm sure Sage has examined every bit of writing that she could get her hands on. I don't think she's turned up anything significant yet. I mean, she would've told me."

"How could the CO be so public about bringing stores over to their side and no one else think it's fucked up? Sure, the others were probably a lot more compliant than we've been. But Joe over at East End just shook his head when I told him about what happened. Either he thought it was unreasonable that this is going on, or he was letting me know that I'm an idiot for putting up a fight."

"Has anyone looked for sources beyond other co-ops?" Louise asked.

"I don't know. Like who?"

"Like the guy driving the Corvette for one."

"He's probably just the getaway driver." Mark looked up. "Paul's here. It's gonna get noisy in here."

Louise sighed, excited for the repair work to move them forward but wishing she could get the damn puzzle finished. She hopped down and covered it with an old towel. "What's today's plan?"

"Finishing off the shelving. Sherrie's coming by after class to paint a new sign. Sticking around?"

"Nah. I'll be back tomorrow. You still want the food deliveries to come in tomorrow, right? Randy and I have a couple of stops lined up."

"Absolutely."

"Cool. I'm off then. Good luck today!"

"Thanks, Lou. Catch you later."

Sage unloaded the stack of newspapers she'd acquired from the filing cabinets in the basement onto her desk. It felt as if months had passed since she first stepped foot into Living Waters, but it had only been just a couple of weeks. And in that span of time, she'd learned about the cooperative model, that the food co-ops were governed—mostly loosely—by a board of directors, with occasional meetings held at the People's Warehouse to spin ideas for the future. But when the CO formed, many of the co-ops moved away from the warehouse group and instead joined the CO. Promises of more shoppers and higher profits seemed the logical reason for the changeover, but these folks weren't in it for the money, if Mark and Peck represented food co-op ideals as a whole.

She'd also perused the aisles of Central Co-op and Real Food Co-op, where she found cans of tuna and bags of organic tortilla chips alongside walnuts by the scoop and ripe watermelons picked that very morning. None of them were stocked with supermarket variety, yet they certainly had a different vibe than that of Living Waters, as if teetering uncertainly on the edge of consumerism.

In talking with managers and staff, Sage had learned that the policies of the CO didn't allow volunteerism within their stores, that they were each to be organized similarly, to sell similar foods, and to keep the important—though very thin—CO manual easily accessible. While she understood uniformity, Sage couldn't determine why such a high level of control was necessary when the entire food co-op movement was, to her understanding, designed for less control. Sure, CO members could vote on certain aspects of running the stores, but a governing board had the final say. What went unanswered, however, was who oversaw that board. From what she could decipher so far, the governing board was very loosely defined, with a president or director presumably as head honcho. It seemed to Sage that no one really knew who this person was. The answer was somehow blotted out.

She plopped into her chair, exhausted by the nonstop perusal of headlines over the past few days to see whether they revealed anything of interest. So far, her efforts had provided her with less than thirty column inches of co-op happenings—none of them mentioning anything outside of city council approvals or the announcement of an opening.

After a while, Sage decided that it was time to visit Living Waters again, where she hoped Mark would be available. With all that had been going on over there, there had been no opportunity to spend any time with him, or Peck for that matter.

She pulled up to the front curb and was surprised to see a final pane of glass being installed in one of the porch windows. Though quite aware of the horrifying confrontation, she had expected that the place would still be in disarray. Instead, as Sage walked through the front doorway, its bells jingling, she spotted Peck arranging onions on a shelf. He saw her and made his way over.

Without reason, words eluded her. Though they'd talked on the phone a few times, she hadn't seen him since their introduction, their initial date having been delayed. *He's simply a man, a person*, she reminded herself.

"Sage, hey. Cool to see you again."

Sage noticed that his Twinkie-colored tank top and faded denim shorts could have used a good scrubbing, not to mention his whiskers needed shaving. Her own nylon blouse, buttoned to the neckline, was tucked neatly into her skirt.

"I'd love to give you a hug, but . . ." He looked down at his clothes and shrugged. "Just a good ole country boy these days."

"Looks like a lot of work has been going on here."

"Yep. Moving on." He smiled at her. "You missed your sister and Randy. They're back out for another farm stop. Oh, and Louise told me you passed your licensing exam. You're a true pilot now—that's far out."

"Well, not a pilot. I mean, I made it through flight school, but I'm not exactly going to work for TWA."

"Ha! You're definitely more of a Northwest kind of woman."

"More like a four-seater kind of woman. Amateur Airlines, at your service."

Peck reached over and placed a kiss on her cheek, surprising her. "I'd fly your airline anytime."

"Where is everyone else?" she asked, ignoring the flush of her face.

"Mark's in the back with Sherrie. Skinny staff. Well, always a skinny staff." He smiled again, and she noticed how white his teeth were against the deep tan of his summer skin. "Here to shop or were you hoping to find your little sis?"

"Actually, I was hoping to see you."

"Hmm. Did you find the assholes who hid my bike? Is it missing again?" Peck asked in mock seriousness.

"Yeah, but it's been hijacked to the remote corners of the Midwest. Its location can only be seen by air, so I can sell you a ticket. It happens to be discount day at Amateur Air."

"Sold! I mean, I'm not saying anyone ought to soar above the earth in a craft that common sense says is too heavy to feasibly take flight, but whatever it takes to get my bike back. You do realize it's a faded, eight-year-old, on-its-last-days, very used bike? Can't get one of those just anywhere."

"Oh, no, of course not. It's practically special order."

He laughed. "I accept your offer."

Sage felt herself go soft inside. She'd been trying to work out in her mind why she was attracted to a guy who differed from her in almost every way possible. He might as well have worn a grass skirt and spoken in Swahili for all the similarities they had. Yet, she'd found herself spending a fair amount of time in recent days considering the possibility of him in her life.

"I was wondering if anything's been happening here recently. Have any more hooligans stopped by since they broke in the other day?"

"Hooligans?" His laugh was like the fast dribble of a basketball. "Well, I guess there are always hooligans of one form or another stopping by."

"You know what I mean. The CO folks looking for trouble."

"No, the assholes have managed to stay away. The city's been working us over, though, looking over our licenses, inspection reports—you know, seeing if there's a loophole to make us surrender in a legit way." Disappointment cast a shadow over his face. "But we're moving ahead. Not about to give up the good fight."

"Sis!" Louise walked in through the front door and wrapped Sage in a hug.

What's with all the hugging around here? Sage couldn't remember the last time she and her sister had embraced each other.

"What are you doing here? Run out of buckwheat?"

"Ha ha. Might go great with the Lucky Charms that's on tonight's menu," Sage retorted.

"Gross. We really need to fix your taste, Sage," Louise said as she set her bag behind the counter.

"I'll volunteer to help with the cause," offered Peck. "What do you say, Sage. Brave enough to let me cook for you?"

Again, she felt a rise of warmth. "Sure, I'll bring the Jell-O for dessert. Lime or strawberry?"

Peck laughed, wiping his hands on his shirt. "I'll go see if Mark has a minute."

"Somebody has a da-ate," teased Louise before Peck was even out of earshot.

"Lou! It's not a date! Stop that!" Sage whispered, then picked up where she had left off with Peck. "Mark seems like he's a busy guy."

"You could say that. I doubt he's slept more than a handful of hours the past few nights. Peck found him sawing logs on the floor in the back this morning."

"Geez. I should probably just wait until things settle down again after the store reopens," Sage said. "The thing is, I have to show something to Bernie, and I'm not able to connect the pieces. Do you think he'd be willing to talk to me? For maybe a half hour, tops?"

"If you're wanting to work with him to solve the riddle of the CO, he'll give you half a week. Maybe it'll help him sleep."

"Can't imagine how stressful this must be for him."

"He was telling me some suspicions he has about everything going down. Something about things not really adding up, I think." Louise looked off to the side. "Well, look at that. Your Watson has arrived."

Sage looked over and saw Mark standing in the doorway that led to the back room. "I can't just run over to him," she whispered to Louise. "How should—"

"Hey Mark, Holmes is back!"

"Louise!" Sage quietly admonished her sister once again.

Mark handed a crate to Peck and approached Sage, who wondered if she was in for yet another hug. "Good to see you again, man," he said, stopping short of a hug but linking his hand through her arm to guide her toward the back of the store, where his office was located. "Sorry we haven't met up again until now. It's been a little hectic around here."

"Are you sure you have time? I just have a few questions, but I don't want to take you away from your work."

"Nah. Have a chair."

"Thanks."

Sage took out a notebook and a freshly sharpened pencil. "I've been doing a lot of research on co-ops in the Twin Cities: background, how they're run. And the recent tension. I won't bog you down with tedious questions about things I already know, but there's a gap in the story."

"I'm interested." Mark leaned forward, crossing his legs. Sage couldn't help but notice the sincerity of his demeanor, as if nothing else in the world mattered at that moment other than to help another human resolve an issue.

Sage, too, leaned forward. "You seem to be one of the only co-op managers who won't be persuaded by the CO. My understanding is that you're less about profit, more about quality."

"Correct."

"The CO lowers the overall quality, but people that I've met who appear to have the same passion for providing quality food didn't seem to care a whole lot that their products are changing." Sage watched Mark, his look unchanged. "Then what is it that changed them? Why aren't they holding out like you are?"

"Maybe because they're all new to this. I've had experience."

"I understand that, too, but . . . it's just too easy an answer, if you don't mind me saying. When talking with a couple of people, I felt like I was watching a performance, but the actors were still in acting school. Only one woman, Pam, didn't put on the same show. She just refused to talk to me. Do you know Pam from Central Co-op?"

"I met her once, quite a while back."

"Do you remember how she was then? As in, is being abrupt just her personality?"

Mark sat back, quiet for a moment. "From what I remember, Pam was a whip. Witty and sharp. Someone you might find teaching a college lecture by day and dancing at a frat party by night."

Sage raised her eyebrows. Pam had looked like she was not much older than herself, but she also appeared to be bent with the burden of metaphorical weight.

"She was with her partner at the time, I don't remember her name, but I remember how she reached for Pam's hand when I introduced myself. As if to let me know Pam was off the market," he said.

Sage noted this before continuing. "Louise mentioned that you have an unsettled feeling about what's going on. That it's more than a food fight. Would you mind telling me why?"

"Yeah, man. I don't mind at all." Mark nodded. "The thing is, I keep feeling like we're dealing with automatons."

"Automatons, what do you mean?"

"Robots being fed ticker tape. Doing their job, emoting the feeling input by the mastermind." Mark looked at her as he spoke, as if watching to see whether he'd gone too far.

Sage's eyes narrowed, her pencil tapping against her chin as the concept took shape—one that might be the turning point she'd been looking for. Her assignment had just become more than a notation for the cloistered shelves of the historical center library.

"Automatons," she repeated.

Chapter 23

—— Elizabeth, October 1948 ——

The persistent wind was not in our favor, accelerating the cover of metal-gray clouds and hastening us back to land. Yet, we were surely miles from shore as we continued full sail ahead. Despite the libations he'd consumed throughout the day, Stephen remained masterful at the helm as the boat bumped over the white-capped water like a pickup truck on a deeply rutted road.

"We're getting closer, darling."

It was the only information he'd provided, and I realized after twice inquiring that my question was an unnecessary burden to him. And so I remained quiet from where I sat on the nearby bench, scanning the horizon for signs of land. More and more the dark colors of the sky and water blended into one. I moved to the opposite bench, where I could see inches of blue sky that remained in the distance, continuing to look forward hopefully every so often. I saw, then, what looked like a hint of the city skyline and stood to better focus.

"Look!" I said, pointing ahead.

Lights had begun to burn early in the darkness of the storm, creating a small but visible glow to the south. We were making headway.

"I'm afraid we're still farther away than you realize, my love," Stephen called to me, his voice elevated against the sound of movement. "Eight nautical miles is how far the eye can see over the horizon. We're closer than that—I'd estimate six—but we've a bit of a jaunt yet." He picked up his glass. "I may need another nip. Would you mind, darling?"

I reached out, not wanting to fill it, wanting him to direct all of his energies toward greater speed and toward the shoreline—toward depositing us safely back onto land. "How long does a six-nautical-mile boat ride take?" I asked, stalling on the scotch.

"Are you so properly concerned about reaching the shore?" he asked, looking not at me but straight ahead, his playful demeanor having slipped away. Did Stephen think I was questioning his abilities? Was he fearful himself? Or was he simply focused? I grew silent once again and descended into the cabin.

Movement was more pronounced inside where I couldn't see the water. In the dim light I pulled open a cabinet door within the galley and patted around the space until my hand landed on the cool glass of a scotch bottle that had been tucked into a secured spot. I set the tumbler on top of the wooden counter, momentarily letting go of it as I hurriedly uncorked the bottle and poured cautiously, stingily, before returning to the deck. Once there, I was relieved to find Stephen where I had left him, a strange notion that he might have disappeared having passed over me.

"Here you go," I called out as I handed him the drink, raising my voice to win out over the noise of the water that was now slapping more forcefully against the boat. He smiled at me, and my concern over his previous response was quelled.

"What's that, up ahead?" I asked, noticing two black images in the distance, long and lit by several lanterns.

"They could be barges."

"What is a barge?"

"Like a freight train on the water."

"Oh." I paused. "We must be getting pretty close then?" The restraint in my voice belied the surge of hope I felt at seeing another craft, especially one heading away from shore. It must be okay to be on the water after all.

"We're moving along at a fine clip, darling."

I reached down and took a sip of his scotch, welcoming its potent distraction, feeling a need to keep a conversation going, to engage my mind with thoughts other than those of fear.

"Stephen, do you imagine?"

He looked over at me as if to seek the meaning behind my question. "Yes, I do." He turned back ahead but continued talking. "I imagine the boyhood taste of my mother's shepherd's pie when I am as hungry as a tiger. I imagine standing upon the shores at my home in England, looking over the ocean. I imagine being with you in, shall I say, the 'biblical sense.'" He paused, nodding. "A day like today needs no imagination, however. A day like today, together with you, was beyond any imagination. It was perfect." He looked at me with a smile that soared directly into my heart.

"Darling, I need you to take the wheel whilst I dig up the lantern from the cabin," Stephen said, breaking the spell he had cast.

A flood of doubt seized me. I wanted nothing to do with taking control, as I had been so keen to do just a few short hours ago when the sun was bright and the water calm. Yet, I knew that he wouldn't have asked if it wasn't necessary.

"Of course." I stepped up and laid my hands beside his on the wheel.

"Hold it steady, just like that. I shall be quite quick."

He pulled his hands away, and I gripped the polished wood tightly, immediately feeling the force of wind fighting against us.

Stephen quickly returned and affixed a brass lantern to the stern. It rocked back and forth, its metal shell knocking unremittingly against the wooden post. The light it produced was minimal, its beam not nearly powerful enough to guide our way, if it were even to stay lit.

"For safety, so that other boats can spot us," he said, taking over the wheel.

The wind had begun to vacillate between strong gusts followed by an easing, as if catching its own breath. Inhaling. Exhaling. Inhaling. Exhaling. The *Winsome Lady* swayed unsteadily with the headiest gusts, my sense of balance tested more than once. Stephen directed me to sit below deck, or even lie down there, but I couldn't imagine hiding away in that disorienting cave, being away from Stephen, unable to see how close we were getting to land. No, I stayed on deck but moved off the bench and sat with my back against the cabin door.

I didn't move from this position, even once the rain began, the cold, daggered rain of a grand storm. The lantern was quickly extinguished, and any sight of the city skyline from which I had gathered hope was now surely obscured by the weather. I grasped a nearby rope and focused on silently reciting the rosary. A splendid devoutness seemed to have been born within me, my words quickly becoming a plea to God, a plea for guided safety.

Hail Mary, full of grace, the Lord is with thee . . .

"Hold tight, darling. I'm afraid this bloody storm is quite angry," Stephen called to me.

I kept my focus on him. He leaned into the wheel, the cling of wet clothes outlining his body. Repeatedly, he wiped his face with his forearm, pushing his soaked hair to the side, but the spitting rain drew it back down where it created a curtain of rivulets.

Blessed art thou among women, and blessed is the fruit of thy womb Jesus . . .

My thoughts began to roil with the waves, churning and churning. I could feel my focus waning in the disorientation. How had I come to find myself in this situation? How had this happened? This couldn't be real. How was it that I was on a sailboat on Lake Michigan with a man from England in the middle of an ominous storm? My mind scrambled to find logical answers, answers made of stone, not water.

Holy Mary, Mother of God, pray for us sinners . . .

I braced my heels and with my free hand clutched the thin inch of wood that overlapped the bench.

From the portside, a distant flashing light appeared. A lighthouse? Was it nearing us or were we nearing it? Or was it not nearing at all?

Another gust sent a wave crashing against the boat, my sense of consciousness swaying and dipping with the movement. We'd dissolved into the landscape—the sky, the lake, the maddening rain, all the color of steel.

But I had seen a light—yes, there it was again! It was closer now. But was it our rescue? Or our warning?

A sharp pain struck my face, a sensation that quickly amassed over my body. What had been rain was now stabbing pellets of hail. I ducked my head between my legs leaving my back exposed to the punishment.

"Stephen!" I called out, though surely he could not hear me over the roar.

Another burst of thunder detonated from above. I lifted my head briefly just as a streak of lightning lit up the sky. Stephen was not at the wheel.

"Stephen!" I called out.

Again, no answer.

What did Daddy used to say about storms? I searched my shallow memory bank for the answer. Count . . . count the seconds between thunder and lightning. If it booms before five, go right inside. Yes, that was it.

Another flash. "One, two . . ."

Craaack! The boat swayed fiercely.

Now and at the hour of our death. Amen. Hail Mary . . .

I had to maintain focus. Where could Stephen have gone? He must have gone below deck. "Stephen!"

"Hold tight, darling!"

Thank god! "I can't see you! Stephen!"

The bright light was back; it was right there, so close to us. A deep guttural blast split the heavy air. I wanted to cover my ears, but I couldn't let go.

Louise and Sage, I was so glad they weren't here. But were they okay? Were they sheltered from the storm? Ah, yes—there they were, in the kitchen. And where did Will go? Why wasn't he there with them? Why were they left all alone with the rain blowing in through the window?

"Shut the window! The floor'll be ruined!"

Why couldn't I let go of the doorknob and go to my girls? I was stuck, my hand somehow glued to it. The baby, he was right on the other side of the door too.

"Will, get the baby! My hand is stuck! Will! Frankie is on the porch!"

Oh, now he was wet. The tiny baby was all wet and no clothes on him, just a skinny blanket. He'll catch a cold. But why wasn't he crying?

"Will!"

My hand finally loosened from the doorknob, and I went back outside, the sun now shining. At the other end of the yard, cinnamon candies were falling from the branches of the apple tree. Daddy! There he was, sitting in the tree, tossing down candy! Why wasn't he at the ball game selling the candy from his truck? The girls were there, too, filling a basket with the candy. But where was Will? He must've gone to the barn. Of course, it was milking time.

Oh, the baby's blanket has blown off! There it goes, into the branches of the apple tree. Daddy caught it! Oh, Daddy, he should've been out there playing ball, not selling candy to the onlookers. Grandma always said he was as good as any of them.

"You were just as good as any of them, Daddy!" I called out and looked again toward the barn.

"Elizabeth! Elizabeth!"

Whose voice was that? I turned back toward the tree, where a man now stood underneath. A handsome man. Lovely eyes.

"Hello!" I called out, waving.

He looked at me and waved vigorously, a wide smile crossing his face.

And then, in a singular moment, a sense of stillness overcame me, a wash of peace. Everything would be fine, perfectly fine.

Craaack!

With a dazzling flash of lightning, the man disappeared.

I was in bed, the blanket rough against my skin. I wanted a different blanket, but a throbbing pain in my head prevented me from getting up. I wouldn't move. I would not move just yet.

Chapter 24
— August 1975 —

Upon returning home, Sage once again approached the box in which the Ley family cross remained housed and removed the balls of crushed newspaper surrounding it. She pulled out the weary-looking thing and set it on her kitchen table, where it consumed the space of the meager rectangle of wood.

Tracing her family name, she imagined the distant relatives who might have commissioned the cross to be made or made it themselves. Was there an ironsmith in her lineage? A family of wealth? She realized how little she knew about her heritage. Daddy's parents had died before Sage was born, his only brother living in California after returning from the war. The lives of Mother's parents, too, had ended tragically many years before when they had borrowed a neighbor's car to drive to the Thursday night dance and had hit a deer, sending the car tumbling down a steep embankment. Maybe that's why history intrigued her: she knew so little of her own.

Sage popped the top from a cold bottle of Pepsi. As she put the opener back into the drawer, she noticed a spoon lying perpendicular over a knife, forming a cross. Looking out the window, it occurred to her that crosses were, oddly, everywhere within sight: a hose in the yard lying on top of a fallen branch, an antenna on the roof across the street. All at once she knew what she must do. She lifted the receiver and rotated the dial. After the fourth ring, Elizabeth picked up.

"Mother, when's the last time you were in Decorah?" Sage asked, niceties forsaken.

"What an unusual question," replied Elizabeth.

"How about the farm? The last time you were there was the day we moved, right?"

"That's right. Why the game of twenty questions today?"

Sage held her breath for a beat. "I'd like to go there. And I'm asking you if you'll come along."

An expected pause followed, and Sage quickly filled the space. "This isn't a pleasure trip, but it needs to be done. I need to go to the farm. To see where the cross was found."

"You seem to be engrossed by the cross lately. What is it that you want to find? Or expect to?"

"I . . . There are just so many weird things happening lately, and I have a feeling that I need to visit the farm. Maybe even . . . I don't know . . . say goodbye to Daddy as an adult. Really, I don't know exactly why. I just know that it feels important to be there. Just a short trip. Louise too."

"Sage, is everything okay?"

Sage knew her explanation was cryptic, but she also had no clue how to express this need—or why it was there in the first place.

"Yeah, everything's fine. It's nothing to worry about. It's more like . . ." She paused momentarily. "Like an enigma."

"I'm intrigued. And a bit worried, to be honest."

"No, don't be worried. I have to run, but if you're in maybe we could go soon, within the next couple of weeks? I want to see for myself where this cross was and, I don't know, look around or something."

Sage looked down at the cross, once again tracing over the family name.

"Sage, I would love to accompany you on a trip to Decorah. It's due time."

"Really? Thanks, Mother. I really appreciate this. I can use the airplane rental certificate that Jim gave me when I passed the final exam."

"Yes . . . Yes, how nice."

Elizabeth hung up the receiver and walked tentatively back into the kitchen. The conviction of Neil's necessary departure had quickly taken a back seat, concern for her daughter and a surge of anxiety over the thought of flying now demanding the space of her thoughts. It was as if the threads of her daughters had crossed on a loom. Had Louise made this request, it would have been entirely normal, simply another whim, but coming from Sage, it felt dramatic.

"Is your daughter well?" Neil asked, looking up from the newspaper that he had picked up when the phone rang.

"Yes, of course."

He gave the paper a shake before folding it, then uncrossed his legs. "I admit that I don't know you all that well, but it seems as if something unfortunate might have happened."

The sound of his voice had become like the unwelcome howl of a dog in the quiet of the night. There was nothing about her life that she wanted to share with him, yet she wasn't prepared to let him go—to let Stephen go. As irksome as it was to have this man in her home, he was necessary.

Neil may hold the key to Stephen's fate, but she couldn't shake the feeling that he was using Stephen—their one connection—for his own shady reasons. Yet, had he really done anything outwardly malevolent? Not since he'd been here, she had to admit. In the past, in Chicago? She felt a strong urge to search her memory for evidence, but now was not the time. Now she had to press. If she didn't insist that he provide her with answers about Stephen, how would she ever know?

"There are things that have challenged my life in recent days, yes," Elizabeth answered unequivocally, twisting her small pearl earring. "Though nothing I am incapable of dealing with."

She reached down to straighten a pillow on the sofa and retrieve a tissue that had fallen from underneath it. Neil settled back into the chair and relaxed his arms upon the armrests.

"We shared a past, you and me," he said.

Shared. She turned, facing Neil directly, a rush of anger rising.

"No, we didn't. We may have known the same person, but you and I did not share a past. You and I, Neil, are not friends. We never were. You and I have but one commonality."

She stood up and took a step toward him, folding her arms protectively in front of her. "You have been here on several occasions now. What is your purpose, Neil? Why do you keep returning to my home? What is it you know about Stephen?"

"Perhaps the letter reveals all."

"A letter that you have never opened yourself."

"That is correct."

Neil stood, once again the topic of Stephen queuing his exit. "I suggest you read it, Elizabeth. You seem somewhat unraveled."

"What would you know of my mannerisms? I am simply asking for any knowledge you might have of a mutual acquaintance. I've extended plenty of courtesies to you. I ask that you do the same for me."

"Unfortunately, the time you spent on the phone used up my free time for the day, and I must be going." He looked at his watch. "Did I mention that I am leaving for Chicago tomorrow? Though, I'll be back again very soon. I'd like to call on you again when I return." He looked her in the eye. "That is, if you don't mind."

Apprehension billowed from Elizabeth, pricking at the tips of her fingers. She couldn't stop Neil from leaving, but neither did she want him to stay any longer. Perhaps if she never were to see him again . . . perhaps life would drift back into the realm of the ordinary. But, Stephen . . . the window to him had been opened, opened wide.

She nodded curtly. Neil retrieved his fedora from the coat rack.

"May you have a pleasant afternoon," he said, smiling crookedly, and closed the door behind him.

"Cessna one-seven-two cleared for takeoff. Runway two, straight-out departure approved."

Sage scanned the runway, then the sky. The full power of the engine induced a familiar vibration within the cabin, and she removed her foot from the brake, steering toward the converging lines before her. In a rush of speed, the plane lifted its weight into the thick air with an unintentional wave of its wings.

Elizabeth, sitting beside Sage in the front of the plane with her eyes closed, gripped the sides of the seat beneath her as the noise of the engine asserted its way through the thinly insulated headset. It wasn't until the plane leveled that she dared to open her eyes and saw that the objects below were already significantly shrunken in size. If not for the fuss of engine noise and mysterious bounce of the air, swooning through the sky might not be so bad, she thought. But instead, it gnawed at the serenity. She glanced sidelong at Sage, who was nothing if not self-assured in her role as pilot.

"Woo-eee! Outta this world!" Randy called out from the seat behind her. "Yo Sage, take a dip over to the right. Let's get a close-up of that guy over there, the spot of dust on the road. Just give him a little buzz right over the top of his big rig."

"That's a negative, Randy."

"You gotta have some fun. How often do you get to fly higher than a kite?"

The small craft sliced through the air providing a 360-degree view displaying rectangles of verdant crops, organic thickets of trees that ushered lengths of river into seclusion, roads meandering the landscape in a shrewd labyrinth. Though the air was punctuated with humidity, the lack of clouds allowed the sun to illuminate the view for miles.

"Copilot, where'd your color go?" Sage turned to her mother with a raised eyebrow. "Are you hanging in there?"

"Of course. I'm practically Anne Lindberg," Elizabeth shouted back.

Sage laughed. "Okay. But if you change your mind, there's a sick bag a hand's reach away on your right."

Elizabeth took note of the pocket.

Twenty years. Elizabeth had meant to return to Decorah after moving away. She'd meant to do so many times over, to reopen the locket of memories on which she'd closed the clasp, but the timing had just never seemed quite right. An early season snowstorm, the catching of a cold, Louise's slumber party—it hadn't been difficult to summon an excuse, time and again, to turn down an offer to visit former neighbors or church ladies. The girls had transitioned quickly and smoothly to their home in Minnesota after Will's death, to their new school and friends, and she didn't want to disrupt that flow by returning them to the only other home they'd ever known. At least, that's what she'd convinced herself of. Eventually, the calls came to a stop. But now, as the aircraft carried them ever closer to their destination, she was surprised at her eagerness to return to the distant familiarity of the place in which she had spent so many years as Will's wife.

After an hour or so they approached the farm. Elizabeth allowed herself to look out of the window now, at first with little recognition from their vantage point. Sage then angled the plane toward the acreage below, and Elizabeth saw the once-white house now painted a cheery peach with burgundy trim, the white barn still lording over the handful of outbuildings. An enormous garden remained between the gravel driveway and adjacent field, and on the south side hardwoods had begun a slow spread, the spring-fed brook hidden by thick summer foliage.

"The playhouse, it's still there!" called out Louise.

Elizabeth saw the tiny roof of the old pumphouse that the girls had made into their second home.

"Remember all those hours we spent in that shack, tending to our babies?"

"Yes, and surgery day. Every Friday was surgery day. We swore we'd get Lucinda's leg sewn on for good one of those times, but sure enough by Monday we had to put the stuffed leg on ice waiting until surgery day came around again."

"Of course, Lucinda never minded," returned Louise. "She just laid there with a blank expression on her face. Best patient ever."

"Probably because I read stories to her until she became catatonic," said Sage with a laugh.

"Yeah, you may want to ease up on that if the real deal ever comes along."

The chicken coop and pole shed, the three apple trees under which Sage would read for hours while Louise climbed its branches—so much familiarity remained, as if held bound in a time capsule.

"Sage, circle around again, would you?" asked Elizabeth, surprised at her own request, considering her eagerness to be back on solid land.

"Roger that. Three-sixty, coming up."

As the plane veered to the right, Elizabeth grabbed the side panel with one hand, the ceiling with the other. "Look. There it is," she said, easing her hand from the ceiling and pointing to an expansive field of what appeared to be soybeans just to the east of the barn.

"What are we looking at?" Louise called out.

"It's the field. The field where the cross was likely found by Hans."

Sage once again dipped the plane a notch lower. She was eager to get a closer look, as if the precise location where the cross had been found would reveal itself in a punctuation of color. But no signs appeared, and Sage turned the plane back toward the municipal airport, coordinating the controls for landing.

Chapter 25

—— Elizabeth, May 1952 ——

Turning the quilt onto its long edge emphasized the displacement of the rusted fishing hook. Rather than being submerged in the river, the hook dangled on the surface, unable to reach the toy boat that lay in the depths. I studied the piece, wondering if I ought to add another strip of fur to the riverbed.

"We're going to the woods to build a fort," Sage called out as she poked her head through the doorway.

"No tools," I called back, recalling Louise sauntering off to the woods last week with the old hand saw that Will kept hanging on the wall of the tack room.

"Can we bring the puppies?" Topper, the coon hound, had recently given birth to a litter of five, a source of delight for all of us and a way in which to build patience in the girls.

"Still too young, sweetie. You can pour a thermos of lemonade though."

I could hear the hurried scuffle of shoes on linoleum as she scooted around the room, opening the cupboard, then the icebox, followed by careful pouring. With Sage I was never concerned about finding a mess left behind.

"And cookies?"

"And cookies, but just two."

I wasn't sure about the fur, but also needing adjustment were the watery strips cut from a navy-blue wool skirt that overlapped to create the effect of surface waves. They were too smooth; more turbulence was needed.

I pushed back from the table to sift through the boxes of discarded junk I'd saved, things that I thought might one day have a purpose, when I remembered the science kit that Sage had been given two Christmases ago that she oddly refused to use. My daughter was curious about everything—except chemistry, it seemed. The rush of bubbles streaming from a test tube when vinegar met baking soda was not nearly the thrill that handing tools to Will was as he brought the Model H back to life.

"Aha!" The test tubes lay prone in their original box just underneath Grandmother's enamel colander, one V-shaped leg missing from the trio. I would attach the tubes onto the quilt, all six of them, adding life through water. But ought I use clean water or water from the creek, I pondered? And how to ensure a lasting seal?

It was the week after I'd returned from Chicago that I had begun quilting, not yet four years before. There was no introduction to it, no sewing group that I belonged to or instruction manual that was followed; rather, it was simply a thought that entered my mind one morning after the breakfast dishes were put away. I had glanced through the kitchen window at the imposing white barn juxtaposed against a piercing blue autumn sky, the flaxen color of a few rows of corn remaining in the distant field. The scene had struck me as one of individual patterns, a form of living art that Monet might've captured in his interpretive watercolors or Picasso might have redesigned into geometrical confusion.

Abstract expressionism had become a trend in New York City, reaching as far away as Chicago, where I had seen the works of some of the greatest artists in the world. I recalled standing beside Stephen staring intently at Rothko's *Sea Fantasy*, the first of a handful of paintings we had approached at the Chicago Art Institute that belied traditional form and subject matter, contrasting childlike creatures from the sea against a surprising gold background. I had studied it only briefly when I'd turned and caught my breath at the sight of a different piece.

Across the room was a colorful painting of a life-sized woman in a long flowing dress, her figure bordering on disjointed, a moon painted black with a greenish eye looking off to the distance. Surrounding her were symbols and lines and smears of paint, all in garish colors that felt more ominous than spiritual. I stood before her for several minutes, enraptured by the colors, the lines, the questions that the painting provoked. How surprised I was when I looked at the placard next to it and saw *Moon Woman* by Jackson Pollock (a name I would never again mention to Will) after having read a feature on his dubious art in *Life* the night before I left the farm.

In that moment, the exhilarating touch of Chicago, the grace of the great lake wide open with promise, the fullness of love and unexpected passion—all of it had encircled me, elevating me to new heights. Yet, I couldn't help but notice a sense of murky turmoil loitering on the fringes. I was the Moon Woman, guarding over my life, while inside I had been dancing rhapsodic around Chicago.

And now, back on the farm, I had the thought to capture my own world, to sew it all together: the disparate, the desperate. They would be my secret stories, my healing elixir.

My first quilt was a collage of colorful scraps of cloth taken from the clothes my girls no longer wore, used to frame the shape of a barn, with denim from Will's faded overalls used to fill it in. In the middle I had sewn a blue heart with layered fabric that rippled like water, onto which I had attached a pair of earrings that I had worn that first night in Chicago at the Blue Window. I'd finished piecing it together by early January. *Marrow*, I called it, for it felt like a resurrection, like the vessels of my bones were beginning to rebuild life inside of them.

So different was quilting from sewing clothes, for there were no bodies to wear my designs, no styles to consider. My quilts were my personal art, sewing the only time in which I allowed myself to coax out the splinter of loss. Since my return, I had been picking my way intently across the stones of familiar paths, but now with Stephen nestled deeply within. He was there alongside me as I ran clothes through the ringer and raked up the last of the leaves, as I sipped on morning coffee at the table beside Will. He was with me when I turned off the light at night, an undeniable presence, yet one I couldn't touch.

While quilting I was able to disassemble memories, rework them thoroughly in my thoughts and expel bits and pieces onto fabric for safekeeping. A violet-colored satin blouse became a fish. A faux fur stole formed the facade of a modern steel building. A black silk camisole turned into mud. I had begun collecting discarded objects from our house and farm, too: gunny sacks, a useless brass key, feathers, pieces of broken porcelain dishware, barbed wire, fossilized stones from the creek. All representations of my life, in one way or another.

At first, nobody understood. But how could they have?

After *Marrow*, I immediately began working on the next quilt and didn't stop creating. Usually the design was expressive, yet at other times I ebbed, creating simple scenes. Budding spring trees were crafted from fallen twigs and decorated with leaves of fabric against a background of white felted raindrops. For a winter scene, fencing wire was shaped into a Christmas tree holding shiny glass beads and surrounded by snow made of cotton batting. Those were the ones that sold at first. Those were the quilts that people wanted to see, scenes that brought contentment into their lives.

But conceptual quilts were those most authentic, those whose stories I held hostage. I was living a parallel life in which my fantasies of Stephen and the pain of being unable to live them out with him emerged onto fabric.

"Mama, I found babies! Come look!" The squeal of Louise's voice brought me back to real time, and I pushed myself away from the sewing machine and followed her with as much concern as curiosity. Many creatures had made their way into our home throughout the years by my youngest daughter's hand, most recently a bucket of frogs that, it turned out, could hop out of after all.

I stepped into the garage and immediately stiffened. Proudly displayed on top of a gunnysack was a huddle of black and white fur.

"Louise Jean, you step away from those skunks right now! Why are you not covered in spray?" I scolded.

"They're just little ones, Mama. They're not gonna hurt anyone."

"Not all babies are meant to share a home with us. Where is Sage? You two stay put while I race these babies back to the woods before their mother returns. Where did you find them?"

"They were over by the oak, the big one that fell down."

I scooped up the bag of skunks, calling back to Sage to check the bread in the oven in five minutes, and hurried toward the old oak at the edge of the woods. I'd just arrived at the tree when I heard a wretched holler coming from the field beyond the corn bin in the opposite direction. I froze. *Will?* I had never heard such a harrowing sound come from a person, certainly not from Will. But yes, there it was again.

I dropped the bag and ran with alacrity up the hill, past the barn and outbuildings, and into the field, my lungs and legs burning with the effort. I saw the tractor in the distance and forced my body to keep moving until I finally reached my husband. There he lay on his back, a few yards from the tractor.

Will was moaning weakly, his shirt torn off. The lack of color in his face was a shocking contrast to the deep scarlet, nearly violet imprint that had already covered most of his abdomen. From the strong smell of chemicals, I deduced that the insecticide from the sprayer had somehow spilled onto him.

"Will, tell me you are with me," I shouted. His chest was moving rapidly—too rapidly. I had to hear it from him, my intrepid husband. I had to know that he was lucid, that—despite what I was witnessing—he was somehow not dying. He nodded his head once before his eyes began a jittery roll toward the back of his head.

"You stay awake, Will!" I demanded, noticing that his hands had begun to twitch. "You keep your eyes open and stay awake until I get back!"

I got up and ran again, this time away from him and toward the house that now seemed so far in the distance. The girls were in the yard, and I shot past them, bursting through the screened door to the kitchen, where I grabbed the phone and called for Dr. Grimmsud.

"Get him away from the spill right away," he advised.

"He already is; he must've moved himself. When can you be here?"

"I'm leaving now, but you need to stay calm for him, Betty. Get a pitcher of water and a soft towel. Pour some water over the wound real gently. But only use a wet towel if there's any oozing. I'll be there in less than ten minutes."

"Thank you, doctor. The northeast field."

I filled a pitcher to the brim and shoved the lid on, then grabbed a cotton towel from the kitchen drawer. I was out the door, racing back through the yard, yelling to the girls as they watched me pass by. "Daddy's hurt, but I'm going to help him. Stay here. Dr. Grimmsrud is on his way."

"Mama!" Louise yelled. "I'm coming too!"

"No!" I stopped and looked directly at her. "You stay here."

I broke into another sprint, away from my terrified daughters and back toward my husband, whom I hoped to god was still breathing.

"Wiiiill!" I yelled as the tractor came into view. "I'm almost there, Will!"

The soybean field was thick and wet. I moved as fast as I could until I found myself abruptly lying on the ground. A sharp pain coursed through my leg, but adrenaline compelled me to stand up and move forward with what meager strength I had left.

Will had remained on his back, there on the black dirt. It was difficult to distinguish life from death until I fell onto my knees beside him and saw the quickened, though shallow, rise and fall of his chest. The powerful insecticide, undiluted I'd suspected, stung my eyes as I poured water gently over the burning blotches of his skin. Even with that, his only movement was the ongoing twitch in his hands.

I forced my voice to calm as I spoke to him, but it wasn't long before my words were replaced with sobs. It was for Will's pain that I cried, not only the physical pain, but the emotional pain I had caused over the years. The pain I caused him by leaving for Chicago, as if he somehow knew our lives would never be the same.

That morning, the day of my leaving, Will had walked from the bathroom at the end of the hall and tripped over a doll dropped earlier by Sage as she fled the house to rescue a bluebird that had smacked against the kitchen window.

"Ga-dammit!" he called out.

I looked at him, surprised that he'd sworn. Knowing I was about to leave surely had his emotions on edge; that the cattle had found a leeway in the fence line and wandered into the neighbor's cornfield had done nothing to ease his mind.

His err was but a slip. He didn't chastise his daughter, but there was a clear message in the look he gave me. "See what you're doing to us," it said.

I picked up the doll and went back into our bedroom to make one last run through the contents of my suitcases.

"Got your ticket handy?" Will asked, following me into the room.

"It's in my purse."

"Window seat?"

"Yes. D14."

"We probably oughta leave by eleven. Don't want you to miss your ride to paradise."

The tension hadn't dissipated over the course of the morning, and by the time my train arrived we'd departed with a quick, obligatory kiss.

But now, seeing Will lie before me, both of us awaiting an unknown future, the underlying detachment of emotion that had haunted me began to peel away in layers of sorrow, revealing a rush of love for my husband. With one hand I continued to gently wash his skin. With the other I held tightly onto his hand in an outpouring of prayerful pleas, for the second time in my life.

Chapter 26

— August 1975 —

Randy sat behind the wheel of the rust-infused car rented out by Decorah Airport and, guided by Elizabeth, drove the five miles to the farm. As they turned into the driveway and made their way down the first stretch, Elizabeth noted that the trees near the house had matured significantly, especially the locust in the front yard that had shaded her hosta bed. A new shed had been erected, too, large enough to fit two tractors and a pickup truck inside. Otherwise, outside of the different house color, it appeared that little had changed in the nearly twenty years of her absence.

As they came to a halt beside the garden, a group of well-fed hogs bathing in the sun behind the barn came into view, a few rooting through the trough for any remaining scraps of fodder. Two calico cats stretched languidly on top of an abandoned doghouse, eyeing the car with disinterest.

"I can hardly believe we are back, after all this time," said Elizabeth.

Memories whispered from every corner. Will eyeing her through the kitchen window as he walked from the barn toward the house during their first night there—the pride she had felt for him. The four of them sipping hot cocoa as the sweet scent of burning leaves brought an outdoor fire to life on a chilly autumn evening. The windowpane of their bedroom vibrating in the riled winds of a blizzard. The white clawfoot tub and the soak she had taken in it the night she'd returned home from Chicago.

"Oh, um, what's happening?" Randy's question drew Elizabeth back to the present.

Walking toward their car was a man in faded green bib overalls, sheared off midthigh, and work boots covered in a layer of dried muck. A head of generous white hair deeply contrasted with bushy black eyebrows that framed the top of his wire-rimmed glasses.

"Yah, can I help you?" he asked, approaching the car.

Elizabeth poked her head out the window, ignoring Louise's giggle from the front seat. "Yes, please. My name is Elizabeth—Betty—and this is my family." She gestured at them with a nod and smiled back at the man. "Betty Ley. We used to live here years ago."

The man's eyes widened. He clutched his head and stumbled backward, crouching so low that his backside grazed the gravel. Elizabeth was about to jump out and help him, sure that he was having an attack of some sort, when suddenly he spoke.

"You mean to tell me that you're the Leys? The ones I called a vile ago?"

"Yes. Yes, that is who we are. We thought it would—"

"Vell, almighty! I sure didn't expect you to drive on down from the city. Vhat that take you? Ten, tvelve gallons?"

"Ah, well we didn't drive here. We flew in an airplane," Sage said.

The man shot up. "Vhat's that?" He leaned in toward Randy's window to inspect the occupants, close enough to reveal several smudges on his glasses and three wily hairs stemming from a significant mole on his chin.

"We, ah . . . flew here," Randy stammered. "My, um, girlfriend"—he nodded toward Louise at his side—"her ma and her sister," he continued, tilting his head in the direction of the backseat.

"My daughter has recently become a small engine pilot. We are Sage's passengers," explained Elizabeth.

"Sage? Like the herb?"

"Yes indeed," Elizabeth replied. "Sage like the herb, not the spice."

"Spice? Vhy vould you call sage a spice? That makes no sense!"

Elizabeth smiled, taking an immediate liking to this stranger.

"You run into any birds? They get in your vay, you know. Took down a plane outside Davenport just last year. You can't predict vhere they'll fly."

Elizabeth's heart quickened, still not entirely comfortable with the idea of having to return home by air. The car, with its four sturdy wheels cruising over the solid ground, had been a welcomed respite.

"Flying is the safest mode of transportation," said Sage, leaning across her mother in the back seat. "You may want to read up on it in the latest issue of *Newsweek*."

"If God vanted us to fly, he vould have given us a propeller on our head and a powerful engine on our ass. Pretty sure gravity vas put here on purpose, young lady."

Randy burst into laughter, but Louise was not as entertained.

"Tell me, did you or your ancestors arrive by boat, or did you all swim here?" she inquired. "Cuz I'm seeing arms where your fins should be."

The man looked at her for an expressionless moment before he cracked, laughing so hard that he was forced to squat once again.

At the same time a woman emerged from the house, her white-streaked hair hanging in wet strings that reached to her buttocks. A long, flowing skirt covered her legs, but a fitted T-shirt revealed a shapely bosom beneath. "Hans, what're you doing on the ground, and who's this here?" she called out.

"Siri! You vill not believe how these folks arrived. They flew in an airplane!" He stood, shaking his head in disbelief as he dusted himself off.

"Hello. Welcome." Siri greeted them with a smile. "Hans and I have never flown in an airplane. But you've probably figured that out."

"They're here about the cross," Hans said. "Say, did you get it? I sent it to you in the mail, you know."

"Yes, I did," said Sage, pointing behind her. "We have it with us."

"Oh, no! I don't vant it back!" Hans called out.

"No, no. We don't want to see that thing again," chimed in Siri. "We had to have some special person come out here and fix the plow."

"Ve couldn't even finish the plowing. Who knows vhat that vill cost us in the end too," Hans added.

"No, I didn't mean that we are returning it. It just seemed that we should have it with us, to . . . I don't know . . . solve the enigma while on location, I guess."

"It's in the trunk," Louise added.

"Vell, it can just stay there. Siri has a new Polaroid if you vant to take a picture to carry vith you, but it can just stay right there in the dark vhere it belongs."

"Hans . . . um. Mr. . . . What is your name?" asked Sage.

"Hans Schvamman, that is my name."

"Mister Schvamman," Sage began, noting the German name.

"No, Schvamman."

"Yes, Schvamman."

"No, Schvamman, vith a double-u.'"

Sage glanced at Elizabeth who raised her eyebrows and gave a slight shrug of her shoulders.

"Mr. Schwamman!" called out Randy as if a contestant on a game show.

"Yah, that's it: Schvamman!" replied Hans.

"Mr. Schwamman, we will happily leave the cross in the trunk. But would you mind if we were to perhaps take a look at the field where you found it?" Elizabeth asked.

"Yah, yah, of course you can do that!"

"Hans, you mean to tell me you haven't even asked them to step out of the car yet? What's the matter with you?" Siri scolded, pinching him on the behind.

"Hallelujah, Siri! Save that for later, vould you?" Hans reached over to tickle his wife, but Siri bolted away in a fit of giggles, smiling coyly back at him as she slowed her gait near the house.

"Vell, let's go see the field then," Hans declared. "Ve'll cut through the barn, and I'll show you our prize-vinning hogs. Vonderful beasts!"

Elizabeth, Sage, Louise, and Randy unfolded themselves from the car, and the five began the impromptu field trip at the barn where Hans extolled the leanness of his pigs and the shape of their hams, while fluffing the straw bedding of a corner stall.

Next they moved toward the field, where soybeans were in full summer growth, though noticeably less bountiful than what was typical. Here, Elizabeth took the lead, her stride certain as she stepped high over the rows of plants. The others followed, listening to the unending chatter of Hans as he expressed his opinions on topics ranging from chicken feed—"giving chickens ground corn is like drinking cola; you don't vant to ruin their innards,"—to the necessity of adding earthworms—but not too many—to the garden before planting. "They give air to the soil so it can breathe!"

A small gathering of clouds had begun to move in from the west, carrying with it a hint of a breeze. There was but a moment's hesitation in Elizabeth's gait, during which she altered her direction slightly as she aimed toward the spot they'd come to see. A dozen or so yards farther, she came to a halt.

"Here it is."

The others formed a circle around the nondescript spot, staring down at it.

After a moment, Randy broke the silence. "So Mama Betty, this is where the cross was?"

"No," Elizabeth said. "This is where I found Will the day of his accident. This is where he lay, where Dr. Grimmsrud met us."

"Whoa," said Randy, linking his arm through Louise's. "Feels like we're on sacred ground."

"Yah, yah. The cross vas over there. This isn't vhere I found the cross!"

"I know. I know just where the cross was, Mr. Schwamman, but I felt that my daughters needed to come here first," explained Elizabeth. "You may have heard that my husband had a farm accident. I'd never allowed my daughters out here after it occurred."

Sage crouched down, brushing her hands over the plants as she studied the area indicated. Nothing out of the ordinary appeared, no noticeable scar on the earth. She'd always envisioned an obvious marking, a permanent memorial to her father. A wave of disappointment passed through her.

"Okay then. To the cross locale," Louise announced after an uncomfortable lull in conversation. Randy raised his head in relief.

"Yes," said Elizabeth and marched ahead, Sage hastening to match her stride before falling in step beside her.

"Mother, you didn't even remember the cross until Hans sent it to me. How could you possibly remember where it was located?" Sage asked, her voice hushed.

"Thirteen," said Elizabeth. "It was thirteen strides from where I tripped to where your father lay." She stopped, pointing back toward the house. "Considering where the house is and where I found your father, the object I tripped over would have been right about there." She pointed a few feet ahead.

"You know, I just planted these beans here for the first time. Alvays been corn, but the experts are saying ve need to put nitrogen back in the ground. The dirt is more than just little brown microbials, you know. And like ve humans need milk and meat and bread and good vegetables, the dirt needs nitrogen. You see, the beans feed it to them so the corn can be healthier. Who vould've thought!"

"It's a complicated world we live in," said Elizabeth. "May I ask, do you use chemicals on your crops?"

"I was wondering the same thing," said Louise. "Your methods remind me of some of the farms I've been to."

"No, chemicals don't touch my crops! I know not everybody agrees vith my vays, and my fields might not yield as much as some of the neighbors' do, but I vill do vhat I think is best. These beans here," he continued, indicating the field in which they stood, "they are not for the animals. They are for people. Either vay, I vouldn't go near that stuff vith a ten-foot-long vooden pole! They make people go crazy, they do!"

"Do you mean to tell us, Hans—Mr. Schwamman—that you are an organic farmer?" asked Louise, astonished. Though she had come to know the handful of farmers near the Twin Cities who were committed to using organic methods, she never would have guessed that such methods were being used on the farm on which she'd been raised.

"That's precisely what I mean to tell you. You've heard of organics?"

"Yes, I've heard of it!"

"Those chemicals, they not only destroy the microbials in the dirt, but they destroy us, the people. Ve are vone big circle," he continued, drawing a loop in the air. "If vone part of us gets sick, ve all get sick: the dirt, the plants, the people."

"Now *that* I can dig!" Louise said, her hands forming peace signs as she shot her arms into the air.

"Yah! Yah!" exclaimed Hans, lifting his hands, too, as he began dancing in a circle. Louise joined in, the two oddly coordinated in their impromptu pagan celebration.

Elizabeth shook her head and couldn't help but smile as she moved ahead, the others following behind. In a quick moment, she declared the arrival of their destination.

"Yah, this is it!" agreed Hans. "I vas plowing the field as I vas vhistling a little ditty I come to like. Johnny Cash, ever heard of him? He's got a voice like a bassoon playing in the forest. Vhen, *CRULLLKKSHH!* The plow hit the cross and made the darndest noise! I thought Johnny come crashing through the sky to scold me for ruining his song vith my vhistle! So I hit the brakes, and I threw her in park, and I jumped off the tractor so quick-like you vould have thought I vas a gosh darn jackrabbit, you vould have. I valked back to the plow and there vas an old cross, pulled vight out from its burial place!"

"So, your plow hit the cross and must've made shit of the blade," said Randy.

"Gosh darn right it did! Cost me forty-seven dollars to have it repaired!"

"I'm so sorry there was damage to your machinery. And we thank you for sending us the culprit," said Elizabeth. "As I've shared with my children, the cross was buried there by my husband years ago."

"In the field? Vhy in the field? That's a gosh darn place to bury a big chunk of metal!"

"I honestly don't know," said Elizabeth. "It is an odd place to bury a cross, but my guess is that he wanted to somehow consecrate it, honor his ancestors who had been farmers for generations."

"That sounds like something Daddy might've done," said Sage, looking up as a small smattering of clouds passed by.

"Is there anything else you can tell us about what happened, Mr. Schwamman?" asked Elizabeth.

"Vell, no. No I can't. I guess that's it."

"Thank you, Mr. Schwamman," said Sage. "We appreciate everything."

"Yeah, especially honoring the Earth," added Louise. "Happy dirt, happy beans!"

Hans put his arm around Louise and began the return from their pilgrimage, Sage and Randy following behind. Elizabeth brought up the rear, feeling the shadows of their lives following them, the past commingling with the present. In the distance, she caught sight of the emerald-green hayfield, early layers of mown hay drying in perfect rows at the bottom of the slope near the creek. She could almost smell the rich alfalfa on Will's clothes after having been in the field all day. But now, the field looked different, the bank of the creek higher, steeper. There was something about it that pecked at her, an inaccessible perplexity.

In a short time, they arrived back at the house and stood under the shade of the locust tree preparing to leave, when Elizabeth turned toward Hans.

"Mr. Schwamman, earlier . . . Did you say chemicals kill weeds, insects . . . and people?"

"Yah, they do. Just last year another one bit the dust."

"Another person?"

"Yah. Burt, he died many years ago vhen he fell into the vat at the chemical plant down in Dubuque, God rest his soul. But Elmer, he vent crazy, plum crazy, before he upended."

Elizabeth covered her mouth. "What do you mean by 'went crazy?'"

"Vell, you hear about these accidents happening vonce in a vhile, but it's always a little burn here or a scar there. Elmer had all that, but he vent in and out of the hospital many times. And I don't mean to fix his burns. No, he vent to Independence, vhere they kept him. The nut house, they call it. Some said it vould be forever."

"How was he acting? Did you see him or talk to him?" Elizabeth asked, reaching out for the tree, minuscule beads of sweat forming on her forehead.

"Yah, I saw him. Saw him at the livestock sale just last month before they took him avay. I vent to buy a new pair of pigs. I bought the vhite vones vith the black spots that look like a Dalmatian dog. Gloucestershire, they are called. Not so popular anymore, but I'm going to breed them vith each other for the first batch, then mix them up vith my Durocs and see vhat comes of it. Siri's already been painting pictures of the little vones. You should see our kitchen table—it's covered vith paintings of the darned cutest little pigs you ever did see!"

Sage, sensing her mother's growing urgency and beginning to feel some of her own, brought Hans back on track.

"Vone thing I noticed is that he couldn't smile if his life depended on it. Elmer, he used to have half a joke told before he even got to your door. But he slipped away after the accident. Never complained of pain, but it vas like the chemicals burned the fun right out of him."

"And he was in a mental hospital for depression?" Elizabeth asked.

"Depression? No! Elmer stopped laughing because he couldn't remember a single joke anymore. Blacked right out of his brain like a big eraser came along and rubbed them out."

"When you say blacked out of him, do you mean that he also had blackouts? Times when his mind sort of went away?"

"Yah! That's it! You know Elmer?"

"No. No, I don't know Elmer." Elizabeth now put a second hand against the tree trunk. "Randy, could you help me to the car? I'm . . ." Elizabeth's knees buckled beneath her as she slumped to the grass below.

Chapter 27

—— September 1953 ——

For twenty-seven days, Will had remained in the hospital. By the time Dr. Grimmsrud had arrived, his F-1 Ford rutting across the field, Will's face had turned from pale to ashen in color. The skin of his torso had begun to erupt in a mass of bleeding blisters that leaked slowly but alarmingly. Seeing my husband lying there on the dirt, powerful chemicals eating away at his flesh, knowing that there was nothing I could do . . . He was at the mercy of the doctor and of the ambulance, whose flashing red bulb seemed to take an endless amount of time to appear. But it finally did, and moments later the blaring sound was reignited, the ambulance carrying my husband toward an unknown destiny. Dr. Grimmsrud had assured me that Will would survive, that his burns were indeed severe, but that he would survive. My confidence did not equal his.

Those first days Will had spent in the hospital felt like watching a fireworks show. He'd awaken with outbursts of pain or startle over the shrill ring of a phone at the nurse's station. The girls plied me with questions about their father, and I was distraught, not knowing what our future would hold.

Day by day as Will healed, the fireworks lessened, and the clouds that had been hovering over us began to lift. A grafting surgery had been performed, removing a portion of the damaged skin and replacing it with layers taken from his thighs, leaving a smattering of scars upon a partially hairless chest, like a map of a new world.

An eyeblink before, my husband had been robust in health. Now, at age thirty-five, he had morphed into a different man. The scars were minutiae; the underlying issues were those that altered his life.

Will's muscles often cramped in agony or twitched as if in self-assault, and his joints nearly always pulsated with some level of pain. The headaches and the vertigo took several long months to subside but never entirely left. And he had become instantly asthmatic, unable to be near chemicals of any sort. Spic-and-Span was replaced with white vinegar. Clorox bleach no longer whitened our laundry.

It seemed that every moment spent with Will and the girls back then had been one of strength laced with angry energy. What were we to do? How were we to move forward? So little time was there to even consider answers with all the work there was to do.

A familiar melancholy arose, its persistence more potent than ever. Memories of previous arguments and of tension, of my trip—my infidelity—poured from my thoughts, a loosened spigot. Skirting death was a communion my husband and I shared, unbeknownst to him.

I had spent the previous four years mastering the art of dismissal. If I'd awakened from a nightmare—always involving a lake or ocean—I would imagine myself in a field of butterflies, the sun shining its warmth onto me. If I had made an egg salad sandwich and recalled the cool touch of air against my skin as Stephen and I ate the very same sandwiches aboard the *Winsome Lady* on that fateful day, I pinched myself and pushed those thoughts to the far corners of my mind, until I could sit at my sewing machine and purge the memories onto the canvas of a quilt.

But as I watched my husband suffer, knowing that his former life would likely never return, the window to my own past anguish had been thrown wide open. The two of us suffered, side-by-side, each in our own quiet agony.

The following morning, after the wondrously perfect day that Stephen and I had shared sailing before the shattering storm had approached, I had found myself in a hospital room in Chicago. Still heavy with sleep, at first I couldn't comprehend where I was or whether I was dreaming. Beneath me the mattress was firm, so different from the comfortable bed I'd grown used to at the hotel. The air smelled sterile yet identifiably sickly. Had the maid entered my room during the night?

As I had awakened more fully, I noticed that a dim light shone from beneath the door and another, that of the sun coming up over the horizon, cast a pale but strengthening light into the opposite end of the room. I studied my surroundings and realized that I was in a hospital room.

It had taken but a short while to regain my knowledge of the events that had led me to this point. Sailing upon the *Winsome Lady*, the sinister storm that had gathered as if by wizardry from the previously clear skies. Lights in the near distance. Calling out to Stephen, who was no longer at the helm. Or was he?

"Stephen," I whispered.

Silence. Of course, he wouldn't be in the same room as I.

Again, I turned toward the door. "Stephen," I called out with as much force as I could muster, but still only a whisper emerged.

I reached for the bell at my bedside and shook it. A weak but audible ring resounded, and before I could set it back on the table a nurse had arrived at my side, checking my pulse, noting numbers on a chart.

"Hush, now," she said as I whispered his name again. "You're awake, but that doesn't mean you need to make noise." She reached for my chin, pulling it down. "Here, open up."

Before I could say anything further, a thermometer had been pushed under my tongue, leaving me with my growing fear for the next two minutes as I waited for the mercury to settle into place.

"Do you know where Stephen is?" I asked Nurse Wilma the moment I had the opportunity to do so. My throat rebelled in pain.

"Shh. Now, I need to roll you onto your side," she said as she pulled at my torso.

"Is he here? Did he come here with me?"

"Take a deep breath in."

"I need to know."

"Deep breath in. Now."

The inhalation had sent me into a fit of coughing, and Nurse Wilma stepped back, letting me find my way through the painful explosion from my lungs. Afterward, I lay still, silently pleading, waiting for her to tell me that Stephen was next door. But she didn't. She didn't say anything. She only held my gaze, expressionless, her eyes mimicking the set of her lips, until she was satisfied that the coughing spell was over.

I turned away and fell into a deep sleep despite the weight of my dreams.

Will's accident had taken place in early May; by late July he was determined to resume farming. Roger, the hired man, had begun to leave buckets of grain for the milk cows outside the barn door, where Will could access them and pour the feed into the outdoor troughs. But no longer was Will able to enter the barn with its dank, pungent air. Though he would check the wire fencing in the pastures and tinker with machinery, none of his activities lasted more than a couple of hours before he'd tire out. The hired help, now expanded to two men, had become indispensable.

It wasn't until late September, after the beans had been harvested, that I had ventured back out to the field, to the very place in which our lives had been so fiercely altered. Sage and Louise were back in school, and Will was fishing at the pond down in the valley.

This time my gait was slow, vastly different from the adrenaline-induced run of a couple months prior. Disturbing emotions swirled around me as I neared the barren spot, and I allowed each to voice its sentiment—pity, misery, indignation—letting them settle in as I sat down. In time, I laid onto my back, the prickle of recently harvested plants poking painfully at my legs and shoulders, but my torment was temporary; Will's never entirely left him. Here, I let the agony of his changed life—of our family's life—seep out of me and into the tainted land beneath my body.

I thought back to my return from Chicago, the first time our collective life had changed, even if it was only I who had realized it.

My return had been a silent reception, my family having awaited my arrival at the train station in La Crosse. I had stepped off the Midwest Arrow, and Sage was there to greet me with affectionate hugs, Louise with a running lunge of an embrace. I instantly felt the uncoiling of motherly love spill over my daughters. Will had wrapped his arms around the three of us as if to form a seal around our family, and together we walked toward the car, my cold hands held tightly on either side by Sage and Louise's warm counterparts.

Once on the road, Sage had begun to belt out stanzas of "Buffalo Gals," Louise chiming in with a prolonged "moooon." I didn't sing along, suggesting that I had caught a cold near the end of my trip.

"You do look a little unwell," said Will. "I don't suppose the train ride helped you get any rest. Must be kind of noisy in there."

"It's not easy to sleep in those seats. It'll be nice to be back in my own bed again."

"It'll be nice to have you back." He looked at me tenderly as if to say the tension between us was forgiven. Yet, I could only think that he didn't have an inkling of all that called for forgiveness. I leaned my head back.

"Honey, you sure you're okay?"

I nodded. "I'll be fine. I might need a little extra sleep."

I turned toward the window, gazing out at the bluffs as we drove past, rain glistening upon them in a sunless shine. I listened to the voices of my daughters from the backseat, felt Will's hand on my shoulder, gently massaging. I closed my eyes and thought back to my final day in the city, unwilling to let it go just yet.

I hadn't learned whether Stephen was at the hospital. "Patient information is confidential," I had repeatedly been told. "But he is my friend. We were together," I'd insisted.

"He is my fiancé," I had even desperately declared at one point. Nurse Wilma had only looked down at the wedding ring on my left-hand finger and didn't say a word. "Please, I don't have to see him. Just let me know if he is here." This plea had, like the others, had fallen on silent ears.

At the hospital I had created a different identity, using my maiden name. A phone call to Will was out of the question, and I'd therefore claimed not to have a phone or a husband, despite the ring. I was weak and desperately tired, but other than a cough, I had not sustained any injuries. And I had a train to catch in two days.

The following day I had been set free, my cough having already subsided significantly.

"We just needed to get you nice and cozy for a while," said Nurse Wilma after the doctor had given me the anxiety-relieving news of my release.

I had returned to the Dominican via taxicab and slept long but fitfully. The next morning, I had packed my belongings and taken a taxi to the train station.

Stephen had been nowhere to be found. He was not at the hospital. He was not waiting for me at the Dominican. He was not at the other end of the desperately ringing telephone. I had to decide whether to remain in Chicago for what by all appearances had become a futile search or to return to my home, from where I could continue my search from afar.

———◊———

It was late when we had arrived home from the train station. I tucked the girls into their beds and met Will in our own bedroom. We made love, a perfunctory act, after which he held me for longer moments than he had in years. I abided. I acted. He slept soundly. I hardly slept.

I had begun to see the world through a different lens, a crisp sense of loss having become the beneficiary of my life turned inside out. I was back home, a mother of two who was playing the role of wife. As memories arose, I learned to diligently brush or tuck or heave them aside until I was able to sit in my sewing room and stitch together quilts.

Will's distant, confused glances hadn't gone unnoticed, but I couldn't bring myself to ask him what his thoughts were, nor did he inquire too deeply of mine. He seemed to know, as if with animal instinct, that something was amiss, but breaking the bubble of assumed contentedness was not an option. At least not yet.

We carried on as husband and wife, and I poured myself into family life. Meals became more bountiful, whites became whiter, and dust was nearly obliterated from our home. I withdrew from Ladies' Circle, claiming that my work held me back, which was not entirely untrue. I couldn't have surmised that I would one day be lying in a newly harvested field feeling the sharp stems of beanstalks impress upon my skin, my husband beyond my reach, his body and mind scarred for life. Where I would realize, with a nagging sense of certainty, that no matter how much I hoped or prayed for Will—for a full recovery to buoyant health—he would not be with me into our golden years.

At length, I pushed myself up and was making my way across the shorn stalks toward the house when I saw something thick protruding from the field, bringing back a flash of memory from the day of Will's accident. I walked the few short steps over, where I discovered a piece of rusted iron partially exposed. I tapped it with the toe of my shoe. I pulled at it using the heft of my body. But it would not budge. I turned around and made my way to the barn in search of a shovel.

Weeks had expanded into months, the snow heavy that winter, pushing at the walls of our personal space. I had begun walking daily, an activity that allowed a small sliver of time in which I could be alone. When spring finally arrived, warmth washed over me like a pleasant bath as I trod through the woods, and by summer, the trails were clearly laid out in several directions throughout our acres of woodland. Somehow, September had already slid into place, and it was a walk that was on my mind as I readied breakfast.

"Roger's here," I called to Will, seeing the hired hand's pickup come to a stop next to the chicken coop in a cloud of dust.

"He'll start the milking without me."

I dipped the last slice of bread into the egg and milk mixture and laid it on the baking sheet. Though it had happened before, it was rare for Will to miss a milking—the chore he had been most eager to resume once he was able to tolerate the barn air.

Wiping my hands on the kitchen towel, I approached the bed where he still lay. His hand was on his forehead, calloused palm facing up. The blanket was turned down, exposing the raspberry-colored mark on his chest.

"Your head," I said. "I'll get you some aspirin."

"Ice this morning."

"I'll bring both."

Headaches were no longer frequent, but when they did arrive it was usually with a vengeance. Aspirin and ice were hardly cures, but at least they provided some relief.

"The fence in the northwest field, downhill from the gate. Have him replace the barbed wire. First thing after milking."

"But wasn't that fixed on Monday? When you two put up the new gates?" I asked as I set down the aspirin, fluffing the feather pillows as much as I could during the few moments that he sat up. This wasn't the first time his memory had failed him.

My husband gave me a distant look and laid back down. I closed the door gently and returned to the kitchen where I slid the pan of French toast into the oven.

Never a garrulous man, Will had now folded even further into himself. When he did talk, it was at times tinged with confusion; at other times he was quick to ignite spurious interactions—a far cry from the amiable man I'd been married to these past several years. Life was different now, but we adjusted. He adjusted, and I adjusted. We ate, we slept, we moved. There'd been talk that our marriage had fallen into a sad predicament, and I suppose they were right, in a way.

By midafternoon, Will roused himself and was readying to meet Roger in the hayfield. I was pouring a thermos of iced tea and reminded him to drink plenty, but he walked out the door as if he hadn't heard me.

A low-pressure system had pushed its way in, resting heavily upon the late summer day as the girls arrived home on the school bus. Sage was sent out to the garden to gather beets and potatoes for supper. Louise was pushing the old baby carriage across the backyard with a handful of kittens desperately peering over the edge, their terrified meows heard clearly through the open window of the kitchen. I shook my head and laughed at Louise's never-ending desire to mother creatures.

I had decided to work on some sewing. It was unusual for me to be in the sewing room in the middle of a summer's day, but the patching had to get done, especially now that both of the hired hand's jeans were added to the stack. I had just finished turning a pant leg inside-out and was positioning the denim patch when I heard Will return and pull the thermos off the counter. The kitchen door closed with a bang, the spring having broken the week before.

I watched through the sewing room window as he climbed onto the tractor, the rake attached behind, and heard the groaning *putt, putt, putt* of the engine catch to full roar. The sound receded as Will drove away. The thing is, I expected him to return, as he always had.

In my memory, I've outlined these ordinary moments—setting the sewing machine to a zigzag stitch, the clang of the screen door, the starting of the tractor—as reminders that life gives no warning to its capricious ways. Will had driven away on the John Deere, thermos of iced tea tucked beside him, and the next time he was seen was in the creek bed, the tractor lying silently on top of him.

It was first surmised that the tractor's brakes had given out and Will had tried to jump off, the cuff of his jeans catching on the pedal. It was later discovered, however, that the tractor's brakes were in fine working order, as were the clutch, axles, and steering wheel. Like all of Will's machinery, it had been meticulously kept. The tractor and rake were not at fault.

I wasn't oblivious to the talk that breezed through the community. People knew there'd been trouble between us, but now the timeline of our changed relationship had been pushed back from Will's accident with the sprayer to my trip to Chicago.

"Ever since then, Betty's been so quiet. Remember how she pulled out of the Ladies' Circle as soon as she got back from the city? Makes a person wonder why the sudden change."

"Will was never the same either, like that sparkle in his eyes just burned right out of him. Seemed to me it happened right around then."

"She never should've gone away without him. City of sin."

"Ruined poor Will to his very core."

Their words became a scarlet letter sewn onto my garments. They wondered to each other aloud, some without concern that I was nearby, perhaps even with intention. But no one ever chose to ask me—it was much more fulfilling to use one's imagination. And so, it had been determined that in Will's despair, he had driven the tractor precariously close to the steep edge of the bank, unable to live with his marriage in ruins, and took his own life. The mystery of Will Ley's unusual death had been settled.

But I wouldn't settle for it.

Though the coroner revealed nothing unusual, no one knew Will like I did. No one understood the insurmountable control he had over the bearings of life, even as the pain of his disability bore into him. To have let it all go by taking his own life would have been to erase his belief in the order of the world and of God. That, Will would not have done.

But I was just the wife, a solitary raindrop in the gathering storm around me with little chance of convincing anyone otherwise. Not that I had tried; I was too numb. I'd lost my son. I'd lost the man I loved. And now I'd lost my husband. I was thirty-one years old, and a period had been placed at the end of my brief cycle with the male species.

It wasn't long before I came to understand that the girls and I would not be staying on the farm. Because the farm had been Will's. Because the farm was the pincushion holding in the pointed memories of all that had been lost.

— August 1975 —

"What's happening?" Louise lurched toward Elizabeth. "Mother!" Sage fell into place beside her mother and quickly confirmed the rise and fall of her chest. "She's breathing fine. Her pulse is somewhat slow but steady."

"Maybe the heat got to her," Randy suggested.

Sage thought of her mother's recent disclosure of infidelity. Of her visitor, Neil. And the fact that she was now back at the farm for the first time in over twenty years, the place where she had last seen her husband. "Mother, can you hear me?" she asked, her voice raised unnecessarily.

Elizabeth stirred and nodded slowly, her lids heavy but intentional as they reopened.

"How many fingers am I holding up?" Sage asked.

Elizabeth held up three of her own.

"Can you breathe okay?"

She nodded slowly. "I think I fainted."

"Yeah, you really bugged us out," said Louise, wiping away the sweat from her mother's forehead.

Elizabeth began to push herself up onto her elbow, but Sage ordered her to lie back down. She insisted, however, and Randy reached a hand under her back as Sage and Louise each held an elbow, slowly moving her into a sitting position under the shade of the locust tree.

"How embarrassing. I'm sorry," said Elizabeth, confusion crossing her face.

"No apology needed, Mother, but what the hell just happened?" asked Louise.

"Maybe we should give her a minute, butterfly," said Randy. "Here, Siri's coming with something to drink, Mama Betty."

From the direction of the house came Siri, scurrying toward them with a pitcher of water. Elizabeth felt as if she were reliving a scene from years ago when she herself had carried a pitcher of water toward her injured husband in the field just beyond where she now sat.

She took a long drink, then looked back toward the bank of the creek, toward the site of Will's death, recalling Hans's description of Elmer's mental state, the result of an accident not so dissimilar from Will's. At the time of his accident, nobody—not even Dr. Grimmsrud—had believed that a chemical burn had the power to cause an eruptive blackout over a year later. To now learn that another man had been impacted by a similar menagerie of horrific symptoms and subsequently sentenced to a life of insanity was like the resurfacing of a wound, but one that could now be treated. One that might even be healed.

When Sage had first suggested returning to the farm, Elizabeth understood that doing so would most certainly reopen doors that she had previously locked securely after having taken the girls and left for Minnesota those many years ago. But this—this she didn't expect. Hints of a long-delayed explanation for his death—could it be possible?

Sage followed the line of her mother's sight toward the creek, the way she scanned the broader expanse of land from the mild slope of the field they'd just walked to the one across the driveway where a creek bed had been dramatically carved along the base of the steeper hillside. Questions began to sprout, connections dancing elusively on the stage before her. Visions of Daddy, of crosses and fields. Of a tear sliding down Daddy's cheek—and now Mother's cheek. Was there a connection? Could it be a message?

She inspected the scene more closely, taking note of a row of oak trees that grew nearby, and of one in particular, a leafless skeleton just like in her visions. *Watch out for that cross. Don't trip.*

"Mother?"

Elizabeth looked at Sage, her lingering lightheadedness quickly forgotten once she noticed the distance in her daughter's eyes. "What is it?"

"How did Daddy die?" Sage asked, still looking beyond. "I mean, I know his tractor rolled over the creek bank. But why did that happen?"

Elizabeth had her elevator story, the one that she had told her daughters, her new friends, and inquisitive others that she'd met in her redesigned life. It was a truthful story, a reliable story. Will had lost control at the wheel of his tractor and, too close to the steep bank of the creek, it had rolled, pinning him against the rocky floor of the creek in an instant death.

But now, over the course of the past few minutes, her story had been exposed to the vivid light of day, unfolded and shaken out, resuscitating the question of Will's death. After all these years, there was a modicum of evidence that he hadn't taken his own life because of a marriage whose legs had become rickety, as so many had insisted, but that it may have been an effect—the after-effect—of poison that caused his demise.

"You look like you're on the verge of freaking out, sis," said Louise.

Sage looked fleetingly at Louise and Elizabeth, lines furrowing between her eyes. She stood and took a few steps in the direction of the creek. "Don't trip," she whispered. "Don't trip," she repeated more forcefully, turning back toward her mother.

"Sage . . ."

"Hush, Louise." Elizabeth held an arm out toward her younger daughter.

The breeze that had accelerated while they were in the field was once again calm, the sun luminous. The distant babble of water over ancient rocks resounded in the stillness.

"Don't trip. That was Daddy's caution in a vision I had," Sage continued. "He was pointing at a cross. A cross stuck in the dirt. He was making me aware of it." She took a few more steps in the direction of the creek. "I think it was his way of telling me something about his death. I feel it. But I don't know what it is." She knotted her hands at the back of her head, averting her gaze toward the sky.

"Sage," Elizabeth began after a moment. "Louise." She paused. "I'd always believed that your father's death was an accident. But I think you must know . . ."

Sage dropped her hands and turned to face her mother.

"At the time the accident occurred . . . Well, even for a few years before that, we'd experienced some stressors in our marriage that . . . that challenged us as a couple. That changed us."

Sage thought back to the story of Mother's trip to Chicago. She noticed a look of alarm cross her sister's face.

"What I want you to understand is that where my life is now is very different from where it was back then. Because I've intentionally sculpted a different life, one that is fitting to who I am," continued Elizabeth, her sights set on Louise.

"Being a farm wife in a small community was not for me, and I couldn't find joy in it beyond being with you, my daughters." She drew in a breath. "As you can imagine, this caused a growing distance between your father and me for a time. All that your father ever really wanted was to raise a family and a farm."

Elizabeth took another sip of water from the stiff pink plastic cup, *Funk Seed, Inc.* printed on the front, its colors faded from wear.

"When your father had the accident with the sprayer, his life changed. Physically, he was no longer able to do the things he'd always done. Eventually he got back to his everyday life, despite his limitations. He was a farmer; he pushed ahead.

"But it wasn't just that. He experienced lapses in memory and became easily angered. Depression set in. He was a changed man." How easy it was to recall those trying times, even all these years later.

"As for my part, after his accident I set aside our differences and gave him my full attention. But by this time there had been a noticeable change in Mr. and Mrs. Will Ley. Or so went the gossip." She reached out her hands, one toward Sage and one toward Louise. "When your father's tractor rolled down the creek bed for no clear reason, it was assumed by many . . . It was assumed that he had taken his own life."

Louise gasped. "Oh my god!"

Elizabeth pulled her daughters in close. "I chose not to mention this before now because I've always known that it wasn't true."

"That isn't what happened," declared Sage. "And something happened today that confirmed this."

"Yes," Elizabeth replied. "I've always intuited that his death had to do with those chemicals. But Dr. Grimmsrud never agreed from a physician's point of view. There was no proof that your father had blacked out—and there was certainly no reason for it, Dr. Grimmsrud had concluded. So, the assumption was that he took his own life."

"But it's not true," reiterated Louise.

"No, Louise, it is not."

"And Hans's comments about Elmer solidified that for you?" asked Sage.

Elizabeth nodded. "But I do think that he knew he wouldn't be long for this world," she continued. "He never said as much, but as I mentioned, your father's changed life took a toll on him. I can't help but wonder if he etched the fourth mark into the family cross during that time."

"Whoa," said Louise. Randy wrapped his arm around her.

"The idea just occurred to me today," said Elizabeth.

"But what's this got to do with you dreaming about black dirt?" Randy asked Sage, whose faraway look had further intensified. "You look like you're dreaming again now."

Sage shook her head. "The visions. They've been ongoing, not just the one I told Louise about. Since then, I've had two more. I never knew when they'd show up, and I never had a clue what they meant. Each was slightly different from the previous one, as if progressing, like a story."

"And Daddy was in them?" asked Louise.

"Yes, always."

Sage described the graveyard and the single teardrop of the first vision and the subsequent one in which an open field lay in the distance, Daddy beside her, again with inexplicable tears. She then revealed the final one in which Daddy had cautioned her to "watch your step" as they walked together over a field of black dirt.

"*Black* soil. His blackout," she explained, her voice beginning to elevate. "Each vision involved water, whether precipitation or tears. And the cross—we wouldn't be here if Hans hadn't called us about the cross he found. The cross that Mother had tripped over."

The look in Sage's eyes now matched the growing excitement of her words. "You see it, right? Daddy led us here. He's given us the answer. I don't just feel it—I know it!"

Elizabeth was certain that Sage was right. These past weeks had felt like an impending storm had been moving ever closer. The surprise delivery of the family cross dredging up the loss of Will, the rehashing of her sins as she opened up to Sage. And the appearance of Neil resurfacing heart-wrenching memories of Stephen and the myriad unanswered questions surrounding him. But now the storm had begun to recede. Now, it was moving back toward the horizon.

"Yes, Sage. I believe you are right," said Elizabeth.

Elizabeth looked over at the hayfield one last time, then to the creek at the bottom of the hillside. Around her, the blue of the sky seemed to have brightened and the heaviness in the air to have lifted, allowing her to breathe deeply and fully for the first time in years. No longer was she a silent mourner whose solitary story stood like a fading star in the night sky. Other secrets would, perhaps, remain just that for now, but this burden—this lasting weight—had finally been lifted.

"Thank you," she whispered and turned back toward her family.

The plane soared through the summer sky, the allure of the scenery below once again commanding the attention of its passengers. The return trip was quieter, and it wasn't long before Sage brought the airplane in for a smooth landing and taxied to the hangar, where her passengers waited as she worked through post-flight procedures.

"Why do you think Daddy would've buried the cross in a field?" Louise asked her mother. "Why not on a hill or next to a big tree? Isn't that what people do?"

"It does seem unlike him to bury it in a tillable field," replied Elizabeth.

"I think Daddy buried the cross in the field on purpose," said Sage, stepping down from the plane.

"It's about time you spoke. Hardly heard a peep from you the whole way home," said Louise as they walked out into the blaze of sun, the broiling heat of the pavement meeting them with a punch.

"When we were flying home, I recalled looking into immigration records for a project on the ore mines up north a few years ago. There were some photos of small graveyards right on the edge of farm fields, just like you still see today. Back then it wasn't uncommon for people to bury their loved ones on their land. Daddy couldn't do that; he couldn't bury his parents on his land, but he could memorialize them—and Frankie too. What better way to do so than on his newly acquired property?"

"He did extend that field the third spring after we moved there. Come to think of it, its burial spot would've been near the edge of the original acreage," said Elizabeth.

They arrived at the car where Sage opened the driver's door, a hot blast of air rushing forth, and reached in to unlock the back door.

"Will used to talk about burying the past," Elizabeth continued. "'Never mind that, it's buried in the past,' he would say. God knows he had every reason to do so, after losing his parents when he was seventeen. His brother no longer in touch. His only son buried." Elizabeth looked up at the sky. "But after today, I think he was telling us just the opposite. I think he was telling us to revisit the past." She turned to Sage. "You, more than anyone, could understand that."

Sage nodded in agreement.

"Maybe the past is where we have to return," Elizabeth continued. "Take a peek inside, without sticking around for too long. Be aware of it. Be aware of the tip of the cross protruding from the earth, but that's enough." A self-realized lesson that Elizabeth would take to heart.

Chapter 29

— August 1975 —

Neil arrived at Elizabeth's door at a prompt four o'clock Monday afternoon. Until now, their conversations had led her no closer to the truth of Stephen's life—or death. At times she was convinced that he'd perished, but subsequent conversations led her to believe that her former lover was very much alive. She'd begun to wonder if this was merely a twisted game to Neil.

But now, with the weight of Will's untimely death lifted, Elizabeth hungered for further peace. She'd had enough of his shenanigans.

Neil made his way into the kitchen, where he pulled a bottle of scotch from a paper bag. Elizabeth watched him remove the cork and tip the bottle forward, its contents flowing freely into the glass that he had garnered from her cupboard. Scotch had been Stephen's drink of choice, and she momentarily recalled the pungent taste that had crossed from his lips to hers during the last kiss they'd shared.

"Neil—"

"Would you join me in a glass of scotch today?" he asked, interrupting her.

"Yes, I think I will."

Neil glanced her way before reaching for a second glass and pouring an inch.

Together, they walked outside and onto the deck, toward the metal chairs that she kept draped with towels to avoid the scorch of heat. Elizabeth sat, resting her glass on her lap, forcing herself to keep her cool despite the thudding of her anxious heart.

"Neil," she began, with no attempt at easing into conversation. "Tell me about Stephen. Did he survive? I think you owe it to me to be straightforward."

Though her gaze was direct, Elizabeth could feel herself quivering. Still, she was determined that this visit would not end without knowing what had happened to Stephen. Too much time had passed with her acquiescing to the unknowns of her past. She took a sip from her glass, the sharp, smoky taste of the scotch punctuating its potency.

"Do I?" Neil responded, his voice somnolent as he rolled up his shirt sleeves.

Since Neil had first arrived on Elizabeth's doorstep, she had mulled over what the discovery of Stephen's fate might ultimately mean for her. What would she do if he was alive and well? She was, after all, an independent woman who was unattached to a man and free to choose her path forward. Would she seek him out? Be unyielding in her efforts to find the man she had never ceased to love? Or would she succumb to the fact that—despite all that she had shared with Stephen—she really hadn't known him well? She couldn't prove that his love had been authentic—certainly not after all these years—even though it felt so very real at the time. How often as time slipped by had she questioned whether his attentions and words were authentic, whether her story was real or fantasy? Could he right now be sailing the Atlantic with another woman? Could he have forgotten her?

"Let me ask you a question, Elizabeth. Why did you never look for him, your lover?" Neil asked, raising the glass to his lips.

"What makes you think I haven't?" Elizabeth retorted.

"Presumably, I would have heard of your return to Chicago. We ran in the same circles, Stephen and I, as you know."

"I had to return to my life, Neil. I couldn't go back to Chicago to look for someone who by all odds and by all indications had not survived." She took another sip.

"Still, you presume wrongly. I did look for him—often and long. For weeks I drove to the library in my town to scour every page of the *Tribune*. Nothing was reported but for a small mention of a boating accident: a recovered woman, a missing man. I wrote to Wini at the Blue Window, but her band had moved on to a new venue, a new city. I had no way to find her."

Elizabeth checked herself, willed herself to remain calm. How she wished that Neil had never reentered her life—this vexing man who left her desperate for answers, reassurance even.

From over by the gazebo the sight of the canoe caught her eye, a reflection of abandonment against the lake that danced and dappled in the magnificent sunlight just beyond. The lake was why she had chosen this place as her home years ago, her way of maintaining a relic of Stephen: the memory of him, of their memories made together.

"Stephen . . . survived," Neil said.

Elizabeth was caught off guard. She heard the words he spoke, yet fathom was elusive.

"How was it that he survived?" she asked after a moment of hesitation.

"Life vest. Just like you."

She shook her head. "But he wasn't in the hospital. I was there, and he wasn't there. Surely, they would have brought him to the same hospital as me. I asked about him. Again and again, I asked about him."

Neil looked at her with a hint of surprise.

"What?" Elizabeth stood. "What do you mean with your eyes? What do you need to tell me, Neil?" She set down the scotch, unwilling to be deterred by a vice that might meddle further with her thoughts.

"What more should I say?"

"What more?" Elizabeth took a step toward him, a rise of fury beginning to flare. "All of it, Neil," she said. "I want to know all of what you know. Don't toy with me. And don't look at me that way!"

"I imply nothing with my look," he said, his voice remaining unnervingly low-key.

Elizabeth reached for the handrail, squeezing her impatience into it. "I respectfully request a full explanation. Did Stephen truly survive? And if so, where is he today?"

Neil shifted his legs, recrossing them on the opposite side. "If I tell you this information, how might it benefit you?"

"How might it benefit me?" Elizabeth stepped directly in front of him. "It might benefit me, Neil, by enabling me to seek out the man I have been in love with for almost twenty-seven years. It might benefit me by bringing an end to an agonizing ache that has lived inside my heart for *half of my life*."

"So, you were in love with him?" Neil looked at her questioningly. "And . . . he with you?"

"Of course I was in love with him! We didn't spend those many days together—nights together—as *pals*. I'm sure Stephen shared some of this with you. If not before the accident, surely after."

"What makes you think I've seen him since the accident?"

The ire that had been simmering turned to a boil, but an explosive outrage was very well just what this exasperating man was seeking, Elizabeth realized, and remained calm as she spoke. "Presumably, if he had indeed survived, you—his closest friend who, from what I recall, sought his companionship as often as possible—would have spoken with him several times over during these past two decades."

Again Neil hesitated, keeping a steady eye on hers. He drew in another sip of scotch and smacked his lips. "Mrs. Ley, people change. And friendships end—for many reasons."

"Did your friendship with Stephen change?"

"Well, I don't have an answer for that. I didn't see him again after the accident."

"But he survived? You know this to be true?"

"I know of the accident, and I know that it wasn't the only boating mishap that night. A barge also lost three crewmen in the same waters."

"What does that have to do with Stephen?"

"You, my dear, were retrieved by a rescue squad. But you were the only one found."

Elizabeth inwardly cringed at the endearment but recalled how, during her haze of convalescence, the doctor at the hospital had mentioned her rescue.

"Two of the crewmen went missing, but still, two men were also pulled from the lake by the crewmen that same night: one dead and one alive." He downed the last of the scotch from the tumbler. "He who survived was not a member of the crew, nor was he ever identified. The survivor, you see, chose to remain anonymous."

Elizabeth finally sat, ignoring the scalding heat of the chair where the towel had slipped away. "But . . . why did this story not run in the *Tribune*? I wouldn't have missed an article about another boating accident that had occurred on that same night in Lake Michigan. Another accident, Neil."

"The answer is simple. The barge was owned by Great Lakes Shipping. The captain had allowed a bit of revelry on board before leaving dock. Turns out two of those who went overboard had had more than their fair share of drinks." He unfolded his legs and leaned forward.

"You see, Elizabeth, Great Lakes is a powerful company. They not only threatened to sue the *Tribune* if the story was exposed, but they paid the publisher a good sum to keep it under wraps. And so, it was never published.

"But, three years later, I happened to meet one of the crewmen who witnessed the scene, drunk as a skunk at a pub."

"And he revealed the story to you."

"He revealed the story to more than me by that point. Fired within six months of the accident for leaking. Exchanged his title of seaman to that of full-time drunk."

"And did any of the newspapers pick it up at that point?"

"No. Not the *Tribune* at the very least. Might've been a paragraph or two hidden in the pages of a smaller press, but I can't say for sure. I never saw anything."

"And you think that the unidentified man was Stephen." Her eyes narrowed. "Why?"

"Because the drunk knew every crewman on board, and this man was not one of them."

"That proves nothing," Elizabeth continued. "What did they purportedly do with him?"

"He claimed that they took him to the ship's infirmary. Later, the captain deposited him at Petoskey, offered a wad of money to keep quiet—money that he declined. The man was never heard from again."

Elizabeth considered this for a moment, but Neil's story still wasn't adding up.

"Surely, he would have let someone know. Friends, family. Ruth—Ruth would have known."

"Ruth and Stephen were in the middle of a quick and fairly hostile divorce, if you recall. The only thing any of us knew is that you and he went out sailing, you returned and left very soon thereafter, and he and the boat did not return. End of story."

"Until a drunk at a pub convinced you that he was rescued by the crew of a barge, that consequently kept him imprisoned in convalescence, offered him hush money, and dropped him off into an unknown life. All of this happened to Stephen."

"You are welcome to believe what you wish. I'm not here to convince you of anything."

"Why *are* you here, Neil?" Elizabeth faced him squarely.

Neil stood up and looked out past the lake, toward the distant cities beyond. "I, Elizabeth, am here to build magnificent things." He turned back toward her. "And I am here with you because you intrigue me."

His eyes roamed downward over her neck, her breasts, her legs, just as they had those many years ago. He stepped forward, sliding the back of his hand up her arm, his eyes settling once again onto hers.

Elizabeth grabbed his hand and pushed it hard against his chest, causing him to stumble backward at the surprise attack. Without hesitation, she reached for his glass and looked him squarely in the eye.

"And I, Neil, will now bring this reunion to a close," she said. "You will leave my home. Never again will you and I see each other."

Chapter 30

—— September 1975 ——

Is the Penguin Planning a Coup?
By Peck Wells

They claim their mission is "for the good of the people," but is the Cooperative Organization—the "CO"—actually flexing its puny muscles under a magnifying glass as a clever ruse to intimidate their kindred?

Three months ago, "Aida" flipped a coin from heads to tails. "Aida," a woman I've known going on four years, has a voice as groovy as silken tofu, a never-ending smile that you can't help dreaming about, and wit quicker than instant coffee. This city girl can dole out a shovel of shit like she's been farming all her life.

But Aida has never farmed; instead, she answered phones and handed out keys and smiled with delicately practiced acceptance as customers from the hotel in which she worked unloaded their complaints onto her. She rented a single room in a house, walked to the bus stop under both warm summer sun and freezing rain. She probably could have stood to take more time off or eat more food than she did. And, she volunteered at a food coop nearby.

You see, not so very long ago my friend Aida, giddy with the excitement of a schoolgirl recently asked to prom, told me that she'd "been invited." Not to prom, but to a meeting with a group that was all about helping people just like her, a working gal, move up in the world—a seemingly authentic, change-inspired group. She couldn't say much about it—she didn't know much about it—but she understood that if everything worked out, there was a chance she'd be enrolling in college. "Imagine, me grooving a backpack!" she'd exclaimed.

Aida got her backpack. In exchange, her operatic voice was muted.

Last week I came upon Aida downtown, where she was waiting for her ride. I grabbed ahold of her hands as I always had, but those hands pulled away like they'd been seared by an iron. Then I noticed her new pantsuit (pantsuit!). I noticed her fleshed-out frame. I noticed her reticence to answer my friendly inquiries with anything other than two-word sentences. She had become, in effect, her upside-down self. And when a blue car packed with bodies drove up, she pulled at the door handle and sank herself into the remaining space without a goodbye.

Sound familiar, anyone? Sound like a big hungry bear might be in town, looking for more meat to fill its belly? Perhaps more co-ops to gulp up, more power to yield, more demands to

> make—all in the name of "anticapitalism" for "the good of the masses?" A bear that leaves behind a trail of shit laced with tin? A bear that leaves others wondering how their values had come to suddenly crumble in their hands like a dried-up sugar cookie?
>
> Aida had stepped away from the opera of her own life to become the last-row, second-to-the-right voice in the church choir. She got a backpack in exchange. But the question remains: for what? Or perhaps more so: for whom?

Sage closed the cover to *Sensationally Alive* and realized that her jaws were clamped shut. The disquiet caused by Peck's words morphed swiftly into apprehension at the thought of the fury his editorial could incite if read by the wrong person. Already the CO was on a rampage of angry victory—no further fuel was required.

Inflammatory writing was his way, she realized. Now that they'd been on a couple of dates, she began to understand him better and knew that he would continue his quest to bring humanity to their senses. His kind eyes belied his insatiable desire to stronghold the world into making it right, as he saw it, to plant a tree in the center of a path where it could not be missed. Peck was bent on nailing to its trunk neon signs with words that ended in exclamation points.

Even so, even though his style was acutely fearless, astonishingly fiery at times—and her manner one of reticence—she knew that she would support him in his choices. Peck had become a dash, a sudden break from the predictable flow of her days. She'd spent what had felt like her entire lifetime in search of definitiveness, of details to support unarguable sense, tirelessly scanning black print on white pages in a technicolor world around her. But never had she felt such an awareness of another's presence as she did with Peck. And now, after reading his latest editorial, a sense of fear arose that both exhilarated and frightened her. Fear for Peck, for his forwardness into a danger zone in which he could become a target. If there was one thing she didn't want, it was a premature period on their budding relationship. She would keep searching for the answers he sought. She would do her best to protect him through her research.

Sage was reasonably certain that Peck was right. Mark too. The CO just didn't add up. Someone, some force, had to be behind the bizarre acquiescence of the other co-ops in the area, just like someone had to be behind the assumed threats to this girl, "Aida." But to what avail? This was food, not weapons. Marxists, no doubt, but not gangsters.

With dim recollection, she thought of the Corvette that Louise had told her about, the driver having watched the fight at Living Waters from his car. Who was he? And why did a black Corvette seem so familiar?

Bono ambled over to her, the rope of his leash between his teeth. She clipped the leash onto his collar, slipped on a pair of sandals, and headed toward the park on Linden Avenue. There, she let him off leash as they roamed through the woods on dirt trails, Bono slowly loping ahead, stopping often to sniff at a tree trunk or something hidden within a tuft of grass. The echoing sound of cicadas rose and fell around them as she continued her thoughts. And then it came to her: the airport.

A couple of weeks back when Sage had arrived at the airport, she'd noticed a tall, blond-haired woman, perhaps in her mid-twenties, walk through the small lobby and toward a shiny black Corvette that was waiting just outside. Both the woman and the car had seemed out of place, but Sage assumed a randy businessman was having a midlife crisis: new Corvette, new airplane, new woman. She got a brief look at the man in the driver's seat, but he'd peeled out nearly before the woman's door was closed, marking his territory with black tread.

Sage hastened toward Bono and clipped his leash back on, urging him to walk faster as she hurried toward home. The moment they were back inside, she dialed the number to the airport. But as she wound the dial of the seventh number, she realized that a phone call was futile. They certainly wouldn't give out information about passengers, if they even knew their names.

She clicked the receiver and began dialing Terry's number at the *Twin Cities Times*. She'd recently asked him to consider writing a piece on Living Waters, of their attempt to educate others about food, but he didn't think there'd be enough interest. Now, she hesitated for a moment before continuing to dial, unsure that she ought to be asking for another favor so soon. But she'd helped him out plenty of times; it couldn't hurt to ask.

Within a half hour, Terry called her back. Three speeding citations had been given out to owners of black Corvettes in the past six months alone. One was a woman. Another was someone test-driving a car. But the third, one Theophilus Smith, had an additional record of a domestic disturbance tagged to his file.

"I don't like the feel of this," she said to herself after hanging up the phone.

Ignoring a pang of hunger, Sage picked up the White Pages. There was no listing for Theophilus Smith, not that she expected it would be that easy—she didn't even know if he lived in the city, after all.

But she realized that she was getting ahead of herself. First, she had to compare notes with Louise and Peck. Was the young woman she saw at the airport Aida? She had no idea. Was it the same black Corvette that both Louise and Peck saw? Was there even a connection?

Her growing unease told her that there was indeed a strong chance of a connection. But she wasn't about to rely on feelings when facts needed to be had.

"It goes beyond rights. And beyond who is right or wrong. We've got to build unity together, here and now, as nature intends. Or else division will be created in its void, a separation that goes far beyond business, or neighborhoods, or food. A separation of humanity! You don't want that any more than we do. So embrace, man. Embrace what is unique and celebrate it."

The modest crowd that had gathered on the front lawn of Living Waters applauded in the space of Mark's pause, a sharp whistle of approval from Peck. "Thank God We're Living" Water's Day of Celebration had arrived, and the hard work of the gang to restore the co-op would, hopefully, pay off.

"We're all connected. We are of the same ilk as much as we are one with the grass, your dog, the clouds. It's food, man. It's everything—but it's also just food. An awakening to a different relationship with food."

Mark was concluding his brief speech that was met with more scattered applause just as a shy sprinkle began. Though guests had politely listened in, the real attractions were the young goats brought in by the Sanderson family, along with samples of their Green Acres goat cheese. Next to their display another featured Nick's eggs, free range and grain-free, and a few of the chickens raised on a diet of garden scraps, worms, and bugs plucked from the rich soil on his farm. An array of colorful tomatoes and peppers, along with neatly tied flower bundles, rounded out the vendor displays.

As soon as Mark's speech ended, Louise got up from where she'd been sitting on the grass between Sherrie and Randy. She'd been distracted, thinking about a call from Sage last night. Her sister had asked for details on the Corvette that she'd noticed at the co-op, as well as the person inside it—anything she could remember. Not that Sage searching for details was alarming—she was Sage, after all, full-on Velma mode the norm—but it was the unusual intensity with which she inquired that had piqued Louise's attention.

Louise began to mill about, casually asking a couple of those who lived nearby about a black Corvette seen recently in the area, but no one seemed to have noticed. She gave up quickly, realizing that this wasn't the day for nosing around.

"Hey there, what's your goat's name?" Louise asked a young girl dressed in a checkered shirt and dark red denim jeans.

"This is Cindy, and the one over there is Purple," she replied with a note of youthful pride.

"Well, aren't they little charmers? Are they the cheesemakers?" Louise asked.

"Daddy and Mommy make the cheese," the girl replied with a firm look so as not to let anyone think the goats did all the work. "But they give us the milk. Only because I feed them every day. Else the milk would disappear."

"Why yes, of course it would! Feeding them really is the most important thing."

The girl's younger brother hid behind her, a small bundle topped with dark wavy hair, who peeked out at Louise every few seconds. Louise crouched down and poked her head around the opposite side of the sister wall, forcing a smile from his punch-red lips. He scooted underneath the Sanderson table, and Louise slid over to the side of the goat pen, crouching even lower. She'd always been drawn to young children—to young creatures of any sort—and was about to peek over the pen at him with a "boo!" when a blinding glimmer of sunlight caused her to shield her eyes. She squinted toward the source, the hair on her arms raising at the sight of a small cluster of vehicles pulling up to the curb near the end of the block.

Louise shot up. *This can't be happening again, not today!*

She quickly moved over to where Mrs. Sanderson stood and whispered into her ear before turning back toward the gathering to seek out Mark. Peck was there in front of her, looking directly at the cars that were now draining a sludge of men onto the street.

"Go!" he said with hushed urgency. "Let Mark know, then gather the other girls and get the hell out of here. I'll take care of the guests." His eyes locked onto hers. "Now."

Louise spun around and broke into an easy gait, trying to be as nonchalant as possible as she set her focus on Mark. A bitter sensation formed in her throat—not the first time it'd happened in recent days.

"They're back," she said, whispering into Mark's ear.

Mark nodded, and Louise changed direction and made her way toward Sherrie and the young couple who she recognized as the first new customers since the brawl that had turned the co-op on its heels.

"Sherrie, c'mon," Louise asserted as soon as she saw her. "You too," she said to the couple. "Follow me." She grabbed Sherrie's hand and moved quickly toward the corner of the house, feeling her stomach lurch, a rise of angry bile.

"What's going on?" Sherrie asked, noticing then that Tim was clearing the vendor families and Peck hurriedly ushering away other guests.

"They're back," Louise managed to say before bending over to wretch, the acidic burn in her throat like the deep lick of a flame. *Ugh, what a time to get sick!*

Sherrie saw the battalion of angry men approaching and pointed the young couple toward the back alley. "Don't you worry, girl," she said, turning to Louise. "They're not gonna take us down."

Louise nodded, swiping at her chin with the back of her hand. "They're sure as hell not."

Sherrie picked up the stub of an iron pipe that lay on the ground next to the house, a pipe that had at one time held up a wash line. She handed it to Louise and carefully grabbed a piece of old roof flashing, its sharp, rusted edges capable of causing regret, should it be necessary.

"I can't believe this is happening again. And now," she said in a hushed voice, her nostrils flaring as she stood guard beside Louise.

A small mass of men had gathered, though more than last time. Mark, Peck, and several others, including Mr. Sanderson, stood their ground in the spot that moments ago had been a relatively lively, family-friendly scene. Louise quickly recognized Jerry, the leader who had exuded boisterous machismo during the last go-around—the sole man without a weapon.

"Well, well," said Jerry, eyeing Mark in his approach. "Lookee what we have here." He sized up the displays on the tables, reaching over for a morsel of cheese and popping it into his mouth. "I guess I thought we made it pretty damn clear the last time we were here that you needed to close down." He bowed his head. "Isn't that right, fellas?"

Mumbles of agreement resounded.

Jerry took a step forward, repeating his previous performance, which Louise now realized had merely been a dress rehearsal. "Thing is, this time we're not going to be so nice."

In a swift second, Jerry raised his arm straight up then cut it back down as if to indicate the start of a race. At his signal, his cohorts bounded toward the store, toward the tents, shoving aside anyone in their way.

Mark held up his hands ineffectively, and Peck leaped forward into the swarm of men.

"You!" A man grabbed Peck, twisting his T-shirt in his fist. "You think you can stop a revolution by telling a little bedtime story to your followers? 'The big hungry bear?'"

Peck ignored the threat and gave him a hard shove.

The man briefly lost his balance, then stepped up again, puffing out his chest. "You have no idea what a revolution can do."

In one swift move, Peck wrapped his leg behind the man's ankle, yanked his leg forward, and shoved him back with the force of outrage, landing him hard on the ground. Without pause, he grabbed the man's baton and pointed it at his chest. "Tell me more, asshole."

Louise watched, horrified, as the men of Living Waters defended their fort, some with shouts, others with fists. Any remaining guests ran off as men pinballed around the yard, knocking down tables and each other, upturning baskets of eggs and sending sprays of lemonade into the air. Two brown chickens flapped their way over to the neighboring yard. Terrified goats bleated in fright.

Louise held tight to the iron pipe and looked to make sure Sherrie had her weapon of defense in hand, too, but Sherrie was no longer standing where she'd been a moment ago. Louise looked around frantically, then scurried to the back of the house. Still no sign of her. She hoped Sherrie had had the good sense to hightail it out of there. Like Randy, she couldn't afford a mark on her record this far into medical school.

Louise returned to her corner and was looking over at Hilda's house to check on Mrs. Sanderson and her kids, when from behind she felt the weight of a body stumble into her, the impact blunt but fierce. She fell to the grass with an audible *thud* and felt an immediate burst of pain shoot through her ribcage.

The man's body momentarily pinned her down before he rolled off and roared back toward the knot of men, leaving Louise to gulp for air. She knew she had to move, to get out of the way, but even the slightest movement carried with it flashes of red-hot pain.

Once she caught her breath, Louise closed her eyes and used her hand as a lever, forcing herself up and over to her back. She cried out, the pain like nothing she'd ever experienced.

"Louise!" Sherrie ran toward her and dropped to her knees, scanning for signs of injury. "Where does it hurt?"

"Ribs," whispered Louise. "Knocked down."

Sherrie lifted the flap of Louise's halter top and saw that a lump had already begun forming on her right side. A broken rib, no doubt.

"I hate to leave you, girl, but I can't move you myself and have to find some help." She stood up and ran toward Peck's apartment, where she had just returned from calling the police. "They'll have an ambulance here for you in no time!" she called back over her shoulder.

Louise heard the slap of Sherrie's thong sandals recede, intermingled with the now-familiar sound of shattering windows. She spotted Mark with his Woody Woodpecker T-shirt like a beacon amid the fog of men, face down, though propped up on an elbow. He attempted to raise himself, but his right arm was turned at a sickly angle. Louise watched in horror as he slowly anchored one foot on the ground while dodging a blow intended for someone else, and raised himself up.

Then she saw Randy running up the street toward Living Waters at full speed. He stopped short of the yard, and she saw him quickly evaluate the situation. Both a sense of relief and a renewed fear washed over Louise.

"No," she uttered. Randy couldn't afford this now. Not now, not when he was on the verge of getting offers from more than one law firm. She kept a hawk's eye on him as he pushed his way toward Mark, who said something that Louise couldn't hear. Randy shook his head and ushered Mark away, out of her sight.

Louise continued to watch and wait, knowing that Randy would find her. And then he was there, falling into place beside her.

"Baby, baby! Are you okay?"

"I'm a . . . little . . . hurt."

"Does anyone know?"

She nodded almost imperceptibly. "Sherrie."

"Dr. Sherrie, thank god."

Randy looked down at her ribcage, the open flap of her halter top revealing the angry welt. Before he could react, Sherrie was back again, along with a man Louise recognized from the neighborhood.

"Randy, good. We need your help." Sherrie quickly concocted a makeshift gurney out of a bedsheet and a few planks of plywood, instructing them on what was about to happen.

Randy's gaze flickered toward the store, then the front yard, and Louise knew that he was itching to throw himself into the brawl. "Stay," she said. "Need you."

"I'm not going anywhere, butterfly."

At the count of three, Randy and the other man hoisted her onto the gurney, a bolt of heat searing through her ribcage, forcing her to catch her breath once again as they carried her over to the yard next door and lowered her onto the grass under a shade tree.

"We're heading back." Sherrie grabbed the man's hand, and the two returned next door, leaving Randy and Louise alone.

Nearby, Louise heard the revving of a car engine. "Randy." She inched her head to the side where she had a peek-a-boo view of the street and caught sight of the front panel of a car. A black car. Randy followed her gaze.

"Corvette?"

He nodded.

"Go."

Randy gave her a questioning look, then hopped up and jogged toward the street, where a black Corvette was pulling away from the curb, its windows closed but the license plate visible. He noted the combination of letters and numbers, along with the Wisconsin registration.

The car stopped, and the driver's window slowly lowered. From where she lay, Louise could see the man behind the wheel, his skin a shade darker than Randy's, his dark eyes dead set on his. From the opposite direction, sirens sounded, and the driver sped off.

Chapter 31

—— September 1975 ——

The nurse stepped aside as the doctor entered the room. His lab coat and stethoscope could have been a black robe and gavel, Louise a defendant waiting for her judgment to be decreed. Without a word he placed oversized sheets of X-ray films on the backlit board before retrieving the chart from the foot of her bed.

"Ms. Ley, you have one broken rib and two fractured ribs on the lateral side, as you can see in the X-ray." Dr. Gustafson looked at the glowing screen as he spoke. "Though it's not common, it could lead to lung damage or chest infections. How is your breathing, now that you've had some pain medication?"

"Better."

"No inability to breathe normally?"

"Not if this is my new normal."

The doctor turned toward her, his face devoid of humor. "I don't see any sign of a punctured lung, but if your ability to breathe changes, ring the nurse right away."

Louise held her forefinger and thumb together in an "okay" sign, thankful for the morphine drip.

He ignored her and looked down at the clipboard in his hands. "There's one more thing."

This time he looked first at Randy, then back to Louise, though she seemed only able to focus on the grayish skin that hung loose below his eyes, pools of mud that were beginning to slowly swirl. It occurred to her that doctors ought not to look like a foreboding caution to their patients.

"The blood tests revealed chorionic gonadotropin." He paused. "A pregnancy hormone, Ms. Ley."

Louise lay motionless, attempting to understand. She turned to Randy and saw that the whites of his eyes were large and bright. Whatever was happening, it was something groovy. Way groovy.

"We . . . are going . . . to have a baby?" he asked, his voice incredulous.

Randy grabbed ahold of her shoulders, momentarily forgetting about the reason they were in the hospital. Louise winced from the pressure, and he immediately threw back his hands.

His eyes looked misty now, she realized. And then the announcement sank into her consciousness. *Pregnant?* They had talked about parenting somewhere down the road, but . . . *We're having a baby?*

"Butterfly, we are having us a baby!"

"Oh my god," Louise whispered. She reached out for Randy's hand. "I am going to be a mama? And you a daddy?"

"Folks," interrupted the doctor. "You must be aware of the risks of this pregnancy, considering the injury Ms. Ley has sustained. There's a fair likelihood that the embryo may have become injured during the fall."

Their smiles disappeared, and Dr. Gustafson continued without pause.

"The nurse will take Ms. Ley in for an ultrasound. That'll give us a much better idea of what to expect."

The nurse, who had remained standing near the door, now took a step forward.

"I'll return with the results," the doctor said and left the room.

Randy laid his head on the pillow next to Louise's and gently stroked her cheek. "Baby. Butterfly. We've got this. We're together."

Louise found herself calmed by the sound of his voice. She wanted to hold him, to wrap her arms around him and burrow into his chest, to take in the peppery scent of him as she had so many times before. But instead, she lowered her hand to her belly. "Oh," she murmured.

"What is it?" Randy pulled away. "You hurting?"

"Yeah."

"Your ribs?"

"Lower."

Randy looked at where Louise's hand rested. Just below, a small crimson spot had begun to take shape against the white of the sheet. He turned back to her and brushed her hair aside, then kissed her forehead, his lips lingering.

She didn't have to see it for herself. Louise knew that this newly discovered life that had begun to grow inside of her had now ceased to be. The first teardrop slid across her temple and onto the pillow.

"Nurse?" Randy looked up at her.

"I'll get the doctor," she replied and disappeared through the doorway.

Randy brushed away Louise's tears with one hand and rested the other on top of hers. They both closed their eyes and waited.

Chapter 32

—— September 1975 ——

"But where's the lime Jell-O? With chunks of fruit cocktail suspended in it?" Sage asked jokingly.

While she was open to trying new foods, a meatless, box-free meal was not what she'd expected when she agreed to let Peck cook for her. Tonight's menu included lentil salad with walnuts; tofu cooked with garlic, ginger, and curry powder; and a bed of steamed vegetables.

She kicked off her Dr. Scholl's, not the most comfortable shoes to wear when ascending the steep flight of steps leading to Peck's apartment. While waiting for the door to be opened, she had looked down at the boarded-up co-op below that had recently been on the verge of becoming a promising business. Though Sage was glad that the battle over food sales had ended, she was also saddened, as if she had lost a friend, even if a new one.

"How's Lou doing?" Peck asked.

"Still sore, and pretty wiped out from everything."

Sage thought about the unexpected aftermath of what had transpired last week. Not of the final ruin of the co-op, but that of her sister, of the surprise pregnancy that was over before it could even be celebrated. How her mother had handled it worse than anyone—Mother, a pillar of strength who'd twice in the past month buckled during two very different situations.

"Glad she's doing better. That was a hell of a thing to happen."

"Yeah, she and Randy were pretty distraught." Sage paused and changed direction. "I see everything is boarded up downstairs."

"It is. The CO assholes have now shut down two storefronts and taken over four others. They've managed to effectively wipe out the *true* food cooperative model."

"With all that pressure, I can see how some might've thrown in the towel a lot quicker than Living Waters did."

"I still don't believe that petulance is the reason behind the CO. A toddler will stomp his foot only so many times before moving on. It's more like a game of puppetry, these assholes dancing around on strings. But who's behind the marionette?"

"You really think there is someone, as in one person?" Sage asked. Lately, she'd been thinking that the idea of an authoritative figure had become more and more likely.

"I think it would resolve some of the mystery behind the avalanche of control. Shit!" Peck quickly turned the burner off from under the lentils and lifted the lid, the simmering bubbles releasing an earthy aroma.

Sage winced a little, realizing that it was probably a good thing she was extra hungry. She stayed quiet as Peck handled the lentil emergency, then decided that it was as good a time as any to bring up his editorial. "With all the chaos lately, I haven't had a chance till now to mention that I read your latest."

"Yeah? What'd you think?"

She sat down at the table for two, noticing a single flower in a vase, a daisy. "It seemed . . . I don't know . . . daring, I guess. Full of suspicion, of course."

"Yeah, I was wondering how that'd pan out."

"Why did you write it?" She squirmed a bit in her chair. Their relationship had developed agreeably over these past weeks but was still young enough to make questioning his actions uncomfortable. "I mean, it's one thing to write about food or crops being maliciously manipulated by industry, but to propose that a young woman might have been hijacked from her own life? Isn't that like throwing fuel on a fire?"

"I wouldn't say fuel . . . just blowing a little oxygen at it." He smiled.

"To what avail?"

"To the avail of letting the public know how deep the evil goes. Sage, I really do think there's something more than food at issue here. It just doesn't add up. No matter how I look at it."

"I agree," she said after a beat.

Peck added a final pinch of mystery seasoning and returned the lid to the lentils. "Why? I mean, what's your take?"

"I've been doing a little sleuthing." She smiled.

He turned up the heat under the rice and walked over to where Sage sat. "That's my girl," he said, reflecting her smile.

Sage laughed and shifted again.

"Just what flavor of dirt have you uncovered?"

"Well, I'm pretty sure I found out the name of the guy who owns the black Corvette," replied Sage.

"Shut up."

She jerked back.

"No, go on! I meant 'shut up,' like 'no way, man.'"

She raised her eyebrows in surprise.

"Sorry, I'm not used to checking my words." He looked up at her and smiled with mock politeness. "Please tell me more, ma'am."

Sage laughed again.

"I gotta step back to the stove, but keep talking," Peck said. "I'm all ears."

The lid on the pot of rice began to tap out a hurried rhythm. Behind it, another larger pot of water was just beginning its hungry boil, and Peck added two large handfuls of vegetables, then unleashed a concoction of golden-brown spices and coconut milk into a fourth saucepan that punctuated the room with another spike of unfamiliar aroma. She helped herself to the apple tea from the fridge and poured a glass for Peck too.

"Last week, during the uproar, Louise saw the Corvette leaving the co-op. Randy was there and got the license plate number. It's a Wisconsin-registered car."

"You don't say."

"Registered to a man named Theophilus Smith."

"Theophilus, an odd name."

"I thought so too. But apparently it's not that uncommon a name for Black folks down South."

Peck grunted a surprised *hmph*. "So, is he from Wisconsin or down South? Or don't we know that yet?"

"I had Terry run a background check on him. He lived in Arkansas for some time, then moved around the Midwest for a few years, including Minneapolis, and now he lives in Sheboygan, over in Wisconsin. There are a few minor incidents on his record—unpaid parking tickets and speeding, along with a domestic call—but nothing criminal."

"Nothing else out of the ordinary?"

"Well, not from the police report, no. But Randy got the willies from him."

"No shit? What happened?" He lowered the temperature of the sauce and added cubes of white tofu. The kitchen was clearly Peck's element, Sage thought admiringly; it surely wasn't hers.

"It was a look the guy gave him. A knowing sort of look, he said, as if Randy would understand what he was thinking."

Peck had begun pulling soup bowls from the cabinet above the sink but paused midaction. "As in a 'yo, brother' sort of look, or 'I got your back' look, or 'you're going down next' look?"

"Well, you'd have to run those options past Randy to be sure, but I think he meant more of a brother-to-brother look. Revenge, maybe, but not on Randy. On . . . White privilege."

"Which is just what those assholes think Living Waters is about, catering to the privileged."

Sage sat back. "That's an excellent point."

Peck was now scratching a match along the black, chalky strip of the blue and red box, making a second attempt at lighting it before the *whoosh* of a small flame came to life. He lit a single candle and carried it over to the table.

"But why in the world would a bunch of White people follow him or fall into his trap, as your editorial suggests? I don't see how that would happen," Sage continued.

Peck set down the candle, the small flame reflecting off his eyes. "It would happen if they didn't realize it was a hatred of White privilege. If his motives were under the guise of building a monopoly—and therefore wealth—through food supplies."

Sage leaned forward again. "Peck! This is making sense! There's got to be money in this for him—maybe along with revenge. And certainly power!"

"I've been thinking about this a lot. It always comes down to money," said Peck, scooting his chair closer to hers. "Even though one co-op buying from the CO wouldn't make much of a difference, several buying from them would turn a pretty good profit, especially as they continue to grow and boost their own profits."

"True."

"But combine money with revenge and power, like you said, and that makes it a whole different game."

Sage thought about this for a moment. "And the girl? Aida? What might've changed her demeanor so drastically?"

"I don't think this Theo guy is an ordinary boss, handing out 'well done' notes and serving up cupcakes on birthdays. If this guy is doing what we're suggesting, he's more like a 'da boss,' if you know what I mean. Get caught up in his web and you'll have a hell of a time clawing your way out."

"Geez. Scary stuff."

"Scary as shit. If it's true."

"This is adding up to the makings of a cult. Have you ever heard of the Children of God?"

"As in the one where those who had sex with a cult member received the salvation of God? Sure have."

"How do people fall for such idiotic concepts?"

"I don't know, but I think Aida would've done just about anything for a better station in life. She always seemed to have an air of desperation about her, like she'd believe anything any asshole told her if it would give her a chance to take a step forward in life." He paused. "I imagine there are a lot of folks out there like that. Desperate to belong. Desperate to move ahead."

"Good point."

"And with the right level of charisma, a guy like Theo could probably snare women and men, absorbing them into his lair with relative ease."

This was it—Sage was sure of it. She and Peck had found the hidden key to the mystery of the CO. She looked at him, her eyes glowing with victory, and saw a growing smile crossing his face. He reached over and grabbed her shoulders, then moved in and kissed her deeply.

"Hey babe, I brought you home some extra lovin'." Randy set down a basket he'd carried in and knelt beside her.

Louise was lying in bed, reading the last few pages of a book she'd begun yesterday. Being inactive had been a struggle, but at least it gave her time to read and more so to think about all that had occurred.

"How's my butterfly?" Randy asked.

"Never been better," she said with a wan smile.

"I know this is hard, but each day is a little better. We'll get through it together."

Louise nodded. "I love you."

"You too, butterfly. Always will." He kissed her forehead.

"I got you a little something that you might want to share some of that love with," Randy continued, sliding the basket closer and reaching inside. "How cute is this little guy?"

Louise sat up with deliberate care, her pensive mood liquefying into delight as she scooped up the bundle of black and white fur from Randy's hands. "Oh, Randy. He's adorable."

"I thought you might like the company," he said, ruffling the fur of the kitten's head. "Looks like life is going to be changing very soon."

"Oh . . .?" Louise looked at him questioningly.

"Watch out, Madison—here we come!"

"Randy! You took their offer!"

"That's right, butterfly. You are looking at Randall J. Oates, Esquire, Attorney-at-Law with the practice of Von Ruden, Keller, and Anderson."

Madison had secretly been Louise's first choice, even though the firm in Minneapolis was slightly more generous in its offer, but she wanted the decision to be entirely his.

"I figured it'd be good to start somewhere fresh, you know? It's taken all my willpower to avoid tracking down and beating the hell out of the gang from the CO. Not easy to let go of that."

Louise knew it was time to leave, to start fresh in a place that was far away from the disappointments of the past weeks. To plan for their future children not by surprise, but with intention.

"I couldn't be prouder of you," she said. "I'm with you, babe, all the way."

The kitten meowed delicately as it peered over the edge of Louise's arm, eager to explore its surroundings. Louise released it, and together she and Randy watched as it took a few tentative steps toward the edge of the bed before it leaped with faith to the floor below.

The notice of death for Helena Graham in Sunday's *Times* jolted Elizabeth.

> Mrs. Helena Graham, age sixty-eight, of St. Paul, died suddenly in Chicago in the lobby of the Congress Hotel. Mrs. Graham, unmarried, left behind no survivors.

The photograph appeared to have been taken several years earlier, perhaps not long after the two had met on the Midwest Arrow and again briefly on the streets of Chicago. An ageless ghost with whom she'd had but two encounters. She immediately recognized Helena's clear eyes, eyes that glimmered with certainty and goodwill, and the smile that had the ability to easily morph into graceful laughter. Her unsolicited mentor throughout all these years, now departed.

> Ever a staunch supporter of women's rights, Mrs. Graham spoke at venues throughout the Twin Cities and Chicago, her last appearance at the Chicago Women's Club the day before her passing. Her fortitude and presence will be dearly missed by many.

Elizabeth sat back in the chair. Years ago, she had spent a considerable amount of time thinking about Helena. How she had made Elizabeth feel welcomed into a new experience—a new life, ultimately. From Helena she'd learned the art of grace; she was who Elizabeth silently summoned when planning a dinner party with new friends or negotiating quilt collections with gallery owners. After Will's death, she had asked herself what Helena would do and found the courage to sell the farm and begin anew in a different community, a different state. And it was the spirit of Helena whose courage Elizabeth had summoned when she closed the door against the vandalism of Neil's presence. Helena, who was practically a neighbor—perhaps an hour's drive away—but one Elizabeth had never called upon. Surely her address had been readily available in the phone book. Surely a knock at Helena's door wouldn't have gone unappreciated. But now, the only thing that remained was a black-and-white image and the recollection of their brief encounters.

Elizabeth rose from her chair and walked outside, where the view was brilliant on this early autumn morning as the sun still rose toward its peak. Her thoughts turned to her other lost friend, Wini, and their fortuitous introduction at the Blue Window. Of the afternoon they'd spent in each other's company, there, in Chicago. Elizabeth wondered what had happened to her, a woman of singular talent, and hoped that she'd found success far beyond employment as an animated piece of furniture in a basement lounge in Chicago. So often she had longed to let Wini know what had happened, that her leaving without a goodbye was unintentional. But the mists of time had shrouded the opportunity, and memories were to be the only means of ever again seeing this friend too.

She walked down the steps and toward the gazebo. There, Elizabeth paused beside the canoe and wiped away a smear of black mildew from its side. Each spring, she'd dragged it out from its canvas covering at the edge of the woods and parked it next to the gazebo, knowing full well that she would not sit on its seat, that its oars would not be rowed by her hands.

Yet many years ago, before they'd had children, she and Will would scamper off to the invigorating water of the swimming hole. Under the moonlight, they'd shed their clothes and slide into the clear spring water, their bodies pressing against each other's with the mischievous sensuality that young marriage allows. They'd challenge each other to see who could hold their breath underwater the longest, counting . . . counting . . . until they'd been forced to jump up and gasp for air, teasing and laughing over their silly game.

But the sailing accident changed Elizabeth. Her intrigue of water had been unplugged, had funneled down the drain on that fateful day.

Too many losses had been endured for one lifetime.

Frankie. What would have become of him, her son, defenseless against nature's will?

Her husband, who only wanted what she could not give him: pure, lasting love.

Stephen . . .

Elizabeth pushed the canoe onto its belly, where it rocked momentarily. She gathered the wooden oars, faded by nothing but time, and a life vest from the gazebo that had been used by one of her daughters a few years back. Was it Sage who wore it? Sage, so steady in her beat, her mind endlessly observant. Or Louise, drifting toward wherever the clouds might lead her?

She worked her arms into the puffy orange vest and felt a shiver of memory as she pulled snug the dusty white straps, lacing them into a double knot in front of her chest. She nudged off her sandals and positioned the oars inside the canoe before tugging at the heavy rope clipped to the bow, which she now aimed toward the lake. It was surprising how easily she was able to drag it over the grass, over the small pebbles along the shore and into the water, where the bow bobbed in a nod of agreement.

Elizabeth rotated the canoe until she stood between it and the shoreline, then tossed the rope inside and held it into position with both hands. With Sage's steady heartbeat and Louise's capricious manner, she raised one leg out of the shallow water and stepped inside, then hoisted herself over the edge and onto the seat, her legs dripping small streams of water onto the floor.

The canoe rocked unsteadily, and Elizabeth sat still, suspended in the moment until it had settled back to steadiness. The radiance of the sun over the breadth of the lake, the motionless surface, the beckoning air—all of it was reminiscent of the day spent on Lake Michigan with

Stephen long ago: October 20, 1948, a date so importantly locked in her memory.

She picked up an oar and gripped it with unskilled hands, pushing it downward, where it quickly met with the rocky bed below. She gave a shove, now aiming the bow toward the wide-open mouth of the lake, and began paddling with slow, unfamiliar strokes. The caw of nearby seagulls and the swishing sound of water steadied her mind as she diligently paddled the water from in front of her to behind her.

Enough of that which has passed.

Reaching a point not too distant from the shoreline, she dragged the oars through the thick water, bringing the canoe to a natural rest. She stroked along the starboard side until she had made a half turn, her house now in view, where the canoe held its position.

Elizabeth had never seen her home from this vantage point, the whole of her scant acreage abutted by the protective fortress of the lake. To the east, apples had begun to ripen on their branches, a blush of color against emerald-green leaves. Coneflowers and mums stood out against the light color of the house, and on the west side the hardwoods had just begun to display their autumn colors. Everything had its place and time.

Turning away, she looked down at the water upon which she floated and was surprised that the bottom of the lake was still visible, that its depth wasn't limitless. It wasn't an abyss into which she might lose herself; indeed, it possessed a level of beauty that took her by surprise. A small fish floated by, guided by the movements of its generous tail fin. Tall grasses waved in greeting. All along, life had been teeming just below the surface. Life, where she had only assumed death.

And there, too, was her own reflection, an aura of light surrounding her, shining and certain.

Elizabeth turned her face toward the sun, breathing in deeply. Exhaling, she felt her pain-laced history unknot, its decided usefulness expiring like spent oxygen. Easing her hand over the side of the canoe, she swept her fingers through the enchanting clarity of the water, disrupting her reflection into dozens of ripples that carried it far away.

Chapter 33

— June 1977 —

Louise set two floral-patterned plates found at a garage sale on the porch table and topped them with summery orange napkins. She lit a candle, its layers of beeswax tapering from the bottom upward like a cone. The demand for her craft surprised her—she wasn't the only person in Madison making this type of candle—but she was glad that she was able to contribute to the family funds.

Once a week Louise made deliveries to various shops, including the new food co-op that had opened across town last month. There, she had quickly befriended the manager, who shook his head in disbelief more than once as she regaled him with stories of the takeover of co-ops throughout the Twin Cities and the brawls that had occurred at Living Waters, along with its ultimate demise. Nor could he believe that, despite the thievery of business funds, a cult-like leadership, and even kidnapping, some would say, Theophilus Smith had never been captured. A man on the run. But maybe, Louise thought, running away from life was his personal conviction.

Randy would be home soon, his work week finally at an end. He had found his niche in civil rights cases, and though not all his cases were victories, his tenacious yet respectful reputation for effecting change did not go unnoticed. Already there was talk of partnership in the law firm looming in the not-too-distant future.

Despite the long hours of overtime, both Randy and Louise were grateful that he'd chosen Madison over Minneapolis. Here, they'd found a community of like-minded people with whom they often gathered to discuss current events and hash out political views or, at other times, for potlucks and game nights. In fact, this was a rare Friday evening that they would be dining alone.

Ivan leaped onto the table with easy effort, where he could keep watch on other cats in the neighborhood. Louise picked him up, stroking his soft fur as she opened the porch door and set him on the front stoop. She noticed Randy just a few blocks away, pedaling his Schwinn toward home, and scurried back inside and down the hall.

Willamena, or Willow as they called their daughter, lay wide awake in her crib under the spell of the dangling mobile that Elizabeth had made: felted balls in bright colors dangling from a puffy rainbow. Louise picked up her baby girl and gave her a snuggly kiss on her belly before dancing their way back toward the kitchen. She'd long pined for the day that she would become a mother, a change that had catapulted her into a domestic life that she'd never envisioned for herself, but one that now felt as necessary as living itself.

Randy had just come in through the kitchen door and was loosening his tie when she and Willow turned the corner. He opened his arms toward them, a space into which the two fit perfectly.

———◇———

"What do you say, stop in Decorah for lunch?" Sage asked Peck, her new headset a vast improvement from the old one that had come with the very used airplane she'd purchased.

"Roger that, darlin'."

The air was spectacularly smooth as the two flew back to Minnesota from Peoria, where Peck had been the keynote speaker during the first annual environmental conference for the state of Illinois. Both were eager to tell Hans and Siri about the event.

When Sage had first met the Schwammans, she never would have imagined that they'd form a lasting friendship. But when she and Peck flew down a second time so that Peck could meet Hans and get his views on organic farming, they'd both become smitten with the quirky couple. Now, Hans would be thrilled to hear that hundreds of concerned people had attended the event, primarily a blend of students and farmers, most of them eager to learn more about what exactly insecticides and pesticides were doing to our waterways and soil and what steps were needed to promote healing.

Some had shared stories of their own. One farmer described how a runoff pond had been infested with an inordinately high number of frogs with five legs and even two heads on one occasion. Another spoke of sections of rivers that had once teemed with fish, now many of them belly-up. Still another man talked about the high rates of pancreatic cancer in a small community that was no different from those surrounding it, except for being situated next to an insecticide test site.

In a short time, Peck's passion for a clean Earth had affected Sage too. She never used to consider where her food had come from, but only the ease with which it could be prepared and whether it would satisfy her hunger. But now, she'd come to understand that the innovations we inflict upon our agricultural lands come with detriments. She was certain that Daddy had a hand in leading her to this point, just as he had in leading the family toward closure, back when she'd had a handful of visions that ultimately returned them to the farm.

Sage continued her work for the historical society on a part-time basis. The rest of her working hours were spent researching alongside Peck and flying him around the country to attend meetings, rallies, and conventions. Environmental awareness was reaching beyond the food co-op scene and into mainstream life. People were beginning to question what the chemical salesmen weren't revealing, and they weren't liking the answers they were hearing.

"What do you suppose ever came of Theophilus?" Sage asked Peck. "After the dust settled, his name just disappeared."

Peck was tapping out a song with his pencil, still energized from yesterday's successful event. "The asshole's probably holed up with a harem somewhere in the Virgin Islands."

Sage laughed, something she found herself doing often in the company of Peck. And now that they were soon to be married, a whole lifetime of joy awaited her. "After one woman finally stepped up and opened up about what was happening behind the scenes at the CO, it was like he disappeared into thin air. How does someone do that?"

"No shit. Guess it's a good thing he did though. The fire he had built was pretty intense for a while. Living Waters could've been one hell of a thriving store by now, but it's good to see some other co-ops doing well again in whatever way they want."

"True, but to think of a cult in our own city! Still seems surreal. And knowing how close you were to it. And Louise too."

"The ultimate food fight."

Sage remained quiet, realizing that it was that but also so much more. Who would have thought that a single man could garner that much control over a group of people and do so entirely from the sidelines? Theophilus had appeared in the Twin Cities, unknown, and convinced a small group of co-op managers to start a buying club. The idea was sound enough—expand the co-op market and make some extra profits through the wholesale business, the Cooperative Organization—but it had quickly grown out of control. Only a select few from the co-op scene had personally met Theophilus, yet almost everyone who was involved with him, even indirectly, became like worker bees pandering to keep the queen content while building a base of golden honey to have at his disposal.

But it turned out that many didn't realize his leadership went beyond organizing co-ops for greater profit—in particular his own profit—even if it meant doing so via threats, as with Living Waters. He had also commandeered a handful of women who played the role of his wives, though not legally, a few of them having given birth to his children.

There was "Aida"—Christine. Sage had met her not too long ago when she and Peck were in Chicago, where they happened to eat a late lunch at the restaurant in which she worked. She'd walked in to collect her check, carrying a baby girl with a mocha complexion and dark head of curls so different from Christine's Scandinavian look. Christine's eyes flitted about nervously when Peck waved and called her over, cutting their conversation short by using the excuse of her daughter's naptime. Christine, whose only true goal was to go to college and to make something of her life, had found herself alone in a city in which one could hide, with a young child to care for and the degree-bearing frame on her wall empty.

"Do you really think Theophilus could be the dad of Christine's baby?" Sage asked Peck. "I mean, we have no actual evidence."

"And Christine won't talk. Of course."

"Besides, she may not have even known him as Theo. Maybe he was Steve or Jim. Maybe Harry. We have no idea, considering he'd had at least three detectable aliases."

"Yeah, good point."

"At least she got away."

Sage veered left, aiming the plane west. She was glad all of this was behind them despite the demise of Living Waters and the unrest that had occurred during that tumultuous time.

"Have you heard from Mark lately?" she asked.

The final battle in the co-op wars was the last straw for Mark, who had shortly after moved to Bellingham, Washington, where he opened the state's first food co-op.

"Yeah, he's swell. He's thinking of taking the train out this way in the next couple of months."

"We'll have to have him over for supper. I'm sure he'll love my Snickers-bar salad," Sage declared with a wink.

Peck chuckled.

Sage had come around to enjoying a host of new foods but still clung tightly to the *St. John's Church Cookbook* given to her by a neighbor as if it were *the* holy book. Tater Tot Hotdish and anything Jell-O were her favorites, though she occasionally forayed into the "Desserts and Bars" section and managed to turn out an awesome pan of homemade lemon bars.

The pencil tapping tapered off, and Peck turned the page of his notebook, picking up writing where he had left off. After another few minutes, he closed the cover and tucked it into his backpack.

"What's the latest?" Sage asked.

"Oh, a little something that, with your approval, I'm planning to publish in the next issue of *Sensationally Alive*."

She gave him a sidelong glance, her eyebrows raised.

"Something I think your dad might have approved of."

A whisper of certainty passed through Sage, leaving a smile in its wake. She took in the view below, where the juxtaposition of man's blueprint upon the land against nature's invincible design spoke volumes. It was here, up in the sky, where everything came together for Sage. Where maybe, just maybe, Daddy's spirit soared alongside her, where he, too, looked down over the land that he had so loved.

The Life and Death of a Farmer
By Peck Wells

William "Will" Ley was simply doing his job. The thirty-four-year-old farmer sat upon his John Deere tractor during an overcast late spring day in 1952, the new sprayer hooked behind, releasing DDT onto his fields. The chemicals would, he was assured, stop destructive pests from decimating his fields, allowing the year's soybean crop to produce higher yields than ever before. If it was good enough to destroy the mosquitoes that had infested our troops with malaria back in the war, then it would surely be effective against other insects too.

But when a mechanical glitch occurred, Will, having retrieved a wrench from his toolbox to repair the sprayer, found himself a victim of angry pressure that had built up against the nozzles. DDT shot out toward him, covering his chest and abdomen, instantly saturating his thin cotton shirt.

He couldn't have surmised that such an accident would occur on this day, and he surely hadn't surmised that this mishap would eventually take his life—not because of the massive burns that ate away at his skin like a hungry beast, but because of the residual effect on his psyche.

And you can bet your bottom dollar that Mr. Ley also hadn't surmised that spraying these chemicals onto a field of soybeans grown to feed animals—animals that went to market, then moved on to the slaughterhouse, and ultimately onto the dinner tables of hundreds of people—could potentially steer them, too, toward an untimely death. No. Will just knew that the increased yield in his crops would eventually outweigh the cost of buying DDT and the sprayer needed to spread it. He was told that the chemicals were designed to do just this, and so he played the game.

Did Paul Hermann Muller, the Swiss chemist

who created the insect eradicator, surmise that a farmer in Iowa would begin his journey to death from his concoction? Or did the Nobel Prize-winning chemist see only the beneficial effects of his discovery in lowering the mosquito population, and therefore the high rates of malaria, on the war front?

The Life

Will Hermann Ley lived an accomplished and, most would say, satisfying life. He married his love, Betty, at age twenty-two, and the couple began a family, raising their two daughters on a farm in northeast Iowa during the years following World War II.

On the south side of the house were two tree swings—one with a wooden seat and another with a tire—both fashioned by Will. During summer afternoons or after chores were done, he'd push his daughters as high as their bravery allowed, spinning the tire to their delighted squeals.

On weekends, he would spend hours with his girls sitting alongside the creek or pond fishing for trout, putting a humorous twist on stories about the bugs and birds and trees that surrounded the very entertained young ones.

And during winter months, he would enjoy the sledding hill as much as his daughters and didn't blink an eye at pulling the little ones back up the hill toward the house where Betty would have mugs of hot cocoa ready for the rosy-cheeked crew.

Together with Betty, the two accomplished their goal of succeeding as parents, as farmers, and as genuinely kind neighbors and upstanding community members. But sadly, the goal of retiring together would never be achieved.

The Death

Will Ley spent four weeks in the Winneshiek County Memorial Hospital after his accident. And then he was sent home, his burns under control, though armed with the knowledge that the scars would likely remain for a lifetime. Never a proud man, Will didn't care about scars. He cared about his family, about his farm. But had he known the most lasting scars would be those that marred his mind, he might've been damn worried.

Betty had immediately noticed the mood changes—a new development in her mild-mannered husband. She brought him ice when headaches developed, and when they became so severe that he cringed in pain, she left him in the darkened bedroom alone and kept their daughters' voices hushed. Later, after the shock of her husband's unexpected, and certainly unusual, angry outbursts wore off, Betty became the most agreeable person he'd ever known. And when he stumbled into the deep wells of depression, Betty learned how to skirt around this newly arisen challenge too.

But late that summer, when her husband's tractor rolled down the steep slope of the creek at the bottom of a hill, landing on top of him and closing off his lungs, Betty would no longer skirt. She couldn't skirt—her husband was dead.

The community had conducted an unofficial investigation. Why had this happened to a man who'd driven a tractor along this same hillside for nearly a dozen years? There was no slick mud, and the tractor's mechanisms were in fine working order.

But folks demand answers, so they formulated theories based on unverifiable speculation, spreading the sickly virus of gossip. But no one—not one deputy, doctor, or medical examiner—had suggested that it might have been caused by the DDT that had soaked through his shirt, through his protective layers of skin, and into the life of his body, his mind. A delayed aftereffect that caused him to black out momentarily at exactly the wrong time.

But I am here to suggest just this.

Science is now more advanced than it was in the '50s. We now know that those exposed to DDT in the manner in which Will Ley had been are subject to long-term health effects. Uncontrollable shaking. Horrific migraines. Bouts of dizziness. Blackouts. Seizures. Death.

And I also suggest, if this can happen to a man who was unfortunate enough to be braised in DDT, what is happening to those who unintentionally ingest similar chemicals through the food they eat? Do they know how many birds have died? Fowl and fish?

Yeah, I know—DDT was recently banned. But what is the substitute? Rid-Away? Do we assume this one is safe because it has less potency than its predecessor?

Don't be fooled, readers. Don't be blinded by what the big corporations tell you is safe. Demand proof—or stay away.

Epilogue

—— September 1978 ——

Elizabeth removed her sweater and hung it on the back of her chair before sitting down at the black iron bistro table to which the waiter had led her. With the first sip of Earl Grey, she felt the tingle of caffeine begin cascading her senses into awareness. And what a morning to be aware, felicity nipping at her from all sides. The intimate patio of the seaside bistro offered a spectacular view of the Brighton Marina and beyond, where the sun's blinding glimmer reflected off the mast of the single sailboat working its way back toward shore.

Though she had just eaten breakfast, Elizabeth glanced at the menu, noting the Guinness steak pie, then set it down and picked up the flyer that she'd taken from the stack near the entrance of the café. The picture of her that they'd chosen was taken earlier in the year at an exhibit in Chicago where Elizabeth had just been introduced by the curator and was about to say a few words on how the city had inspired her art, her life.

She had been surprised at the peace she had felt upon returning to Chicago. Peace that distance had allowed. There, she'd walked the nearby streets after the artist's reception, past shops and restaurants, past the entrance to what had once been the Blue Window, and on toward the Dominican Hotel. Inside, the decor of the lobby had been slightly altered, but its grandeur, though somewhat antiquated, remained. No longer had it caused her to gasp in amazement; she had become used to finery, used to a life of travel, of worldliness.

Tomorrow, Elizabeth would make her appearance at the West End Gallery of England, just down the street from where she now sat. There she would once again discuss the details of her quilts, revealing snippets of her life that went into each piece, always alluding, never explaining. Bits of her life that encircled her like motes of dust floating through the air, mostly invisible but never completely dormant.

Elizabeth took another sip of tea and looked up at the small sailboat that was now close to the marina, its lone skipper lowering her sails, ready to bring her in.

She turned her gaze back to the flyer, to the image that had been imprinted onto glossy paper just below her photograph. It was one of her original works of art, the vials taken from Sage's chemistry set still intact, the creek water within floating above the sediment that had settled at the bottom. Water and earth—so essential to each other yet always finding means to separate.

Elizabeth finished the remains of her tea and placed the flyer inside her purse next to the two envelopes that she carried with her, always. One, a gift from Stephen, brought to her the night he had surprised her by showing up at the door of her hotel room, the night she had fallen in love. The other delivered by Neil, its contents a replica of the first, down to the personal stationery upon which it was written.

She stood and faced the marina, smoothing her skirt and patting her hair into place. Breathing in the fresh sea air, Elizabeth stepped forward onto the cobblestone street, an easy smile crossing her face, one that reached all the way to her heart.

Just as snow falls from the heavens,
whispering wings of angels curling soft flurries into singular patterns,
their destiny given from above yet dedicated to the earth,
laying claim to every barren inch below;
just as this do I love you,

with lavish artistry,
with elusive mystery,
with infinite abundance.

—— Author's Note ——

In the 1970s, the Twin Cities was a hotbed for the emerging food co-op scene as young revolutionists sought out and fought for social change. During this time, anarchists and Marxist-Leninist groups battled for control of the industry using both verbal and physical attacks.

On the surface, the quest for control by the Cooperative Organization, known as the CO, was about co-ops maintaining cohesive guidelines and policies and using the CO's warehouse as a central place from which to buy sellable goods. More so, the CO believed that co-ops should be affordable to all, which meant selling goods beyond fresh produce and locally raised bulk items—staples of early co-ops—to include canned and prepackaged goods that could be bought and sold for lower prices via the warehouse. Purists (anarchists) fought against this idea, claiming that their practices were not catering to the middle class and the wealthy, as the CO claimed, but to anyone and everyone interested in pure, wholesome food. While several co-ops at the time either folded into the CO or closed shop, some held out, fighting for their beliefs.

Yet there was also an underlying secrecy to this drive for control that few knew about at the time. The significant level of control seemed unwarranted, and those at the top of the CO were strict in avoiding disclosure of who it was they answered to. Men and women who were drawn into the uppermost levels of the organization found themselves unable to untether themselves from the group, some of whom were forced into marriages or specific jobs.

It wasn't until years later that a charismatic man by the name of Theophilus Smith was discovered to be the founder of the CO. Originally a lightweight criminal who had moved to the Midwest from the South, Smith used psychological manipulation to coerce those in the cooperative community into joining him, which for a few meant following him into a cult-like lifestyle over which he lorded. Many years later, Smith was convicted of second-degree murder for the killing of a man in Minneapolis. Overall, little is known about this man who had several aliases and of whom no known photos have been found.

It is important to note that several liberties were taken in fictionalizing the events that occurred during this period in Minneapolis-St. Paul history. For a more accurate account and further information, I highly recommend Craig Cox's book, *Storefront Revolution: Food Co-ops and the Counterculture,* or the Twin Cities PBS special, "The Co-op Wars." Both provide a well-researched, insightful look into this turbulent time in the history of the Twin Cities.

—— Acknowledgments ——

You may have heard that writing a book can take a long time. Yep, it's true—at least for me.

Yet, Here We Are was begun several years ago, a story that inched its way out of me even though I had set it aside repeatedly to be a mom, hold down a job, further my education, and for a number of other likely excuses. But little by little I cobbled it together, until it eventually morphed into the story it is today.

Even though writing is a solitary endeavor, the abundant and seemingly ubiquitous encouragement I've received has been there with me during each of the countless hours spent creating this book. Had I not been buoyed by my husband, Theodore, and children, Skuyler, Rainah, and Aspenn, I would likely still be stuck midmanuscript trying to recall the details of what I had written in previous months and years. I hope you know just how deeply anchored my love and gratitude for you are.

My appreciation extends also to my parents, Fritz and Jo Ann, for teaching me the values of love, family, and hard work; to my beta readers, Aspenn Ward, Rainah Ward, Kari Clark, Kristin Bell, Alice Carson, and Sheri Acosta, for carving time out of their busy lives to read the early manuscript and bring clarity through the eye of a well-read reader; to my fabulous book club friends of twenty years for their cherished friendship and wide-ranging conversations that occasionally involve books; to numerous other friends and family members who have championed me in achieving this long-term goal; to my work colleagues who are as supportive as any worker bee could ask for; to Craig Cox for putting into the world *Storefront Revolution*, the book that sparked the storyline of the co-op wars; to Cap'n Joe for helping Sage learn how to safely land a plane; to the accomplished authors who took the time to read and endorse this book; and to the many writing greats of the past and present whose work continues to inspire others and to better this world that together we inhabit, ideally in peace.

Last, to John Koehler and the entire crew at Koehler Books: thank you for believing in me and for bringing this book to life. Collaborating with you has been an extraordinary and delightful experience.

Yet, Here We Are

—— Discussion Questions ——

Elizabeth had a devoted husband, a solid man to whom she was married, yet she was deeply unhappy. In contrast, her relationship with Stephen made her feel whole. Considering this, what are your thoughts on her infidelity? Was it justified? Did Elizabeth act appropriately in keeping her secret after returning to her family life?

Were you familiar with the so-called co-op wars that took place in the Twin Cities before reading this book? If so, how did the story differ from actual events? Did it make you want to learn more about this unusual part of food co-op history?

Elizabeth fell in love with Stephen, a man she didn't know well and one who had his faults. What did you see as Stephen's faults, and why did Elizabeth overlook them?

Why did Elizabeth reveal her love affair to Sage and not Louise? How did each of the Ley women thrive or suffer in their own love relationships?

What did you think of Neil? Did you believe his story of Stephen's survival? Did Elizabeth make the right choices in allowing him into her home time and again? How did the experience with Neil change her?

Peck's character was feisty and impassioned yet loving. In what ways was he an important, if not essential, character in the book?

Which character did you most relate to or enjoy? Why?

The author left the ending open to interpretation. How did you interpret the epilogue?

www.ingramcontent.com/pod-product-compliance
Lightning Source LLC
LaVergne TN
LVHW091712070526
838199LV00050B/2361